Jaded

NYT AND USA TODAY BESTSELLING AUTHOR

TIJAN

Paperback formatted by Elaine York/Allusion Graphics, LLC
Publishing & Book Formatting
www.allusiongraphics.com

Chapter 1

"Hey, baby."

Corrigan Raimler was my school's most popular leech. He's the guy who's at the top of the food chain and hits on anything with two legs and a vagina. That's this guy. Didn't help he was stereotypically gorgeous to boot with shaggy blonde hair, green sparklers for eyes, and perfectly formed lips. They were sculpted by a goddess, or Corrigan liked to brag.

He took two things seriously, his friends (Bryce and myself) and women (sex).

"Hi, Corrigan," I murmured as I grabbed my calculus book. I checked my mirror. I wasn't really vain; I just wanted to make sure that my hair didn't look like a bird's nest or something. It didn't, but I usually always had it under control. My hair grazed the tops of my shoulders. I turned my head and grinned when I saw the dark brunette color shimmer black from the light.

Corrigan draped an arm across my neighbor's locker and ignored their weak-kneed protest as he turned his back to them.

I didn't look. I already knew he wanted something and he had his trademark panty-melting grin on that face of his.

The green eyes helped, trust me.

"What are you doing this weekend?"

"Why? What do you want?" I moved down the hallway and Corrigan snapped my locker shut as he kept pace.

The flies flew around us and no one jostled us.

"Harris is throwing a party."

Shock. Not. Harris always throws parties.

"So?" I drawled out, bored as I turned to my class. Corrigan followed behind and draped his arms across the back of my chair. He wrapped his arms around me and breathed into my ear.

My table partner, Leisha, nearly fell off her chair. No joke.

"I was hoping you'd go."

"Why? Want to get laid?" Corrigan always wanted to get laid, but the joke was that he'd never get laid by me.

"Well..." He glanced to Leisha and shooed her away.

Leisha shooed and he dropped into her seat.

"You've got the hookup with Steele, right?"

Here it was.

"You want to get laid by Denton Steele? I didn't know you swung that way," I teased. Denton and I weren't friends. We weren't even screw-buddies. It was a one time deal and I wasn't looking to extending it to a two-time deal. He might've been the locally grown national heartthrob, but I hadn't wanted another go with the movie star.

Corrigan ignored that as he leaned closer to me, for my ears only, "Word is that he's got a hot sister coming home for the summer. You should go visit, make friends, and bring her to the party."

"Why would I go and visit the female Steele?"

"No, no. Not her, but him. And *then* make friends with her!" Corrigan nudged my knee.

"Mr. Raimler," Mr. Aldross barked with a frown. He wasn't a Corrigan fan, but not many were. Although, they liked myself and Bryce even less and *that* said a lot.

"Yes, Mr. Aldy?" Corrigan returned smoothly and leaned back in his chair. He removed the arm around my shoulder and the one that had been kneading my leg.

"This isn't your class. What are you doing here?"

"Well, Mr. Aldy..." Corrigan took a deep breath, ready to jump into his charming act.

Mr. Aldross shook his head and barked, "Get out before detention. I don't have time to play your game."

There was a spark of disappointment in Corrigan's eyes, but he stood slowly, winked at me, and moved to the door. Just before he left, Mr. Aldross called out, "And Mr. Raimler…"

"Yeah?"

"I enforce a no-mauling policy in my classrooms. You and Miss Jeneve can pick up your 'mauling' elsewhere from now on."

Corrigan barked out a laugh and suggested to me, "What do you think, Sheldon? You, me, janitor's closet in forty eight minutes?"

The classroom laughed. Mr. Aldross frowned.

I winked and drawled back, "Which one?"

"Get out," Mr. Aldross barked again and Corrigan left, satisfied.

"Miss Jeneve." Mr. Aldross frowned my way.

"Yes?" I yawned and stretched, knowing my breasts were nicely outlined against my thin top. Sometimes the game was so easy… sometimes.

"Would you please write your answers to questions eight and ten on the board?"

"Sure thing, Mr. Aldross." I stood and walked to the board. As I grabbed the chalk, I spoke up, "And Mr. Aldross?"

"Yes, Sheldon?" He asked, weary.

"Corrigan can maul me, but I don't maul back." I sent him a seductive grin and whispered, "Just wanted you to know."

Mr. Aldross shook his head, probably in disappointment while more than a few coughed behind me.

Just then the door opened again and Bryce Scout strolled in to take a seat at my table. Bryce was Corrigan's exact opposite, but the two fitted the best friend duo perfectly. Corrigan smoozed anyone and everyone he chose while Bryce produced the same results with his silence. The quintessential gorgeous bad boy: black Mohawk, sea blue eyes, and cheekbones that couldn't compare to how the rest of his body was chiseled. Anyway, Corrigan talked and Bryce listened. It worked for the two and they were the top of the social hierarchy.

I heard the swift intake of breath from nearly all the girls in the room, but I often wondered why half of them fell over backwards when Bryce was around. He didn't give so many the time of day.

"Mr. Scout," Mr. Aldross sighed. "You're late. Again."

Bryce greeted him by laying his head down on the table. He closed his eyes and the class watched as he promptly fell asleep.

I laughed.

A few others laughed and Mr. Aldross stood in shock. The disrespect was damning and it didn't help to come on the heels of the Corrigan and Sheldon show.

"Mr. Scout, you will wake up as you progress to the principal's office." And Mr. Aldross must've had enough.

Bryce lifted his piercing blue eyes and grinned triumphantly as he looked right at me. He quickly grabbed his books and left, but I knew that's what Bryce had wanted.

Mr. Aldross glared, "Miss Jeneve, please return Mr. Scout to the classroom. You can inform him that I've changed my mind." No doubt, he wanted to torture Bryce by making him actually stay in a class.

Everyone knew why he sent me. Besides Corrigan, I was the only other person that Bryce would listen to. Whatever, I didn't mind. I wouldn't have to write the answers on the board for the homework that I hadn't done.

As I strolled out the door, I glimpsed Bryce turning a corner that didn't lead towards the principal's office.

"Bryce," I called out. A second later, as I turned down the same hallway, I saw Bryce was at his locker.

"Hey," I greeted, lazily, as I leaned against the locker beside his.

"Hey," Bryce greeted, his head still in his locker. A second later, he raked his eyes over me and grinned as he reached for my book. He placed it in his locker, grabbed my hand, and led me farther down the hallway.

"What are we doing?" I already knew.

"Why'd you come after me?"

"Mr. Aldy wanted me to inform you that you weren't going to the Principal's office anymore." I left the rest out on purpose.

"I wasn't going to go. You know that." He grinned as he pulled me into a janitor's closet. And when that door closed, no more words were needed. Once inside, I wrapped my arms around his shoulders as his head dipped and took my lips in his, fiercely. Hot.

This is what Bryce and I did. We weren't together, but most everyone assumed we were.

Neither of us did commitment, but if we had, it would've been to each other. That was another unspoken agreement. If anyone wanted out of the situation, the other would let them go with an easy smile, but probably no well-wishes.

Our clothes were still on, and would've remained on (I had some class), when the door opened abruptly and the janitor stood frowning at us.

Before he could muster a lecture, Bryce pulled me out and we both meandered towards his locker. He kissed me deeply once more before the final bell rang and the hallway was flooded.

Our hands fell apart when he opened his locker and produced my book.

"Thanks," I murmured, ruefully.

Bryce looked to say something, but Corrigan interrupted as he bounced up to us and threw one arm over both of our shoulders.

"How are my greatest friends?" Corrigan asked, cheekily.

Bryce smirked.

"I'm not making friends with Steele," I retorted.

"Oh, come on. I bet she's hot. She has to be hot. Be friends with her for me."

"What's up with Steele?" Bryce questioned. I searched his face, but there wasn't a hint of anything. Bryce had been doing our thing for years and he'd known about the Denton Steele event. He'd never commented on it and I'd never offered any explanation, but—really—how do you explain that?

"He's got a super-fine sister coming to town. I want Shell, since she's hot and heavy with Mr. Sexiest Man Alive to seduce his sister around to our social crowd."

"Seduce?" I grinned. "I don't do girl on girl."

Bryce chuckled as a bright smile lit on Corrigan's face.

"That'd be perfect! You can do that too." Like it hadn't already been his secret hope.

"Hi Bryce. Hi Corrigan. Hi Sheldon."

Becky Lew was one of the head cheerleaders and the queen of the underworld minions. She ruled all her little queens: cheerleaders, dance team, some of the cross-country, yearbook, and all the skinny blonde girls who aspired for popularity. Some brunettes and redheads too, but there just always seemed to be more blondes than any other hair color.

I didn't *not* like her, but I didn't like her either.

Becky hated me, but was nice to me. I was pretty tight with Bryce and Corrigan so she needed to be nice to me. To tell the truth, I would've handled it on my own anyways. I could turn bitch when I was heated enough, but it didn't happen that often.

"Becky," Corrigan grunted and turned his back.

Bryce leaned his back on his locker and watched.

Two minions gasped behind Becky and we all knew why.

Corrigan had snubbed Becky Lew.

I didn't care about that.

Why had Corrigan snubbed Becky Lew?—that is the real question.

"So, Sheldon—let's talk about this weekend," Corrigan continued, ignoring his own snub. "I'm thinking that when you go to reacquaint yourself with Steele, you should wear one of those pink lacy thongs. You have about a million anyway."

"How do you know what my thongs look like? You snuck into my room, didn't you?" I should've cared. I didn't.

Corrigan looked affronted, but I saw the mirth that sparkled in his eyes.

I swore, good-naturedly.

"I just went up once to look for Bryce. Any decent red-blooded male would've looked."

"Corrigan," Becky spoke up. She had decided that she wasn't one to be ignored.

Corrigan resumed, passionately, "And then you should ask if Steele's sister has a matching pair of pink lacy thongs. That'd be awesome. You could both wear them when you bring her to the party."

"Corrigan," Becky said again.

I laughed and shifted so my side pressed against Bryce's when I noted, dryly, "Someone's knocking at your door, Corrigan."

Bryce snaked an arm around my waist and cupped my hip.

Corrigan grew still and sighed. He turned to Becky and asked, "What do you want, Lew?"

"I'd like to know when you're coming over tonight." She pressed, eagerly, happy for her opening. "My dad's coming home for dinner and it'd be nice to make sure he won't walk in on us."

Corrigan froze in place.

Becky smiled sweetly.

And hot damn—the minions seemed to preen.

Corrigan said slowly, "Becky, if and when we hook up—you can be sure that your dad's going to be scheduling around us. Not the other way around." The statement made no sense, but it didn't matter. Corrigan was being his usual cocky self and to add insult to injury, he tsk-tsked her—such a dismissal.

Becky tightened her mouth and started to retort, but I drawled, "Corrigan, I never knew. Were you hoping for a twosome with Steele's sister and Lew?"

Becky hissed, but caught herself in time. She knew better than to play her games with me.

Bryce must've grown bored because he straightened away from me and left the group.

"Where you going, Bry?" Corrigan called after him and eagerly left to follow.

Bryce had given him his 'out.'

Don't ever say best friends don't look out for each other.

"It's true, you know." Becky tore my attention from the guys back to her.

"What is?" I asked, suddenly tired of the game. Baiting her wasn't fun without Corrigan to suffer the consequences.

"Me and Corrigan. We hooked up at Bryce's party on Friday. You weren't there."

No, I wasn't. I knew everyone wanted to know where I was, but I told none.

"You and Bryce have a fight or something?" Becky shifted closer to me, like it was a whispered secret between the two of us.

"Well, if we did then we just kissed and made up."

"I don't get the two of you. You're on his arm half the time and the other half, he's got someone else on his arm. What's the deal?"

"So…you and Corrigan, huh? Good luck with that." I patted her shoulder and pushed past to my own locker.

I wasn't really surprised to see that Corrigan had waited for me.

"Your girlfriend's a bit too nosy for her well-being," I murmured as I opened my locker and stashed my book.

"She's not my girlfriend," he muttered.

"Where'd Bryce go?" Spanish for second period wasn't looking too enticing. Sex was.

"I don't know," he shrugged. "What am I going to do about Lew?"

Spanish it was. Sadly.

Corrigan fell into step beside me when I pointed out, "It'd help if I knew what happened."

"We hooked up," he evaded. That was a duh, but what else happened? There was always something else.

"And went back for seconds last night?" I guessed the 'something else.'

"Please," he puffed his chest up, arrogantly. "*Thirds* was last night."

His cockiness just rolled over off his shoulders.

"And you suggested a fourth tonight?"

"Something like that."

"So Becky Lew is your new screw-buddy and she doesn't know it?"

"She thinks she's my girlfriend."

Bingo. We just found the problem. So many thought they were the girlfriend.

"And that's why you want me to bring Steele's sister." It made sense. A movie star's sister would trump Becky Lew on any day.

"Oh no, I just want to get laid by a movie star's sister. You know me better than that, Sheldon. I can dodge Lew all week." He flashed another arrogant smile.

I think the girl behind me fainted, but I didn't care. I called him a not-so-nice word instead, but I did it with a sparkle in my eye.

"Please," he huffed. "You and Bryce are always all over each other, but the minute emotions might come into play, the two of you are all over someone else. Who's the bad guy between us?"

Coolly, I promised, "Watch it." He knew where to step and where to avoid. He'd just stepped wrong. Corrigan knew the conversation that had words like Bryce, myself, and emotions were automatically off limits.

"I'm just saying, help me out."

"You don't need my help getting laid, Corrigan." Had he not just left Becky Lew in his dust?

"It's different. Girls in school are different. Seriously, make friends with Steele's sister for me?"

"How do you even know if she's hot? Maybe there's a reason why she's not known. She could be ugly and fat."

"She's not. I've already met her." He cursed at his slip.

I arched an eyebrow and asked, "You didn't want me to know that?"

"Look." He glanced up and down the hallway and moved closer. One of his hands rested at my hip as he whispered, "She's not exactly a fan of mine."

I slapped his hand away and said, "You already shagged her, didn't you?"

"Not quite," he sounded pained, but shook his head. "Just do it for me? Please, Sheldon?"

Whatever.

I sighed and replied dully, "Yeah. I'll make buddy-buddy and bring her round."

"To the party?" he pressed.

"To the party." I was such a sucker.

Chapter 2

When I entered Spanish, I saw the normal crowd in the back. Bryce sat, listening to whatever Chad Yerling was saying. A few of the other guys were also listening while some of the girls either gossiped or had perched on the guys' laps.

Stephanie Hills was perched on Bryce's table, but not his lap.

As I moved forward and dropped to the empty seat at Bryce's table, she shot off and scurried away.

Bryce switched his attention to me and leaned closer.

"What were you talking to Corrigan about?"

I shrugged and refused to meet his eyes.

"Wanna skip?" he suggested.

I smiled slowly and asked, "And do what?"

"You know." His eyes fell to my lips and stayed there. One of his hands rested on my knee and started a slow rhythmic caress.

"Scout," Chad called loudly.

Bryce ignored him and asked me again, "Now or never. Wanna go?"

I bit my lip, knowing it'd turn him on, but murmured, "You're in a weird mood today."

Bryce sighed and leaned back. His hand stayed in place.

"So a no, then?" he asked. Bryce and I had our own language. And we both knew my response was an evade.

I could never say no or yes. Neither could he.

"Scout," Chad said again, a little huffy now.

I leaned forward and pressed a slow, torturous kiss to Bryce's lips.

He grasped the back of my head and held me in place as he explored me in return. I'm pretty sure I heard Chad groan in frustration. He'd effectively lost the battle for Bryce's attention.

"Mr. Scout and Miss Jeneve."

Our teacher, Mr. Dwellsworth, banged a ruler on his desk.

I tried to pull back, but Bryce finished the kiss, languidly, before he released me.

I was a little relieved to hear Bryce panting right alongside me.

"Mr. Scout and Miss Jeneve!" Our teacher tried again.

"Yeah?" I asked, knowing my voice was hoarse.

"I don't want the two of you to sit at the same table. Mr. Scout, please switch seats with Miss Veera."

"Who?" Bryce asked as he stood, relaxed and confident.

A girl in the back, tiny and pissed, stood up as she grabbed her books. She glared as she retorted, "That's me." She brushed past him, her red hair smacked him in the face as she dropped into his vacated seat.

Bryce chuckled as he took her seat.

She glanced my way, but hunched her shoulders as she opened her book to read.

"What's your first name?" I ignored her silent request to be left alone.

She ignored me so I reached out and plucked her book away.

"What's your name?" I asked again as she paled. I wasn't one to be ignored—ever.

"Her name is Shelly Veera and you need to leave her alone, Miss Jeneve," Mr. Dwellsworth said sternly.

When he started his lecture, I leaned forward and whispered, "Why are you all pissy?"

She made a sound like she was in pain, but didn't reply.

I felt a tap on my shoulder and turned around to see that Chad held out a note for me.

We should've skipped.

I looked to Bryce and nodded. I bit my lip again and he coughed.

"Mr. Scout!" The teacher again.

I rolled my eyes and turned eyes front.

"Yes, sir?" Bryce questioned, politely, sarcastically.

Mr. Dwellsworth became red in the face and sputtered, "You continue to disrupt my classroom day after day. I have had enough, Mr. Scout."

Bryce didn't say one word.

That was something I'd always been envious about. Bryce had the hot body that could get him into a magazine, but it was the air that surrounded him. The air drew in all the attention. He could muster anyone to do anything for him without a single spoken word.

Sometimes it turned me on and other times it pissed me off.

Today was the former.

I raised my hand and decided to join the foray. "Mr. Dwellsworth."

You could feel the enraptured tension in the class. All eyes slowly trailed towards me.

"Yes, Miss Jeneve?" Mr. Dwellsworth asked cautiously.

"Bryce didn't say anything to disrupt your class. He just coughed."

Mr. Dwellsworth weighed his words, but he responded with forced politeness, "Miss Jeneve, when I ask to debate the decisions of my classroom, you may talk then. Right now, I am the teacher and I will tolerate your disrespect no longer."

"So are you going to have us leave?" I asked, looking almost bored.

His eyes narrowed as they took in my relaxed state and saw that Bryce mirrored my look. It had been practiced and perfected throughout our lifetime because of unjustly parents who thought they could tell us what to do. Or, at least, that's what my third shrink told me when I made the not-so-startling revelation that I struggled with authority. It was because my parents were never parents to me. The little they chose to stick around didn't grant them the right to suddenly turn parent on me for two holidays of the year.

I had liked that shrink, but my parents hadn't.

"No, Miss Jeneve." He sighed and shook his head. "No, I am not. Unlike every other adult figure in your life, I'm going to make you learn something. I think, from now on, you and Mr. Scout will be tutored in the library by two of my student aides."

Shelly gasped beside me and I cast a curious look her way.

And to this, she ducked her head back into her book and tried to ignore everything else. Interesting.

"Are you serious?" Bryce yawned. "We get an hour to ourselves in the library instead of coming here?"

"Trust me," Mr. Dwellsworth grinned, in all his evils delight that a teacher could muster. "You won't be enjoying yourselves."

I didn't really care what our 'discipline' was, but I spoke up, "Are you serious? Just because I spoke up for a friend doesn't give you the right to suddenly expel us to the library. You have no reason to remove us from this class."

"Oh, Miss Jeneve." Mr. Dwellsworth shook his head. "You are not being removed from this class."

"Shut up, Sheldon," Bryce murmured. "We get out of here."

It wasn't the point.

"You may both leave now, but if you are not in the library when my student aides report there, you will receive detention for the rest of the week."

Well, it was pretty obvious to everyone what we were going to do. Detention it is!

Bryce stood and waited at the door for me.

I heard Chad starting to laugh just before the door shut behind us.

In the hallway, Bryce asked, "What was that about?"

I shrugged, "I had a point."

"Whatever. I think he's getting used to us after two years." Bryce chuckled. "Wanna skip?"

"That's what got us into this punishment in the first place." But we both knew we were going to go.

Bryce shot me one of his melting grins. He tugged me close and rested his forehead against mine. As his lips rested just above mine, he said again, "Let's go somewhere else."

"And do what?" I smiled and enjoyed the brush of my lips against his. Bryce transferred my book into his hands and clasped me closer to him. I reached around his neck and brought my body flush against his. Bryce turned and backed me up against a locker. He started to kiss my neck.

"You guys need a room."

Who else? Only a few would dare...

Corrigan.

Bryce didn't stop.

"What are you doing out of class?" I asked as I remained in Bryce's arms and tilted my neck for better access.

Corrigan leaned against the locker beside us and stuffed his hands into his pockets. He looked dejected when he mumbled, "Nothing. I could go for some food."

If memory served correctly... I teased, "Isn't Becky Lew in your second period?"

Corrigan rolled his eyes and pushed off from the locker. "You guys coming or not? My treat."

I sighed and Bryce felt it when he stepped away.

We shared a glance and both turned to follow our best friend. When we got outside, I saw that Corrigan had taken up residence in my car.

"Of course," I said sarcastically as I took the driver's seat. "You're the one who's up for food, but I'm the one driving."

Corrigan grinned cheekily at me and remarked, "You like driving stick, Sheldon. We all know it."

I shared a resigned look in the rear-view mirror with Bryce before he laid down in the backseat.

"No sleeping," I remarked as I pulled out of the parking lot.

"Yeah. Yeah," Bryce mumbled back, but Corrigan turned and punched his best friend in the stomach.

Without shock, pause, a reaction, anything—Bryce reached up and slammed Corrigan's head against his headrest. It happened so quick…this is why we were best friends.

I shook my head, grinned, and pulled out into the street.

"Oomph," Corrigan breathed.

Bryce laughed and punched Corrigan in the shoulder before he laid back down.

"So what's up with this impromptu food trip?" I asked, shifting gears.

"No reason. I'm just hungry," Corrigan murmured, vaguely, as he turned back in his seat. He tapped the dashboard absent-mindedly and reached to change the radio station.

Bryce sat up and our eyes met again, but not in shared lust.

Corrigan was evading my question. Corrigan only evaded when he was upset.

"Right, you're just hungry," Bryce murmured sarcastically as he studied his best friend.

"If you wanted food, you would've gone to the vending machine," I added and pulled into my house's driveway.

"Thought we'd go to a restaurant or something," Corrigan half-heartedly protested.

I didn't like restaurants. He knew that.

"Whatever," I brushed it off as I climbed out and led the way into my kitchen.

Having rich parents had its benefits. When I requested a chef to come in, a chef came in.

I rarely ate so the chef was only requested when Corrigan and Bryce ate through my stock. As they did now—they both attacked the fridge to find some lasagna while I ate grilled chicken.

We all headed for the media room and I curled on the couch as the guys sat on each end and inhaled their food.

After Corrigan got up for more, I leaned forward and punched Bryce on the arm.

"What?" he asked as he cradled his arm.

"You start it."

We both knew what I meant.

A pained look crossed his face. "Oh, come on. You're the girl. Be girly."

I punched him again.

"Ow! That one hurt."

"Bryce," I warned.

"Fine. Alright, just stop hitting me."

I raised my fist again, but Bryce caught it and hauled me onto his lap.

He grinned in satisfaction as he leaned back against the couch. Both of his hands moved to my hips and he held me in place when I moved to slide off.

"This will be more enjoyable if you stay exactly where you are."

Hearing the microwave door open and shut, I leaned forward, kissed Bryce quickly and twisted his nipple.

"Ow! That hurt too," Bryce cried out.

I slid off his lap and kicked him for good measure.

Corrigan returned and started to eat his second helping when Bryce groaned and spoke up, "Alright, man. What's up?"

Corrigan froze mid-chew and looked us over.

He finished chewing, swallowed, and slowly settled back against the couch. He kept his plate on his lap.

Bryce looked at me with raised eyebrows, but I watched Corrigan instead.

Finally, Corrigan spoke up, "Alright...you should know...I'm moving."

"What?" I sat up and asked in shock.

Bryce's eyes widened—a feat that I'd never seen before, but he didn't say anything.

Corrigan watched us another moment and then threw his head back in a laugh.

"I'm so joking, you guys. God—look at you." He kept laughing until Bryce punched him in the shoulder.

"Ow!" he yelped and moved away. Corrigan shook his head and continued eating in between laughs. "Seriously. You guys looked like I'd died or something. That was hilarious."

"Not funny." I glared.

"It was funny." Corrigan chuckled as he finished the rest of his food. When Bryce and I continued to stare at him, he threw his hands in the air, "Come on, guys! Seriously! You don't want to go there."

"What is wrong with you?" Bryce asked, more curious.

"Nothing's wrong with me. Why do you automatically assume something's wrong?"

"Because we were making out and you interrupted. You never interrupt us," I spelled it out. That was my first clue anyway.

"If you want to make out right now, don't hold back. I have no problem with it." Corrigan flashed his charming grin again.

I blinked, stunned at how slippery he could be. Then I said, "No. Tell us."

He glanced at Bryce for a second and shook his head again. "Seriously. Nothing's wrong."

He didn't want to share and it was starting to become more work than it deserved. I rolled my eyes and asked, "How do you know Steele's sister? What's her name?"

Bryce glanced to him and asked, "You already know her?"

Corrigan stiffened, but answered, "Her name is Mena and yes, I've met her. It didn't go so well."

"What happened?" Bryce flashed a grin. "You hit on her, but shagged her best friend."

Classic Corrigan and as his jaw tightened, Bryce had hit the bulls-eye.

"Oh come on, Corrigan. How are you expecting to make a better impression over that?" I laughed.

The charm was back when he replied, "I've got a few tricks."

I narrowed my eyes and then rolled my eyes. Corrigan was in one of his moods and I lacked the energy to play his game.

Bryce studied for a moment longer and then decided the same as me. Corrigan would do what he always did.

"Come on. I'm ready to go back. How about you two?" Corrigan stood up and waited.

I did have three cars at my beck and call. Mine, plus my parent's. They didn't need them in Europe or wherever they were.

Bryce watched me. I turned to him and we both shared a wolfish grin.

I dug my keys out and chucked them to Corrigan.

"Crash her and you pay for her," I warned and he sent a suggestive leer at us before he jiggled the keys.

"Thanks, Sheldon. Feel free to tape it so I can watch later," Corrigan called over his shoulder as he jogged up the stairs and out the door.

Bryce watched me, trying to gauge me.

He always did this too.

Sighing, I uncurled my legs and stood. As I stretched gracefully, Bryce enjoyed the show with a half-grin curling at his mouth. I bent forward, holding his gaze intently, and reached for his plate. I grabbed my own and then traipsed up the stairs.

Bryce followed as I placed the dishes in the sink and proceeded upstairs to my room.

I left the door open and fell on my bed as Bryce followed inside.

"When are your parents coming back?" he asked as he pulled his shirt off. My eyes traveled over his muscular chest and stomach.

"They're in Italy and won't be home until Thanksgiving," I murmured, huskily, as I knelt on the bed. "Between you and me, I don't even think they'll be back by then."

Bryce left the door open since my room could get stuffy and moved closer to me.

"You told me they'd be back this weekend. I remember," Bryce stepped closer and closed his eyes when I slid my hand down his chest. I hooked a finger on the inside of his pants and he said hoarsely, "Because that was your excuse for my party on Friday."

I unsnapped the front button and slid the zipper down.

I pulled him down on top of me and whispered, closing my eyes as his hand started his own exploration, "Maybe I just didn't want to go and see you hit on all those other girls."

"Baby." Bryce rolled me underneath him and propped himself up on one elbow.

I opened my eyes and held his sapphire ones.

He bent forward and pressed a kiss to my jaw when he murmured, soothingly, "You're always my first choice. You know that, don't you?"

In truth, I hadn't gone because we'd had a 'near emotion' event that day. That's what Corrigan called them when I witnessed a cheerleader pawing the front of Bryce's pants that afternoon. Bryce hadn't known I was around, but my jaw clenched and I turned away.

Corrigan had shaken his head when I left down the opposite hallway and out the door.

The sight of a girl mauling Bryce wasn't anything new, but the sight of Bryce enjoying it had cut deeper than I wanted to acknowledge. I begged off the party and my excuse had been weak. At the time, Bryce registered the feeble excuse with a flicker in his eyes, but he hadn't said anything.

I entwined a hand around the back of his neck and pulled his head to mine. Against his lips, I whispered, as I twisted one of my legs over his, "I better damn well be."

Bryce smirked once before he captured my lips with his and his full weight fell on me.

Moments later, both of us were panting as the rest of our clothes followed to the floor and Bryce gasped, "Condom."

"Usual place," I whispered against his skin as I stayed wrapped around him.

Bryce groaned and I pressed against him.

We hadn't been together all weekend.

"Baby," he grunted. "I have to go. Condom, now."

The haze disappeared enough for me to remember the importance of that little piece of rubber and I let go. Bryce was off the bed in a flash and he grabbed a condom from my dresser drawer. He met my lips when he returned and it didn't take long before the condom was applied and Bryce rolled me underneath once more.

He slid in and both of us groaned in pleasure.

As the tempo sped up, slowly, Bryce continued to kiss just underneath my ear. It was one of my spots that he'd discovered early on.

I tilted my head back, ran a hand down his back, and moved to meet his lips with mine.

I knew that was something he liked.

He groaned into my mouth and increased his thrusts.

After awhile, both of us just held on as we climaxed together and our bodies shuddered. We stayed put, wrapped around each other with Bryce still inside of me until our bodies had stopped convulsing.

I sunk down onto my pillow and nearly purred when Bryce ran a hand down the side of my body, from my shoulder to my knee. It was soothing and I rolled to allow him to move to the other side of my body.

Chuckling, Bryce pulled out and pressed a kiss to my hipbone as his fingers finished their exploration of my body.

He moved to the side and pulled my bedcovers over both of us before he turned and wrapped an arm around me, spooning from behind.

I yawned, feeling contented, when I glimpsed the clock.

12:45.

"We should go back for the rest of the afternoon," I murmured, tiredly.

Bryce chuckled into my ear and asked, "What for? We'll just get reamed out by the principal."

"So what? We should stay in bed all day?"

"Why not?" He propped himself on an elbow and looked down on me as I fell to my back. He smiled and murmured, "It wouldn't be the first time."

"Because you have soccer practice in three hours," I pointed out. "If you're not in school, you can't play."

A shadow of weariness passed over him as he sat up and moved to the edge of the bed.

"What?" I asked and sat up.

Bryce shook his head and reached for his pants.

"What?" I repeated and reached for my own.

"Nothing," he clipped out and moved to the shower. When I heard the water running, I dropped my clothes and crossed to the bathroom doorway.

I could see Bryce in the shower and his eyes found mine through the translucent glass shower door.

He finished and stepped out a moment later.

He moved aside and was dressed when I finished my own shower.

Bryce sat on my bed and waited for me to finish dressing.

Finally, I asked when I put my hairdryer away, "What is it?"

"Nothing. Are you done?" He stood and grabbed a set of car keys on my nightstand. He knew I kept keys to all three cars on any set. I always kept an extra set in my bedroom, one in my purse, and another set in my pockets.

"Are you mad?" Even as I asked it, I felt my chest tighten a little. This was encroaching onto a conversation I didn't want to have, but I'd already asked.

"I don't want to fight so let's just…" he waved towards the door. "Let's go."

"What fight? Did I say something to offend you? Is this about soccer practice?" I felt myself cringing with each question. Seriously. I feel like I had lost control of my mouth. I couldn't stop asking questions. I was annoying myself.

Bryce opened his mouth, but no sound came out. He closed it and turned towards the hallway.

I followed behind and neither of us questioned it when Bryce drove us to school in my mom's Chrysler.

Chapter 3

The fifth period bell must've just rang because we saw a bunch of students in the parking lot when Bryce turned off the engine.

Neither of us moved, but watched the crowd just outside the door.

It was warm and we had an extended break between fifth and sixth period. It wasn't uncommon for nearly everyone to flock outside, either in the back or in the front of the building.

I couldn't stand the tension, but I also knew I didn't want to get out of the car with how things were between us.

Finally, I said weakly, "I don't know what to do right now."

Bryce bit off a bitter laugh and shook his head. "You don't have to do anything."

"What?"

"You're always saying that. Get a clue, Sheldon," he snapped and slammed the door behind him.

I sighed and watched as Bryce was greeted by Chad, Trenton, and so many others.

Get a clue? What did that mean? And why did I actually care?

I followed behind, feeling just…uncomfortable. I didn't care that most of the students had knowing looks on their faces.

I didn't want to stop and chat. It must've shown in my face because a path cleared for me so I was able to walk inside without any hassle. As I stopped in the girls' locker room, I grabbed some deodorant from my locker. I had forgotten to apply some at the house.

There were three girls at the sinks and when I turned back, all three had their eyes on me.

"What?" I asked, tiredly. If I was Bryce, I just would've snapped at them. It took a lot to get me heated.

All of their eyes widened and turned away.

Thank goodness…for them.

I washed my hands and saw that one of the girls stayed behind.

She had jet-black hair that streamed to her waist. She was petite with a cute green tank top over a faded trendy miniskirt and black boots that stopped just underneath her knee.

"Hi?" I asked. What'd she want?

"You're Sheldon Jeneve, right?" she asked and tamed a strand of hair that was out of place. She didn't look nervous, just confident.

"Yeah. And you are…?"

"I'm Mena Cruiw. My brother is Denton Steele."

Oh. I studied her again and saw a faint resemblance in the eyes, but that was about it. Oh, and the nose curled at the same spot.

"You have a different last name?" I asked the obvious question.

"I was adopted by my stepfather, but they're having problems so they sent me out here to live with my biological dad."

"You and Denton are half-siblings?"

"No," she said shortly and leaned against a sink. "We're full brother and sister, but he still loves our dad. Me, I'd rather not have anything to do with him. You know my stepmother and biological dad."

This sounded complex. "Look," I murmured. "I don't really want to hear your family's genogram."

"That's okay," she said brightly. "I don't really want to tell you my family's genogram. We're messed up, that's the gist of it."

"And why are you talking to me…?"

"Because you shagged my brother and didn't give him the time of day afterwards." She grinned and it lit up her face and eyes. Corrigan would've called her hot without the smile, but he would've considered her deadly with the smile. "I wanted to meet you."

"Nice to meet you," I said dully and dismissed her as I turned my back to leave. I expected her to say something, but she didn't. When I got to my locker, I realized why—she'd followed me.

"What?" I grabbed my sixth period book.

"I thought maybe," she shrugged. "I don't know. Maybe we could be friends? You know who I am and you don't care about my brother. I like that. And I heard around that you don't have a lot of friends."

"I don't do friends."

I cringed inside. Bad choice of words.

"This isn't about popularity. Trust me." She assured me and gestured to the hallway. I glanced around and saw a good portion of the guys were eyeing us, up and down. I'd grown immune to the attention, but I shouldn't have been surprised they were watching her.

Mena waved them off and added, "I know who my brother is. I can be popular off his name. I can be popular on my own too. I was Homecoming Queen at my last school for the junior class. I went to the largest high school in Manhattan. I'd like to think that says something."

"Becky Lew likes friends," I mentioned. Becky Lew liked followers.

Mena parroted my thoughts as she snorted, "Becky Lew likes to be followed around and fanned. She wants errand girls, not friends. I was lucky to get a few good friends at my old school. I like you. I heard all about you from Denton and this morning around school. You don't give a crap what people think of you. It works for you." She stepped closer and said, "And you don't play those childish games that all girls inevitably do. I'm tired of that life."

I frowned and moved away from her. To be truthful, I didn't know what to think of this girl. Luckily, Corrigan interrupted us as he stopped and asked, his back turned to Mena, "Do I need to know what happened between you two?"

Corrigan did that so efficiently. It was a perfected technique that effectively cut out anyone else.

For a moment, I thought he meant me and Mena, but then comprehension dawned and I whispered, "No. You don't need to know because I don't even know."

He meant Bryce and myself.

"Bryce is furious. I'm asking." He shifted closer to me. "Should I know what happened?"

"You want to know all the dirty secrets?" I teased. "You want the play by play?"

Corrigan took the hint and returned smoothly, "You taped it. Right? Tell me you taped it."

Mena shifted farther to the side as Corrigan dropped to lean against the locker that she had been standing against.

She frowned at his back, but all of our attention was thwarted when Bryce stopped beside us.

He ran his eyes over Corrigan and myself before he drawled, "Principal wants to see us."

I groaned and buried my head in my locker.

"Hope your nooner was worth it. I heard you guys were supposed to be at the library instead." Corrigan leered knowingly.

"We skipped because you were hungry," Bryce pointed out.

The leer disappeared.

Becky Lew chose that moment to stop with her usual crowd of minions behind her. She smiled seductively at Bryce and ran a hand down his chest while she purred, "Hey, guys."

No one knew what to do.

It was common knowledge that Bryce was off-limits when I was around. There was a reason why Stephanie Hills scampered off his table when I arrived. It wasn't because I turned sudden bitch, it was just because Bryce really did choose me first. Girls just got humiliated when I showed up.

I frowned and watched Corrigan instead.

Jaded

He tensed and looked at me.

I burst out laughing, which earned a few puzzled looks.

"I'm sorry." I tried to hide my smile behind a hand. "It's just... you were all after Corrigan this morning and now you're into Bryce?"

The seductive gleam vanished from Becky's eyes. They narrowed in anger at me instead.

I caught a relenting glint of amusement in Bryce's eyes so I moved forward and leaned my back against him.

Bryce tensed a moment and then slid his arms around my waist to dip his hands inside. I felt his thumbs caress against my thong, but that's all they did.

Becky frowned and stepped back.

"What are you doing here, Lew?" Corrigan leaned against my locker now.

She paused and studied him a moment. Then she glanced at Bryce and myself.

She'd tried the girlfriend bit with Corrigan, which hadn't worked and now...I couldn't understand her thought process. She probably wanted to make Corrigan jealous. And I had ruined it because I had laughed at her and then stole the show as Bryce had his arms around me, not her.

I looked up and caught an appreciate gleam in Mena's startling green eyes before she turned and sauntered away.

Becky was flushed, but she retorted, "I thought I'd say hello to Bryce since you've ignored me all day."

"There's a reason for that," Corrigan said swiftly and bounced on his heels. He was ready for a fight. The malice was mixed with enjoyment.

Bryce chuckled in my ear and I leaned fully against him. The two continued when I let my head fall backwards to his shoulder and I asked, my mouth beside his ear, "Truce?"

Bryce pulled away slightly to look at me. His eyes searched my face before he sighed and murmured, "I was just touchy before."

"Yeah, but…" I pulled away and turned so my stomach rested against him.

"I don't get what you were mad at before," I reasoned, ignoring the warmth that spread over my body.

This was just how it was between us.

"I wasn't. Can we drop it?" Bryce straightened and I pulled away.

"I'm the one who avoids. Why are you avoiding this? I don't even get what you're avoiding."

Neither of us were aware that Corrigan and Becky had stopped to watch us. The entire hallway watched us too.

"I'm not avoiding anything. I just don't…"

"What?" I cried out, more annoyed that I didn't understand. If I understood what I'd said to piss him off, then I could understand what he was avoiding. I just didn't understand and…we were nearing one of those 'near emotion' events.

I'd had enough. My red flag had been thrown up.

I pushed through the group and shrugged off, "I'm out."

A second later, I heard Bryce curse.

I ignored the principal's heed and headed to my art class. The teacher was cool. Mr. Sayword wouldn't say a word, even if the principal did track me down. Seriously, though, how can one truant student be so important?

I managed a grin to Mr. Sayword when I entered the room and swiftly entered the darkroom. I clicked the switch that let others know now not to interrupt because I'd be working on films. Instead of grabbing some film, I pulled out my drawing pad and started a portrait.

No, I wasn't upset. No, this wasn't a self-coping mechanism. I just wanted to avoid any and all. The darkroom gave me that.

After ten minutes, some students pounded on the door and I called out, "What?"

"Are you almost done developing? We have some pictures we need to develop too, you know. You're not the only one."

I stood and opened the door.

There were three students and all of them took a step back, startled when they saw who it was.

"Oh. Sorry, Sheldon. Seriously," a girl said quickly as she grabbed her camera and hurried to a corner.

The other two gaped. One was a boy with wire-rim glasses and messy black hair. He used gel to make it stick out on its ends. It looked trendy, which was accentuated by the plaid vest that was snug over a black silk shirt. The other boy was tall, lanky, and wore a Suns tee shirt.

Neither looked familiar.

"What are your names?" I asked since they still hadn't moved out of my way.

"Um…I'm Teddy." The plaid vest guy mumbled and pointed beside him, "This is Brent."

"Hi."

They didn't move.

"Move," I spelled it out.

"Um…" Teddy began again.

Just then I looked up and saw Bryce enter the room.

He glanced at Mr. Sayword and then scanned the room. His eyes stopped on mine and he approached me.

"We're supposed to be at the principal's office. I've told you twice," he snapped.

"And I said that I was out."

"Then you should've left school. They know you're here so we gotta go and pay our penance or something," he growled and skimmed his eyes over Teddy and Brent.

Both snapped to attention and ran off.

"Were you talking to them?"

"No," I sighed and moved back into the darkroom for my drawing pad. Bryce followed and looked around.

"I've never been in here," he murmured and leaned against the counter.

I eyed him up and down and made my decision. I shut the door again and flipped the same switch.

"What is up with you today?" I demanded to know. Enough was enough.

"Noth—" he started to say, but I interrupted.

"Bryce. Seriously. I'm here and I want to have this talk. Tell me what's up with you."

His eyes locked with mine and I saw that he was considering it, considering something.

Finally, he cut out, "Why'd you bail on my party?"

"Are you serious? This is what that's about? Because I bailed on your party?"

"Yes and no." He sighed and pushed off from the counter, but kept a hold of its edge. He bounced back and forth, doing reverse push-ups from the counter. His arm muscles bulged with each movement.

"I don't know," Bryce mumbled with his chin tucked downwards. He looked at the floor. "I just...I don't know. I'm on edge today."

"Why?" I was dumbfounded. Yeah. I had bailed on Friday night, but so what? He still got laid. Corrigan said he saw Bryce disappear into a backroom with one of the cheerleaders. And Saturday night, Bryce had been all over some cross-country runner.

"I don't know," he shrugged. "We should go before we get in more trouble."

"Since when do you care how much trouble we get into?" They couldn't do anything to us. Bryce was the soccer team's captain and recruited heavily. The school needed that attention. And I just didn't care. The school knew that and had given up on me a long time ago. They just wanted me to continue attending school and classes. At least, that's what their school counselor had confided in me once.

"I don't, but it's a big practice tonight. I don't want my coach more worked up than he needs to be, you know."

Understanding finally dawned on me and I felt like smacking myself in the head. This was the beginning of Scout Week. Those same recruiters and more were visiting the school's teams. They came to the practices, games, and talked with the families.

"Which ones are coming to your practice?" I asked and I saw I was right. A flicker of tension passed in Bryce's eyes.

I moved closer and slipped my arms around him. I looked up and grinned, "Which ones?"

He hugged me back, slowly, and murmured, "Brown. Stanford. And Florida."

"And you want Brown, right?"

"Yeah."

Just then, someone pounded on the door again. It stopped after someone hissed, "Bryce and Sheldon are in there. Ssshh!"

There weren't any more interruptions.

Bryce chuckled in amusement, but he shook his head a moment later.

A discreet knock sounded at the door and Mr. Sayword murmured, "Uh…Mr. Scout and Sheldon, the principal requests your presence in his office. Please finish your developing as soon as possible."

Bryce cracked a grin as I laughed.

"We're almost done, Mr. Sayword," I called back.

Bryce murmured, his hand at my back as we moved outside, "He seems cool."

I flashed a grin to my teacher who'd moved back behind his desk.

"Yeah. He is." I waved to Mr. Sayword as we moved into the hallway.

Before we got to the main office, we both saw Corrigan in the hallway, hunched over an open locker.

"Seriously, dude." Bryce clapped a hand on his shoulder.

Corrigan jumped around, eyes wide, and nudged the locker shut with his heel. When he saw it was us, he relaxed.

"Jeez. Don't do that!" he hissed and opened the locker again. He was on a mission.

"Don't you ever go to class?" I asked.

"Not if I can help it," Corrigan muttered.

"Whose locker?" Bryce reached inside and plucked a book out. He opened the cover and read, "Theodore Campbell."

Theodore Campbell?

I said lazily, "That's Teddy. I just met him. He's in my art class."

"Yeah, well, he's going down." Corrigan mumbled as he looked through Teddy's bag.

"What are you doing?"

"He spray-painted 'Greco' on my car. The douche is going down. I'm looking for his keys."

"Greco? What does that mean?"

"I don't know, but it's on my car," Corrigan growled. Corrigan never growls. In fact, a serious Corrigan was a rare event.

"What are you going to do?"

"Steal his car and give it to Hoodum."

"Isn't that excessive?"

Hoodum ran the local gang. They specialized in the economics of refurbished cars. They stripped cars, stolen or 'legitimately' donated.

"He spray-painted my car," Corrigan spelled it out. "No one does that and gets away with it."

Fair enough.

"How do you know it was Teddy?"

"Chet saw him do it. He did it when we left school. He's going down." Corrigan produced the keys and took off, triumphantly.

"Mr. Scout and Miss Jeneve!" Our names were shouted down the hallway. The principal's secretary, Mrs. Walker, was irate as she pointed at us. "If you do not get your butts in this office within thirty seconds, you are both expelled from this school."

Yeah right, but… Bryce and I headed towards the office. I know that I liked to see an irate Mrs. Walker. It was funny to watch.

Chad Yerling grinned widely when he saw us walk in. He leaned back in one of the waiting chairs, his arm rested over two more, and had kicked up his shoes on another pair of chairs. Three students were forced to squish together in the remaining two chairs across the waiting room.

"What are you guys doing here?" he asked and removed his legs. Bryce and I sat down while Chad rearranged himself to lay sprawled over three chairs. His feet propped onto the stand.

"What are you doing here?" Bryce asked in amusement.

Mrs. Walker harrumphed as she sent a withering glare our way before she walked into the employee's lounge.

Chad beamed and folded his hands underneath his head. "I got caught getting a blowjob in the boiler room."

"You did? By who?"

Chad shrugged. "Just some girl."

I narrowed my eyes and studied him. He was lying, but whatever. I saw that the other students had froze at his words. Chad's coolness would rise another level.

He nodded in our direction again, "So what are you guys doing here?"

I shrugged and Bryce replied, "Mouthing off? I don't know."

Chad smirked, "Did you guys go to the library in second? Word is that you took off." And had sex.

He hadn't said the words, but they were still there.

"Nah. We skipped to eat with Corrigan," Bryce murmured and the sneer disappeared from Chad's face.

The office door burst open and a student sprinted inside. He panted as he babbled, "Corrigan Raimler is—"

Bryce moved in a flash and dragged the kid outside.

Chad glanced to me and asked, "What was that about?"

I shrugged and moved to follow. I glanced over my shoulder to make sure that Mrs. Walker was still absent—she was. Chad moved to follow too, but I said firmly, "You stay and cover for us. Tell them I'm sick."

He could've come, but I didn't like Chad—never had. He just gave me the creeps.

"Okay." Chad nodded, but watched through the window as I quickly darted around the hallway.

Bryce had dragged the kid outside and was already interrogating him by the time I got there. "So what were you going to say?" He prodded the kid with a finger in his shoulder.

The kid looked like he was about to pee his pants. He trembled when Bryce towered over him.

"I...I..." he stammered and glanced up at me. Terrified.

"Just tell us what you were going to say," I spoke, calmly.

"I...Corrigan..." He took a deep breath and rushed out, "Corrigan Raimler just stole one of my friends' cars. I know it wasn't his because it's Teddy's."

Bryce and I shared a look.

"You were going to tell the staff that Corrigan stole your buddy's car?"

He paled when Bryce repeated his words.

"No...nnnnoo. I wasn't. I was just..."

"Corrigan is my best friend." I wanted to make sure he understood.

The kid shrunk back against the wall.

"He's my best friend," Bryce murmured soothingly, but we both heard the lethal promise in that voice.

Seriously. I even got shivers.

"Um..."

"What's your name?" I asked as I shifted closer to him.

His eyes widened further and he stuttered, "D-d-Darrell."

"Darrell? And you're friends with Teddy?"

"Yeah."

I nodded and brushed against him. Bryce shifted backwards to give me space and I crooned into Darrell's ear, "When you hear that Teddy's car is gone, you're going to *not* remember anything about it. Okay?"

He nodded quickly and swallowed tightly.

I ran a hand down his arm and murmured, silkily, "And the reason you're not going to remember anything is because my friend could get into a lot of trouble. And I don't want that. Bryce doesn't want that."

I moved back and stared him in the face.

"And if we hear that Corrigan's name was slipped, by anyone, you're the one that we're coming after. Got it?"

He jerked his head up and down. His hands covered the front of his pants as I stepped back. He rushed past us, inside.

Bryce swore and yanked his phone out of his phone. He pressed Corrigan's number and barked into it, "You idiot! You were seen by a kid. Do you know what would've happened if the kid had told?"

I breathed in relief as I fell back against the bricked wall of our school.

Bryce swore again, "No. It's criminal charges, asswipe. You could've gone to jail or…" He hung up and stared at me.

I spoke the obvious, "It's not the first time we've bailed Corrigan out of jail."

"I know." Bryce slumped next to me and slid to the floor. "But they would've pressed him harder because he'd be connected to Hoodum."

It was known around town that the cops had a vendetta against Hoodum and his gang. They wanted to shut 'em down completely, but they were having a hard time. Hoodum was pretty slippery and pretty damned smart.

The door opened again and Chad poked his head out.

"Hey, just so you know, Mrs. Walker is freaking out that you guys are gone. You might want to get in here."

"You were supposed to cover for us," I said sharply.

Bryce looked at me, surprised, but Chad shrugged and muttered, "I tried, dude. Jeez."

When he went back inside, Bryce asked me, "What was up with that?"

I shrugged and moved inside.

Relief was evident on Mrs. Walker's face when she saw us.

She snapped two fingers at us and pointed to the seats. "You two, stay put and don't move. I don't care if you're sick, if you have to vomit, or the school burns down. You stay put or face expulsion."

Bryce and I sat.

The other students were still there and had mixed looks of fear, awe, and trepidation.

I closed my eyes and leaned against the wall when Bryce started to chat with Chad.

Each of the students had already gone inside the principal's office until it was just me, Bryce, and Chad. It seemed to take forever and probably did.

Mrs. Walker received a phone call and repeated her instructions sternly before she left the office once more.

"Seriously, guys. What'd you do? I haven't seen Mrs. Walker that pissy since Corrigan got caught screwing the Spanish teacher's daughter."

"Oh yeah," Bryce laughed.

Corrigan's popularity had skyrocketed that week. He'd been suspended for three days, but his arrival to the Friday football game had been to a standing ovation. None of the parents had stood, but some had been amused. Corrigan had saluted the crowd.

Mrs. Walker walked back inside with Miss Connors behind her.

"Sheldon," Miss Connors said softly. "Can you come with me?"

I snapped to attention and shot up.

"No," I said firmly.

Mrs. Walker looked taken aback, but Miss Connors wasn't surprised.

Chad avidly watched the encounter while Bryce stood slowly beside me.

"Sheldon, please." Miss Connors said again. She frowned at Bryce's hand that had moved to cup my elbow.

"You can't make me talk to you," I declared. It was the truth.

"Miss Jeneve," Mrs. Walker said promptly. "You will talk with our counselor or you will be expelled."

I narrowed my eyes at her and called her bluff.

"Expel me then."

Mrs. Walker gasped.

"Sheldon, this is ridiculous." Miss Connors stepped forward. "I just want to talk to you. That's all. I just want to know how you're doing."

"No, you don't," I spat out. "You want to try to figure me out. I'm not one of your subjects to understand and test."

"You have so much potential," Miss Connors pressed earnestly. "I don't understand why you're wasting it all away. I want to help you."

"I'm fine with how my life is." I stepped back. The chair pressed against the backs of my knees.

Bryce was extremely still beside me. Just watching me.

"No, you're not. Sheldon, you spend your time with these boys..."

Bryce whipped his head towards her.

Miss Connors faltered, but resumed again, "You are so intelligent, Sheldon. You could already be in college. Your IQ tests were—"

"You can't say any of that!" I shouted. "That's confidential."

"Sheldon, please..."

More students had filed into the office, but they all stopped abruptly.

I shook my head and clenched out, "You can't do this. You can't make me talk to you. Expel me then. I don't care. Screw you." I shoved past them. At the door, I stopped and met Bryce's gaze, "Call me later."

He nodded, his jaw was clenched.

Mena was at my locker when I swiftly kicked it and grabbed my bag.

"Hey," she called after me when I turned for the parking lot.

When she caught up to me, she asked, "Are you okay?"

I ignored her and shoved through the kids who hadn't seen me coming. Most of them darted out of my way, but a few weren't as lucky. We met Corrigan on his way back into the school, whistling with a contented smirk on his face.

He took one look at me and the smirk vanished.

"What happened?" He turned and walked on my other side.

"Nothing," I said tightly.

"Did they threaten you guys? Did that kid say anything?" he pressed.

"It has nothing to do with you!" I cried out and unlocked the Chrysler.

I threw my bag inside and turned to Corrigan, "Drive my car home, alright?"

"I'll just give you a ride tomorrow morning. Or Bryce will. You can drive it home then."

"I'm not coming to school tomorrow." Or the next day.

"Why not?" Corrigan looked at me again and seemed to get it. He asked softly, "What happened, Sheldon?"

"You can get the play by play from Bryce. I'm leaving." And I slammed my door shut and tore out of the parking lot.

Mena and Corrigan watched.

Chapter 4

I went home and showered again. After I had changed into some baggy clothes, I moved downstairs to my father's study.

Inside, I sat behind the computer and typed 'Greco' in a search engine. A moment later I searched through the results and found out that 'Greco' stood for a Greco Defense, named after Giachino Greco. It was a chess move that's used by amateurs who are stupid.

Corrigan had been right. The word had been an insult, but a nerdy insult.

I forwarded the article to Corrigan's email.

The doorbell rang when I lay down to watch a movie a little later.

Muttering an irritated curse, I moved upstairs and was surprised to see Mena at the door.

"Hi," I murmured as I held open the door.

"Hi." She looked nervous.

"Come on in." I gestured inside and we walked towards the kitchen. "Do you want anything to eat? Or drink? I was just going to watch a movie."

"Oh. Um..." She laughed again and shook her head. "I can't believe this."

"Believe what?"

"This. Me. You." She waved between us. "I'm nervous and I'm never nervous. I've gone against some of the richest snobs in the nation and I'm nervous around you."

"Why?" I took out a Diet Coke and slid it across the counter to her. "You want a glass with some ice?"

"Sure." She sat on a stool at the counter. She explained, "I'm nervous because… I don't know. Dumb, huh?"

"I told the school's counselor and the secretary of our principal to expel me today," I stated bluntly. I hopped onto the counter and dangled my foot over the edge. "It's not dumb, but there's not a lot that makes me nervous."

"I know. I heard. That was pretty balsy."

I shrugged. "Had nothing to do with balls." I just hadn't cared about the consequences.

"So…" She took a deep breath. "Have you thought about what I said before?"

"About being friends?" Who outright asked for a friendship?

"Yeah. I know…it's kinda stupid, but I just wanted to know before I entered the social scene tomorrow."

"Actually," I smirked. "I'm supposed to become friends with you anyway."

"Why?" She asked suspiciously.

"Because of Corrigan. He asked me this morning to make friends with you. He wants you to come to a party this weekend."

"Oh!" Disgust flickered over her face before she contained it. "He recognized me after you left school. He did a double-take and started muttering about second chances. I don't believe in second chances for scum like him."

I frowned and pointed out, "He's one of my best friends."

"Oh." Her eyes widened. "I'm sorry. I just—"

I waved her off. "Don't worry." I laughed and drank some of my own Diet Coke. "Corrigan's an ass. I told him myself this morning."

"I'm sorry. I knew he was one of your best friends. I just…when I met Corrigan, he slept with my best friend and never called her. She cried for an entire week."

That sounded exactly like Corrigan. I smirked.

Mena grimaced again. And then she cringed when her phone rang.

"It's my brother," she mumbled just before she answered it and moved into the living room.

When the front door slammed again, I heard Corrigan call out my name, "Sheldon! Where are you, you freak?!"

I waited as I heard his voice grow louder. Just as he turned the corner, a sly grin spread across his face and he shook his head.

I laughed.

"I cannot believe you," he stated as he patted his chest. "You are my idol. I love you. I will always take your side whenever you fight with Bryce."

"Shut up," I chuckled and glanced down.

"Seriously, though," he sobered. "You're a living legend at school. Again. You told the counselor to go to hell."

"No, I didn't," I corrected.

"You told her to expel you. That's the same thing. You said 'screw you.' I've never heard of any student who had the balls to say that."

"Yeah, well…I was pissed."

"And frantic," he added as he hopped up next to me. He patted my knee. "Bryce told me what happened. And thanks, by the way, for covering for me."

That's right. I'd forgotten.

"Corrigan, if that kid talks…" I started, concerned.

Corrigan stopped me, "Don't. It's covered."

"I know, but…Bryce is right. If the cops find out, you know they're not going to be nice. They're after Hoodum."

"I know and seriously—shut up about it," he said firmly.

I snapped my mouth shut.

"I'm sorry," he muttered in the next second. "I'm just worried about you, okay? Bryce said you freaked about the counselor."

"I know and seriously—shut up about it."

Corrigan flushed, hearing his own words, but he shut up. He jumped off the counter and raked a hand through his hair.

And then we watched each other, at an impasse.

Corrigan didn't want to be reminded how stupid his actions had been—not for the action, but because someone had seen him. And I didn't want to talk about my counselor freak-out.

"Look," he began. "Want to go grab something to eat? Let's go do something."

Just then Mena came back into the room and stopped short at the sight of Corrigan, with his back to her.

She stood silent and shook her head to me.

I asked, "Like what?"

Mena mouthed 'thank you' and moved to walk down the front hallway. A second later, just because I was listening for it, I heard a soft click.

"What was that?" Corrigan stopped in his list of possibilities.

I shrugged, but remarked, "Did you know that Mena already goes to our school?"

"Oh yeah. I meant to talk to you about that. You know her. I saw her talking to you when you took off," Corrigan accused me as he grabbed my hand and pulled me off the counter. He dragged me up the stairs and into my bedroom.

"What are we doing?"

"You're changing and we're going to go out," Corrigan replied, his voice muffled as he pressed his nose in my closet. A moment later, he produced some leather pants and a barely-there halter top.

"Nice try, but no." I shook my head and fell on my bed.

Corrigan nearly giggled as he dove back into the closet and pulled out a barely-there skirt with the same halter-top.

Laughing, I pushed him, "Get out. I'll find my own clothes. And where are we going?"

Through the closed door, Corrigan called out, "Let's go play some pool or we can go swimming at Chad Yerling's house."

I finished dressing and yanked opened the door.

I wore the barely-there skirt, but my sweater nicely covered the top. It hugged in all the right curves.

"Bryce is a very lucky man," Corrigan mused as his eyes lit up. He suggested, "You have those black boots that come to your hips. You can wear those…"

I slipped on my flip-flops and walked past him. "Let's go. You're driving."

"Then I'm driving your car." He jangled my keys in the air.

I whisked the keys from his hand and quickly locked the front door behind us. Inside the car, I suggested, "How about we go and hustle us some money?"

Corrigan cringed.

"What?"

"Let's just play. Why do we need to hustle?" He glanced at his knuckles.

"Because just playing isn't fun. Hustling is so much more fun and you won't get into a fight. Promise."

He sighed, "I don't like that look." He waved a finger in my face. "That look has gotten me in jail before. I don't like that look."

I grabbed his finger and pushed it down. "Stop waving your finger in my face. And you go to jail plenty enough on your own, you don't need me to get you there." It was true.

"Stop giving me that look." Corrigan sighed when the look intensified.

I stopped at the school's hangout, The Café Diner. Dumbly named, but everything else wasn't. It had the best burgers, salads, shakes, and some of the employees would slip us alcohol. Corrigan gave me a twenty when I went inside and marched past the back counter. He stayed inside and moved to one of the tables to chat.

After I struck a deal with the head cook, I walked through the main area and I couldn't find Corrigan, but Chet pointed him out.

As I moved around the back corner, near the phone booth, I saw Corrigan had his tongue shoved down some girl's throat.

I took pity and turned to leave.

I didn't get far when Chad stepped into my path.

"What do you want, Yerling?" I asked as I crossed my arms over my chest.

His eyes trailed down and then back up, but not after it lingered on my breasts.

"Eyes up front, Yerling. Now," I snapped. "And I'm waiting."

He grinned ruefully. It was the same grin that I'd seen him use on more than a few drunken girls.

I just sighed on the inside. It wouldn't be my eyelashes that I'd bat at him.

"You don't like me much, do you?"

"What makes you say that?" I asked sweetly.

He didn't answer that, but said instead, "Are you and Scout exclusive? Because I've seen him with a lot of other girls, you know."

Nothing new here.

"If Bryce and I are exclusive, then it's Bryce and me who should know that."

"He slept with Lew on Friday at his party." He shifted when I tried to move around him.

I sighed and regarded him.

"What?" Chad sent another of his grins that he'd perfected to get into so many pants. Corrigan had a look. Bryce had a look. And Chad had a look.

"Are you telling me this because you're hoping you have a chance with me?" I asked bluntly.

His eyes widened a bit, but he recovered instantly. "Why? Would you be interested?"

I leaned closer and whispered, silkily, "I get approached by a lot of guys. I don't know why you think that you'd have a chance."

The grin was wiped clean when I leaned back and commented, "Now move before I move you."

I heard a slight hush fall over the diner. Everyone had been watching. Chad knew it. I knew it. I hadn't cared, but now Chad was all the more humiliated for it. We were at a stand off now…

what would Chad do to protect the little dignity he had as a piece of scum?

We stared each other down.

"What?" I asked and crossed my arms again. Still, Chad didn't move. He just stayed there, angry and fighting for control.

I noticed that Chet stood up, along with a bunch of other guys in the room.

Chet was good friends with Bryce and Corrigan, but he was also on the football team with Chad. In fact, a lot of the guys that stood up were football players. I wasn't sure if it mattered because the male dominance placed Bryce and Corrigan at the top, but Chad was just below him.

This might've been a showdown to change the social status and Chad might've chosen me to be that symbol.

"You don't want to do this," I said smoothly, calm.

In the back we could hear a moan. Corrigan chuckled and hushed her.

"Do what?" Chad asked, feigning innocence.

"What I think you're doing," I said firmly.

Chet stepped closer and said quietly, "Leave her alone, Yerling."

Chad narrowed his eyes at him and asked, softly, eerily, "From what? I'm not doing anything. I'm just standing here."

Chet came to stand behind me.

He grabbed my elbow and moved in front. He warned, softly, "Step back, Yerling."

"What? You're going to escort her out? All safe-like and be her knight in shining armor?" Chad taunted. I saw the malice in his eyes and instead of a shiver; I stood at my tallest height.

Two more guys moved around behind Chad, Tatum and Holster. They were both football players, but they were loyal to Chet first. A part of me was relieved.

That pissed me off. I shouldn't need to be relieved at the sight of these guys, not here, not in my territory.

Chet prompted me forward and out the door.

Once outside, he asked tightly, "You okay?"

"Yeah," I bit out, my jaw tense.

Tatum had followed us outside, but we all looked and saw that Holster remained inside, right beside Chad.

"What the hell was that?" I clipped out.

"I don't know," Chet murmured, tiredly, as he continued to hold Chad's stare through the diner's windows.

"I'm thinking you do." I raked my eyes over his face and saw I was correct.

Chet glanced at me, studied me, and then relented, "Chad's been…a loose cannon lately."

"He hit on me and I turned him down."

Chet bit back a grin and guessed, "You humiliated him."

"No." I had, but he'd chosen the when and where. That wasn't on me.

"Great, well…I don't think it matters. He's had his eye on you since eighth grade. Just…be careful, okay? Tell Bryce about this."

I nodded mutely and climbed into my car. Instead of going to the pool hall with Corrigan, I turned around the back door of the kitchen and got out to put the beer inside. And then I headed home, alone.

I was home for another hour before I heard my doorbell ring again. I knew Bryce would probably stop over, but I had locked the doors anyway.

When I got to the door, I saw Corrigan outside, jumping up and down.

"Hey." I opened the door.

He brushed past me and demanded, "Why didn't you say anything?"

I moved past him and headed back downstairs to the media room.

Corrigan followed and continued, "I was just around the corner. I would've helped, Sheldon."

It wasn't the point. I waved him off, "Chet was there. It was fine."

It wasn't.

Corrigan agreed with me because he cried out, "Are you delusional? Are you stupid? How screwed up are you?"

I bristled and sent a warning glint his way. I didn't like insults.

He caught it and bit back his next words, but he said, "Seriously, Sheldon. That was scary, even for me. Chet said it took him, Tatum, and Holster to stand up before Chad finally backed down."

More than those three had stood, but I guessed that Chet hadn't informed him of those details.

"This is huge," he breathed out, slightly still in shock.

I groaned and pulled a pillow over my head. "Shut up."

"I cannot—" Corrigan stopped abruptly when the front door slammed shut.

We glanced at each other before Corrigan took off running upstairs.

I stayed put and waited, tense, for what seemed like forever. I even shut off the television and listened, but I didn't hear a thing. I should've gone upstairs. I should've contained the situation, but I knew it'd come down to an argument between Bryce and myself or Bryce and Chad Yerling.

I chose to be selfish.

I groaned and moved into the media room where I started playing pool.

I was good on a normal basis, but all my shots were spectacular under pressure. And my mind wasn't even on the game. It was on whatever was going on upstairs.

And then I heard the door slam again. I cursed as my arms jerked in reaction.

I waited, held my breath, but I didn't hear any movements down the stairs. After ten more minutes, I slowly, gingerly, placed the pool stick on the pool table and moved upstairs.

Instead of finding Bryce or Corrigan or both of them, I found a note that had been quickly scrawled on the kitchen counter.

Went out. Be back later.

B & C

Chapter 5

I skipped supper, shot another hour at the pool table, and even watched a movie.

My mind was reeling, but I couldn't bring myself to call Bryce or Corrigan to find out what was going on.

It pissed me off because I wasn't relaxed, laughing, or being satisfied.

I was anxious, pissy, and tense. All three emotions that I hated.

When the doorbell rang at 10:32 that night, I shot off the couch and raced upstairs.

Instead of seeing Corrigan or Bryce, I opened the door in surprise to find Denton Steele. He grinned at me and skimmed his eyes up and down my body. I had changed to a skimpy tank-top with no bra and pajama bottoms that rested low on my hips. Coral toenails peeked from underneath. I brushed my hair behind my ears. The slight movement teased my shoulders and I felt goose bumps break out over my arms.

"Steele," I greeted, confused. "What are you doing here?"

"You look good, Sheldon." He nodded. "I like your hair like that, when you let it loose."

I touched my hair. It wasn't anything special, but it was straight, shiny, and the guys seemed to like how dark it was.

Denton added, "Can I come in?"

"No." But I held the door open and waited as he passed by.

He glanced around the place and whistled, "It looks just like I remembered." He flashed a grin that girls nationwide swooned over. With his brown locks that were styled to frame his face and those hazel eyes, I remembered why I'd made a play for him before and grinned at the memory of my orgasm.

He'd been creative.

"Remember my garage?" he teased. His thoughts must've paralleled mine.

"I remember the feel of the couch in your garage," I replied, dryly. I actually remembered the echo of my orgasm around the building.

Denton chuckled and moved into the kitchen.

"So what brings you to my doorstep at 10:32 at night?" I asked.

"Aren't you going to ask if I want anything to eat or drink?" He frowned. "I think that's what you offered my sister."

"Is that why you're here? Are you here because of Mena?"

The flirtatious glint was wiped clean when he replied, coolly, "Look. I don't want my sister hanging around you."

My eyebrows arched at that one.

"How come?" I asked, curious.

"No offense," he said quickly and I shrugged. He added, "I just—you're not the type of girl I want around Mena right now. She's," he frowned. "She's vulnerable right now."

"Because of your mother's divorce?"

"Mena told you about that." A scowl flashed over his face before it was replaced with concern. "Yeah, but it's more than that. She's going through some stuff and she's not adjusting well to being back home with our dad. I'm staying at the house for awhile to help her out, but…I can't stay forever."

Actors, especially movie actors, traveled a lot.

"Can you just…can you say something to her?"

"Like what?" I laughed. "Should I have a pre-break-up talk with her before we're friends? How do you even talk about that stuff? Does she know how you feel?"

"She does. I've told her my concerns."

"What are your concerns?" I'd heard most of them anyway.

"Just that…" he frowned and halted as he considered me. My face was void of defensiveness. I really was just curious. "I told her that you're just more experienced in the guy department than she is. She talks big. I know she does, but she's only dated one guy."

"Are you sure it's just one guy that you know?" I teased.

"No," he answered, seriously. "It's just one guy. She dated him for a year and they never had sex."

"How do you know that?" And I couldn't believe I was having this conversation.

"I just do," Denton shrugged. "She's not ready for the world that you live in, Sheldon."

"And how do you know what world I live in?"

He gave me a knowing look and replied, ruefully, "I learned some tricks from you that time. You didn't learn anything from me and I'm a guy who's a famous actor. That says something."

"Maybe she could learn to toughen up," I challenged, but my heart really wasn't in it.

Denton stiffened before he replied, coolly, "Look, I'm just going to be honest with you. Our family has its problems, but we've got two parents in each home. Mena might have some serious anger problems against her biological dad, but…she's got her parents. And you…" Don't.

I felt my heart slam back into this conversation. I slid off a stool and asked, coolly, "What exactly are you saying, Denton?"

"I really didn't come over here to piss you off or hurt your feelings."

"But you are, so say what you came to say," I bristled.

Denton sighed and studied me a moment. I felt like everyone did that when they were carefully picking their words. People did it a lot around me.

He broke, "I don't want my sister to become a girl that screws her movie star neighbor because she's pissed off at her parents."

I felt a punch to my gut. "You're in luck. You don't have a movie star neighbor. You just have a girl that screws her movie star neighbor because she's bored and he's pretty good in the sack."

He grinned tightly and shook his head. Denton raked a hand through his hair and considered me again.

The silence was thick, but he broke it when he murmured, "I'm out of line. I know that. I know I had no right to say what I did and if a guy ever said that to my sister, I'd beat him down."

"Was that an apology?" I asked in disbelief.

"Yes. No. Kinda." He shook his head and chuckled in disbelief. "I cannot believe how I'm just stumbling over my words. I'm an actor and I never stumble over my words. It's one of the reasons I've gotten most of my jobs."

I didn't care.

He caught my look and stopped, "But then again, you probably don't care."

I tilted my chin up.

"Okay. Look...I just don't want Mena to become as tough as you."

That was different. I sighed and stepped back. "For what it's worth," I murmured, "I think that's why your sister wants me as a friend. I'd give her some protection at school."

That caught his interest.

"She's your sister," I added. "That's going to get out and she's going to be eaten alive by some of those girls in there." Mena might've thought otherwise, but she was wrong. In fact, she was delusional.

"I never thought of it that way," he admitted and skimmed his eyes over my figure again. "You're hot when you're pissed off."

I grinned silkily and shot back, "I'm not that girl who screws her movie star neighbor because she's pissed at her parents anymore."

Denton barked out a laugh and glanced away.

"Wow," he whistled. "That was good."

Just then the door shoved open and slammed again.

"Sheldon," Bryce called out before he turned the corner. "We gotta go. Corrigan's in jail..." His voice trailed off when he saw I wasn't alone.

Denton sent me a frown as he glanced between the two of us.

This was ironic.

I said weakly, "I'm not in jail. It's my friend who..."

"Would be Mena's friend too," Denton finished. He walked past Bryce and threw over his shoulder, "Just talk to her and let her down gently, please?"

When the door shut again, Bryce asked, "What was that about?"

"Big brother thinks I'm not a good example for his precious little sister," I muttered.

"You haven't even met her yet."

Never mind. I asked abruptly, "What's Corrigan in jail for?"

Bryce hesitated, but said, "Fleeing the scene of an accident."

"What accident?"

"Corrigan smashed up Yerling's car. When he tried to leave, the police flashed their lights and he took off." Bryce chuckled. "He led a high-speed chase. He's so proud of himself for that one."

I sighed, but darted to my room and quickly changed. Again.

I threw a bulky sweatshirt on and replaced my pajama pants with a pair of baggy jeans. "I'm ready," I said as I moved back downstairs.

Bryce nodded and held the door open when we moved to his car.

I caught a glimpse of his knuckles as my motion-detector flared on. They were bloody and bruised.

"Whose blood?" I asked, but I already knew.

Bryce shot me a look, but didn't answer.

"Is that what you guys did? You beat up Yerling and Corrigan beat up his car? For what? For good measure?"

He shrugged and started the car.

I shook my head, "Is this just because of me? I just had one older brother come over to my house and tell me that he doesn't want his little sister to grow up and have a life like mine."

"What?" Bryce shot me an incredulous look as he pulled into traffic.

"Nothing. How much money do we need?"

"A thousand cash, just to be safe." Bail varied on the crime.

"Stop at the ATM at Garrity's. You can wash your hand off in the bathroom."

When he pulled into the gas station, he murmured before either of us got outside, "Look. This wasn't just about you. A lot of the guys were behind this. Yerling's been off lately and he's made some of the guys nervous. And the girls."

"I was the last straw?"

"Something like that."

"What if he presses charges?"

Bryce shrugged, "He won't. He knows better."

"Or what? He'll get beat up by everyone else?"

"Something like that."

"I'm starting to hate that phrase," I muttered as I threw open the door and moved to the ATM machine.

When I got the cash, I bought a soda and an energy drink. In the car, I handed the energy drink to Bryce and drank my soda.

"Thanks," he murmured as he opened it and put it in the cup holder.

A moment later, we pulled into the jail and approached the front desk.

"Can I help you?" A deputy glanced up and raked his eyes over each of us. His eyes lingered on Bryce's bruised knuckles.

"Yeah. I'm here to post bail for a friend of mine," I spoke up.

When he asked, I gave Corrigan's name and a moment later we were given some paperwork to fill out. It seemed to take forever, but in truth it was probably fifteen minutes before we saw Corrigan smirk cockily when he was hustled from the back holding area. They took off his handcuffs just before he was allowed his personal items and moved through the gate.

"Hey," Corrigan greeted us both with a hug.

Bryce thumped him on his back while I punched him in the stomach.

"Ow," Corrigan grunted, feigning pain, but he grinned a second later and wrapped me in another big hug.

We trailed back out to the car in silence and I took the backseat.

Once we were inside, he asked Bryce, "So did you…?"

Bryce flexed his knuckles in response and let out a hiss in pain.

"Man," Corrigan whistled. "You did him good."

I rolled my eyes in the back, but remained quiet.

Corrigan twisted in his seat and asked, excitement in his eyes, "Wanna hear about the chase?"

I groaned, but a chuckle slipped out.

"They could've shot you, Corrigan," I pointed out.

"Nah, man," he laughed. "When they cornered me, I got out all slow with my hands in the air. It was awesome, but they *were* rough when they cuffed me."

Bryce asked, "They pull their guns?"

"Yeah. A few. They put 'em away quick though when they realized I was just a kid. I bonded with my arresting officers. I was cracking jokes on the way to the station. And I told them all about Chad, what he did."

"What?" Bryce asked sharply. "Why the hell did you do that?"

"They said they'd keep their eyes out for him."

"Man," Bryce groaned. "If they go over there, they're going to want him to press charges against me."

"What? Nah." Corrigan shook his head, but a cautious look flashed across. He laughed again and exclaimed, "No way. Yerling won't say a thing. He knows what'll happen if he does."

"What is this? Like Fight Club?" I mumbled.

"Yes," Corrigan answered while Bryce replied, "No."

They glanced at each other and shared a meaningful look.

Corrigan corrected himself, "I mean, it's not anything like Fight Club."

"Right," I scoffed in disbelief.

"The first rule: no one can talk about it. The second rule is: no one can talk about it. And the third rule is: if they do, they're out. Did I get it right?"

"It's not like that." Bryce met my eyes in the rearview mirror. "Yerling's pulled some other stunts lately. He just needed to be put back in his place. That's all."

"Let's grab some food. I'm starving." Corrigan pointed at the closest fast food and we trudged inside.

One of the girls whispered to her friend behind the counter and soon two additional employees were at the counter.

I groaned when Corrigan literally licked it up.

I sat at a nearby booth and waited as the two morons got their food. Bryce grabbed a soda for me, but neither moved for a moment when their food had been placed on their tray.

I marched up and grabbed the tray. As I moved past, I bumped shoulders with both of them on purpose.

"Hey," Corrigan protested when he spilled his drink.

"Oops," I deadpanned.

Bryce came to sit beside me on my side of the booth. Corrigan sat, inhaled his food, and grabbed the rest of his burger. He stood at the counter while he finished it and his drink.

Bryce relaxed against the booth and slid an arm on the back. He purposely stretched and slid his leg beside mine.

"Stop," I murmured.

Bryce chuckled and leaned closer to me. He whispered in my ear, "It'll be fine."

I shrugged him off.

Bryce frowned and asked, "What's wrong with you? You're usually up for this stuff."

I was, but I acted like a 'girl.' That pissed me off more.

"Nothing," I mumbled.

"What? Is it Yerling?"

Nothing.

"Is it what Steele said to you?"

Nothing.

"Oh." He got it. "It's the counselor thing."

I tensed beside him.

He leaned closer and pressed a kiss underneath my ear.

I relaxed slightly and closed my eyes when his hand slid onto my leg. He massaged just inside my thigh before he continued his exploration around my neck. I hung my head down, helpless and turned so he could capture my lips with his. I felt his fingers dip inside my pants and murmured, huskily, "If you wanted to take my mind off that, its working."

Bryce chuckled and his breath teased my skin.

"Let's go. Now," I breathed.

Bryce shot up. "Corrigan, we're leaving."

Corrigan finished talking with one of the girls and jogged over with a suggestive smirk. "You two go on. I'm going to grab a ride home with this girl."

Bryce and I looked over and saw that she was giggling with another friend. They both blushed when they realized they were the center of our attention.

In the car, Bryce kept a hand on my leg. It stayed in place.

When we pulled into my driveway, I hit the garage opener on my keychain and Bryce pulled his car beside my mom's Chrysler. Mine was still parked outside.

"Sheldon."

We were startled when a figure spoke up from the driveway's darkened edge, but she stepped forward and the light shone over Mena's strained face.

Bryce swore.

I let out a breath I'd been holding when I murmured, "Mena. What are you doing here?"

It was almost midnight.

"My brother came and talked to you, didn't he?" she asked, anxious.

"Uh...yeah." We moved inside and into the kitchen. Mena followed and perched on the stool she'd earlier occupied. She hugged herself.

"I knew he would." She shook her head. "He's just being an overprotective brother, but he doesn't understand anything."

Bryce frowned at me. He nodded towards the kitchen table, but I shook my head. He went to the fridge and grabbed a beer before he disappeared upstairs.

"Wow," Mena breathed out.

"What?"

"Bryce Scout. Wow."

"Are you serious? Your brother is Denton Steele."

"And my brother is my brother," she replied, dryly. "Believe me. I don't see the allure."

Let's hope not.

"Uh..." I shifted uncomfortably. "I've had a really long night, so..."

"Right. Cut to the chase." Mena nodded. "I can do that."

I relaxed slightly.

"Here's the thing...my brother thinks I'm this innocent little girl. He doesn't want me to be as worldly as you. That's a load of crap. Denton just wants to shelter me from all the bad stuff in this world and he thinks that you've seen more than your fair share."

Um... This was nearing a 'near emotion' event.

Mena proceeded, unaware, "I am a little sheltered. I'll own up to that, but he thinks that I haven't even had sex. That's not true. I've had sex with lots of guys, he just doesn't know about any of them."

"He seemed pretty sure that you hadn't had sex with your boyfriend."

"Because I hadn't," Mena said bluntly. "Justin was Denton's errand boy. He told him everything. Justin and I never went further than kissing on the lips."

Ewe. I cringed and asked, "He asked your boyfriend if you guys...?"

"Yeah. He was like Denton's spy. I figured it out pretty quick and realized that Justin was the perfect cover for me to live my life *my* way."

I sucked in my breath. This talk was *really* becoming too uncomfortable.

"Listen, I uh..." I glanced towards the stairs and gestured upstairs. "I've got..."

"Okay." Mena grinned widely and nodded, "I get it. You have more important things to do than listen to me complain. I'll see you at school tomorrow?"

"I doubt I'll be there."

"Oh. Oh yeah because of...that thing that happened, right?" She watched me intently, but I smiled.

"Okay." Mena laughed again and moved to the front door. When she left, I locked the door, hit the garage button, and reset the security system. I stopped in the bathroom before I moved towards the light that shone out of my bedroom.

Bryce leaned against my headboard, shirtless, with an empty beer beside him. ESPN was on my flat-screen.

I shut off the lights and shimmied out of my jeans and sweatshirt. I crawled underneath the covers and felt Bryce pull me into his arms. I could smell my mint toothpaste on his breath.

"Who was that girl?" he asked.

"That was Steele's little sister. She started at our school today and asked to be my friend." I still felt weird about the whole thing.

"That's the girl that Corrigan wants to bag?"

"Yeah, but I don't think he knows how protective Denton is of his little sister." I turned over and grinned up at Bryce as he looked at me.

"It's kinda freaky," he frowned.

"What is?" I slid a leg up and nestled it between his.

"That dude was here before and she showed up tonight. That's what's freaky."

"They're just…I don't know. Messed up or something. He cares about his sister and she's trying to have a life. I can relate."

"You can?"

"No. Not really, but I think it's sweet."

"Because you haven't had that," Bryce bit out.

I slid my hand around his neck, but we both swore when his phone rang.

Bryce reached over me to grab it and cursed swiftly before he flipped it open. He sat up and murmured, "Yeah, mom?" He yawned a replied, "No. No. I'm at Corrigan's house. We were watching the game. It's still on."

A second later he closed his phone and placed it on my bedside table.

Since he was up there, I shifted smoothly underneath him and wrapped my legs around his waist.

Startled, Bryce shifted more comfortably, but bent and kissed my chin, then my cheek, lips.

He finished under my ear and I moaned.

Chapter 6

I woke and instantly knew Bryce wasn't beside me. I knew that without feeling for him or opening my eyes. He rarely was. Whenever he did sleep over, he was the first up and he rarely woke me for a morning round.

It was just something weird about us. We didn't do the morning quickie.

What he had done, though, was left my bedroom door open.

That was another thing about Bryce. He liked to leave my bedroom open. He told me once that it was because my room got unbearably stuffy, but I didn't mind. When I got up to close the door, I was surprised when I saw Bryce walk back in and pull his shirt over his head. I sat back and watched as he tugged it down to cover his chest.

I whistled appreciatively.

Bryce ignored me and shuffled some things underneath my bed until he emerged with a pair of men's sandals.

"What are those doing under there?" I asked as I fell onto the bed.

Bryce fitted a belt around his waist and replied, distracted, "I dropped them down there awhile ago. It's going to be seriously hot today."

"I thought you were home."

"I'm going, but these are my favorite pair and since I remembered they were down there..." He looked up and raked his eyes up and down my figure.

My sweatshirt had ridden up and a wide amount of skin showed. I didn't move to cover up.

"So what are you thinking about Corrigan's new girl from last night?" Bryce turned away and leaned against the wall.

What'd I say? No morning quickies for us. Someday I might ask why that was, but not today.

I grinned slyly and sat up. I removed my sweatshirt and scooted up in bed, knowing that my pajama bottoms would get caught against my bedcovers. My movement would pull them down further. And they did.

Bryce noticed too.

"I think it's pathetic," I said flatly, but I grinned slyly as I watched Bryce watch me.

"She's cute. What are you pissed about?" His eyes lingered at my hipbone where my thong peeked out.

"I'm not. I'm a little tired of watching Corrigan roll over those girls, though. They let him do anything to them."

Bryce swallowed slowly. He watched as I wiggled further up and my pants wiggled further down.

"You let me do anything to you," he said huskily. "And you haven't even met her."

"I don't have to meet her to know she's just like all the others," I said evenly. "And I don't pant after you and I don't pin my heart on my sleeve." Here we go, a conversation about the two of us was now on the table. The game was over.

His eyes whipped to mine and stayed there.

I sighed and stood. I moved to the closet and grabbed some clothes.

"What's your problem?" Bryce asked as he moved to the doorframe. He watched me strip down and step into the shower.

Over the water, I said, "Nothing. I'm just kinda tired of having to be nice to those girls. They're around for, like, two minutes and then he's got another girl over." If he wasn't going to say anything about 'us', then two could play at that.

"Are you serious? You're actually mad that Corrigan plays these girls?"

"No," I said tightly and finished rinsing my hair. I held Bryce's eyes and knew we thought the same thing. Bryce played the same games, but he played them when I wasn't around. And I did my own thing.

Bryce sighed and moved from the doorway. When I dressed in my bedroom, I heard the front door slam shut.

I wasn't planning on going to school, but I'd already gotten dressed so I figured…

Outside, just as I climbed into my car, I braked suddenly. Mena stood on her house's patio with a blank stare on her face. That was odd. I frowned, but reversed and drove to school. I wasn't about to put much thought into Mena's life when I barely thought about my own.

When I walked into school, I saw a group of guys surrounding Bryce at his locker. He was turned with his head bent as he listened to whatever Chet was saying. Corrigan stood on the outskirts with a girl with dark brown hair that fell to her waist. She was short, but had exotic eyes. They glowed when she looked at Corrigan, but she still looked awkward.

My guess, this was the girl from last night. And I smirked when I saw that Becky Lew stood on his other side, just behind him. Becky chatted with her friends while New Girl glanced self-consciously around. She hugged her books to her chest and averted her eyes when they trailed and met mine.

Holster nudged Corrigan and nodded in my direction. Corrigan immediately left the group and fell in line beside me. He threw an arm around my shoulder and said, cockily, "So what do you think?"

"I generally try not to think."

Corrigan laughed and tightened his hold around my shoulders. "No, about Logan. What do you think about her?"

"Are you serious?" So that was her name.

"Yeah. Why?"

I kicked my locker open.

"Because," I murmured as I reached inside, "you just ignored the girl."

"Well, yeah, but…it's the first morning. You know how it is."

"The school hierarchy, you mean. If you're all into her, everyone might think you have a girlfriend and they can't think that."

"Yeah." He said like it made perfect sense.

"Sometimes," I started and leaned against my locker, "being the arrogant womanizer that you are might bite you in the rear."

"What do you mean?" He shifted on his feet, but listened intently.

I shrugged.

"Corrigan, someday you're going to meet a girl that's going to know her place with you and not be alright with that."

"Huh?" he questioned.

"Look, you know me. I don't care about these girls as long as you don't ask me to be nice, but one day one girl that you're going to actually want won't be okay with your chain of command."

"Not following."

Bryce walked to us just then and punched Corrigan in the arm.

Corrigan ignored him and asked me, "Seriously. What do you mean?"

Bryce glanced between the two of us.

I saw Becky Lew pass behind us. She skimmed her eyes over all three of us and her mouth tightened.

"Do you really want a girl that's okay with all the other girls you got going on?" I continued.

Bryce went still beside me.

I ignored him and waited for Corrigan's answer.

He shrugged.

"Not really thinking about that right now, you know," he responded thoughtfully. The moment vanished when the first bell rang and self-assured Corrigan fell back into place.

He threw an arm around my shoulder and walked beside me.

Bryce disappeared in the opposite direction.

"Seriously." Corrigan asked, "Should I take Logan, Mena, or Becky to Harris' party?"

"Since when do you take girls to the party? You usually just show up and pick."

"That's right." He laughed. "That's why we're friends. Sure you don't want a ride with me?"

"A ride?" I teased, my eyes darkened. "Or a *ride*?"

Amusement leapt to Corrigan's eyes and he smiled slowly.

"You know which one." He nudged me with his shoulder and patted my ass as he left for his own class.

I stayed in place and watched as he passed his first period classroom.

Corrigan didn't go to classes. That was a universal law. And someday, sometime, that law would come back to bite him in the butt.

Leisha smiled warmly as she approached the classroom and asked, "No Corrigan this morning?"

"Nope," I murmured and walked to our table.

We both sat down and I asked, "Why can't we have coffee in our classes?"

"No doubt," Leisha huffed and yawned dramatically.

Leisha was pretty cool. She wore the most outrageous outfits. She had on a taffeta shirt with ruffles on her neckline that spread past her shoulders.

Outrageous.

We had grown used to each other since we were assigned table-mates in the beginning of the year. I hadn't known who Leisha was before our first day in Calculus, but she had informed me that she'd always known who I was. At first she'd been on guard around me, but when she figured out that I wasn't going to screw with her, she started to relax. Now we almost seemed friendly to each other.

Just then Mr. Aldross entered the room and said, "Miss Jeneve, you are wanted in the counselor's office."

I stiffened and asked, tensely, "Why? What for?"

He started to write on the chalkboard and responded, "That is none of my business, Miss Jeneve. I would not know that information."

I stayed in my seat.

Leisha watched me. So did the rest of the class.

Mr. Aldross wrote the daily set of questions from our assigned homework.

"Okay, class…" He turned back around and saw I had remained. His lips tightened as he stared at me. Clearing his throat, he asked, "What are you still doing here, Miss Jeneve? You are wanted in the counselor's office."

"And I told the counselor yesterday that she can expel me. I'm not going to talk to her and you can't make me."

He started to say something, but the words died in his throat.

Bryce walked in, late like normal.

Irritation flickered across Mr. Aldross' features before he spoke, "Mr. Scout."

Bryce dropped in his seat and leaned back in his chair. He didn't respond.

"This is becoming a daily routine that grows tiresome."

I met Bryce's eyes and smiled haughtily.

Bryce looked amused, but he stayed quiet.

"Maybe you should sleep some more," I suggested.

Our teacher snapped his attention back to me.

"Why do you say that?" he asked, but looked cautious.

"You just said that it's getting tiresome. If we can't get enough sleep at night, you should let us bring coffee. That's what I think."

"You shouldn't even be sharing your opinions, Miss Jeneve. You are supposed to be in the counselor's office."

"Yeah, well," I crossed my arms over my chest. "I'm not going." I raised my chin up and stared back, steadily.

Mr. Aldross stared at me and I knew he was wondering what he would do with me.

"Then you may go to the principal's office," he quickly named his only other alternative.

I rolled my eyes and stood up. When I was at the door, Mr. Aldross commented, "Please wait, Miss Jeneve."

"Changed your mind?"

"May I please see your homework?"

"I don't have time for that, Mr. Aldross. The principal needs to see me," I taunted him and dramatically threw open the door.

I hadn't gone a few steps before the door opened again and Leisha ran to catch up.

"Hey," she gave me a tentative grin.

"Mr. Aldross asked you to escort me?" I asked, already knowing.

"Yeah." She ducked her head. "Sorry."

"It's cool," I shrugged. "I'm not going. You know that right?"

At my locker, I traded my books for my purse.

"So are you skipping?" She asked, her shoulders hunched.

I eyed her outfit again. The taffeta clung to her skin. She wore some type of tight khakis that were pinned to itself with large black buttons that ran up and down her legs. She almost looked like a naughty librarian.

"Where'd you get that outfit?" I asked.

"What?" Confusion crossed her face as she glanced down at herself. "This?"

"Yeah. Where'd you get that?"

"Hot Topics. Why?" She frowned.

"It's cool. I like it." And I did, I wasn't lying.

Just then the door opened again and Bryce strolled out. He grinned at the sight of us and moved to lean beside me.

"Hey," he murmured.

"Did he kick you out or send you after us?"

"He's got his ass all twisted," Bryce commented.

"Nice articulation," I joked and Bryce grinned ruefully.

I yawned and asked Bryce, "Wanna go for coffee?"

Bryce frowned, but said, "Sure."

I eyed Leisha and asked, "Wanna come?"

Her eyes widened.

I saw the glint of a smile at Bryce's mouth, but he just watched.

"I shouldn't." She shifted on her feet and glanced at the classroom door. "I should go back. I mean, Mr. Aldross is expecting me."

"You're right." I grinned wolfishly. "You should go back."

"Um." Her eyes glanced between Bryce and myself again, anxiously. And then she exclaimed, "I'm going to go." She disappeared down the hallway, but was back within a moment with a black purse tucked underneath her arm. And she looked nervous, very nervous.

I felt a pang of conscience and said, "You don't have to come."

She bit her lip and asked, "What do you mean?"

"Leisha, you're a good kid. Lying to a teach is not your forte. You can't really want to skip with us."

"I do. I really do," she insisted.

"Okay." I exchanged a look with Bryce. He raised an eyebrow, but that was the extent of his feedback. "Let's go."

Bryce took shotgun in my car and Leisha hopped in the back. She giggled as we left the parking lot and confided, "You're right. This is the first time I've skipped school. I kinda like it. It's a rush."

Bryce and I both chose to remain quiet on that matter.

When I pulled into the coffee shop, I informed Bryce, "You're paying."

"What?" Bryce asked. "Why am I paying? We're not on a date."

Leisha giggled behind her hands.

Maybe bringing her wasn't such a good idea.

"You're paying because you're the man. Men buy things."

"And women put out?" Bryce finished the sentiment and flashed a suggestive grin.

"Exactly," I murmured and pushed inside. I wasn't serious, but I grinned a little at the Leisha's sudden intake of breath.

She hesitated at the door when Bryce held it open for her. "Girls first." Bryce ushered her inside with a hand at her back.

Leisha looked like a deer in headlights.

The clerk frowned at us, but filled our orders. I moved to study the magazines when Bryce dropped onto one of the couches. After we'd gotten our coffee, we sat there in silence. Bryce leaned back and closed his eyes. Leisha watched Bryce, shyly, and then nibbled at her nails when she looked to me. And I drank my coffee while I watched her. I almost felt sorry, she was out of her league and she knew it.

When the door's bell jingled, Bryce sat up and bumped his knee into mine.

"What?" I asked and he gestured towards the front door.

It was Mena and Denton.

Mena had a glazed look in her eyes and Denton looked bored.

I remembered the blank look that had been on her face when I first left for school.

"Do you guys know them?" Leisha asked and then gasped. "That's Denton Steele."

"They're weird, Sheldon." Bryce murmured and leaned for his drink.

I was starting to agree.

"Oh my god. Do you guys know them?" Leisha pressed again, eagerly. All her virgin-blushes and awkwardness was gone now. The presence of a celebrity could work so many miracles.

"Something like that," I murmured and plastered a warm smile on my face when Denton noticed us. He did a double-take, but left Mena's side. Mena remained at the counter.

"Hey, Sheldon." Denton flashed a smooth grin my way and took the seat beside mine.

Bryce leaned back and watched underneath his eyelids.

"Skipping school?" Denton managed to condemn and flirt with me at the same time.

"I have first period free," I lied smoothly.

"Really?" He raised his eyebrows.

"Hi." Leisha stuck her hand out. "I'm Leisha Summers."

"Hi." Denton turned celebrity in a flash.

"Can I have your autograph?"

"Sure." He winked at me. "Sheldon, do you want an autograph?"

I looked at him coolly and murmured, "I think I gave you *my* autograph."

"Oh right." He flexed his back and added, "I never knew nail marks stung so much."

Mena sat beside Leisha at that moment and handed a drink to her brother.

Denton dropped the celebrity façade and turned into big brother immediately. It was impressive.

"Thanks, Mena," he said softly.

She ignored him and gazed at me. "Hey, Sheldon."

"Hi, Mena."

She glanced warily at Bryce. Her eyes lingered a moment and Bryce raised an eyebrow when he looked at me.

Denton's jaw clenched. He thrust a hand out, "We didn't meet yesterday. I'm Denton."

"Bryce," Bryce grunted as he shook hands.

"Did you guys get your friend out of jail?"

Bryce and I both grinned and enjoyed the startled looks on Leisha and Mena's faces.

"Sure did." Bryce lifted his cup in a salute.

"Who was in jail?" Mena asked.

"A friend," I answered and switched the topic, "So, Mena, you're not going to school today?"

Denton frowned and answered first, "She's not feeling well today."

"Looks fine to me," Bryce commented.

"Looks fine to me," I repeated.

Mena gave her brother a forced smile and said tightly, "I'm feeling fine, but Denton thinks he felt a fever coming on."

"Coffee's a good antidote," Bryce deadpanned.

Denton scowled his way, but recovered almost immediately.

Bryce and I both caught it and shared a look. I shifted in my seat and introduced, "Mena, this is Leisha. Leisha, this is Mena. Mena's first day was yesterday at our school."

"Oh really? I don't remember seeing you." Leisha said warmly. I enjoyed her naiveté.

"So why was your friend in jail?" Denton said abruptly. I don't think he enjoyed the naiveté.

I ignored him and murmured, "Mena, do you have a fever now?"

"No," she said quickly.

"See? Coffee heals anything," Bryce said easily, but kept his eyes on Denton, alert.

"Look, man, I was concerned for my sister. What's your problem?" Denton bit out and flexed his hands.

"I think I skipped my second day when I started high school too." I laughed and shifted in my seat, getting comfortable.

Denton caught the insult and glared at me. "You're a real bitch, you know that?"

"Me?" I asked innocently, fighting a smile.

Bryce bit back a smile.

Leisha gulped and had the whole deer in headlights look again. Mena just frowned.

Denton leaned forward and retorted, "It may work wonders in bed, darling. In real life, people are going to stop dancing to your tune real quick."

"Funny how you're still dancing," I mused.

A wall slammed in place over Denton's eyes and he stood up. "Let's go, Mena. You're feeling better. I should take you to school."

Mena stood reluctantly.

I suggested, "You can ride with us. We should get going too."

"No," Denton said quickly with a hand at his sister's elbow. "I'll take her. I don't know if she'll actually get there with you."

Bryce laughed.

"Was that an insult?" I joined in Bryce's amusement.

Denton shook his head and dragged Mena behind him. We watched through the window and saw him shake his arm in the air at her. Mena shrugged him off and got into the passenger seat. A moment later Denton followed and his tires squealed out of the parking lot.

"What…" Leisha breathed out. "What was that?"

I shrugged and stood, "Let's go." Game over.

Leisha led the way and Bryce fell in step beside me. He ignored my back pocket and slid his fingers into my thong's top strap. His thumb gently caressed the outside of my pants and he murmured into my ear, "Big Fame Steele's got a temper on him."

"I know."

He held me back and the coffee shop's door shut with us on the inside and Leisha on the outside. She stopped at my car and glanced back for us.

He nipped at my bottom lip and murmured, huskily, "Can we please ditch this girl?"

"And do what?" I nipped back.

Bryce slid his tongue against mine before he replied, "Do what we should've done yesterday."

"Spend the whole day in bed?" I laughed and pushed away from him.

"Why not?"

I looked in surprise and saw that he was serious.

"Whatever, Bryce. You have scouts all this week." I moved to leave, but he caught my arm again.

"What?" I asked again, breathless.

"I'll still play. Let's skip. Come on."

"You won't play and you know it." His coach was strict, which was needed with Bryce. Coach Bewer was also a pseudo father figure to Bryce, including punishment and discipline. The soccer field was probably the only place that Bryce didn't get away with our games.

"Seriously, Sheldon."

"Seriously, Bryce," I said firmly. "No." I slipped out of his hold and was outside before he could drag me back inside.

Bryce followed reluctantly and shot me a dark look as he sat in the passenger seat.

Leisha just watched us both warily. She was like a breath of fresh air.

Chapter 7

Bryce didn't comment the entire drive back towards school, but it wasn't a long drive until I turned the engine off.

A group of students stood just outside the school's doors. Some smoked, some just chatted.

"There's Yerling," Bryce noted and gestured towards the door. Sure enough, Yerling and his posse stood amongst the group.

I sat back with the keys in my hand. I wasn't sure I wanted to be around for whatever was going to happen.

Leisha had moved to the door handle, but she paused and waited for us.

"Go," I said briskly and she left. Bryce and I both watched as Chad stepped to the front of the group. He threw his cigarette to the ground and watched my car. His eyes trailed to Leisha, but he let her pass without a second look.

He still looked bloodied. A large bruise had formed at his jaw and at the corner of his eye. His nose was swollen and his eye was bloodshot.

"Holy," I murmured. "He looks awful."

Bryce bristled beside me.

"Your knuckles didn't look like they'd done that."

Bryce didn't comment on that, but he said instead, "Let's go back to your place." He grinned charmingly, "You can put ice on my knuckles."

"It's not the only thing that needs ice."

He grinned faintly, but moved across and kissed the underside of my jaw.

"Seriously." I put a hand on his chest, intending to push him away.

He slid a hand down the inside of my thigh until I firmly pushed him back.

"What is up with you?" I demanded, seriously. "Contrary to what you might think, I don't spend my days on my back." At the glint of amusement, I added, "Or straddling some guy or on my knees. What is going on with you?"

"Nothing," he said tightly and settled back in his seat.

I watched him, concerned.

"Bryce," I said softly. No more games.

He glanced away, but I heard his breath of surrender.

A moment later, he relented, "I don't need to be at practice anymore."

"Why not?"

"Because I'm off the team."

"What?!"

"It's not like that," he said hastily. "I already got the scholarship. They don't want me to play high school anymore."

Oh.

I sat back stunned. And then I cried out, "That's not fair. They can't do that." He'd miss everything. His senior games, play-offs, even state—and that's if they got there without him.

"They already did. Dad met with them last night and finalized everything."

"You're really not playing for the rest of the year."

He nodded.

"How's your coach feel about that?"

Bryce's jaw clenched and he replied tightly, "He's not happy."

"Did you go to practice last night?"

"Yeah, but I didn't need to."

"Why didn't you tell me?"

"Because I didn't want to be having this conversation," he pointed out.

"Bryce, you're such a shit."

He chuckled.

"Does Corrigan know?"

"Yeah."

"Corrigan knows and I didn't?"

"Because of this. You're acting like a girl."

"I'm acting like your best friend, idiot," I retorted and slammed the door as I got outside. As I stalked away, Bryce called my name. I ignored him and kept going.

I had moved almost all the way to the door before Chad caught my elbow.

"Back off," I snapped as I wrenched my arm free.

In a flash, Bryce was at my side. He maneuvered to stand between me and Chad.

"Hey, hey." Chad had a feral smile on his face. He raised his hands and backed up. "I'm not going to hurt her. Oh, that's right. I never hurt her in the *first* place."

"You're a wounded animal." I grinned at him, back on familiar ground. "You've been put down, but you just keep coming back for more."

Bryce moved so his back was to me. He had effectively cut me off from Chad's glare.

"What's wrong, Scout?" Chad taunted. "You don't even want your girlfriend talking to me?"

"Back off, Yerling."

A sophomore had come to the door, but turned back when he noticed what was going on.

"Or you're going to mess up my face again? I heard Raimler got arrested for my car. Thanks, by the way. Now I know where to send my insurance information. Are you going to pay for my medical bills?"

Bryce remained silent. Again, he didn't have to say anything.

It seemed to infuriate Chad even more because he shook his head and spat, "You know what pisses me off about you, Scout?

You, Raimler, and your little girlfriend walk around this school like you own it. The only reason you get away with everything is because you do to everyone else what you did to me and to that kid from the office. Someone goes against your unspoken rules and you knock him down."

The door shoved open behind me and Corrigan pushed his way to Bryce's side.

Chad glared at him now.

"What do you want, Raimler? You weren't a part of this conversation."

Corrigan grinned, self-assured, and shot back, "Maybe I should've been. You mess with my friends and you mess with me."

Bryce shifted on his feet. Corrigan moved forward, just a slight inch of a step, but everyone knew that Corrigan was the threat now. Bryce had moved to the background.

I had become nonexistent to the guys. It wasn't even about me, not anymore. I wondered if it had ever been about me. I remembered Chet's words and Bryce's. They had both said that Chad had been off lately. He'd pulled some stunts that weren't okay with the guys.

There was a code among the guys. They could do a lot, say a lot, but nothing would be done as a reprimand. It makes a person wonder what was so bad for Chad to be taken down. And to have all the guys be okay with it.

I glanced over my shoulder and saw a bunch more had followed Corrigan. Chet, Holster, and some others must've left through a side door. They came from behind us and had formed a circle around Chad and his group. Some of *those* guys started to look nervous.

Corrigan was saying, "You know what you did, Yerling. You better watch it."

"Or what?" Chad sneered. He took a step closer. "You're going to hurt me, Raimler? You and Scout. You can't hurt me by yourself. We both know that."

Corrigan bit back his words, but Bryce shifted again. That same inch and suddenly he was back in charge. He murmured, seemingly relaxed, "I can hurt you."

Chad's glare seemed to darken and his eyes skimmed over me. Whatever he thought, he didn't share. A second later, one of the guys murmured, "Teacher."

Immediately the group dispersed. Chad and his friends took off into the parking lot while everyone else either took a lounging stance or walked back inside the school. And me? I headed inside and actually went to the rest of my classes. I even disappeared to my art room during lunch. I wasn't eager for a replay with Chad Yerling and the rest. I didn't even want to banter with Corrigan.

Mr. Sayword glanced at me questioningly, but he didn't say anything. When I was in the developing room later, a brisk knock sounded and I called out, "Yeah?"

Mr. Sayword called through, "Can I come in?"

I flipped the switch and the door opened. He closed it behind him and flipped the switch back.

I waited. He'd never come in before.

"Uh huh." Mr. Sayword cleared his throat and shuffled on his feet. My art teacher was nervous. He tucked his longish sandy-colored hair behind his ears and straightened the wire-rim glasses over his nose bridge. His buttoned-down shirt was a little rumpled, but his pants were still nicely pleated.

"Yes?" I asked.

"Uh…Miss Connors called me into her office for a consultation."

"What?" I asked sharply.

"She has heard about our unique teacher-student bond."

What bond? I respected the guy. That was a bond?

I remained silent.

"Yes, she—uh—she wanted to ask my opinion on your state of well-being."

"What'd you say?"

He blinked, his eyes were magnified behind the glasses, but he gazed in stupefaction to me. He stared another moment and I noticed that his eyelashes were rich and plump. I was jealous. I wish I had those eyelashes.

"I said...well, to be quite honest, I told her that I had always thought you were a magnificent student. You've always been on time. A hard worker. You've never talked back to me or bullied another student. Your projects are always done wondrously with a touch of genius."

What the hell? I blinked.

"Miss Connors was...she was, well...she was—she seemed a bit taken aback by my opinion and thought perhaps we have an unusual bond."

My smile was barely constrained when I guessed, "She thinks we're sleeping together?"

He coughed and pounded his chest. He needed to turn away and cough some deep wrenching hacks before he was composed. When he turned back, he gulped and looked at me.

I held firm and stared him down. That's when I saw the truth.

The one teacher that earned my respect is the one rumored to be my lover. Poetic, really.

"What do you want me to do?" I asked.

"Well," he began, "I really just wanted to make you aware of the situation. Miss Connors seemed to have quite a list of concerns about you."

"Do I quit the class?"

To this, I saw my first glimpse of anger in my normally-composed teacher.

"No." He said it short, simple, and final.

I grinned despite the situation and replied, ruefully, "I'm guessing Miss Connors doesn't know about those balls."

He frowned, but replied, "Well, Miss Jeneve, now that you have been apprised of the situation, I will leave you to your work." He nodded and I saw some amusement that tickled the corner of his mouth.

I finished a drawing for the rest of sixth period and headed to the cafeteria for study hall.

Chet moved down and I took his seat. The rest of the group all moved, grumbled, saw it was for me and shut up. I hid a smile at their expense. Bryce dropped his history books on the table across from me and sat beside Becky Lew.

No one reacted, but—like always—they watched me for the reaction.

I disappointed them all and focused on my homework. I finished my calculus and got up to buy a pop. When I returned to the table, Bryce was back at his seat across from mine. Becky Lew and her friends had moved to the open section of the cafeteria. They were painting signs for the soccer and basketball team. The rest of the cheerleaders had moved into the cafeteria so it must've been a planned event.

I ignored Bryce and started my history homework until the final bell rang. Bryce walked beside me towards my locker and asked, "What are you doing after school?"

I ignored him, but then he tapped my arm and leaned closer when we arrived at my locker. His arm draped across the top of the locker and he effectively entrapped me against the locker.

"What are you doing now?"

I shook my head and slipped out from underneath.

"Sheldon," he called out.

"I'll see you later," I called over my shoulder and disappeared around the corner.

The counselor's office was vacated, but the back office doors were still open. I walked to Miss Connors, knowing from prior trips where her office was located and watched her shuffle papers around her desk. She gripped a pencil in her teeth and frowned at her computer screen. The day must've been long for her because there were sweat marks down the back of her silk blouse and her skirt was rumpled where she would sit on it.

She sighed in frustration to herself and wrote a note on a pad near the phone.

I cleared my throat.

As Miss Connors whirled in her chair to see me, I said tightly, "So I hear that you think I'm sleeping with a teacher?"

"Sheldon," she murmured, reproachfully.

I walked in, shut the door, and took a seat in the lounger besides her desk.

"It's out of line and I'm a bit disappointed in how unoriginal you are," I said firmly and leaned back.

She smiled tensely and retorted, "Got you in here, didn't it?"

"So you know it's a lie?"

"I know that you're not sleeping with Mr. Sayword, but you have to admit that it's a bit suspect. You mouth off to the teachers except him. You are either consistently late or you don't show up at all, except sixth period. You've never been tardy to one of his classes and you've had him for four years now. The days you do skip, you always stay after the next day." She sighed. "You do the math."

"I respect him."

"Your other two friends have never shared an art class with you. Is that why? Do you act out because you're reacting to their influence?"

I didn't even dignify that with an answer.

"No." Miss Connors ran a hand through her straw-colored thin hair. "I didn't think you'd respond to that one either."

"What do you want?" I asked, my eyes flat.

She seemed to consider me for a moment before she replied, "Honestly?"

I nodded, mute.

"I care about you and I think you're wasting an unfair amount of potential. You could be in college. Yes, I know that you've heard this already and I don't care. You could be the captain of track, volleyball, and yearbook staff. You could have any number of prestigious scholarships if you wanted. I've read some of your essays. You have so much talent and I cannot stand the fact that you just waste it away."

"I'm living a typical teenager's life."

"A typical teenager is not rumored to screw an entire sports team."

I hadn't been aware of that one. It made me smile.

"I see." Miss Connors groaned. "You think that's funny. Granted, I've watched you around campus and I'm impressed at the amount of power you seem to hold with the other students. However, I'm not stupid." She shook her head as her bore into mine. "I know what girls have to do to earn that spot."

"Did you call me a whore?"

"What? No!" Miss Connors looked horrified and flushed. "That's not what I meant. I just..." She caught the amusement in my eyes and sighed in disappointment. With a gentled tone, she asked, "Have you heard from your parents lately?"

"No." I stood up and shook my head. I moved to the door.

"Wait. Please, Sheldon?"

"I'm not some wasted space due to negligent parents. That's not me, not who I am. I'm not going to talk to you about my hurt feelings because the last time I heard from my parents was three months ago." I left the room and walked down the hallway. Just before I opened the counselor's door that connected to the senior hallway, I stopped and heard a resigned sigh from her office.

My hand paused for a moment, but I hardened inside and left.

Chapter 8

I drove past the Café Diner and saw Bryce's car in the parking lot. Corrigan's was somewhere else. As I continued home, I sent a text to Bryce and Corrigan telling them that I had beer waiting at home.

When I got home, I removed one of the cases that was still in my car from our previous trip to the diner. I stuffed it underneath the steps leading to the connecting door. As I moved down the hallway to unlock the front door, I found a note that had been stuffed underneath the door. I opened it and read:

Whores get stoned to death. Are you the stone or whore? Or maybe you're death.

I laughed and crumpled it up. After a quick toss to the garbage, I pulled out a frozen pizza and warmed the oven. It took two minutes for the oven's pre-warm up bell to ring and as I slid the pizza in, my front door opened. Bryce and Corrigan were both laughing as they made their way inside.

"Grab the beer from my trunk," I shouted over their laughing.

Corrigan hollered, "Will do."

Logan was the first to appear around the corner. She was hesitant, but seemed to relax when she saw an easy grin on my face. I still hadn't formally met the girl, but I was determined to be in a gracious mood. There was no bitchery allowed when it was beer and pizza night.

I crossed my feet as I leaned against the corner and stared at her.

She changed her expression back to caution and edged, hesitantly, onto one of the stools.

Neither of us said a thing.

Logan stared at anything except me. Her hands also seemed to fight with each other. She'd hold them still, then they'd start trembling, and she'd jerk only to start it all over again.

When I heard footsteps jog down the stairs, I smiled to myself at her predicament. She's with a guy, one of the most popular, and thinking she's his new girlfriend. She's in his other best friend's house, who's a girl, who's known to get her jollies by taunting girls just like her. What to do?

Predicament.

A moment later, Bryce and Corrigan both walked in with a case in their arms.

Awkward silence time was done…for now.

I raised an eyebrow and murmured, "You could only handle one case?" I said it in disdain.

Corrigan wasn't affected and grinned cockily. He jumped onto the counter right in front of Logan and shot back, "I'm just conserving my energy for more pleasurable activities."

He ran a hand down the side of Logan's face and lingered at her lips.

Logan flushed, but didn't move her head back. She even relaxed her lips and Corrigan slipped his finger inside where, after a moment's hesitation, she sucked it. Her eyes looked somewhere else. Not at Corrigan, Bryce, or myself.

Bryce whistled in appreciation and asked, "Why don't you do that for me?" He held up his hand.

I punched him in the arm.

"Ow!" He cradled his arm, but smiled endearingly at me.

Corrigan sniffed the air and asked, "Please tell me that I'm smelling pizza?"

"You are." I knew my eyes were frosty as I watched Logan take two of Corrigan's fingers into her mouth.

"Hey," Corrigan suddenly said as he noticed something in the front hallway. "You have a voice message on your machine." He looked at me, confused, "Since when do you use your machine?"

I'd been distracted with creepy notes. I hadn't noticed.

"When was the last time someone even called your landline?" Bryce asked.

Corrigan jumped off the counter and hit the play button.

A second later, I stiffened when I heard my mother's voice echo around the house's hallway and kitchen.

"Hello, dear. This is your mother. I am calling because your father and I are getting a divorce. I won't be returning home for Thanksgiving and I have no idea what your father is planning over the holiday. I'll be in touch with my new number. Love you, honey. Hope you stay out of trouble."

The air was thick in silence when the machine clicked it's end.

All three watched me, but I was paralyzed.

Finally, I choked out, "God."

Corrigan reached inside one of the beer cases and offered a bottle. Bryce took it, opened it, and moved it into my numb fingers.

I downed it.

Another beer came along and I downed that one.

A third proceeded the same until I spit it out and threw the bottle across the kitchen.

The buzzer rang on the oven, but I ignored it and walked upstairs. I passed my bed, headed straight for the bathroom, dropped my clothes, and stepped into my shower. I turned it to a scalding temperature and stood there, with my head hung downwards. After awhile, I slid down and wrapped my arms around my legs, hugging them to my chest.

I don't know how long I stayed there, but I stayed when I felt the first chill. I didn't move until my entire body trembled from the cold. And I wasn't too surprised to see that Bryce had taken root on my toilet seat when I climbed out. I wrapped a towel around my body and moved into my bedroom. After I closed the door, I just crawled into bed and pulled the covers over me.

Bryce stood beside the bed. He watched me.

After awhile he slid to sit on the floor beside my bed. He didn't watch me, but just stayed there.

I didn't cry. I didn't do anything.

"Do you want a beer?" Bryce asked sometime later.

"Yes."

"Okay." He stood up and returned a little later with four beers. He uncapped two and handed one to me. I sat up and downed it. I passed him the empty bottle as he held out the second. The third and fourth went down the same way.

After the fourth, I looked up and asked, "Is this a wrong coping mechanism?"

Bryce flashed a grin and my heart beat.

He leaned down and whispered, just before he touched his lips to mine, "Coping is coping, baby. Either way, you get through it."

I captured his lips in mine and found myself in his arms. I had one knee firmly between his legs on the bed and raised my body so I was kneeling above him.

"I don't want her in this house."

Bryce nodded and left. I heard the front door shut a few minutes later. With a tentative knock at my door, Corrigan called from the hallway, "Can I come in for a minute?"

I didn't answer and the door was pushed open.

I had laid back down, still wrapped in my towel, but I knew my face was void of emotion.

Corrigan's eyes skipped over the empty beer bottles.

"Hey," he murmured and moved to sit beside me. His hand came out to smooth down my hair, but I shoved it away.

"Sorry," Corrigan breathed, ruefully. He took a deep breath and commented, "So…drunk orgy is the way to go?"

Drunk orgy was the way to go.

He nodded and patted my shoulder. As he moved to the door he stopped short said, "If you want to go hustling, give me a call."

"I will," I murmured, hoarsely.

Corrigan threw me a tender smile and moved through the door.

I laid there and heard a murmur of voices from the front hallway. A second later, the door shut again. Another minute and Bryce appeared in the doorway. He had the case of beer underneath his arm.

A grin slipped past my lips at the image of him.

He grinned back and moved to sit on the side of the bed.

After setting the case on the floor, he asked, "You want another one?"

"Yes." I sat up and leaned against the headboard.

Bryce took two out. He handed one to me and downed his own.

I didn't down this one, but took some sips as I watched him stand up and empty his pockets. He placed his phone on the nightstand and then pulled his shirt over his head. He grabbed a handful of condoms and placed them on the nightstand before he sat back on the bed.

He met my gaze.

I took another sip and asked, "Do you think I'm a whore?"

He frowned, but asked, "How many guys have you slept with?"

"Three." I didn't hesitate.

"No," he answered and I knew it was the truth. He had thought about it.

I murmured, "Brian Kincaid. He was my first."

"Our first time was the end of freshman year."

"He was before that, long before that. He was my first boyfriend and I thought...I thought it was what I was supposed to do."

Bryce took a drink from another beer and rubbed a hand over my leg. It wasn't meant to be seductive, but soothing. Comfort.

"Nah," he murmured. "Girls don't have to do anything they don't want to do."

"I know that now." I hadn't then. I took a deep breath and finished my—I hadn't been counting—. Bryce took it out of my still numb fingers and placed it in the case.

"We've been friends for a long time," I said quietly and laid back down.

"Yep." Bryce nodded. "We became really good friends in…?"

"When we were ten."

"That's right. And in seventh grade, you kissed me."

"You kissed me."

"No." He shook his head and moved to lay beside me. He flipped on his stomach and threw one arm over my waist. His head rested on my shoulder and he gazed up at me.

"Yes. I remember because it was during recess."

"No." Bryce smiled at me, a beautiful sight. He inched closer. "It was during lunch, but you kissed me because you wouldn't let me go and play football with the rest of the guys. I wasn't happy with you at all. Why would I kiss you if I wanted to play football?"

I noted, "You're supposed to always say that you were the one who kissed me. That's what a gentleman does."

Bryce laughed a full laugh and teased, "You admit that I'm right? You kissed me."

I poked him in the arm. "You're supposed to be a gentleman and say that you kissed me first."

Bryce studied me and then said softly, "You're right. I kissed you first."

"I know. That's what I've been saying this whole time." I flashed him a blinding smile.

Then I remembered my mom's call and the smile vanished.

Bryce lifted his head, cupped my cheek and kissed me softly. It was the softest kiss I'd ever gotten. I think my heart stopped and then it slammed back into me. And it didn't take long before I straddled him. My towel was shoved off as Bryce lifted up, his mouth still fused with mine. I worked hungrily at his pants. When I managed to get the zipper down, Bryce lifted me up and kicked his pants down with his feet and legs.

When he would've rolled me over, I pushed down on his shoulders and tightened my thighs.

Bryce fell back and I slowly nipped at his mouth, his bottom lip, his chin. I slid my mouth down his neck and lingered over his chest.

He groaned, but held still for me. I needed to ravage him.

I inched backwards until my mouth lingered at his trim waist.

I swooped down and I grinned when I heard his sudden intake of breath. His legs convulsed and his back arched slightly.

He swore and I pressed on. Later, when I heard his gasp, I finished it off and licked my way back to his mouth.

Bryce groaned and flipped me over. With a condom already in hand, he sheathed himself and slammed inside.

This time, I was the one who collapsed against the pillow, wrapped my legs around him, and hung on.

It was hot, savage, and I melted as I curled onto my side.

Bryce padded barefoot into the bathroom. After a quick shower, he dressed, and pressed a kiss to my forehead.

"Where are you going?" I asked, the bedcovers wrapped around my naked body.

"I'm going to run home and get some clothes. I'll be back."

"Take one of my keys. You can let yourself back in then."

He pressed another kiss to my forehead and lips before he grabbed one of the sets and darted down the stairs.

I got up, showered, and dressed in a jogging suit. I wasn't planning on jogging, but it looked cute and it was comfortable. Plus, I'd gotten a little drunk from the beer. Sex with Bryce had helped, but it always helped no matter the circumstances.

Bryce had already placed all the empty bottles in the case, so I took it downstairs and placed it beside the other. The pizza was still left, untouched, on the stove. I wrapped it up and put it away in the fridge as leftovers.

And then I took a deep breath and took my cell phone onto the patio that extended off of my parents' bedroom. As I curled on one of the patio loungers, I dialed my father's phone number.

"Hello?" he asked, slightly confused. My father always seemed to be confused.

"Hey, dad," I said quietly and wished I had grabbed a blanket.

"Oh, sweetie. How are you?" He even sounded cheerful.

"Mom called. She left a message."

"Oh. I'm so sorry, sweetie." He didn't sound it. He still sounded cheerful.

"What happened?"

"You don't need to bother with those details. What's important is that your mother and I are making the best choice for all parties."

"Where's Mom?"

"I think she may be in Paris, but who knows with your mother. She could be in Japan, for all I know."

"Are you coming home?"

There was a slight pause before he said, unapologetically, "Oh dear. I'm sorry. I can't bring myself to come home. The memories, you know, sweetie."

Again. I didn't know. I hadn't even known there were problems.

"I haven't heard from you in three months and the first I hear anything—it's a voice message saying that you're getting a divorce?"

"Oh honey. That's not fair. You could've called too, you know. Communication is a two-way street."

"In marriages," I said, surprisingly unemotional. "Not when it comes to parents and their children. I haven't seen you guys for five months."

"We've been over this before. Your mother and I wished to spend time in Italy. Your mother wanted to reconnect with her family roots—"

I couldn't believe—I stared at the phone. I could still hear my father, but I slowly, ever so slowly, closed my phone.

My father's voice was no longer and I was left without even a dial tone.

I took a deep breath before I stood and moved back inside. I wrapped a blanket around me and moved back into my father's study. I slid one of the bookcases aside and revealed his hidden liquor cabinet. Inside was champagne, crystal, wine, whiskey, bourbon. Anything and everything. There were even a few imported beer bottles.

I grabbed the rum and walked to the media room. I turned on a television station that played music videos and tipped my head back for my first shot.

I grimaced and then took another.

It took forever, but slowly the world faded away.

And then Bryce's arms were there and he had lifted me against his chest. I offered him the bottle of rum and he took a shot.

He hissed from the burn and I tried to make fun of him, but it was work. Words didn't make sense in my mind or from my mouth. Something just didn't connect.

When I felt my bedcovers, I came alive and pulled Bryce on top of me. He held back, which irritated me. I knew what I wanted and I wanted him. It didn't take long before I was on top of Bryce. I rubbed my body against his and nipped at his lips. It seemed to finally infuse him and he took charge, like he always did.

This time I didn't want the same. I shook my head numbly and moved to my knees.

Bryce groaned, but he stayed where he was.

I glanced at him and turned around.

It took a little bit, but all the sudden he was on top of me and he slid into me from behind. I felt him wrap an arm around my stomach as he plastered himself to my back. From the first thrust, I had to brace myself against the wall so I didn't bang my head against it.

We'd never tried it this way before.

It just felt different for me, but Bryce seemed to explode. I'd never heard the guttural groan that escaped him before as he collapsed onto my back. My own body shook. Bryce slid out, kept his arm around my stomach, and tugged me back down to the bed. He tucked me into his side and flung a leg over mine. He seemed to engulf me into him and his face rested just underneath my jaw.

I remember wondering where the rum had gone when I faded off.

Chapter 9

When I woke, Bryce was still beside me. He nuzzled the back of my neck and ran a hand down the front of my body. It caressed and rubbed at all the right spots to spark tingles. When his hand slipped between my legs, I gasped but closed my eyes. The pleasure soothed some new aches that didn't quite make sense.

A little later, Bryce tucked me underneath him, sheathed himself and slid inside. We didn't look at each other, but it was slow and sensual. I ran my hands over his shoulders and back. Bryce seemed to tremble.

At the final thrust, I curled back on my side and Bryce moved behind me. He didn't wrap his arms around me, like he did sometimes. He rested on his back and a second later, I heard his even breathing. He had fallen asleep.

I checked the clock and saw that it was a little after eight in the morning.

When I made my way into the shower, I shook my head past the fuzz. Something had happened last night, but...

I dropped the bar of soup when I remembered. I remembered everything.

The soap remained on the floor as I stood frozen in place. I ran over every word, action, and each thrust of warmth that had spread throughout my body.

Groaning softly, I finished in the shower and stepped out to dry off.

Bryce was still asleep when I slipped into some clothes.

I padded barefoot down to the kitchen and saw the near-empty bottle of rum.

Grimacing, I capped it and replaced it in my father's hidden liquor cabinet. I moved the bookcase back in place and left the study. It didn't look like it had even been touched in the first place.

When I heard my shower running, I filled two glasses of water and returned to my bedroom.

Bryce was still in the shower so I laid on my bed and snuggled into the bedcovers.

A little later, he came back and stopped short.

Our eyes met and he smiled a very satisfied smile.

I laughed and then cringed from the rum's revolt in my stomach.

Bryce chuckled and sat beside me. He ran a hand down my arm and murmured, "So, that was new."

I laughed again, but stopped short from the nausea inside.

"We could get to school in time for second period."

Bryce swore and remarked, "Who needs Spanish, anyway?"

"Only anyone who doesn't want to look like an illiterate idiot."

He snorted, but dressed in some clothes.

That's right. He'd gone home to pack a bag.

"Did we..." I started, but stopped.

He looked up and watched me intently. He sat back down and prompted, "Did we...?"

"Did we venture into new lands last night?"

A humorous smile spread across his face and Bryce nodded, "We did indeed."

"Oh," I breathed out. "Things are a little blurry, but I just wanted...I wanted to remember it all."

"Are you..." he asked slowly. "Are you having second thoughts?"

"No." I leaned upwards and captured his lips in a thorough kiss. "No, I'm not."

"Good," Bryce whispered and kissed me thoroughly. He stood again and asked, "So you're coming to school?"

"What else am I going to do?" I sighed in acceptance.

Something flickered in his eyes and Bryce admitted, "You're taking this pretty well."

"Not counting the drunken fog of orgies last night?"

"That makes sense, but I would've thought you'd be…angry, furious, something. I figured you'd want to get even or something."

I shook my head and stood to change my clothes.

Bryce watched me the entire time, but it wasn't from lust.

"What?" I asked, irritated.

"Nothing." He shrugged and grabbed the keys to his car. "Ready to go? I'll drive today."

"How will I get home?"

"I'll drive you or Corrigan will."

Bryce pulled into the school's parking lot a few minutes later. Some other stragglers were just arriving. Still others had decided to skip after the first torturous period of school. So there were more than a few students who were leaving and entering school at the same time we did.

Just as I left my locker, I locked gazes with Leisha as she passed by. I nodded in greeting and she gave me a fleeting smile. When I turned into my Spanish classroom, I saw Collette Chantal smiling seductively down at Bryce. She sat on the table just above him with her legs spread invitingly.

He was paying attention to whatever Chet was saying. As she touched his knee and started to slide down to his lap, Bryce brushed her off.

She looked insulted and about to protest, but Bryce ignored her.

"Doesn't it piss you off?" Chad had come up behind me.

"Does what piss me off?" I gripped my book and turned to face him. Cold.

He nodded in Bryce's direction. "Come on. Everyone knows what you two do and yet he's always got a new girl hanging on him. It has to piss you off, make you just burn inside. Tell me I'm right." He grinned cockily and moved to stand too close.

"Is this your card?"

His smile vanished.

"Because, really, it's been played by so many others. Try a new one, please, so I don't die from boredom."

His eyes had a glint of malice, but I evaded him and dropped into the seat beside Bryce.

I didn't have to look to know that Bryce was pissed. He would've seen Chad talking to me, but whatever. I had other things on my mind.

For one, my ass hurt.

Thankfully, the rest of the day passed without event. Chad sent a few glares our way and enjoyed licking his lips when his eyes met mine. He did it more when Bryce or Corrigan was around. And speaking of Corrigan, he must've been filled in by Bryce about my mental health state because he didn't pester me with questions. Then again, I didn't talk. They both knew that.

I dealt with it on my own. Drunken orgies had been a very pleasurable coping mechanism.

Lunch seemed to be declared wanton-free. I think maybe the guys had sent out a bulletin because no girl approached them or the table.

I sat with Bryce on one side and Corrigan on the other. Chet and Holster sat across and they all chatted about the upcoming soccer game. The word had been leaked that Bryce was no longer on the team and everyone seemed to have sent questions through Chet and Holster to ask Bryce. Lunch eventually became a Q & A about Bryce's plans for soccer.

After sixth period, I grabbed my purse just as Corrigan wrapped his arms around me from behind in a hug.

He chuckled and picked me up as he squeezed me.

"Oomph." I laughed and asked, "What's that for?"

He shrugged and fell down on the locker beside me.

We both knew what it was for.

"Yerling's a dick," Corrigan said abruptly. He watched him as he passed by and sent the same leering stares.

"Forget him. He's a loser."

"A loser that needs another pounding." Corrigan frowned abruptly. "Seriously. He's going to be a problem."

"You said the cops already knew about him. They were going to watch him, right?"

"Right," Corrigan scoffed in disbelief. "They don't unless a complaint's been filed or he's harmed someone."

Something in his voice had me frowning. I leaned closer and asked, "Has he harmed someone?"

Corrigan glanced at me sharply, but abruptly straightened and asked, his eyes on my purse, "Are you leaving?"

"I just like taking my purse to classes," I said dryly.

He smirked and suggested, "Let's take off."

"And go...?"

He shrugged and stuffed his hands in his front pockets.

"You want to go and hustle?"

He gave me a sharp glance and retorted, "Already been to jail this week."

"For me?" I murmured, huskily, and ran a finger up and down his arm.

Corrigan sucked in his breath, but didn't move away from the touch. He was thoughtful and finally shook his head, "No can do, Shell. I love ya and all, but I know I'll be sleeping next to some fat guy named Pervy." He shuddered and said shortly, "Not going to happen."

By unspoken agreement we turned towards the parking lot. We were outside the door when we heard a shout from behind us.

Turning, we saw Logan at the end of the hallway. She waved with a smile on her face, but she didn't move to us.

And Corrigan didn't move to her.

I glanced at him, but he was looking towards the parking lot. He had a stoic expression on his face.

When comprehension dawned, I punched him in the stomach.

Corrigan didn't grimace, cringe, or laugh. He sighed and moved towards his car.

"You're a dick," I declared.

Corrigan rolled his eyes and muttered, "Get in the car."

Inside, I said further, "No, I correct myself. They're the dicks."

"She's not a dick," Corrigan said quickly, but seemed to stop whatever else he was about to add.

I grinned now, "So you're the only one."

"Come on." he whined and wheeled out of the parking lot.

"Look, just—why do you have to bring them around?"

Disbelief crossed his face and he asked, "What are you talking about?"

"She knows about my parents. If you were going to drop her, why'd you bring her around in the first place?"

He shrugged, but asked, "Why do you care? It's not like you're nice to any of them."

I laughed, "I just laugh…at them. And have contempt for them."

Corrigan grinned from the corner of his mouth. As he pulled into the mall's parking lot, I remarked, "You know, if you were with her to make Becky Lew not your girlfriend, you put her through hell."

He glanced sharply at me, but didn't say anything.

"I'm just saying…she put up with a lot. Me. And you know that Lew's making her life hell. Not to mention, Lew's mindless bubble-heads."

Corrigan grinned and said, "Can we not talk about this? This is weird."

That was true.

"I'm a little off—parents and all," I relented.

Corrigan glanced at me, closed his mouth, and then wrapped an arm around my shoulder. Instead of the usual squelching hug, it was a gentle touch.

It was gone just as quick as it came.

Corrigan coughed and said, after a brief hesitation, "Yeah…uh… how are you doing with that?"

"Drunken orgies was the way to go." And I thought, for a moment, that the orgies had gone too far.

"Sweet," Corrigan remarked suggestively. "That's what I thought."

And we were back on familiar ground.

"So tell me—how many times with the latest reject?"

"Six." The answer was so quick, I was taken back a little.

"Six?" I narrowed my eyes. "You've been waiting for that question, haven't you?"

Corrigan didn't reply, but suddenly stopped, threw an arm over my shoulder and leapt onto my back.

"Oh!" I exclaimed, but grabbed his legs just in time.

We were the picture.

Corrigan was known as the player with a temper while I was known for having my walls up against people. My second shrink had told me that I set up multiple walls to close myself from others. People needed to break through the walls before they found me, but Corrigan and Bryce had never needed to break through the walls.

I rather thought it was because of this—Corrigan had been jumping on my back since seventh grade. The abrupt piggy-back ride brought a delighted smile to my face. It had been too long. We'd become almost adults for too long.

Corrigan pretended to swap my butt as he laughed in my ear, "Giddy-up, ho-bag."

"You're the whore, playa," I retorted with no heat behind my words. Laughing, I arched my back and threw him off.

He caught himself just before he would've fallen and managed to keep one leg around my waist. With my momentum, both of us fell on the cemented parking lot.

Still laughing, I staggered to my feet while I turned and kicked him in the side.

He howled, but lunged for my feet the next instant.

Not wanting to fall on my back, I fell forward onto Corrigan's stomach.

Corrigan caught me just before my elbow connected with his groin, but he flipped his body as a wrestler and had me pinned to the ground instantly.

"Am I supposed to tap out?" I asked as I panted. I knew that I had a stupid grin on my face, but I didn't care at that instant.

"Tap out, bitch." Corrigan growled, but giggled at the end. This made me giggle.

We hadn't wrestled like this for years. This was the kid that I had befriended so many years ago. This was the real Corrigan behind all of his walls that I sometimes forgot were there.

All of the sudden, I felt my throat choke and I blinked back some tears.

I scrambled to my feet and started to walk away quickly. Horrified.

"What—Sheldon!" Corrigan called after me as he jogged to catch up. When he saw my tears, he fell silent beside me.

He looked away. I looked the other way.

When we entered the mall's food court, Corrigan cleared his throat and looked slightly embarrassed.

"What?" I asked forcibly, my voice hoarse.

He looked away again. If I hadn't known better, I would've thought that he looked panicked.

"What?" I said again and was grateful that my voice sounded more normal.

He stuffed his hands inside his jeans, hunched his shoulders, and asked in a quiet voice, almost too quiet for me to catch, "Are you…I mean…never mind."

"I'm good. Don't worry," I murmured quickly and bumped my shoulder to his.

A grateful smile spread over his face and he bumped back.

From there a short arm wrestling match ensued and it ended with Corrigan getting another piggy-back ride in the mall.

We walked around for an hour. I modeled some lingerie to his wolf whistles. He tried on some flannel pants to my suggestive comments about the crotch-flap. Even though the modeling had started as a joke, Corrigan bought a pair of flannel pants because of 'easy access.'

The clerk had given us both a knowing and slightly disapproving look, which Corrigan had loved.

From there, he brought some smoothies and we ended our mall tour in the tattoo parlor. Corrigan already had two tattoos and was considering a dragon design for the back of his left leg.

I briefly considered a tramp stamp, but decided against it. Even with all my hype, I wanted to get a tattoo when it meant something.

We left the mall, stopped at a place for sub sandwiches, and headed to my house.

Just as Corrigan turned into my driveway, we both heard a sudden pop and the car swerved. Corrigan cursed and slammed on the brakes. He was out of the car in the next instant and I followed to hear him cursing some more.

He kicked a tire and spat out, "A flat."

"How?" I asked and glanced at my driveway.

My eyes found some spikes with steel-pointed edges that had been laid across my driveway.

"What the hell?" I asked as I knelt for a closer look. They were attached to a cord. Each end had been clamped down by some steel rods that were used to secure tents into the ground.

Just then we heard a squeal of tires and a truck roared past us. As they passed, the window opened and a brick was thrown at us. It smashed into Corrigan's back windshield. After it peeled around the corner and the engine sound faded, I didn't have to look at Corrigan. I already knew he was furious. When Corrigan was livid, he was silent. When he was pissed, he cursed, complained, and threatened.

Corrigan was silent.

"Do you know—" I managed out before he cut me off.

"Yerling," he spat harshly and cursed savagely. "Yerling."

He fell silent again.

I sighed and pulled up the rods that had been stuck into the ground. I rolled up the cord with all the spikes and stood there. Corrigan hadn't moved. His jaw clenched every now and then.

We stood there for awhile before I started his car and moved it to the side.

When I got back out, Corrigan must've clamped enough control over his fury because he opened his trunk and changed his tire. He threw his old one into the trunk and grabbed the keys from my hand. He peeled out of my driveway without a goodbye.

Chapter 10

I sighed as I walked towards my house. I already knew Corrigan would get revenge. He was the joker, the player, but he also had a temper and a penchant for ending up in jail. I figured I should make a trip to the bank, just in case I got another phone call asking for bail in the middle of the night.

When I entered my house, I walked through the garage to make sure my cars were all fine and left untouched.

They were.

Yerling hadn't broken into my garage. If he had broken into my house, the alarm would've sounded and my phone would've rang with a police report.

As I passed the front entrance into the kitchen, I noticed something on the ground.

Another note.

You didn't take the first note serious. It wasn't a warning. Adhere the grave circumstances if this note is thrown to the side as well.

To the trash it went.

I grabbed a can of soda and got into my car. The first stop was the bank, just in case. I withdrew two grand because I never knew what would happen with Corrigan. His bail had been a thousand one time and three hundred another time. Judging from his fury, I didn't think he would be content just trashing Yerling's car.

When I pulled into the Café Diner's parking lot, I saw that Bryce's car was there. He sat at the same booth in the back section. Chet, Holster, and Evan Harris sat with him. Becky Lew sat at a different table, across from theirs. The guys seemed to be ignoring the girls, while the girls were pissed that their flirting wasn't getting them attention.

Bryce's eyes found me and he nodded in greeting.

Chet stood and moved beside Holster and Harris.

I took his seat beside Bryce.

"You talk to Corrigan within the last hour?" I asked.

The guys quieted.

Bryce frowned slightly and shook his head. He asked, "Should I have?"

"Yerling put some tire slashes on my driveway. Corrigan lost a tire from it and his back windshield got smashed up. Yerling threw a brick as they drove off."

Chet started laughing. The rest of the guys all mirrored his amusement.

Bryce shook his head with a resigned look in his eyes. He murmured, "I should head to the bank."

"Already did," I told him.

Chet barked out a laugh at that. "Oh god. That's hilarious."

Harris leaned forward and asked, delight in his eyes, "So Sheldon, are you really coming to my party? It's tomorrow night, you know."

I cast a lazy eye over him and shrugged, "I'll try."

Bryce wasn't listening.

"What do you think he'll do?" I asked.

"With him—who knows," Bryce muttered, frowning.

"Didn't Corrigan light a shed on fire once because someone messed up his locker?" Chet asked.

Bryce swore.

"Imagine what he's going to do for his car getting messed up."

I swore.

"Yerling's going to the morgue if he keeps pissing off Corrigan," Holster remarked.

The guys all had the same sudden wariness now.

"Keeps pissing off Corrigan? What do you mean?" I was in the dark here. And I knew I didn't enjoy being in the dark, something else had happened.

Chet frowned and glanced to Bryce.

Holster and Harris both looked away. Sometimes I thought they were spineless, but then again—they were followers. I'd witnessed when those guys had waded through fire if Bryce, Chet, or Corrigan told them to. They weren't spineless, but wary at times. And they had reason to be.

"What am I missing?" I looked at all four of them and ended with Bryce. He had been watching me with an emotion I couldn't name. A knot of dread suddenly took root in my stomach.

Oh god.

"What is going on?"

"Uh…" Bryce started, but fell silent.

Chet cleared his throat and leaned forward. "Uh…Yerling's been pushing the envelope lately. He's been…he's been—"

"A psycho lately," Holster said flatly.

Chet threw him a frown, but resumed, "Yeah, well, he's been off his rocker lately. Remember that day in here when he…"

"I remember," I said dryly. I'd been there. I didn't need to remember when he'd made me scared—pansy.

"Well…the truth is that Yerling had done something to another girl this past weekend. And—" Chet gave Bryce a beseeching look.

Bryce coughed and finished, calmly, "Yerling hurt a girl at my party Friday night."

"What?" I hadn't heard anything about that.

"And on Sunday night, he made a few not-pretty comments about you—about what he'd like to do to you. We've been kinda watching him ever since then."

"He knew the score!" Harris burst out. "You told him that if he hurt anyone else or even looked like he might hurt someone that you'd put him down. He's asked for what's coming to him."

"He seemed fine on Monday and Tuesday. He was joking with Brent at lunch that day." This was from Chet.

"I know. We saw him in the principal's office Tuesday. He was fine," Bryce remarked.

"He said he'd gotten caught getting a blowjob," I said shortly. "He lied."

"Or he was trying to make someone give him a blowjob," Holster mumbled without thinking what he'd just said. His eyes widened when he did and he glanced at Bryce.

Bryce said slowly, "If that was the case...who was the girl?"

"I haven't heard a thing," Chet remarked as he swallowed tightly.

"Me neither," Evan parroted.

"Right," I scoffed. "Because girls who are forced to do sexual acts really go around and proclaim it." I sent a scathing glance at them. "You guys are idiots."

They looked at me.

"If you guys were forced to do something like that, would you tell people?"

They all grimaced and looked anywhere, but at me.

"Ignorant, ignorant, ignorant. And you're idiots," I chastised before I caught a glimpse of Becky Lew, who had been watching us. "Why is she looking at us?"

The guys seemed to sigh in relief at the same time. The topic had been changed.

Bryce relaxed beside me and threw an arm across the top of the booth. His hand brushed my shoulder.

"Because she's hot for Scout," Harris said with a cocky glint.

Bryce smirked and reached for his drink. His hand started to rub up and down against my shoulder.

He asked me, "You want something to eat?"

"I'm good."

"I could eat something. Let's go to Donadeli," Chet requested and the decision was made. The guys stood one by one and all trailed towards the door. I caught a sneer from Becky Lew, but she turned and flung an arm around some other guy. As we cleared the back section, I tucked my fingers inside of Bryce's back pocket and stopped him.

"Who's the guy?" I gestured behind us.

"Braven Locke. Why?"

Why? Because the guy next to him was salivating just as much and I remembered seeing that same guy with Leisha. She had been blushing and had even ducked her head, flirtatiously. I wanted to know, that's why.

"Is he friends with the other guy, the blonde?" That's who had caused Leisha to blush.

"I guess. His name is Carlos Hunstville." Bryce shrugged. "Why do you care?"

I shrugged and moved past him. When we got outside, I threw over my shoulder, "You're driving."

Bryce nodded and I sat shotgun with Harris in our backseat. Holster rode with Chet.

Bryce flipped some music on and it drowned out any conversation until he pulled into Donadeli's small parking lot. Donadeli was a locally owned Italian deli with red plush booths and floors that had polka-dotted tiles. They specialized in meatballs, but served sandwiches to the majority of their customers. The guys' liked the deli because they gave large helpings and Becky Lew's crowd generally looked down their noses at the Italian eatery. It was a place to hide when the mood struck.

I liked going to Donadeli because the owner's son had a crush on me.

"Hey Marcus," I said warmly, sultry, as we strolled inside.

He dropped the menus from his hand and stood paralyzed for a second, which didn't seem too far from his normal blank-eyed stare. I somewhat felt sorry for Marcus at times. He stood around five feet and nine inches. His hair were black strands that just seemed to hang off his scalp. And his eyes were always covered by his glasses. I never looked long enough to notice what color they were. Over all, Marcus was just blah and most of the time, he acted blah.

Bryce reached around me and grabbed a few before leading the way to our table. That was another thing. We sat where we wanted. We never waited to be seated. It had annoyed the owners at first, but Marcus must've said something for us because they never said anything.

I lingered at the hosting table and flirted with Marcus, my normal routine. This time, I got us free breadsticks and drinks, but Marcus said we needed to pay for the entrees. He almost choked in fear as he told me this.

He put our order through while I moved to the seat across from Bryce.

They all waited until I commented with a proud smile, "Breadsticks and drinks."

A collective 'nice' sounded around the table.

"And he put your orders in."

Another collective 'sweet' went around.

The guys always ordered the same thing. With the quick order, we usually got our food faster than the customers who'd already ordered before us.

Just then Corrigan dropped into the one empty seat nearest the aisle. He sighed dramatically and looked irritated.

Chet, Holster, and Harris quieted.

Bryce and I shared a look before I ventured, "What'd you do?"

Corrigan ignored me and griped, "Did you order already? Where the hell are our drinks?"

"Dude," Bryce said quietly, watching. "We just got here."

Corrigan swore and turned his chair around to straddle it. He looked a bit frazzled, but it was the anger in his tone that made my knot of dread double in size.

"What'd you do?" I asked again.

He ignored me again and asked abruptly, "What free stuff did you get us?"

I gave him a pointed look.

"I didn't do anything." He cursed. "Back off."

If anyone except Bryce had spoken to me like that, Corrigan would've been the first to throw a punch.

I never needed his protection before and I didn't need it now.

I slid a knife out from the silverware wrapped in a cloth napkin and stabbed it in his chair's cushion, right between his legs.

Corrigan yelped and jumped off the seat. Startled, he cursed some more before he settled back in his chair, now watchful.

He snapped, "What?!"

"What. Did. You. Do?"

"Are you going to jail for it?" Bryce asked instead.

"No. No jail." Corrigan answered Bryce and looked at me. "And I'll tell you later. It's not dinner talk, you know."

Fine.

Marcus brought the drinks and two orders of breadsticks. He grabbed another drink for Corrigan and said, with his head hung downwards, that he'd put in Corrigan's order too.

Corrigan ignored him and downed my drink. He stood up and refilled it behind the cook's doorway.

Marcus stood helpless behind him.

Corrigan returned to the table and sat it in front of me.

"You're a jerk," I murmured.

Corrigan shrugged, but he patted my knee underneath the table.

"So we got a game going." Chet spoke up and the conversation was off and running. Corrigan lapped it up. He wanted a distraction from whatever he didn't want to talk about.

A few minutes later, Marcus brought the drinks and our food wasn't too far behind. I sat back and poked at my salad as the guys talked more about soccer and Harris' party. They started planning an elaborate drinking game that consisted of a chart with relays when my phone rang.

I didn't recognize the number so I answered.

"Hi, sweetie," my mother's sickening sweet voice drawled across the other end.

I stilled and asked, tensely, "What do you want?"

"I wanted to let you know my new number, sweetie. You should've gotten my message, but I know you don't always think to check the house's line."

Her voice disgusted me and I had to take a deep breath to clear the nausea.

"Fine." It was all I could manage out as I choked on the inside.

"Honey." Only my mother could make concern sound like contempt. Not to mention condescension.

"I'm fine. Really." I gripped the phone harder, but I knew my face looked fine, probably a little bored.

"Do we need to talk about this? I want you to know, Sheldon Eva, that I am your mother and I love you very much."

Funny. She sounded like she'd been drinking.

She continued, "This is for the best. It really is. Your father and I just reached a point in the marriage when it was time to part ways."

"Did you sleep with someone?" It's something she'd do.

"Sweetie." Sharon hadn't liked that. She heaved a dramatic sigh. "Are you angry with me? This really is for the best. A harmonious parental unit benefits the child better. Neil and I were not harmonious. This is for you really, honey, more than your father and myself."

"What?" My eyes went cold. "Did you pick up that language in therapy?"

She was quiet for a moment and then said stiffly, "Your father and I did try some marital counseling."

"You went once and said it wasn't for you?" I guessed.

"Sheldon, you need to watch your tone with me."

"I am watching, Sharon. My tone is completely calm and ladylike. I am not angry," I bit out. "I am not bitter," I spat. "I am not sad," I chewed out. "And I am most certainly not feeling abandoned at all." I finished with a smile.

She drew a sharp breath and said flatly, "Fine."

"Fine."

"I love you, sweetheart."

"Sure you do," I said smoothly.

"I really do. I'll see you over the holidays."

"You're coming home for Thanksgiving?"

"Yes. I'll need to pack my things and look for a new home."

"And who'll be looking with you?"

"You don't need to worry about that. Just a little friend."

So she *had* slept with someone.

I asked, "You're still sleeping with him?"

She sucked in her breath again and admonished, "Sheldon Eva, I will not put up with your tone of voice any longer. You are to respect your mother. This is hard on all of us, trust me, but I think it's a bit more tiring on your father and myself. You've told us many times to get a divorce."

"Great, mom. So you're just fulfilling one of my wishes." If I could cut glass with my voice, it would've happened then and there.

She sighed, sounding rightfully tiresome. I rolled my eyes.

"Have you heard from your father?"

"Yes." I didn't share our conversation.

"Is he well?" Sharon really wanted to know what he'd said and if I loved him more than her.

"He is well." And I'll let you worry if I love my father more than you. You deserve it.

"Alright, well…I love you, sweetie."

I hung up.

The table had fallen silent throughout my entire conversation. I didn't need to look to know that Bryce and Corrigan were both watching like hawks.

I breathed out one clear breath and stood up.

"Where you going?" Corrigan said quickly.

"I'm going home." The calm was forced in my voice. I knew my eyes spoke volumes, but only to Corrigan and Bryce.

"Sheldon..." Bryce murmured.

"I'm fine. I'm going home to do schoolwork. Beg off...please." The request was sincere.

The guys took it as such and both remained in their seats.

The drive was too short for me. I had plenty to stew over and my hands shook as I parked in the garage and hit the button to close the garage door. I didn't look for any more notes or messages as I made a beeline for the case of beer still on the kitchen table.

I dropped my purse and at the same time I uncapped a beer. I downed that one and did another.

With three clenched in my fingers, I moved into my father's study. I decided to start with the computer and I effectively deleted every single business document he had kept as a reserve on the home computer. After I made another search, I emptied the trash can and then removed the hard-drive.

From the hidden liquor cabinet, I placed all the liquor bottles on his desk. When that was done, I grabbed a poker stick from the fireplace and swung it hard at every crystal vase in the library, every picture frame, every and anything that would break. I left the couches and chairs untouched and moved into my parent's bedroom with a bottle of bourbon in my hand.

With a knife in hand, I visited the closets and slashed the most expensive clothing. I threw all of Sharon's undergarments and lingerie into a box that'd go to a local thrift store. Neil's tuxedos were next for the knife. And all of the neckties, socks, and suits went into the thrift store box.

I ripped his shirts to pieces and let them fall on the floor.

The shoes—they'd started to go a little blurry by that time so I left them in one piece.

I lay on the couch in one of the rarely-used sitting rooms and thought I might save my mother a trip. I could hire some movers to pack it all up. She needn't bothered.

I'd decided to divorce my parents in turn, not like they'd even notice.

Chapter 11

When I woke up, I heard my cell phone beeping first. Bryce and Corrigan had called. And then I realized I heard scuffling from the inside of the house.

I glanced at the clock in the sitting room and saw it was 2:54 in the morning.

No doubt the scuffling was from the guys. They must've come looking for me.

Yawning, I made my way slowly down the back hallway. I knew it by heart so I left the lights untouched. Even though it was nighttime, the moonlight filtered in through the windows and lit the side hallways that ran around the house. I passed our backdoor and I was able to see the bench that ran the entire length of the wall. My mom had stored various items into bins that were all underneath that bench.

The dining room opened onto the kitchen. There were two hallways that connected to the dining room. I had walked down the side hallway that's never used.

So it was a bit disconcerting when I walked into the dining room and saw a man in the kitchen.

I didn't recognize him and he didn't know I was there. I had walked silently, like I always do, but the guy wasn't Bryce or Corrigan. He wasn't my father. And I hoped he wasn't my mom's newest bedmate.

Just then a walkie-talkie that was attached to his belt crackled to life. "Jimmy, are we clear?"

The guy snatched the radio from his belt's holster and answered, "That's a right-o, Jimmy John. We are in the clear."

"You've checked your entire section."

Jimmy sighed impatiently and snapped into the radio, "What did I just say? Did I not say that we are in the clear? That's a right-o."

It was surreal. He stood in the moonlight with his back turned to me and he was shifting through my kitchen's drawers. I stood thirty feet from him, five feet from my doorway.

If he had looked, I might've resembled a ghost.

My heart pounded in my ears and I stepped slowly, silently, backwards. He kept shuffling through the drawers and I kept reversing until I was hidden in the hallway. At the back door, I took a calming breath and kneeled on the floor. Blindly I felt around until I found the flap that kept our security keypad hidden from eyesight.

I coded in the alarm and a second later, an earsplitting alarm sounded throughout my home.

Jimmy cursed savagely. And I heard more curses and shouts.

"Jimmy, what the hell happened? That code came from your section. We aren't clear. We aren't clear!"

Jimmy dropped whatever had been in his hands and a second later, I heard his pounding footsteps on the floor.

He searched the dining room. I could see his shadow get bigger until it engulfed where I had kneeled.

I scooted back until I was curled in a small hole just underneath the bench, in between two of the bins.

Jimmy couldn't have seen me unless he walked into the back hallway and knelt literally right in front of me.

"There's an entire hallway back here," he cursed to himself.

He swept a flashlight beam up and down the hallway. It hit on some of the bins and just as he started down the hallway, his radio crackled, "The police are coming. We have to go, Jimmy."

Jimmy continued to curse, but turned and sprinted from the hallway. It only took another second until the front door slammed shut and I heard two pairs of vehicles squeal from my driveway.

I slowly crawled back from my hiding spot. My legs trembled so much, I couldn't quite stand so I crawled to one of the windows and pulled back the curtain.

I saw a lone figure dart across my yard, but it paused just before the shadows. It turned and I swear that it looked right at me. Startled, I dropped the curtain back in place and scooted into my hiding spot. I hugged my knees and rested my forehead against them until I heard my doorbell ringing.

My heart still pounded in my ear, but I was able to hear the doorbell.

Glancing up, feeling the blood drained from my face, I felt like weeping in relief when I saw the circling red lights of the police.

They rang the doorbell again and then knocked on the door with their batons.

It took me longer than normal because my legs were so unsteady, but I finally opened the door for them.

There were two of them. One was an older muscular guy that was balding on the head. His partner was a young blonde female. Both looked fit. Then I looked again and saw their grave expressions. The female stepped forward and asked, "Miss, we got a call from your security company. Can you tell us why it went off?"

The male stepped back and raised a hand to the radio he had clipped to his shoulder. I heard him requesting back-up officers.

"I…" I had to cough and clear my voice. "I…there were men in my home and I was the one who set the alarm."

"Are men still in your home, Miss?"

"No." I shook my head. "They heard the alarm and left."

"Could we do a quick search, Ma'am?"

I nodded and stepped from the front door onto the patio as both of them moved inside cautiously with their guns drawn and ready beside their hips.

It seemed forever, but the alarm was silenced and the female officer returned.

"My name is Officer Patterson. You can call me Sheila, if you'd like."

I nodded and sunk onto one of the patio loungers.

She stood above me. "Can you tell me what happened?"

I told her most of it. I left out the details about my mother, but I told them I had trashed most of my parent's belongings in the office and bedroom.

Sheila gave me a questioning look and raised an eyebrow. "You trashed your parent's belongings?"

"Just the important ones. I'm...they're getting a divorce and they told me over a voice message," I said numbly.

Sheila nodded like it made perfect sense. "We'll need you to do an inventory of what you damaged and cross-reference it with forensics to see if the burglars took anything or damaged anything further."

I nodded. Whatever.

"Do you have someone you'd like to call? We'll need you to come down to the station for an official report."

"Can I go in and get my cell phone?"

"Officer Milon will escort you inside, Miss Jeneve." Sheila nodded and stepped off the patio just as two more police cruisers pulled into the driveway.

As we walked around the kitchen and down the back hallway, I shivered as I passed my hiding spot. I knew that guy, whoever he had been, had seen me.

Once I got my phone, I was led back outside and into the front seat of Officer Sheila's car. That's when I called Corrigan's number first.

It rang and rang so I left a message.

I called Bryce next and he answered after the second ring.

"Sheldon?" he asked, tiredly. I heard him yawn and could envision him sitting up against his headboard.

"My house was broken into tonight."

"What?" He was wide awake now.

"Can you—can you meet me at the police station? I have to go there for a report."

"Yeah, yeah. Of course." I could hear him already dressing. "Are you okay?"

"Just come down, okay?"

"Okay. I'll be there as soon as possible."

"Thanks."

"Yeah. Sheldon—"

"Yes?"

"I'm glad you're okay," he said sincerely and it nearly broke me right then and there.

Hoarse, I murmured a thank you and hung up.

The police station looked different arriving as a victim rather than to post bail for a friend. It looked scary, threatening, and I had to blink back tears for the fourth time as Sheila parked her police cruiser.

She had me sit beside a desk and had left to get me a cup of coffee when Bryce walked through the door in sport pants and a hooded sweatshirt.

It was amazing really. I shouldn't have noticed, but immediately some of the cops turned a watchful eye on him. It was something about him—he exuded a silent demand about himself. It made sense that cops would instantly tune into that demand and be alert.

He ignored them and found me with his eyes.

Giving me a tender smile, Bryce nodded to me when one of the officers questioned him. The cop let him through and Bryce was beside me in a flash. He lifted me up and I was hugging onto him for dear life. I hadn't realized that I had wrapped my legs around his waist until Sheila coughed discreetly behind us.

"Let go, Sheldon," Bryce murmured in my ear and I unwound my legs.

Sheila gave us both a small smile and indicated a chair beside another desk for Bryce to grab. He did and he sat beside me, leaning in his chair, looking relaxed and a little bored.

As I gave my official report, I saw that Sheila frowned a few times in Bryce's direction, but she never made a comment. Bryce was either worshiped or disliked. He wasn't a bad guy, he just came off as one to people.

We stayed at the station for an hour. Bryce had looked at me strangely when Sheila had asked me to list the items that I had damaged. They wanted to know where I had placed the computer's hard-drive, when my last communication had been with my parents, when my mother was returning home, and etc.

Sheila asked if I had a place to stay. They'd want to get back into the house the next day.

Bryce spoke for the first time, "She'll stay at my place."

"What?" I asked. "With your mom there?"

He shrugged and seemed to settle back in his chair.

"Alright." Sheila gave Bryce another perusal, but only said, "We'll contact you if we think of any more questions."

Bryce stood and waited for me. He followed behind with a hand in the small of my back as we made our way into the waiting area. Just as we turned the corner, I glanced over my shoulder and saw Sheila frowning. Her eyes locked and held with mine. I contained a shiver from the dark concern in those eyes.

Just as we pushed through the doors, we watched as Corrigan drove past us and slammed on his brakes. He was out of the car in a flash and left his door hanging open to rush over to us.

"Are you okay?" he asked as he swept me in his arms much the same as Bryce had. My legs didn't wind around his waist, but I hugged him tightly. He squeezed once more and as he sat me down on my feet, he ran a hand over my hair. "I got your message. I was so…"

"I'm fine. Really," I said with a gracious smile. I was getting there.

Bryce asked, "Where were you?"

Corrigan's gaze switched to Bryce and he straightened abruptly. His hand fell away from me as he took a step backwards.

"I was sleeping. What's your problem?"

"She needed both of us, a-hole. You should've been here."

"What are you pissy at me for?" Corrigan asked, confused and slightly defensive.

Bryce opened his mouth to say something, closed it again, and walked towards his car.

"What is he mad at me for?" Corrigan switched his confusion to me.

I shrugged and wrapped my arms around me. "He wants to blame someone."

Corrigan rolled his eyes and shot out, "He shouldn't blame me. I'm not the one who broke into your place."

I winced.

Corrigan swore. "I'm sorry, Sheldon. I wasn't thinking."

I shrugged him off. With a tight grin, I said softly, "Its fine. I'm fine. I'm alive."

"Sheldon!" Bryce called from his car.

"Where are you guys going? Do you need a place to stay?" Corrigan scowled in Bryce's direction.

"I'm going to stay at his place."

"With his mother?"

He understood too.

"That's what I said, but whatever."

"Oh...okay. Well, if you need help, call me." Corrigan flashed a reassuring smile and hugged me once more. By that time, Bryce had pulled the car beside us and I smiled grimly at Corrigan as I got inside.

The ride was quiet, but I was okay with that. I wasn't up for conversation, not at that moment. At one point I shivered and Bryce quickly switched the heat on.

I fought back tears and then cursed my own weakness.

When Bryce pulled up to his house and as he parked in the garage, I asked, "Are you sure?"

"Yes," Bryce said firmly.

At the door, he grabbed my hand, shut off the garage light and opened the door. He didn't turn the lights on inside, but led me through his family's kitchen, dining room, and down to his bedroom.

He turned the light on when he closed his bedroom door.

Bryce started to change clothes and I moved into his bathroom.

When I came back in, he stood up from his desk and passed behind me.

I slid underneath his sheets and closed my eyes. The routine was so familiar and I knew it's what I needed. I fought back tears again, but rolled over to bury my head in Bryce's pillows.

It didn't take long before I heard the bathroom door open and his light switched off. Bryce slid in beside me and tucked the sheets around us both as he flipped on his stomach to lay one arm over my waist.

I sighed and tucked my head against his shoulder just before I fell asleep.

Chapter 12

Both of us jumped awake to a slammed door.

"What the hell?" Bryce groaned and ran a tired hand over his face. When his little sister let loose with a blood-curdling scream, he sighed again and moved to the edge of the bed.

I yawned and curled on my side as I pulled the bedcovers over me again.

Bryce stood up, shirtless, in his basketball shorts and padded barefoot out the door. He banged on a door and I heard him mediating between his seven-year-old sister, Savannah, and his fourteen-year-old brother, Luca.

The two were water and oil. And their mother never helped. She either scolded, threatened, or placated. She never disciplined. That was what Bryce told me once and I'd seen enough to agree with him.

From what I could overhear, Luca was sick and vomiting in the bathroom. Savannah needed the bathroom because she felt the same. And a second later Bryce's bedroom door flew open and Savannah let loose another scream as she scuttled to an abrupt stop on her way to her older brother's bathroom.

"Mooom!"

I groaned and pulled a pillow over my head.

Savannah stayed put.

"Mom! Mom! Mom! Bryce has a girl in his bed! Bryce has a girl in his bed! It's *her*, mom!"

Savannah might not have liked me, but AnnaBelle Scout liked me even less. In fact, I think she hated me at times and secretly, I didn't think it was because I was tight with her son. I think she was just jealous I wasn't ladylike and I *still* got her son.

Bryce swept into the room, tucked Savannah underneath one arm, and removed her. He shut the door and I heard him talking on the other side.

There was silence and then Savannah screamed again, slightly muffled, "Mom! Mom! Quick, before she jumps out the window."

"Shut up!" Bryce snapped.

A second later, he walked inside and sat on the bed's edge.

"I am not hiding from your mother," I said softly, seriously.

"I know." He yawned and ran a hand through his Mohawk, which looked flat in the morning.

A knock sounded at the door.

Bryce groaned deep in his throat before he stood and opened the door.

There was AnnaBelle Scout, a shimmering brunette vision. Her glare was ominous as she stood, already prim and proper in her silk chiffon dress and perfectly manicured hairstyle.

All in all, his mother was petite, beautiful, and the perfect lady.

She never drank. She never smoked. And I really thought that she'd never had sex.

"Bryce Elliot Scout." It was all she said.

"Mom…" Bryce started, exhausted.

I huddled in the corner and glared from underneath his bedcovers.

"You know how I feel about this girl," she continued sternly. "I have resigned myself to the fact that you insist on a friendship with her, but I forbid you to further any romantic notions. You need a good girl with morals and a family upbringing that meet your standards."

"Your standards, Mom," Bryce argued as he stood and looked at his mother. "This is my life. You've already got my future mapped out, but this is my life right now."

"You're a bitch," I said softly.

AnnaBelle gasped and whirled to me. Bryce had taken the heat from me and even shifted on his feet so she wouldn't look at me. I was done with him taking the heat for me.

"Excuse me?" she asked coldly.

I sat up and knew the skimpy tank-top would enrage her further. Sweetly, I said, "You heard me."

Bryce frowned, but he didn't say anything.

"I will not tolerate disrespect in my home—"

"Then get out," I interrupted quickly and let the bedcovers fall to reveal my underwear and bare legs. I regretted not wearing a thong instead of my boxer underwear, but at least they were made of black lace.

Her eyes widened.

I explained, "You just said that you won't tolerate my disrespect, but you're pretty damned disrespectful to me."

AnnaBelle Scout huffed in righteous indignation. "You will get out," she managed to bark through her clamped lips. "You will get out now."

"With pleasure." I glared right back.

Bryce moved to grab a tee shirt and his mother snapped out, "You will not leave this house."

"Mom," he sighed. "I have to drive her. She doesn't have a ride."

AnnaBelle ignored her son's comment, but seethed towards me instead, "You are the vilest girl that I could ever wish for my son. You will leave my home and never set foot here again." She stopped and turned back, with a sniff, "I will pray for your soul, Sheldon."

And the wicked witch of the Scout household was gone.

"I hate her. I hate her. I hate her." I exclaimed. "Let's have sex right now."

"Sheldon."

"And make it loud."

"I still have to live here, remember?" Bryce muttered as he went into the bathroom.

I fell back on the bed and moaned, seductively.

"Stop it," came from the bathroom.

I gasped huskily.

"I mean it."

"Make me beg, Bryce." I whispered, throatily.

Bryce came back to the room and shook his head, but his eyes darkened when I smiled, seductively, from the bed. And then he scooped up my clothes and tossed them at me. "Come on, we can grab some breakfast or something. I don't want to stay in this house longer than necessary."

I rolled my eyes, but moved to dress quickly. Bryce waited by the door until I was ready and then held the door for me.

As we left, the house was blanketed in complete silence.

Bryce laughed and remarked, "She took them out, probably to church."

"To brainwash them."

On the kitchen counter, he'd been left a sternly-worded letter to return home as soon as possible. He should expect severe consequences for his outlandish behavior.

He rolled his eyes at the note, but I ripped it in shreds and let the pieces fall from my hands.

When we got into his car, he asked, "Did you really want to get breakfast?"

"I can go for breakfast—or lunch." Bryce had borrowed me a shirt, but I kept my same jeans since I'd fallen asleep in them after my rampage. I even looked presentable by his heinous mother's standards.

It was our usual lunch period and when we got to Café Diner, we saw our normal crowd lingering at the table. They greeted Bryce with high fives and slaps on the back. Each of the guys gave me a friendly greeting while the girls just glared hatred. Like always. Becky Lew seemed even nastier than normal because she didn't hide the loathing when she looked at me.

That was different.

Corrigan was already at the table and he looked up, met my gaze, and traveled to Bryce. Whatever he saw there didn't agree with him because he shoved away from the table and stalked out of our section to sit at another table.

Of course, he chose appropriately. The table was full of blushing sophomores who revealed a little more of their scooped necklines in front of Corrigan's gaze.

Bryce didn't say anything, but sat in an empty booth in the back corner.

"Are you serious?" I asked.

Bryce shrugged and ordered some drinks for us.

Annoyed, I turned and walked over to Corrigan's table.

He quieted when he saw me coming.

"Hey," he said, guarded.

"Hey."

He nodded behind me, "He's still mad at me for absolutely *nothing*."

I shrugged. "It's not my problem."

"Whatever," Corrigan cried out, louder than he had intended. He quieted his voice, "It's because of what happened with you. I was sleeping—I'm sorry."

"Look, just apologize to him."

"I didn't do anything."

"Apologize and we'll all be fine."

"Not me," he retorted.

The sophomores were a captive audience.

"Do it for me."

"Wha—" His initial protest died in his throat. He looked at me with renewed eyes as he remembered and asked, "How are you? Are you okay?" His smile flashed, "You want a piggy-back ride?"

"Good." I pushed it to the back of my mind—once more.

"Okay." He didn't believe me, but I knew he wouldn't push it.

"Apologize for me?"

"Fine." It was wrenched out of him, painfully and slowly. Corrigan sounded like he was being tortured.

"Good!" I sent a beaming smile his way and turned back to slide into Bryce's booth. Chet, Harris, and a guy named Seth Haugen had taken residence around the booth. They were chatting with him and continued when our food orders were taken.

When our food and drinks came, they departed only to be replaced by Becky Lew and Mandy Justice. Mandy was alright by my standards. She was one of the smarter girls in our class and she'd refrained from joining the cheerleading squad. She'd been the Senior Editor of the yearbook last year and everyone knew she'd be the same this year. Plus, she was loyal and funny. The only downfall: she was friends with Becky Lew for some insane reason.

Becky said warmly, "Hi, Bryce. We missed you in class this morning."

Gag.

"Hi, Becky," I said loudly and sent her a sweet smile.

She managed to restrain a look of disgust, but smiled back and replied in a bland voice, "Hello, Sheldon. How are you? You haven't been around that much this week."

"Parent's divorce. My house was broken into. I kinda had a lot going on."

She froze in surprise, but with an eye blink, it was gone. Only to be replaced by the robot cheerleader façade once more.

No sympathy for me.

Instead she turned to Bryce and cooed, "No wonder you've been exhausted this week. You're such a good friend, even loaning Sheldon your clothes."

Bryce gave a full smile and remarked, "I like Sheldon in my clothes."

I coughed back a laugh.

Becky scowled, blinked, and smiled. She ran a hand down his arm and gushed, "I'd love to wear your shirt."

"There's a requirement," I stated matter-of-factly. "You gotta satisfy him first."

Bryce choked back the laugh this time. He failed and had every table in the back section glance towards us in curiosity. It was known that Bryce Scout did not laugh.

"I think I could manage that," she said, meltingly.

I choked back the vomit.

The urge to kick her was really tempting. Her shin was in perfect position. I could kick and smile like it never happened.

"Ow," Becky complained and glared at Mandy. "What?"

Mandy had beaten me to it, but with an elbow to Becky's side.

Mandy nudged her again and indicated towards the front entrance. She moved aside and we all saw Chad Yerling stroll into the diner. If he had looked awful after Bryce's beating, he looked like he survived a bomb this time.

And the crazy look in his eyes didn't help.

He had bruises everywhere, two busted lips, only one good eye, and the way he walked—at least three broken ribs.

As he neared Corrigan's table, the two eyed each other in shared hatred.

Yerling passed by to enter the back section and he stopped when Chet, Seth Haugen, Harris, and a half dozen other guys stood up. A moment passed and then they all walked out.

It was another surreal moment.

A rift had occurred among the best of the best. Chad Yerling, second only to Corrigan and Bryce, had now been ostracized by *all* the guys in his grade. If he looked for friends underneath our grade, good luck to him. I highly doubted it.

He only stood with five or so friends behind him and they'd never be mistaken as one of the 'best.'

When I looked at Bryce, he was staring at Corrigan who was staring back at him.

They shared an unspoken message and I saw approval flicker in Bryce's eyes.

Becky abruptly left with Mandy trailing behind anxiously.

"Did you know?" I asked underneath my breath.

Bryce didn't answer, but he didn't need to. I saw that he had. He probably participated.

"Why?"

Bryce shrugged and finished eating his food.

Sometimes my two best friends pissed me off. Sometimes they did things and wouldn't tell me. And sometimes I knew I should love them for it. Then and there, I knew it was a battle that I wouldn't win so I dropped it and finished my orange juice. I left the rest of my food. I'd lost my appetite that rarely reared its head.

When we were done, most of the 'good' students had left to return to school. Corrigan and some others remained, content to skip, sit, and chat.

Bryce and I stopped by Corrigan's table as we passed to leave.

"Hey, uh…" Corrigan cleared his throat. "You were right, man. I'm sorry."

I was happy again.

Bryce gave him a stiff nod in response and both visibly relaxed after that.

"So…" Corrigan started, shifting between me and Bryce. "What are you guys doing now?"

"I need to go home," I told him.

"Hey, man," Corrigan threw in. "You wanna head to my place for the afternoon?"

Bryce nodded and we left as if there'd been no rift between the two.

The sophomore girls were disappointed, but I flicked them off behind my back. I felt perversely satisfied now.

I heard Corrigan bark out a laugh just as the door closed behind me.

Bryce dropped me off at home and I showered, changed, and looked around for damages. Officer Patterson had left a message on my machine that they'd searched the house and cross-referenced their list of damaged property with mine. She had the full report for me to look over, if I felt it was warranted. She also had a few follow-up questions, but those could be handled at a later date. All in all, I was given the okay to clean-up.

I first started by ordering a different alarm system. When they got there, I went downstairs until they were done. After I'd gotten instructions for setting the alarm, I showered again and lay down in bed, but only after I grabbed my dad's Colt.45. I slid it inside a shelf in my nightstand. With my bedroom door locked, I curled under the blankets and fell asleep, hoping I wouldn't wake to another AnnaBelle reincarnation.

When I woke up, I realized that I'd slept for seven hours.

Violated security was more exhausting than I realized.

And then I heard what had woken me up in the first place, someone was ringing the doorbell.

For a girl who lived alone, it was pretty hard to get some alone time.

With a face-stretching yawn, I made my way downstairs and checked the window first. It was Mena and she looked frantic. When she lifted to poke the doorbell again, I threw open the door and gasped, "Please no more."

Mena flushed. "Sorry. I knew you were here, but probably asleep since you didn't answer right away."

"Or I was hoping to ignore you, but you annoyed me to death," I deadpanned and Mena followed me inside.

I grabbed an ice tea and hopped onto one of the counters. Mena sat on a stool as I dangled my feet over the counter's edge.

"Uh...so are you still going to that party?"

"What party?"

Self-conscious, Mena clarified, "That party that you were supposed to invite me to...remember?"

Harris' party. Friday night. Corrigan had asked me to bring her.

"I guess so," I sighed. I'd forgotten about it.

"Um...," She bit her lip, unsure of what to do or say. I was used to the expression so it was pretty easy to pinpoint. Leisha looked at me that way a lot. The only two who didn't were Bryce and Corrigan.

"Yeah. Let's go." I made my decision.

"It's, like, ten already."

I'd slept longer than I had realized. I almost slept the entire day.

"Fine. I gotta get ready."

As I put my glass away, Mena stayed in place and glanced around the room.

"You can come with me." I indicated upstairs.

"Oh." She sent me foolish smile. "Sorry, I didn't know."

I waved her off.

"So you weren't in school today," Mena murmured, conversationally.

"No."

As we passed the library's door, Mena gasped, "Oh my god. What happened?"

"That's kind of personal, don't you think?" I teased, but when she flushed in embarrassment again, I relented, "I spent a day destroying my papa's things. I'm not all that happy with my parents right now. Plus, my house was broken into last night."

Mena was quiet.

"Don't worry. I don't think they're trolling the neighborhood. The cops said that they singled my house for a reason." I drawled, "Let me tell you, not real settling to the stomach."

Mena relaxed a little, but fiddled with her hands.

I was beginning to agree with Bryce. She was weird.

In my bedroom, Mena eyed the bed warily and perched on the littlest amount of bed possible.

I burst out laughing as I pulled out a translucent chiffon wrap. "The sheets are clean. Trust me. I've had a maid in here since the last time Bryce spent the night. She comes in once every two weeks."

"Oh." She didn't look reassured.

I showered quick and pulled on a pair of khakis jeans that hugged my hips. I wore a pale pink chiffon top that crossed between my breasts. I left the bra behind, but that was alright. Even though the top didn't look like it, my breasts were firmly supported in place and tucked from escaping.

As I did my hair, I murmured, "So where were you? You missed some days of school too…right?"

"Uh…yeah." She fidgeted with her hands some more and finally sat on them. With a flush in her cheeks, she said brightly, "I wasn't feeling that well."

"You looked fine when we saw you at the coffee place."

"I know, but Denton was right. I was a little nauseous that day. The coffee didn't help."

I noticed the glitter that shimmered off of her curls.

"You look nice," I said honestly.

Startled, Mena looked up and I saw a flicker of guilt flash in her eyes. It was quickly gone and replaced with appreciation.

"Thanks," she mumbled.

She did look nice. She was dressed in a white cashmere sweater with a bow-tie that circled the bottom swell of her breasts and tied in the back. Though her jeans were simple, they were stylish and rich. The girl looked like she came from money and she did. Her lips were frosted pink and her eyes were highlighted by white eye-shadow that gave her an innocent, yet knowing look. The boys would go crazy.

Chapter 13

When we arrived at the party, Harris stumbled over to us. He wore a shirt with eight vertical strips of blue tape on it. After he greeted us drunkenly with beer-sloshed arms and a slur in the eyes, I regarded him, "Let me guess. The eight pieces of tape are for the eight drinks that you've had."

His smile exuded booze, but it was still blinding. Harris was a very good looking boy with ruby-red lips that would never need to be touched-up by a camera. His golden locks were misted almost perfectly with sweat. The drunk look worked for him.

"No, no. Eight beer bongs." That was said so matter of fact.

"Where's the rest of the gang?"

Harris shifted and gestured towards the backyard.

"Thanks, Harris." I patted him on the arm and winked at Mena. Harris was busy skimming her figure up and down while she stood in place, self-conscious.

She looked about to say something, but I was quickly swallowed in the crowd.

Harris' entire backyard was crawling with other students. Most stood in smaller groups and cliques, talking and drinking. Some couches had been placed around a bonfire near the patio and I saw Corrigan sitting there with Bryce beside him. Collette Chantal sat on the arm of Bryce's couch. Her legs weren't crossed over his, but her knee rested against him.

It should've enraged me, right?

It didn't.

"Sheldon!" Corrigan's face lit up as he threw his arms in the air. "Come here, girl!"

Corrigan was feeling pretty good. Bryce looked a little glazed over too, which surprised me a little. Even though he drank, he rarely got drunk.

That could not be said for Corrigan.

Collette stayed in place with a look of defiance on her face when she saw me approaching.

Corrigan threw an arm around my waist and I was tipped into his lap.

Uncomfortable, I managed to crawl out from underneath Corrigan's suddenly exploring hands. He managed a few grabs until I finally—accidentally—placed my knee over a certain anatomical organ of his.

As he sucked in his breath from the pain, I moved to the middle.

Collette was eyeing me with disdain by this time.

Bryce had been watching the show in amusement.

"You look rested," he murmured.

"I am. I slept all day."

Corrigan whooped. "That just means you can party all night, Shell!"

I had nothing better to do and just to piss off Chantal, who now had her hand on Bryce's arm; I grinned slyly and raised myself to capture Bryce's lips in a melting kiss.

Bryce's hand moved around and swiftly deposited me in his lap.

I wrapped an arm around the back of his neck and let it hang loose as we continued kissing.

When we pulled apart, Corrigan had an enraptured look on his face.

Chantal was suddenly cramped, but she held firm and didn't leave. I had to give the girl some credit for that.

Bryce kissed me again and asked, against my lips, "Are you okay?"

"I'm fine." I feathered him with another kiss and then stood up. "But I need a drink."

One of the guys stumbled to his feet from his haste. "I'll get you one. Stay. Please."

The other guys were grinning like idiots.

I sat back down, but I moved in between Corrigan and Bryce this time.

"Hey, Corrigan, I brought who you wanted me to bring."

"Who's that?" So many girls, too little time. Mena had already been forgotten.

"Mena."

"Oh…oh!"

Bryce chuckled and murmured, "Going for number two, Corr?"

Corrigan licked his lips and salivated. "I just might be." He jumped up and asked, "Where is she?"

"I left her at the door with Harris. You better go quickly."

And off he went with a little stumble here and there, but he made it through the door upright.

"What happened with Becky? Where'd she go?" Tatum asked, materializing on the other side of Chantal.

"She took off," Chantal said coolly as she flipped her golden hair back.

Tatum asked, amused, "She took off or she got off?"

The guys laughed and Chantal rolled her eyes. "Get another joke, Tatum."

"Whatever," he shrugged and sat beside me. "How you doing, Sheldon?"

"I'm good, Tatum. How are you?" I responded, reserved. He was in a weird mood. He was normally scary, serious, and/or bored. Right now, he was joking, smiling, and alive. "Are you high?" I asked and leaned forward.

Tatum gave me a weird look and replied, "No. Why. You got something?"

"Sheldon Jeneve on drugs. That's new." Acid dripped from Chantal as she sneered at me.

"Tsk, tsk, Chantal." I grinned. "Showing me your teeth just shows me how big your bite is."

She rolled her eyes and sniffed, "Whatever, Sheldon. You know, Becky's right about you."

"About me? Enlighten me, please." This was starting to get interesting.

"She says that you've slept with everyone. The only reason you're friends with Bryce and Corrigan are because you sleep with them."

"That's it?" I was actually disappointed. "No threesome? No kinky behind the back doggy stuff? Nothing except that I sleep with everyone?"

"You can have a threesome with me, myself, and I," Tatum suggested and patted my knee.

"Sounds like you're doing just fine by yourself. There's no room for me in that threesome."

Tatum frowned.

Bryce laughed.

And I was pretty sure Chantal was still figuring out the math.

Mena rushed up to us. "Please help me."

She squeezed in between Tatum and myself and let out a deep breath.

"Help you from what?" Chantal asked as she readjusted her top. Her boobs got bigger and the guys all watched.

"Corrigan," Mena exclaimed. "He doesn't stop."

"Let's not tell the police that," Bryce said dryly.

Mena flushed and mumbled, "You know what I mean."

"Where's your psycho brother?" Bryce leaned forward to see her better.

Mena shifted underneath his scrutiny.

I watched Bryce intently. I wasn't sure I liked where this might be heading.

"What do you mean?" Mena asked.

"I mean, where's your brother? I have a hard time believing he'd want you to hang out with Sheldon."

Chantal's interest piqued as she stopped moving her halter top around.

"What is it with family members not liking me?" I joked.

Amusement flashed across Bryce as he pointed out, "Luca likes you."

"Luca is a fourteen year-old boy. If he didn't like me, we'd know he likes the other side."

"Good point." He looked back at Mena. "Seriously. Is your brother going to show up here tonight? Does he have GPS attached to your phone or something? Is he going to show up at Sheldon's tomorrow morning?"

I tensed. I really didn't like the idea of people at my house anymore. Or myself being there alone when an angry brother showed up.

"What's with the interrogation?" Chantal piped up. She pursed her frosted red lips farther out. One of the guys groaned.

"My brother's on-location. He's not even around."

Bryce relaxed slightly and sat back.

Mena muttered, "Is this what all the parties are like? I didn't know I'd get attacked by your boys, Sheldon."

My eyes sparked at that. "What are you talking about?" I asked.

Chantal purred, enjoying the change in conversation.

Mena bristled uncomfortably. "I mean," she swallowed. "I didn't mean anything."

"No, you did. What did you mean?"

"I just meant…come on. Corrigan throws himself at me inside and Bryce is doing twenty-questions out here. What happened to just 'here's a drink, now sit and flirt'?" She laughed nervously.

"I think your 'hazing' is nothing compared to what your brother said to me."

Bryce leaned forward and watched us intently.

"What are you talking about?" Mena stilled.

Bryce swore and demanded, "Like you don't know. You were at the house when we got back. We were getting out of the car at midnight when you showed up. That's freaky."

I sucked my breath in. Whether Bryce had meant to or not, he'd just destroyed Mena's social credibility. I didn't care about rumors or gossip, mainly because it was junk and normally about me. However, when Bryce Scout said that he thought someone was freaky, so did everyone else.

I almost heard Chantal's own snub as she giggled in delight.

Mena paled.

"Look," I said, a little gentler. "Bryce is right. You knew Denton came to talk to me and you knew what he was going to say. He said some pretty harsh stuff to me, and he *still* hit on me. So between the two of us, I think I was the one attacked."

"That's because you two kept baiting him."

"Because he's weird," Bryce bit out and stood up. "I don't like the fucker."

He walked away and Mena looked at me helplessly.

"Was it bad? What he said to you?"

"Yeah." It was the truth. "It was pretty low."

"I'm sorry."

I heaved a sigh. I didn't know what the hell to do now.

Chantal asked, a malicious innocence on her face, "So...is your brother Denton Steele?"

Wariness flashed over Mena before she said, "Yeah."

"That dude's gay," Tatum grumbled and walked off. The rest of the guys followed except one, who was intent on Chantal's boobs.

Bryce had started it and the other guys followed in line.

I'd only felt pity a handful of times and this was one of those times. I pitied Mena.

Chantal sniffed and stood. Another halter-top readjustment was followed with a shift of her mini-skirt.

"Why do you wear clothes like that if you have to constantly do that?" Mena asked, coolly.

Chantal gave her a blinding smile and replied sweetly, "Because it drives the guys crazy."

When she left, I leaned over and whispered, "And it earns you a reputation as a whore."

Mena gave me a wan smile. "Sorry. I just saw my social career crumble into dust."

"I'm sorry." I meant it.

"I know. I don't think Bryce was even thinking. He was just concerned about you."

I coughed.

Mena continued, scornfully, "And what is *her* name? What is her problem, anyway?"

"Collette Chantal. She's a plastic booby Barbie."

"She's a bit plump to be a Barbie."

"Yeah, but…the guys seem to like the extra meat."

"I should just leave," Mena sighed in resignation. "The rest of the night is going to be awful. Everyone's going to turn on me pretty soon. They're going to throw peanuts like I'm a monkey in the zoo or something." Mena moaned.

I patted her knee. "I'm not going anywhere. They wouldn't dare throw peanuts at me."

"Right. It'll just happen when you're not by my side. Besides, you're going to disappear with Bryce tonight anyway."

I shifted again, uncomfortable.

"Let's get something else to drink," I announced and dragged her behind. Inside the kitchen, where the keg had been placed, Bryce and the guys all stood around it. Corrigan spotted us and stumbled over. He threw an arm around both of our shoulders and announced, "So…I heard there was talk about a threesome." He grinned stupidly. "How about it, ladies?"

I smiled as I slid a hand downwards.

Corrigan held his breath, his eyes widened.

And I pulled his zipper up, purposely catching on something.

Corrigan howled in pain.

I laughed, "That's what you get for walking around with your pants open, Corrigan."

"You are such a…" he fumed.

I waited with an eyebrow raised.

"I hate you," he growled and limped away to grab an icepack.

I laughed in delight.

Mena had been quiet the entire time, but she murmured now, "I don't think I could be friends with you guys. You guys have your own rules or something. You're vicious to each other."

I caught an ice-pack from Bryce and chucked it at Corrigan's back. He turned and glared before he bent to place it over his groin.

"It's called respect, Mena," I remarked. "You have to earn it before you can demand it."

Mena stayed as I pushed through the crowd.

I hadn't gone far before I spotted Mandy Justice flirting with two guys that I remembered from the cafeteria. One of the guys had been talking to Leisha. "Mandy," I called out and Mandy's eyes widened in alarm. "Hi."

"Hey, Sheldon," she replied, guarded.

"Who are your friends?" I asked, flirtatiously.

"Uh…" She shifted and said shortly, "This is Braven and Carlos."

"Hi!" I stuck a hand out.

Even though I didn't pay attention to most gossip, I knew my social hierarchy. At first, I thought Carlos was in Leisha's group, but when I saw him next to Braven—that changed things. That put him in a much higher position. Braven was a Bryce or Corrigan for his grade. That meant that Carlos would be there too and it wasn't a shock to see some of the more-popular senior girls flirting with them.

Braven looked to be the leader because he spoke up, "Hi."

Carlos nodded and watched.

"I know your friend Leisha." I ignored Braven and remarked to Carlos.

"Oh yeah?" Interest sparked in him and he murmured, "She's great, isn't she?"

"I like *her*," I said meaningfully to Mandy, who moved her hand from Carlos' arm. "She's funny. She's a little nerdy, but it works for her."

"I had hoped she'd come tonight." Carlos leaned closer. "But I don't see her anywhere."

"Maybe you should call her. She might come then."

"I don't know."

"I do. Call her."

Braven spoke up, "I thought you were hoping that Cassie chick was here?"

Carlos ducked his head. "So?"

"Cassandra Bens is good for one thing. If you're looking for a girl with class, I'd lay odds on Leisha any day," I spoke up.

Braven snorted in disbelief just as he was pushed out of the way.

I found myself staring into Chad Yerling's malicious eyes. There was nothing innocent in that gaze as he skimmed me up and down.

"What are you doing, Yerling?" I asked, stiffly.

He stepped closer to me and whispered, "I came to collect."

"Collect what? Another beating?"

"Your boys can come after me all they want, but they won't be able to beat it out of me what I'm going to do to you."

Carlos muttered, "Uh, dude...I don't think..."

"Back off, loser," Chad snarled.

Braven suddenly pushed in between us. With his back to me, he growled in Chad's face, "You might want to get out of here before you're sent to the hospital."

Chad smiled and it sent shivers down my back.

"Look at you." He looked Braven up and down. "You think you can hurt me, little boy?"

Carlos stood beside him.

Chad rolled his eyes.

"You two are pathetic." He sneered and met my gaze. "You and me, Jeneve. That's what it's going to be one of these nights. Scout can't always be there and even if he is, it'll be one to all my buddies. You do the math."

His eyes caught something over my shoulder and he froze.

Bryce stepped around me, grabbed Yerling by the throat, and dragged him out the door.

Corrigan stood at the door and closed it behind them as Bryce passed through. Neither of them looked at me, but Yerling did.

I felt that shiver again.

Braven and Carlos watched me, guardedly.

My little finger trembled so I stuffed my hands into my front pockets.

I gritted my teeth and pushed through the crowd to follow. Chet was at the door and he caught me around the waist as I reached for the door handle.

"No, Sheldon."

"Get off," I snapped and reached again.

"It's not just you," Chet reasoned in my ear as he held me back. "We can't have him here. He'll hurt someone again."

"God forbid that you guys say something to the cops about it," I cried out. "God forbid that he's not just locked up. That means that you guys would have to narc on him."

It was a stupid code. The guys ruled and governed each other, but a nark was the lowest of the low.

"Corrigan said something and they didn't do anything," Chet sighed. "This is what we can do. Corrigan already put him in the hospital for a few days. We don't know what else to do, short of killing him. We're open to suggestions."

I had none. My only solution was to hide a Colt.45 by my bed.

I turned away and grabbed another drink from the keg. I wasn't up for conversation and high school drama, so I found an empty room upstairs.

It was gorgeous outside. The sky was cloudless so the stars sparkled bright. With the soft breeze, some leaves were carried over the yard and a few hit the window glass where I stood. I sipped on my plastic cup.

I listened to the party, alone, but it didn't seem long before I heard Bryce's voice down the hallway. A second later, he kicked the door open and he walked inside, carrying cups while balancing three pitchers of beer. Corrigan followed behind with another three pitchers of beer and he kicked the door shut with his foot.

Bryce placed the pitchers on the nightstand before he turned and took the rest from Corrigan. As Corrigan bounced on the bed, Bryce poured the beer.

"So is he in the hospital?" I asked, guardedly. I wasn't sure how I felt about it all.

Corrigan ignored me and continued to bounce on the bed.

"This is a good bed." Corrigan looked at Bryce. "We should steal this bed."

"And you can be the one to tell Harris who stole it when he's going to ask around." Bryce sat against the wall, beside my feet.

"You think he'd even care?"

"His dad would care."

"Isn't his dad some general in the army or something?" I asked.

"Never mind," Corrigan said quickly. "Your friend Mena took off. She said something about running the warpath? Just as friendly as I remembered."

"You're not going to answer me, are you?" I drank my beer.

Corrigan glanced at me. I knew then that he wouldn't. "Hey, uh…if Bryce isn't over at your place, you call me."

"And the douche will wake up this time," Bryce pointed out.

Corrigan glared. "I already said I was sorry. It was four in the morning."

"I answered," Bryce remarked. "I was there."

"Shut up. Both of you. We're not going round three." I needed them. I needed them to not fight.

Both shut up and nodded.

I chuckled and moved to sit on Bryce's lap and stayed there the rest of the night as the guys drank and chatted. They talked sports, hunting, how fake Chantal's boobs were, and anything else.

I sipped my beer and stayed in Bryce's shelter, content.

Chapter 14

We stayed in that room until Corrigan's stomach growled loudly. There'd been one look shared between the two guys and both announced at the same time, "The diner." It was agreed and as we went downstairs, we left with another two cars of guys following. Everyone piled into the diner and we took up two tables. I found myself beside Corrigan with Bryce across the table. After I ordered a refill, my phone rang.

I answered, guarded, "Hello?" I hadn't had good luck with phone calls lately.

"Where the hell is my sister?!" Denton ground out, furious.

I was actually a little bit relieved. "Uh…she's not home?"

"No, she's not home. Where is she?"

"I don't know. Did you call her phone?" Brother or not, the guy was starting to get on my nerves.

"I don't know. Do you think I'm a moron?" Denton mocked me.

"Uh…" He did not just give me the perfect opening…

"Don't answer that. I don't know where my sister is and I know she went to some party with you tonight."

"Look, she left early. I don't know where she went."

"How'd she get there?"

"I drove."

"Did you drive her home?"

"No," I said sharply. "Your sister's a big girl. She can take care of herself."

"My sister is not like you and I don't want my sister to ever be like you."

I sighed. "If you want my help, insulting me is not the way to go."

"I want you and your friends to look for my sister. Now!"

"And issuing orders won't help either." I hung up on his sudden shout.

"Who was that?" Corrigan asked.

"Mena's brother. She's not home and he's blaming me."

"They're not right. Something's...I don't know...they're not right," Bryce muttered.

"He's just worried about her."

"My mom's not harassing you," Bryce pointed out.

"No. Your mom is *praying* for me," I said sarcastically.

Carlos, who'd stayed quiet the entire time, spoke up, "We could drive around and look for her. I mean, it wouldn't hurt, you know. Just in case something did happen, you know..."

"I've got some flashlights in my trunk," Chet offered and stood up. As we all stood, Corrigan hissed in my ear, "You stay with Bryce. Braven's too drunk to be rational right now."

"You think? He's been leering at me the entire time. And why am I adjusting for a drunk?"

"Because you're awesome...and you're sober."

"I'm not really," I glared. "Sober, that is."

Corrigan grinned and shrugged. "I know, but...you're more sober than Braven and I don't want to beat the crap out of him. I kinda like the stupid kid."

Bryce took shotgun in Chet's car when I slid into the backseat next to Tatum.

"Hey," Bryce peered at me, questioning. "I thought you were in the other car."

I shrugged and looked out the window. That was the extent of our conversation.

"Pull up next to him," Bryce instructed Chet and as he did, Bryce rolled his window down. Corrigan lifted himself out of the window and sat on the doorframe with his arms resting on the car's roof.

"What's up, boys?" Corrigan smirked, cockily, across the top.

"You want the back streets? We'll take Hyde Park?" Bryce asked.

Corrigan shrugged. "Sure. I don't care."

"Holster and his crew can check out the riverbank," Bryce murmured.

Carlos asked, "You got some flashlights?"

At Bryce's negative, Carlos jumped out and passed them out to the vehicles. Braven leered at me the entire time until I snapped.

Cursing, I was at his seat in a flash. I threw open his door and dragged him out of the car. As he fell, I kicked him in the stomach, head, and groin. He just laid there and groaned in pain as I knelt over him to whisper, "You stare at boys like that? Keep it up and I'll spread *that* rumor." I flicked him in the ear before I returned to my seat and turned mute.

Some of the guys were taken aback, but others weren't surprised.

Chet drove off when Corrigan started laughing in their car.

Bryce was fighting a grin when I glanced over. "Shut it," I growled and Bryce laughed outright.

Chet announced, "You're my god, Sheldon. I will pray to you three times a day. I will even buy a mat and declare it my 'Sheldonism' praying mat. It's all you from now on."

"Screw you too." But I bit back a laugh.

Tatum saw it and started laughing. He pounded the back of Bryce's seat and shook his head. "You've got to be an animal in bed, Sheldon." He asked Bryce, "Is she an animal in bed?"

Bryce's smile turned lustful as he remained silent, but met my eyes in the rear-view mirror.

Chet launched into a story about his most animal-like lover and Tatum topped it with a story of his own.

Bryce and I were both quiet until we pulled into the parking lot.

Okay, parks are meant for the daytime. Not nighttime. It's not a big leap to think that parks can turn creepy when the sun goes down. Hyde Park, underneath a full moon, is extremely creepy.

I hated to admit it, but I stuck close to Bryce when we started walking around.

We met a few homeless people, more than a few drunk parties playing Volcano Tag on the playground, and one hooker.

She grinned a toothless grin towards Bryce. I felt him shudder at the imagery of her proposition and coughed back my own laugh.

"Shut up," he threw at me.

Chet walked over to us. He gestured to the drunks playing tag behind him and murmured, "Mena didn't come this way. They did see someone else, some girl with black hair. She was wearing a clown outfit or something. I don't know."

Clown outfit?

"Leisha was supposed to come. Carlos called her and said she was on her way."

"Did you see her at the party?" Bryce asked me.

"I…I don't know. We were upstairs the rest of the night."

"Chet, call Corrigan. Have Carlos call this chick and see where she is," Bryce commanded. "We don't need to look for another girl right now."

Tatum lightly jogged over to us. "Nah." He shook his head. "No one's seen anyone like Mena. She's not here. She didn't come this way anyway."

"If she was walking, the river's the quickest way," I murmured and frowned. "She's not stupid. You'd have to be a complete moron to walk the river at night and alone."

"And dressed for a party," Bryce pointed out.

"Let's head over to the river. It's too big for Holster, Nate, and Justin to cover by themselves. It's not far off," Tatum suggested.

Bryce held my elbow as we walked back to the car and it wasn't a surprise to anyone when he slid in beside me in the backseat. Tatum took shotgun and Chet got off his phone.

"Okay." He turned around behind the steering wheel. "Carlos called that girl and he couldn't get an answer. He left a message."

No one suggested calling the parents. That was another code. Just like how the guys policed Chad. We'd figure out Leisha before we absolutely needed to involve the parents. There was a fine line between being a nark and checking on a friend.

We parked next to Holster's car and saw their flashlights just up ahead.

"Okay." Bryce took charge. "Chet, drive me and Sheldon down about two miles. We'll backtrack and meet you in the middle."

"I'll start from here then." Tatum flashed a grin and murmured, "Don't go in the bushes now and have crazy animal sex."

Bryce shot around the seat and punched him in the side.

Tatum grasped his stomach and sucked in his breath. He cursed, but quickly shot out of the car before Bryce tried for seconds. Through the window, Tatum wiggled his eyebrows in suggestion and pretended to howl at the moon.

I raised my eyebrows and gave a pointed look.

Tatum must've remembered Braven because he shut up.

Chet shook his head as he reversed and drove south. "It's the full moon, man. Tatum's weird tonight and I swear—he hasn't done anything tonight, like alcohol or anything else. That's just him."

"He'll get a beat down if he keeps it up," Bryce muttered under his breath.

He sounded tense. I shot him a questioning look and asked quietly, "What's up with you?"

Bryce shrugged, but started to tap his foot against the floor. A nervous movement. Bryce rarely showed any moments of nervousness. I slid over and rested a hand on his knee, stilling his leg.

"Hey, hey," I murmured, soothingly. "What's wrong?"

Bryce turned back from the window, glanced at Chet, who was pointedly watching the street ahead, and murmured, "I'll tell you later."

I searched his face, but sighed, "Okay."

Bryce cupped my cheek and pressed a soft kiss to my lips, meant for reassurance. It sparked into more and we both pulled away a little breathless.

"Sorry, man," Bryce drawled to Chet, who shrugged it off and pulled the car over.

"Here's your stop." Chet turned around. "You both have flashlights?"

Bryce and I waved them in the air and climbed out of the car.

As Chet drove back the way we'd just come, I asked again, "What's up with you?"

"Nothing."

"You said that you'd tell me. What's going on?"

"Nothing," he bit out. "I...just don't ever walk in this town, okay?"

"Huh?" I asked, dumbfounded. "Like ever?"

"No," he breathed out in irritation. "At night. Don't walk around this town at night, alone, and dressed like that."

I grinned and asked smoothly, "Did you just call me a slut?"

"What? No." He shook his head. "It's not even about that. Just... listen to what I said. Call before you do something stupid like these girls."

Walking over to him, I slid my arms around his waist and looked up. "For one thing, I know what goes bump in the night. I'm not exactly naïve about stuff." Call me jaded. "And two...you know that I'd call."

Bryce relaxed and wrapped his arms around me. He lifted me up and I wrapped my legs around his waist. Face to face now, I grinned in anticipation and dipped to meet his lips.

Bryce met me and opened his mouth. I slid my tongue against his and we both groaned.

He cursed and rested his forehead against mine, "We have to look for Mena."

I untangled my legs and jumped to my feet. "And Leisha. We're looking for both of 'em."

Bryce groaned and swore. "Girls." He made it sound like an insult, but I didn't take it as one.

Bryce led the way into the narrow trail that moved down the steep incline to the river's bank. The trail veered up from the river's edge a few times, but it usually circled back to parallel the river. During the daytime, the trail was gorgeous. At night, it was another scary place. The brush was thick enough to hide someone if desired. We needed to illuminate as much as possible, but our flashlights didn't penetrate some of the thickest stuff.

When I tried to step towards some particularly dense foliage, Bryce yanked me back.

"No," he only said to my glance.

We continued up the trail. We met a few homeless on our path, but they only watched us warily and didn't say anything. They sat off the trail and underneath a tree or brush.

Bryce asked about Mena and Leisha. No one had seen them.

Twenty minutes passed before I started, "So…"

I saw the tension enter Bryce's shoulder as he waited.

"Can you be nice to Mena?"

"Why?" he clipped out, uncaring as he swept his flashlight around a rock.

"Because you said she was weird in front of everyone."

"So?"

"So…that's kinda—I like Mena."

"You shouldn't."

"I do, so be nice to her. Okay?" I snapped out.

"Whatever."

"Bryce."

"I said whatever. I don't like her," he argued.

"You don't like her brother and that's just going to Mena."

"No," Bryce said shortly. Firmly. "I don't like her. She's weird. She looks at you weird. So does her brother."

"You don't like Steele because I slept with him."

"No. You screwed him. You didn't sleep with him. There's a difference. And it's not because of that."

"Right," I snorted in disbelief.

Bryce stopped and turned to look at me. "I don't like that you were with him, yeah. It's not about that, though. He's off. Can't you see it when you look at him?"

"What are you talking about?"

"Like he's not totally right. He's weird."

"Can you define weird?" I said tiredly as Bryce started back up the trail.

Bryce shrugged again.

"Fine. He's weird. Mena's weird, but I like Mena and I don't have a lot of female friends."

"You're friends with that Leisha chick."

"Leisha's like a puppy. She's not a real friend," I retorted.

Bryce chuckled. "Hope you don't describe me that way."

I grinned. "Well, some people *really* love their pets." In gross and totally disgusting ways.

Bryce snorted.

I grabbed the back of his pants and stopped him. "Are you going to be nice?"

"No," he clipped out. "I'm not going to pretend to like someone if I think they're fake. She's fake."

"You won't even be civil?"

"No, Sheldon. Drop it. I don't ask you to be nice to my mom."

"Your mom's a bitch."

"So is Mena, you just don't see it." Bryce argued, but stopped abruptly.

I walked into his back, but Bryce snaked an arm around and caught me so I wouldn't fall back.

I was right behind him, so I couldn't see anything. When I tried to peer around, Bryce shifted to block my view.

"What are you doing? Why'd you stop?"

Bryce didn't say anything. He just held me behind him. He had both arms wrapped around me.

"Seriously, Bryce. Move," I ordered.

He coughed and it seemed to strangle him.

"Bryce?" I asked, quietly. "I want to see."

He wouldn't let me.

"Bryce, seriously. I need to see." My voice sounded a little panicked now. Slightly shrill.

Nothing.

I started to hit his unmoving back. "Bryce." My voice sounded weak now. "Bryce."

"Let's go back," he whispered, hoarsely, and started to walk backwards.

Awkwardly, I stumbled backwards. I wanted to see, but he still wouldn't let me.

"Stop!" I cried out. "What is it?"

"Sheldon, let's go. Let's go back to the street. Come on." Bryce turned finally and it was enough.

I sprinted past him, but a leg tripped me and as the ground rushed up to me, a silent scream wrenched from my throat.

I landed beside the leg and I saw the shoe.

There was smeared blood on it and the leg was black and blue, bruised.

"Oh god." My voice was ripped out of me. It was weird, like from another body. I felt weird. I felt...I wasn't really there, but I was there. I was far away, but I was too close to tear my eyes away.

A body lay in the bushes and I stepped forward.

Bryce said something behind me, but I couldn't hear him. My back was turned to him, but I saw him speak. I saw his mouth open and close and open again. He was saying a lot of stuff to me, but I didn't hear it. I don't know how I knew he was talking. My back was to him.

I looked inside the bushes and it was Leisha.

My hand froze as I lifted one of the branches out of the way, but I saw myself bend down and pick something up.

It was an envelope.

I held it in my hands.

Bryce was talking to me again, he was right beside me. He stopped talking when he saw the envelope, when he saw what was written on it.

I didn't move again for a very long time.

Chapter 15

Bryce and I sat at the end of the ambulance. The police had called the paramedics because I started to shiver uncontrollably. Bryce had hugged me to him, but it hadn't helped. I just kept shivering. One of the paramedics said it was shock and he had checked to make sure Bryce was alright too.

The flashing lights highlighted the terrain. It was ugly and pretty at the same time.

We weren't allowed to call anyone so it was another hour before the guys parked beside the police cars and ambulances.

Corrigan gestured for everyone to stay in the cars while he walked over to us.

"Hey," he murmured, hands stuffed in his front pockets. His eyes skimmed over me and Bryce. He swore and slumped beside me while Bryce stayed on my other side. "So, who was it?"

I turned mute again.

Bryce answered, hoarsely, "Leisha."

Corrigan swore again. "Is she…? I mean…"

"Dead," Bryce said flatly.

Corrigan whipped back to us, but didn't say anything. I didn't think he could say anything.

"I wanna go…somewhere," I mumbled. We'd already given our statements and had been ordered to give official statements the next day at the station. I was really getting tired of going to that same place.

Bryce and Corrigan shared a look before Bryce asked, "Where?"

I shrugged. "Not here."

Corrigan jumped up and said abruptly, "I'll cut the guys loose. We can crash at my place."

I thanked him with my eyes and Bryce nodded.

Corrigan left and returned a second later with keys to Chet's car. "Let's go." He dangled the keys in the air and Bryce placed his hand at the small of my back. Corrigan got behind the wheel with Bryce in the shotgun seat. I huddled in the back in a fetal position.

Bryce had stuffed the envelope in his pocket. We hadn't discussed it, but Bryce snapped it out of my hands and shoved it inside before he called the cops. I heard the crinkle of the paper and knew he showed Corrigan.

The envelope was addressed to me. We hadn't opened it yet.

Suddenly, I bolted upright and grabbed the envelope.

"Sheldon!" Bryce cried out, startled.

I ripped it open and found one piece of paper inside. It was a small note and it read,

Queen of Geneva disregarded her lowly subjects. To the grave they went and more to come.

I dry-heaved as Corrigan veered the car to the side. Bryce ripped the letter out of my hands and read it. He swore underneath his breath and Corrigan took it from him. He reacted the same.

I opened the door and took deep breaths from the air.

No one said anything. We sat there until Corrigan asked quietly, "Are you okay to go? Can you shut the door?"

Bryce rested his forehead against his window and didn't say anything.

When I shut the door, Bryce lifted his head up and glanced back at me.

I huddled back down and hugged my knees to my chest.

Corrigan pulled back onto the road and the rest of the drive was passed in silence. The radio had been left off.

The letter was left untouched between the two guys.

I don't think anyone *wanted* to touch it.

At Corrigan's we walked down to the basement and sat on the couches. Corrigan's family had placed three couches around a large screen that fitted against an entire wall. It was their own theater room. The couches matched the grandiose media center. They were plush and large enough to fit two full-length people.

I stretched out on one. Bryce took another and Corrigan dropped onto the third after he'd left for a bottle of bourbon.

He passed it around and all three of us took two shots in a row.

This time, Bryce didn't hiss from the burn.

We kept passing the bottle until it was empty.

Corrigan sighed and flung the bottle at the bar. It ricocheted off the corner and bounced into the recycling bin.

No one commented on the shot.

"The cops should have that note," Corrigan started.

"No," I said sharply.

"Sheldon…"

"I said no. It had my name on it. It's not going. We need to destroy it."

"They could check it for prints. We should've given it to them right away," Corrigan argued. "Why'd you guys even have it in the first place?"

"Sheldon grabbed it off the body."

I flinched at those words. Leisha was cold now.

Bryce added, "I didn't really think about it."

"I don't want the cops to know. I don't want to be…connected to whoever could do something like that," I spat out, feeling my insides gutted out.

"You should tell them," Corrigan said.

"Shut up."

Corrigan didn't say anything.

Bryce rubbed a hand over his jaw and sat up. He stood and paced. "This is…we should do something. I don't want to sit anymore."

"Everyone at school is going to know," I said faintly.

"Let's play basketball or…I don't know. Let's go for a run."

"We should call the cops now."

"Shut up, Corrigan!" I yelled. "I don't want to talk about it."

He yelled back, "You don't want to talk about anything!"

"Shut up both of you!" Bryce hissed, "We're going to wake your parents."

That shut us up.

I stood and spoke, "I'm going to shower."

Corrigan glanced at me and then away. He closed his eyes and laid down.

Bryce watched me leave the room. When I turned the corner, I heard him ask, "You got more alcohol?"

"Yeah," Corrigan said tiredly and got up.

I closed the bathroom door and leaned against it while I slid to the floor. My hands were chalk-white as I pressed them against my legs. It felt weird. I couldn't feel my hands against my legs. I only stared at them in sick fascination. A person should be able to feel, but my legs had gone numb.

When I saw some spots on my shirt, it took a minute before I realized they were tears. I'd been crying and not known it. Then I watched as another one fell to my shirt and realized I was *still* crying.

Weak, I got up and turned the shower on. I turned the water to scalding hot and stripped my clothes off before I stepped inside. I slid to the floor and sat there, arms wrapped around my knees.

The water pounded on me and I watched the water slide to circle the drain.

It was slowly sucked downwards, like a vacuum.

I wasn't surprised when the door opened and Bryce stepped inside.

I just looked up at him and he sighed. He moved me and sat behind where he wrapped his arms around me. I hugged his arms as they hugged me.

He rested his head in the crook between my shoulders and neck. His cheek grazed against the side of mine.

We both shuddered for a moment until I realized it was me. I was trembling and Bryce was trying to stop it.

A choked gasp sounded and echoed in the shower. That came from me too.

"Where's Corrigan?" I asked, huskily.

Bryce soothed his hands up and down my arms. "He called the police. They're going to come and get the letter."

"I don't—"

"They have to have it."

I shut up. The fight had left me. I knew they were right, but...

"I don't want that to happen. I don't want..."

"You didn't do anything," Bryce insisted. "Whoever did that is sick and the cops have to know. He might do it to you."

I closed my eyes as I finally felt the water hit my skin. Finally.

"Everyone at school is going to know," I murmured, wondering why I said it.

"I know. They'll just know that we found her. That's it."

"Her parents," I said softly, haunted. "I bet they'll be devastated."

Bryce frowned next to me and said, "Your parents would be devastated too."

"Would they?"

"Yeah," he said firmly.

"Your mom would pray for me." She should've prayed for Leisha.

Bryce laughed abruptly and then stopped just as quick. He swore.

I slid my hand into his and threaded our fingers. I asked, "Why don't you want me in the mornings?"

"What?" he asked, startled. Distracted.

"In the mornings. We don't have sex. Why not?"

Bryce shrugged.

"Why not?" I pressed.

"Sheldon," he sighed.

"I want to know."

He burst out, "Because it's too hard to make myself give you space if I make love to you in the mornings. It's too hard to go back and remember your 'hands-off' policy."

The emotional ties. That was why.

"I've never given you a hands-off policy," I said faintly.

"It's the same thing. No commitment, right?" Bryce cursed. "I swear, you get pissed if I *don't* let other girls hit on me."

I shifted uncomfortably.

"See," he pointed out. "This is what Corrigan was talking about. You don't talk about anything, especially you and me."

"I just asked why we don't have sex in the mornings." I turned and glared at him. Pissed. No, I was livid.

"No," Bryce said firmly, daring me to argue with him. "I said 'make love' and you said 'have sex.' They're different."

"It's not that different. It's still screwing."

"No," he spelled it out, saddened. "You screw me. I make love to you."

I pulled away and scooted directly underneath the water. It plastered my hair to my face, covering my eyes, nose, mouth, everything.

I sat there, stunned at Bryce's words until he cursed and yanked me out of the water. He brushed the hair from my face and glared at me.

And then he softened and kissed me.

I moaned and clung to him, demanding. I needed this, I needed this kind of warmth.

Bryce grabbed me and lifted me on top of him.

I straddled him and sunk down until he was firmly sheathed inside of me. And then I moved.

Bryce groaned and moved with me. He grabbed my hips and we both tried to drown each other.

It didn't take long until we exploded and I fell limply against him. Bryce swept his arms around me and kissed my shoulder, a tender kiss. He ran a soothing hand down my hair and down my back.

I closed my eyes and rested my head on his shoulder.

Just then Corrigan pounded on the shower door.

Bryce swore and yelled for him to leave.

Corrigan coughed, "Cops are here. Hurry up."

Bryce used some colorful words to describe Corrigan and what would happen if he had listened to us the entire time.

I told him to be quiet. Corrigan joked, but he wasn't like that. We were in our world and probably couldn't hear him knock on the bathroom door. Bryce clamped his mouth shut, but his jaw was clenched tight. Too tight.

We dressed in our dirty clothes and went to meet the police. It was two different detectives this time, but I saw Officer Patterson had accompanied them. She gave me a small nod while a balding guy in a suit started asking us questions like why didn't we hand over the letter, what did it say, where was the letter now.

We answered each and every one. Numbly. I knew I was in a daze at the end of it when Sheila threw me a curveball. She asked, "Why didn't you say anything about the other two letters?"

Bryce frowned.

Corrigan asked, "What?!"

I sat there and swallowed painfully. I surrendered when I met her all-too-knowing eyes, "Because…if I said something then it was real."

"We went over your house after the break-in. We found both of them in the trash," she said further.

This was a nightmare.

"When did you get the first note?"

Bryce and Corrigan sat stunned.

I sighed and answered, "Wednesday."

"And the second?"

"Thursday."

"And your house was broken into that night, correct?"

It was and I felt on trial.

Sheila glanced towards Bryce and Corrigan, but asked all of us, "Is there anyone who's been harassing you?"

Who wasn't?

I glanced at the guys. Corrigan slumped further in his chair. Bryce spoke up, "Chad Yerling. He's been making threats."

"What's he been saying?" Officer Sheila was all business, the epitome of a detective.

"Bryce," Corrigan warned.

Bryce shrugged it off and said flatly, "That he wants to rape Sheldon. He wants to make her scream for me to help her."

I'd figured it was something like that.

Sheila glanced at the two detectives and asked, "How often has he made these threats?"

"A few times. He started awhile back, but last Sunday—it got worse. He got worse."

"What else should you be telling me?" Sheila shared me in her sweeping glance.

Corrigan said quietly, "He did something to a girl last Friday night, a week ago. We warned him to stop and not ever do anything again, but on Tuesday...he threatened Sheldon."

"He didn't really..." I murmured.

"He scared you. That was enough," Corrigan said fiercely.

"And what did you do?" Sheila asked.

"Bryce roughed him up and I roughed up his car."

I looked away.

"I got arrested for fleeing the 'scene of an accident,'" Corrigan quoted, unapologetically.

One of the detectives mentioned, "Chad Yerling was admitted to the hospital for two days last week. Was that your handiwork?" he asked Bryce.

Bryce shook his head and Corrigan volunteered, "That was me and a few other guys. I'll take the fall. We wanted to make sure he wouldn't do anything to Sheldon or any other girl."

"You were at a party tonight. Did anything happen at the party?"

"Yerling showed up. He was doing the same stuff. We took him out back and just threatened him again," Bryce spoke this time. "We didn't hurt him too bad. He was able to walk when we let him go."

"What'd you threaten him with?"

"Just that if he didn't stay away from our kind, we might have to hurt someone of his," Bryce said matter-of-factly. "We wouldn't, but we didn't know what else to do. We're not going to kill the guy or keep putting him in the hospital."

"You think this Yerling guy could've done something like that to Leisha Summers?"

I flinched at the name. She was still so cold.

"I don't know," Corrigan said lamely.

Bryce shrugged. "I thought he was all talk, but you never know…"

I stood up abruptly and asked harshly, "Are we done? Can I go?"

Sheila studied me a moment and said, "Almost. Where's the letter now?"

Corrigan pulled it out of his pocket and handed it over. "We all touched it. I'm sorry."

She pulled a glove on and took the letter. After she handed it to one of the other detectives, she asked gently, "Where are your parents, Sheldon?"

"Getting a divorce. You know that," I spat out.

"Where are they?" she asked again.

I shrugged. "I don't know."

"Have you talked to them this week?"

"About the divorce. That's it."

Sheila nodded and murmured instead, "We talked to your school counselor, Miss Connors. She's been trying to get you to talk to her. Why don't you want to talk to her?"

"Would you?" I clipped out.

Sheila didn't say anything. The other detective commented, "It would be beneficial for all of you to go and speak with your school counselor. Miss Connors has an excellent reputation as a counselor. She offered for all of you to sit together or individually." He glanced at me and said, "She thinks Sheldon, particularly, would appreciate the group setting versus an individual setting."

Miss Connors could appreciate all she wanted.

"We contacted her over the phone. She offered to come here, if you'd prefer or you could meet somewhere if you would rather not visit on school grounds."

"Right now?" Corrigan asked.

"She's with Miss Summers' parents right now. She would be available tomorrow or at a later date."

Leisha's parents.

"How are they—I mean—how are Leisha's parent's doing?" I asked before I knew what I was asking.

Bryce watched me.

Sheila studied me again, she hadn't stopped. She murmured, "They're pretty torn up as parents should be."

The balding detective asked, "You say that Yerling hurt a girl last Friday? Got a name?"

Bryce shook his head. He crossed his arms over his chest and his biceps twitched. "No. It was just a rumor, but we wanted to be safe, you know."

"Okay." The detective finished his notes and glanced at his two colleagues. "I think we're done here. We'll contact you if we have further questions."

"Please don't," I muttered and the cops stopped in surprise.

Bryce and Corrigan looked unfazed.

Sheila spoke, "Look, you're eighteen. You're an adult, but I highly recommend that you call your parents, Sheldon. They should know what's going on with you."

If they cared, they'd know.

"I don't think my parents have the time right now. They're too busy looking for houses and finalizing the divorce," I said faintly.

A flicker of emotion crossed Sheila's features, but she didn't say anything. No one said a thing and then they left.

Corrigan spoke up when we heard the door shut, "Mom's making breakfast if you guys want something."

"No more questions," I said firmly.

Corrigan nodded. "Trust me, I don't want them either."

"I could go for some food," Bryce murmured and it was decided. All three of us traipsed into the kitchen and were met with aromas of pancakes, eggs, toast, coffee, and freshly cut fruit.

Corrigan's mother smiled warmly at us and gestured to the table. She spoke with a spatula in hand, "Sit, sit. Eat."

Corrigan's father brought a cup of coffee over and placed it in front of me. He patted my shoulder and murmured, "Just how you like it, Sheldon."

"Thank you, Mr. and Mrs. Raimler."

"No thanks," Mrs. Raimler said from the stove. "Just eat. And it's Harve."

Bryce and Corrigan devoured their food. When I sat there and sipped my coffee, Bryce snorted in disgust and placed a pancake on my plate.

I didn't move and he said firmly, "Eat."

I glared and Corrigan and Bryce both snapped, "Eat."

I ate.

Mr. and Mrs. Raimler chuckled and filled the plates of food again.

When Corrigan and Bryce were on their third helping, Corrigan's parents sat down and started on their own breakfast.

Mrs. Raimler cleared her throat as she patted the curlers in her hair. She commented, "Bryce, your mother called here. She was very worried, but don't fret. We told her you were here. You and

Corrigan were upset about some news of a classmate. She agreed with me that it was best for you to stay with your friends."

Bryce and Corrigan. No mention of me. Thank god.

Bryce met my eyes in shared amusement and relief. If AnnaBelle Scout knew of my presence, she would've dragged Bryce back to her home, never to be seen again.

I shuddered at the thought.

"Sheldon, honey, I'll ready one of the guest bedrooms for you. Harve can drive you over to your house if you'd like to grab some clothes and toiletries."

Bryce spoke up, "Uh…I'll take her later. That's okay." He glanced at Corrigan and I knew both of them weren't planning on letting me out of their sight.

"Bryce, you can sleep in the other guest bedroom downstairs."

Corrigan hid a smile.

The Raimler household had guest bedrooms all over their home. There were a few on the bedroom floor. A few on the main floor. And two downstairs. We were both downstairs, right next door to each other.

I didn't think it was by chance we had rooms beside each other.

"Thank you, Mrs. Raimler."

"Oh—it's Katrice, Bryce. Get it right next time." She smiled warmly and patiently.

Bryce nodded.

"You always call me Mrs. Raimler and I always feel like your grandmother. I'm not that old, Bryce."

"No, you're not, Mrs. Raimler."

"Bryce Elliot Scout," she said firmly, feigning outrage.

I snorted.

Bryce just grinned and kept eating.

Chapter 16

The rest of the day was spent around Corrigan's house. We all took turns at Guitar Hero. Corrigan was the best, no surprise. Bryce hadn't spent as much time playing it since, until last week, everything centered around soccer.

I sucked. That was all there was to it, but for my defense—my mind was elsewhere.

After awhile, I padded into the guest bedroom and curled into a dreamless sleep. I kept fighting it because I hadn't wanted nightmares, but I was grateful when I woke up with no dreams and no nightmares.

Bryce knocked on my door and poked his head inside.

"Hey. Corr and I are going to go out for a little bit. Wanna come?"

"Where are you going?"

"Harris' parents are out of town for the whole weekend. I think some of the guys are going to hang out, maybe shoot pool."

I could stay and do nothing.

I got up and yawned, "Yeah. Can we stop at my place to get some clothes?"

"Sure," Bryce left to tell Corrigan the plan and within another few minutes, Corrigan was driving us to my house.

As we pulled into the driveway, I asked, "Did anyone find Mena last night?"

Bryce murmured, watching their house, "No, but she must've gotten home alright. There she is."

And there she was. She had already crossed her lawn and was just entering mine. She was there by the time we got out of the car.

"Hey," she said brightly.

Bryce ignored her while I murmured a half-hearted hello. Corrigan took my keys and let us inside.

"How'd you get home last night?"

"Yeah. That," Mena exclaimed, flushed. "Sorry about Denton. I actually…I went to another party last night."

"How? I drove."

"I caught a ride. They told me about the party and it sounded fun. No Collette Chantal or Becky Lew at that party to torment me."

I glared at Bryce's back.

"So," Mena continued. "It was fun."

"Whose party?" Corrigan asked, reserved.

"Grace Barton. Her and her brother, Tim, threw a party." At our blank faces, she explained, "They're in a different crowd."

"Who?" Corrigan asked what we all wondered.

"Tim Barton…he's a swimmer. And Grace is in theater."

"I know Barton," Corrigan said slowly, frowning. "He's a douche and his sister's not hot."

There it was. Corrigan had quickly classified Mena's new friends as 'losers.' Bryce had already set up the fall and Mena had fallen last night into the arms of lesser social levels.

Judging by the embarrassed flush, Mena had already known it. It was just another kick in the gut when Corrigan has said it out loud.

"You guys are bastards," I flared and brushed past them.

"What'd I say?" Corrigan asked.

I darted up the stairs, but I heard Bryce mutter, "Nothing. Let it go."

Mena followed not long later and watched as I packed a bag of clothes. She sat on the bed and asked, "Where are you going this time?"

"I'm staying at Corrigan's tonight."

Her eyebrow arched.

"It's not like that. Bryce and I are both staying there."

She asked as she glanced at her hands, "What? You don't want to live next door to me?"

"No." I changed into a gold slinky shirt that was transparent at the midriff. It was covered by another transparent white sweater that was tailored for me.

"I heard about Leisha Summers," Mena declared and watched me intently. "She was a friend of yours, right?"

I paused and looked at her. "How'd you hear about her?"

"It's all over. I got eight calls today about it and I'm not even popular."

"Yeah. So?"

"So the word is that you and Bryce found her."

It was funny because when I looked at her, she didn't look shocked, perturbed, and a little sick. Nothing. She looked like she was holding a regular conversation about the weather or a party that night.

Maybe I shouldn't complain about Bryce's insights as much.

I shrugged. "Yeah. So?" It was becoming my trademark.

"Do you want to talk about it? I mean, with a girlfriend. It can't be all that sharing with those two downstairs. They don't strike me as the feelings type."

How funny it was.

"I'm good. Thanks." I finished dressing and grabbed my bag and purse.

"Hey, so…is that it?" Mena stood.

"Is what what?"

"I thought we were friends. You're blowing me off."

"No," I said patiently. "I don't want to talk about it. That's different from blowing you off. And we are friends."

"No, we aren't," Mena said shortly. "I know that you'd like to be, but those two downstairs just vetoed that. Corrigan's never rude to a girl unless she's a social outcast. I've been cast out."

She was right and I didn't know what to do about it.

"Never mind. Your lack of speech just told me everything." Mena sighed and left. The downstairs door slammed a moment later and I jumped from the force of it.

I slumped on the bed and that was how the guys found me. Dejected. And feeling weird that I felt dejected.

They just watched me, framed in the doorway.

Bryce raised an eyebrow and asked, "Wanna go shoot pool?"

"Please," I groaned and followed them out.

When we arrived, I remarked sardonically, my gaze on the eight cars in Harris' driveway, "This is a party."

"Looks like."

Bryce chuckled.

"You said some of the guys were getting together to shoot pool. That's Lew's car. She's not one of the guys."

Corrigan shrugged. He grabbed the door handle and threw over his shoulder, "I didn't know. Don't crucify me."

When we walked in, everything stopped. Literally. One guy was even pouring a cup of beer and he stopped—mid-pour. The liquid didn't stop, but he did. He slammed the pitcher on the table and gaped at us. If it had been under different circumstances, it would've been hilarious.

Under our circumstances, I growled. "Looking at someone?"

Everyone scrambled and that was how the rest of the night proceeded. Corrigan and Bryce joked with some of the guys. Most of the girls left, but only after they were ignored by the guys. Collette Chantal tried to rub against Bryce, but he easily shrugged her off and then stayed beside me the rest of the night. It was only later, much later when they brought it up.

Corrigan had dropped down beside me on the couch. Bryce sat in front of me with my fingers entangled in his hair. And I was a bit drowsy from the booze.

Harris was the spokesperson when nearly everyone had mingled their way out the door.

"Did that chick look deformed or anything?" He belched the question as he finished his too-many beer.

Bryce tensed.

I tensed and lifted my head, now awake.

Everyone stopped again and looked at us. They wanted the answer. Even Corrigan watched us intently.

I yanked slightly on Bryce's hair and he remarked, "What do you mean?"

"I mean," Harris looked around. "What'd she look like? It could've been any of us that found her."

"She was dead," Bryce said flatly.

"Was she…we heard she was raped. Was she? Could you tell?"

"Go to a morgue. She looked like that," I said briskly.

"If she was raped, then we should know."

"Why?" I asked bitterly. "So that you can stop this supposed rapist from doing it again? It doesn't matter. She's dead." I sat up. "He's going to do it again. You can't stop him. No one can stop him."

Corrigan looked at me.

Bryce shifted to look at me. I didn't feel his silken hair between my fingers anymore.

I ignored them and continued on a rant, "If the police can't find him, you can't. You might as well go on about your life. Forget you ever knew anything. He's not going to be stopped. He's going to do it again and again and again…" My voice dropped with each word as I felt hope dwindle.

I didn't know the hope had even been there or what it was for.

Corrigan stood up and announced, "I'm drunk. Who's going to drive us home?"

Everyone was still staring at me.

Bryce stood and lifted me over his shoulder.

"Oomph!"

As he smacked my butt, everyone started to laugh…in comedic relief.

"Bryce," I gasped.

He grinned cockily and murmured loudly, "Keep saying it, baby. All night."

They laughed again and the pitcher of beer was passed around the room again.

Corrigan caught it and downed the rest. When he finished, he asked again, "Seriously. Who's driving us?"

Carlos stood up and said quietly, "I will. I'm sober."

Talking started up and Carlos walked ahead of us with Corrigan's arm thrown over his shoulders. He had given me one tentative grin before he grabbed his keys and headed outside.

I'd forgotten about him. In fact, I hadn't even known he was at Harris'.

Carlos had been the one to call Leisha in the first place—at my insistence.

I swallowed painfully as Bryce lowered me to the ground.

At the car, Bryce slid in the back. I was right behind Carlos and Corrigan had turned so he faced all of us at the same time. He threw his arm over the seat and started talking about how Becky Lew ranked among his conquests. He was fully divulging the evidentiary points of slot number four when Carlos pulled his car to the curb just outside Corrigan's house.

It was then that I realized, "Nice. I was going to stay sober so I could drive my car tomorrow. Now none of us have cars here."

Corrigan shrugged and murmured, "We'll figure it out. I'll make Stephen drive us over tomorrow."

"I have my bag in your car," I glared.

He smirked and pointed out, "Like you're going to be wearing clothes tonight anyway."

Carlos looked out the window, I scowled, and Bryce didn't blink.

Corrigan rolled his eyes and shot out of the car. "See you later, losers."

I stayed and Bryce looked between me to Carlos. He said, "I'm going in, make sure Corrigan doesn't decide to light his house on fire."

It wasn't even an excuse.

The car was silent between us when Bryce shut his door behind him.

Carlos and I weren't the quiet ones, it was the car, definitely the car.

He broke it when he said, hesitantly, "I'm sorry."

"For what?" I frowned.

"For calling her. It wouldn't have happened if…" If he hadn't called her.

"That's not true," I said quietly. "It would've happened anyway, but to someone else. Or to her…later."

"How do you know that?"

Because *he* did it to get at me. I couldn't tell Carlos that.

I shrugged. "Trust me. These types…they always find someone else."

Carlos didn't say anything as the motor hummed.

He was a good kid. I could see that. I leaned forward and said softly, "She really liked you. I could tell."

Carlos didn't say anything.

"It wasn't your fault. He did it. Not you. He did." Just like he was doing everything else. I told myself that when I walked to the house. It wasn't my fault. It wasn't my fault.

Corrigan had waited for me when I walked into the house. He let go the curtain and jumped off the couch. When I locked the door, he said quietly, "Just making sure, you know."

I shrugged, but the nonchalance wouldn't set with me. It meant more than I could ever fathom for that little action.

He hugged me tightly and smoothed a hand down my hair.

Neither of us said a word and Corrigan pressed a quick kiss to my forehead before he darted up the stairs to his room.

I headed downstairs.

Bryce wasn't in the hallway or in my room. I didn't think about it and stripped down to my underwear and tank top. When I heard the bathroom door open, I slid out and met Bryce in the hallway.

We both stopped, stared at each other, and I moved around to the bathroom.

Bryce let me go.

When I came back, his door was shut and the lights were off. I stood there from indecision and finally just went to my own room. I crawled underneath the covers and flipped to my side.

To my surprise…the first nightmare ripped through me at breakneck speed. When I gasped awake, my heart pounding, I looked at the clock and saw I'd been asleep for two hours. I shook my head weakly, trying to clear all thoughts, but the shiver still ran down my spine. The goose bumps on my arms weren't from the cold. I didn't think about it. I didn't plan it—nothing. I just got out of bed and crawled into Bryce's.

I slipped underneath his bedcovers and heard his deep breaths. He was still asleep.

I scooted closer and nuzzled into his side, needing his warmth.

"Hey," he murmured, tiredly, as he wrapped an arm around my waist. Bryce nearly pulled me over his body then. He nuzzled against my neck and promptly fell back asleep.

That's when I closed my eyes and I welcomed the fog that settled on my mind.

The next time I woke, someone pounced on me. It wasn't Bryce. I opened my groggy eyes to see Corrigan beaming back at me. He laid down on me with his clothes, my clothes, and the blankets between us.

He rested his chin on top of his clasped hands, right on my chest and smiled.

"Go away," I grumbled and tried to roll out from underneath him.

Corrigan countered my move and merely spread his legs, entrapping me within his hold.

"Corrigan." I yawned as I tried to wrestle my arms out from underneath the blanket. I was paralyzed and gave up. Corrigan's weight held me captive.

To my surprise, Bryce moved awake beside me. He yawned as he placed one hand on Corrigan's shoulder and shoved him off.

"Get off," he mumbled and tucked me underneath his body. He placed a protective arm and leg over me as he glared at Corrigan on the floor.

"Morning, guys," Corrigan said cheerfully and he threw himself on top of us again.

"You are too damn cheerful," I complained and nestled against Bryce's chest.

"Get lost, man," Bryce scowled, but he bit back a grin. The effect was gone.

"Do you guys ever do it doggie-style?" Corrigan asked.

And I came awake. "Get out of here!" I shoved out from underneath Bryce and tucked my body to throw Corrigan to the floor.

Corrigan laughed, "Thought that'd wake you up." He jumped to his feet and exclaimed, "Let's go. Come on. Morning's a-wasting."

Bryce cursed and grumbled as he sat up against the headboard, "I forgot you were a morning person."

I rolled back underneath the blankets and glared.

"I feel very intimate with you guys," Corrigan remarked and flung himself back on the bed. He squeezed into the middle and glanced at us both. "Is this how it's like when you two do your thing? I feel like I'm a part of something. I think my life has been changed forever. I'm going to marry the next girl I bang. I swear it. I want to feel this intimacy."

"Shut up," I growled.

Bryce didn't say anything, he just flipped and rolled Corrigan under him. As the two started wrestling, I went in search for the bathroom. The two were still going at it when I emerged so I headed upstairs to the kitchen.

Katrice was cleaning dishes and said brightly, "Oh! There you are. I'm just finishing up here. Corrigan told me that you like coffee. Would you like a cup? I know that Harve said you seemed to enjoy it yesterday."

"Thanks, Mrs. Raimler."

"Oh. Please," she huffed and poured a cup for me. Setting it on the countertop, she reflected, "You're doing me such a favor, honey."

Huh? "What do you mean?"

"Well," she blinked. "I get to see Corrigan around the house. He's usually out of the house after he's grabbed a quick bite to eat. And heavens know when he gets home at night. He's always gone spending time with his friends. You know, he really adores you and Bryce. He talks about you guys all the time."

I didn't know what to say.

"You two are such a good influence on him."

My mouth dropped, "Huh?"

"You are. Both of you just calm him down. Corrigan used to get so riled up in school. We got called so much because he fought all the time. Harve and I noticed a change in our Corrigan when he started talking about Bryce and Sheldon. The calls stopped after that."

"I think that was around the time of puberty," I said dryly. "Corrigan noticed girls."

"The Harve and I thought about that too. We thought that was the change in him, but Stephen told us about him one time. He saw his older brother at the mall with you two and it was a new Corrigan."

Who would've thought it? I was a good influence. I wasn't buying it.

Katrice busied herself cleaning the counter as she muttered, "At least we don't get calls from the police anymore. That was stressful. We got calls almost once a month, sometimes two times. If we only get one a year now, we're grateful."

Corrigan in jail? Never.

Just then Corrigan sprinted up the stairs, breathless.

"Hey, mom," he greeted and stopped abruptly at my chair.

I noticed two red gashes on his chin and saw another long red scrape that wrapped around his neck. Rug burn.

"Bryce beat you, didn't he?" I laughed.

Corrigan flushed. "He did not. It was mutual."

"Oh, honey." Katrice rolled her eyes to the heavens above and sighed, "You're always getting yourself into these scrapes. We've talked about this. You don't always have to be the alpha male. Sometimes, it's okay to be the beta. You actually have more personality—"

"Mom!" Corrigan interrupted. "We're not talking about this."

"Honey. You have my family's wild side in you. I have atoned for this. Really. I'm to blame, but I've seen your friend, Bryce. He is not a beta male. And you grew up being comfortable as the alpha male in this household. I know that sometimes you're going to rebel, but I really think you'll benefit in the long run when you're flexible and can adapt to being the beta or the alpha male."

"Mother," he hissed through clenched teeth.

I bit my lip. A laugh would not be appropriate, but...I couldn't hold back.

"Shut up."

"Oh my god." I normally hated giggling, but wow.

"See." Katrice patted her son's tense arm. "Sheldon agrees with me."

"Mom." Corrigan shook his head, glaring. "She's laughing *at* me. You humiliated me in front of my best friend."

"She's not laughing at you. I'm sure Sheldon's seen Bryce without a shirt. She probably agrees with me."

I lost it.

"Get out," Corrigan said through gritted teeth. "Get out while you can."

I got out and moved downstairs just in time to see Bryce leave the bathroom without a shirt.

I started laughing again.

"What's with you?" Bryce asked as I walked in front of him and sat on his bed. I laid down as he started dressing.

"Corrigan's mom is hilarious."

"Really?" Surprise flashed in his eyes. "I always thought she was a little weird."

"Oh, she is. But she's hilarious. She just commended me for being a 'good' influence on her son and she's probably still lecturing him how being a beta male is beneficial."

"What?" Bryce stopped and looked at me, dumbfounded.

"Never mind." Still chuckling, I stretched out on his bed.

I didn't see any similar marks on Bryce like Corrigan's carpet burn. He really was magnificent and the Mohawk accentuated his presence.

"We have to get all of our cars today," Bryce mumbled as he looked for his shirt.

I groaned, "Can we not? Can we stay here? Have Katrice be our mother and forget all about high school?"

Bryce sat on the bed as he pulled a shirt over his head. As he poked his head through the opening, he replied, "That'd be awesome, but my mom would have a fit. I'm supposed to make the money—" He bit off the next word.

I sat up. "What are you talking about? Why do you have to make the money?"

Bryce just sighed.

"Bryce," I said sharply. "You're going to college...that's why you stopped playing soccer. They don't want you to play. Are you supposed to get a job now?"

"Let's go. I think Corrigan said something about waking up Stephen."

"No." I scrambled off the bed and stood in front of the door.

Bryce was avoiding me. He was avoiding my questions and it pissed me off. I may not like to talk about stuff, but I wanted to talk about this—I *really* wanted to talk about this.

"What is going on?"

"You're not my girlfriend. I don't have to tell you a thing," Bryce cursed and shoved past me.

Stunned, I stood there. What had just happened?

Chapter 17

I was greeted with blatant stares as I entered the hallways on Monday. I didn't care as I made my way to first period. Mr. Aldross sat at his desk as he waited for everyone to sit and the first bell rang. After it did, he didn't write his twenty questions on the board. Instead, the speakers crackled as an announcement was given to us.

"At this hour, please place all your books in your lockers and attend the auditorium."

I didn't have to hear the sudden whispers to know what everyone thought. This was the announcement about Leisha's death.

"Sheldon," Mr. Aldross spoke up. "Can you wait a moment please?"

I nodded, struck that he'd spoken my first name. Mr. Aldross only greeted me as 'Miss Jeneve.'

As everyone left and the door closed on the last gawker, Mr. Aldross stood up and sat at a table nearest mine.

"I'm sorry, Sheldon. I wanted to let you know that. I was told that you and Mr. Scout were the ones who found her. That must be…difficult, at the least." He cleared his throat. "Have you thought about speaking to Miss Connors? I'm sure she'd be an excellent listener if there were things you needed to get off of your chest."

I nodded and replied, "The cops said that we could do a group thing. Me, Bryce, and Corrigan."

"Of course. If that would be helpful, it might be the best venue for you." He nodded again and stood. "Well, shall we go?"

The teacher had given his sincerest condolences. Now that his obligatory support had been given, onto the rest of the day's agenda.

As we walked through the hallways, there was an overflow of students in the hallway. The auditorium's door weren't big enough for the sudden influx of students and the filtering slowed the onslaught.

Corrigan straightened from my locker as Mr. Aldross and I turned the corner.

Mr. Aldross gave us both a perfunctory nod as he passed by us with no comment or reproach.

"That was weird," Corrigan muttered, still watching the teacher. "I'm used to getting scolded by that dude."

I kicked my locker and deposited my books inside.

"Hey, so, the cops are here."

"What cops?"

"The ones for your protection. Remember?"

No. I'd forgotten.

"Oh." I glanced around. "Where's Bryce?" After a tense afternoon spent together, he'd gone home Sunday evening to face AnnaBelle's wrath. I was a little concerned if he'd been eaten alive.

Corrigan shrugged and remarked, "Can we skip this lame thing? All it's going to be about is the 'offer of counseling services. Everyone shouldn't walk alone at night. Use your buddy-system. And the faculty and staff wish to extend their greatest condolescences to everyone who has been touched by the recent tragic loss.'"

His words were meant for mockery, but they sounded bitter.

"Where's Bryce?"

"Mama Dearest probably locked him in the dungeon." Corrigan shrugged carelessly. I'd yet to meet a fan of AnnaBelle Scout who wasn't her seven-year old daughter.

Just then, Bryce rounded the corner and said as a greeting, "The cops are parked across the street. They're watching your car, Sheldon."

I already felt protected. Not really, but I was a little relieved. Bryce didn't seem as tense as yesterday.

"Did your mom freak last night?" Corrigan asked Bryce.

A raised eyebrow was his response and Corrigan chuckled, "She's so predictable."

Bryce asked me, "Did you sleep?"

"On and off," I said dully and a yawn escaped me. I'd stayed at Corrigan's, but Bryce hadn't been there to help me sleep. I knew another sleepless night would make my pride too desperate and I'd beg for his company.

"Students," Mr. Adlross boomed down the hallway. "We're starting and you are not inside."

There were other lingering students, but he wasn't talking to them. Mr. Aldross looked straight at us as he gestured towards the auditorium doors.

"Today, Mr. Raimler, Mr. Scout, and Miss Jeneve."

The other students breathed in relief. They'd escaped Mr. Aldross' wrath.

"Whatever," Corrigan muttered as he stood and led our slow arrival past Mr. Aldross' disapproval.

A few seats were empty, but Corrigan led us towards the back sections and jerked his head at a few students. They scrambled and the three of us sat in the back row that was shadowed from the overhanging seats upstairs.

As we all waited for someone to approach the podium on the stage, Corrigan tapped his foot against the seat's backrest in front of him. It earned him an irritated glare from a junior girl that immediately turned into a self-conscious smile. Corrigan's eyes lit up and he leaned forward for some time-consuming flirting.

I slumped in my seat and closed my eyes until I felt Bryce's fingers slide onto my thigh.

I looked up and saw a faint grin as he stared back. He didn't look like he fared the night any better so I sat up and slid a hand around his neck. He leaned down and met my waiting lips. I closed my eyes and enjoyed the warmth as Bryce kissed me. It felt satisfying and pleasurable against a night of no sleep. His kisses pushed the coldness of reality away and I relaxed against him when he shifted me to his lap.

The microphone crackled as it was moved too close to a body and Principal Gregory spoke clearly and briskly, "When Miss Jeneve and Mr. Scout finish their morning 'hellos' we will resume with the agenda for this emergency convention."

Laughter smattered across the auditorium, but Bryce took his time finishing our kiss before he lazily looked up and called out, "We're good. Thanks."

Principal Gregory coughed in disapproval and I slid off Bryce's lap.

"Thank you, Miss Jeneve, for putting our good tax payers' money to use. Chairs are meant to be sat upon."

"They're not as comfortable," I replied and I saw Principal Gregory hide a grin while the students broke out in laughter.

Principal Gregory nodded, "Thank you for pointing that out, Miss Jeneve, but that is not why we all have come together in this auditorium."

With those words, I was forgotten.

Principal Gregory looked over the auditorium and took a deep breath. It changed the atmosphere and everyone quieted. We all just waited.

"I am sure, by now, that everyone has heard the recent events that occurred over the weekend. Some schools would not openly address the tragic loss that we have experienced from the death of Leisha Summers, but I disagree. I have invited the local Sheriff to address some questions we all may be feeling and Miss Connors will have her own say about how to handle some of those emotions that you might be experiencing. After school, we will adjourn our last period thirty minutes earlier where a silent candle vigil will take place in the parking lot in memory of Leisha Summers." He nodded once and said, "With that—Sheriff Adley."

Sheriff Adley wasn't there to speak about Leisha's murder. He was there to address further safety in the community. He repeated most of what Corrigan had mocked, but without the buddy system. He said to be smart when leaving your home at night. Check in when you leave and always give an estimated time when you're to arrive and where. Make sure to check in again after you've arrived. Pepper spray is a weapon of choice among many police officers, its use wasn't deadly and still effective. Don't walk in any area with poor lighting. Park your vehicle under streetlights. Watch over your shoulder and if you feel someone is following, don't be afraid to call 911.

After he opened the forum for questions, he gave no comment on all the questions that were about Leisha. He only replied that his staff and deputies were pursing all avenues and hope to make an arrest in the near future.

Disappointment transcended the auditorium, but it was understood.

Miss Connors took the podium next and spoke about how to handle grief.

I tuned her out and left through the back door.

Mr. Sayword wasn't surprised when he saw my entrance in the art room.

The room was empty except for the two of us and he nodded in sympathy, "I'm sorry, Sheldon. I heard that you found your friend."

I shrugged and moved into the darkroom.

It didn't matter that it wasn't my film that I developed. My hands needed to be busy and moving.

After the second bell rang, I heard the murmur of voices on the other side of the door.

I sighed, replaced the camera I'd been holding, and left. Students were lingering around the tables.

I plopped on the nearest empty one and remained there, content to be alone when I heard a soft voice beside me, "Hey." She was teeny tiny with soft golden hair that surrounded a pointed nose. Her eyes consumed too much of her face. And she had the barest hint of lips I'd ever seen.

I studied her a moment, searched my database, and then said abruptly, "I have no idea who you are."

She flushed and hugged her books tighter to her chest. "I'm Grace Barton."

"You're Mena's new friend," I announced as comprehension flooded me.

Caution flashed over her features again and I got the distinct impression that a burst of wind could've knocked her over. "Yeah," She sighed and moved closer. "That's why I came over here."

"What do you want?" I asked flatly after she'd taken a few breaths for bravery.

She jumped slightly at my question, but rolled her eyes in self-condemnation. "I'm here because Mena's really hurt by what you did."

"I didn't do anything to her."

"She said that you're not friends with her because Bryce and Corrigan don't like her."

I laughed and remarked dryly, "She's gotta be pretty stupid to screw that up. Mena's hot. Corrigan always likes hot girls, but if she did something to piss him off—then that's on her, not me. I don't tell them who to like and who not to like."

Grace looked like she was about to fall over again.

"And you didn't help the situation," I said flatly.

Grace frowned and asked, timidly, "What do you mean?"

"You're a social loser. If you want Mena to be liked by me, Corrigan, and Bryce—she shouldn't be hanging out with people like you and your brother. Whoever invited her to your party saw that she'd already been outcasted. Mena could've fought it and been fine, but you guys sent her the invitation because you saw someone 'cool' who could be in your crowd."

Grace gasped and swayed on her feet.

I stood up. "Look, I'm not saying this to be mean. I'm just saying it because it's true. And I'm not going to be duped into feeling guilty that Mena has some hurt feelings. She knows the deal. If she wants back in, she's gotta earn that respect. The rules apply to everyone."

"Sheldon," Mr. Sayword spoke up, across the classroom.

I turned and saw Corrigan at the door, watching me.

"Yeah?" I asked. I saw a note in Mr. Sayword's hand.

"You're wanted in the counselor's office."

My eyes caught and held Corrigan's. We both thought the same thing, group therapy time.

"Fine," I muttered and left the room. Corrigan fell in step beside me when he asked, "What was that about in there?"

"Just telling a social loser that she's a social loser." I remarked.

Three other students were there and we saw Bryce lounging against the wall. His eyes sharpened when he saw us and he pushed off from the wall. Corrigan booted the students off the couch and we sat down instead. Bryce leaned on the armrest near me until Miss Connors stuck her head out and gestured for all three of us.

"Come on back, guys." She said, friendly.

She'd set up three plush chairs around her office and I saw, surprised, that it was cleaner than my last visit. Miss Connors looked tired, but professional with her outfit spot-clean and pristine.

She looked like a therapist.

"So," she breathed out and sent another warm smile at us. At me. "How are you guys doing?"

Corrigan leaned forward and rested his elbows on his knees as he remarked, "I'm having a hard time handling all the emotional distress that my two best friends have recently undertaken due to the traumatic loss that they witnessed."

Bryce and I both laughed.

A grin slipped past Corrigan's lips, but he added as he attempted to sound vulnerable, "I feel left out because I wasn't there when they found her body, but I realized over the weekend that this was a pattern that's been constructed since Bryce and Sheldon started sleeping together. Isn't there a term for that? Peer isolation?"

I fought a grin, but Miss Connors rolled with it. She nodded and asked, "And when did that start?"

Bryce spoke this time, "First time we screwed was in freshman."

"I remember." Corrigan nodded. "It was that party when Trevor Bently thought he could score with Sheldon and you told him that she'd be busy with you instead."

Bryce grinned. "And he punched me, hit like a girl."

There had been no Trevor Bently, punching, or party when Bryce and I had first slept together. And that's why I loved my two best friends so much. They were lying for me. She knew it. And they continued to lie.

Miss Connors shifted in her seat and stared at me. "I'm glad that you think this is a joke because I'm sure your friend would've thought the same about you. Wait—no, she wouldn't have. Your friend probably would've cried if it had been you instead of her. How do you feel about that, Sheldon?"

Bryce commented, "You're a great counselor. You make people feel like shit."

"No doubt," Corrigan added his two cents.

"And when the two of you stop talking for Sheldon, maybe we can actually get somewhere instead of all three of you jerking my chain," Miss Connors said briskly. "Sheldon, I asked you a question. How do you think Leisha would've reacted if your places were switched?"

Bryce opened his mouth again, but Miss Connors cut him off. "I want to hear Sheldon's voice. She's got one."

He closed his mouth and leaned back.

I leaned forward and said simply, "The difference between Leisha and me is that she was a decent person. I'm not."

Miss Connors was cool when she asked, "So is this your martyr bit? Am I suppose to tell you how great and wonderful you are, how much potential you have? I've already said that. If you choose to listen or believe me, then that's on you. It's your life at the end of the day. You're the one who falls asleep at night, but you still haven't answered my question. How do you think Leisha would've reacted?"

"I can't answer that because I'm not Leisha."

"You were friends. That's what everyone says. It's funny that I never saw the two of you converse in the hallways. I usually notice that, but everyone has told me that you guys were friends with her."

I leaned back and said coolly, "I considered her a friend, yes. Not best friends, but I liked her."

"Enough to have a guy she liked call her. Right? Carlos said that you were the one who suggested that he should call her. You were looking out for a friend, weren't you?"

"What?" I countered. "Does that make me a decent person now?"

"No," Miss Connors clipped out. "One act of decency just shows that there is decency inside, but it doesn't make a person decent. No, but that wasn't your question was it? Your real question is if *I* think you're a decent person, right?"

Bryce remarked, seemingly casual, "Why don't you back off of her?" He looked bored, but everyone in the room knew he wasn't.

"And you come stepping to the plate," Miss Connors stated. She waved a finger to each of us, "Is that what you do? You step up and shield Sheldon when you think she can't handle anymore?"

Bryce leaned forward. "Why don't you stop trying to classify us as awful people and do some counseling? That's what you are, aren't you?"

"I think my question to Sheldon was if she wondered if I wondered if she was a decent person. An 'awful person' never came into the conversation."

"What's your point?" Bryce demanded as he leaned back, back in cool control.

Miss Connors watched him and shook her head as a grin tugged at her lips. "Bryce Scout, you'd be surprised how many times I hear your name in this office. Little girls who think they're in love. Some just want to lose a few more pounds so you'd notice them. Some try to convince themselves that you'll love them if they sleep with you or sleep with your friends. And then there's the scorned ones. The ones who finally realize that you don't love them and you'll never love them. Those are the ones that break my heart because they think they've lost everything." She shook her head, astounded. "How do you do that, Bryce Scout? How do you get everyone to want you so bad and they still want you even when you've tossed them out?"

Bryce locked eyes with her and neither budged.

I sighed and stated, "I know what you're doing."

"Hold on, Sheldon. I'm talking with Bryce Scout now."

I ignored her. "You're trying to understand us so you're going after all of us. You went after me, Bryce, and Corrigan's next. You want to know who speaks up for who because you want to understand us."

She ignored me in return and murmured, "So, Bryce Scout, how does it feel to have Sheldon think you can't handle anymore? She just stepped up to save you, like you did for her."

"I'm bored," Corrigan proclaimed.

A smile came to Miss Connors as she reflected, "And your best friend just threw in his bit. He's trying to save you too."

"Maybe they're trying to save you," Bryce said softly.

"Oh yes," Miss Connors breathed in appreciation. "I get why all the girls pander for you so much. You've got this cool arrogance that make them flock to you. It's interesting, though, because everyone in this room knows that the one girl you love, you can't get."

She looked at me without flinching, "So what's it about you, Sheldon? What've you got that all the other girls don't? And Corrigan? How do you feel on the outskirts as you mentioned before? You've got two best friends who circle around each other, sleep with each other, and there's you."

"This is a waste of time." Bryce yawned, pointedly. "You're just attacking us. Where's the sympathy? We found a dead body Friday night. I thought this was about that."

Miss Connors looked at him steadily and replied, "Really? You really want this session to be about that when the three of you came in here and gave a dog and pony show for me? Because all four of us know that when you walked in here, there was nothing I could do to hear the truth from the three of you. How it really feels to know someone that died, to know that you were the ones who found her first, to see a dead body, and to know that she was killed by the same pervert whose sending sick twisted notes to Sheldon." She waved a finger around the room. "All four of us know that went on and yet, the three of you band so tight together, no one can get in. I knew no matter how much education I have behind my belt, the three of you would never let a stranger into that bond."

Bryce fell silent.

Corrigan fell silent.

So did Miss Connors.

So I spoke up, "It's not you, Miss Connors. I don't talk to them either."

She was surprised. I saw a brief flash in her eyes, but Miss Connors recovered instantly and asked, "Have you ever?"

"What?"

"Have you ever talked to someone?"

I had. I had talked to my parents. To my father once.

Corrigan and Bryce didn't say anything, but I knew they both thought the same thing.

My parents were in the room, even though they were across the ocean.

I relented, "My parents."

"And they left, didn't they?" Miss Connors asked, nonplussed. She leaned forward. "For the record, Sheldon, I think you have truly awful parents. They left their child when it was legal to leave their child. I can't do a damn thing about that and they're very self-absorbed when it comes to their only daughter who has every right to be as bitter and angry as you are. I get why you don't respect me. I really do. I wouldn't either if I had a mother like yours. But I want to make one thing very clear—these two guys will not leave you if you talk to them."

She leaned back again and added, "I've talked to a lot of students and the three of you are always mentioned as the top dogs in this school. I'll be honest, until the last few days, I would've thought the worst about you two, Bryce and Corrigan. But I've also heard some great things about you guys. You protect Sheldon. The two of you are incredibly loyal to your friends. So I'll just say, and this is for you Sheldon, that these two best friends you have will not leave you if you talk to them. It'll draw them closer to you. You will not break down if you cry about Leisha. And that's it for today. I want all three of you back in here in two days. Have a good day and don't skip any classes."

Miss Connors dismissed us and we left, slower than when we'd entered.

Chapter 18

After our session with Miss Connor, neither of us wanted to be in school. After we saw the majority of teachers wandering around, comforting students, and only a handful of students were actually attending classes—Corrigan had bailed. Bryce and I gone after that.

And now I tilted my head back as Bryce's lips settled on my neck where he sucked, licked, and generally made me melt. One of his hands held my hip while the other slid up and down my thigh in a slow caress. His legs rested on the bed to my side, but the rest of his body lightly rested over me. He traveled up my jaw and found my lips again. I gasped as his fingers worked the inside of my jeans and his tongue swept inside.

We'd taken our time, but twenty minutes of foreplay stretched our limit and Bryce abruptly sat up and quickly rid himself of a shirt. He started on his jeans when I unzipped my own and shimmied out of them. Shirt and bra had already been stripped away, but when my fingers found the straps of my thong, Bryce groaned and stopped me. His hands left his pants and he bent to kiss my hip, just above my thong.

"Bryce," I moaned, but could only lay there, helpless, against the onslaught of pleasure.

He slipped the thong off and five minutes later, I shoved him away and desperately reached for his pants.

Bryce kicked them off and fell on top of me as he reached for my nightstand.

His body froze as he reached inside and I blinked in confusion, still dazed from lust, when he straightened away from me and sat back.

"What are you doing?" I cried out and moved to him.

Bryce kept me off and raised his head.

"Oh."

He held my dad's Colt.45 in his hand.

"What the hell is this?"

Busted. I sighed and said flatly, "What do you expect? My house was broken into and I have some freak sending me twisted letters. Not to mention…Leisha."

"Jeez," Bryce breathed out and looked from me to the gun and back again. He cursed softly underneath his breath and laid down next to me. He cursed again. "You're not staying here anymore. Not alone," he declared.

I scoffed, "And what? You're going to stay every night? Keep lying to AnnaBelle?"

He shrugged, "If I have to."

"I can stay at Corr—"

"No," Bryce interrupted me coldly. "I'm not okay with that."

I quieted and moved to lay beside on him, on my side. I moved one hand to his chest and I swept it softly up and down in a caress.

He sighed again. "This is…" Screwed up.

"I know," I muttered. "Believe me. I know."

Bryce took a breath and sat up. He leaned over me again as he replaced the Colt in my nightstand. I moved to my back and Bryce stayed above me, staring at me.

"What?"

He raised a hand to cup the side of my face and shook his head, somber.

"What?" I asked again.

"Nothing," he whispered and bent for my lips again.

I grinned against them and tugged him to fall on top of me.

He did and the next time he reached for a condom, he actually pulled one out.

We spent the rest of the morning and afternoon in bed, just like we tried the week before. Bryce wanted to watch some ESPN after we'd retired from the shower and I was okay with that. My legs felt a little wobbly from lack of food and the continuous onslaught of gasping, clenching, and groaning.

I was in the kitchen when I heard the front door open. Dressed in a pair of scrub pants and a skimpy white tank-top that didn't cover anything, I grasped a butcher knife for protection as I tiptoed around the doorway and waited.

The person wasn't alone and our coat closet was opened. I heard the sound of metal hangers and knew they shuffled through the coats so I tiptoed around the dining room table and into the back hallway that had saved my life before. I circled around into the back sitting room and crept to the end of the main floor hallway where a second stairway had been built, but rarely used.

I hurried to my bedroom and it only took one look for Bryce to scramble out of bed. He put on a pair of jeans, moved in front of me and grasped the butcher knife instead. When I moved to the nightstand, he caught my hand and shook his head.

I was too scared to argue and I trusted him.

I felt a slight bulge in his pocket and recognized the feel of his phone. I turned back and grabbed my own as well as a set of keys. At the door, Bryce led the way first and we moved to the second stairs, but I shook my head and pointed towards my parent's bedroom.

Bryce frowned, but he followed me through their room and neither of us stopped short at the destruction I'd overhauled before. We moved to the back patio and just as the door clicked shut behind us, the bedroom door was swept open and we both heard a short scream of horror, "Oh my god!"

I tensed, but threw my leg over the balcony and grasped the window's ledge from the bottom bathroom. Bryce and I climbed our way to the ground and sprinted for Bryce's car. Once we got inside, he reversed and grasped his phone in the other hand. When his finger cleared the nine and moved to the one, I grabbed it and said sharply, "No."

"What? Why not?"

"Those weren't burglars or whoever from before," I sighed wearily and my head hit the seat's headrest.

"Who was that then?"

"My mother," I said weakly.

Bryce didn't say anything, but he glanced at me sharply.

I sighed, "I recognized her voice. That was my mother."

Bryce braked quickly and turned the car around.

"What are you doing?"

"You're going back to talk to her and tell her what's going on. That's what we're doing," Bryce said harshly, his jaw clenched.

"No. Please. I can't see her now. I just—I can't. Not yet." I needed time to regroup. I needed time to…figure out what I even wanted to say to my mother.

He looked over my clothes and asked with a smirk, "Do you have some extra clothes at school?"

"No." The ones I did have were dirty. I used my second set when I'd met Mena for the first time.

Bryce twisted into his backseat and came back with a hooded sweatshirt in hand.

"You can wear this," he said simply. "Sure you don't want to go back to your house?"

"I have clothes at Corrigan's house."

So we went there and we weren't the only ones.

In the basement, we were met with a flushed and shirtless Corrigan. He looked like he'd just ran his hands through his hair because it stood straight up and his jeans were unbuttoned with the zipper halfway pulled up.

Bryce smiled and asked, "You found Logan."

Corrigan cracked a grin and said, "I found Logan so scram. I've only got another hour before Stephen gets home."

I bypassed them and changed into a different set of clothes. Now dressed in jeans and an added bra with a green top, I moved back to the stairway and found Bryce sitting, waiting for me.

No Corrigan.

Just then we heard a moan from a closed door and I rolled my eyes. "Can we please leave?"

"Yes, please." Bryce sighed and stood up.

Back in the car, he didn't move to start the engine, but said instead, "You have to go and see her. You know that, right?"

I did, but... "Fine," I surrendered.

Bryce reversed again and we drove back. We were met with flashing headlights from two police cruisers that were parked where we'd vacated. As we got out of the car, I recognized Officer Sheila on the front porch, talking with my mother and a notepad in hand. Her partner stood right behind her and another man stood behind my mother.

Or a boy, actually. He looked early twenties and he could've been a personal trainer from the sheer white shirt that clung to him. Tight trendy jeans rested over a pair of beaded flip-flops. His hair looked almost wet from the overload of hair gel, which said a lot when I saw it from a distance.

And my mom.

The knot of dread and nervousness exploded inside of me.

My mom looked good, but she always looked good. Corrigan had tried his hand multiple times with my mom. She flirted, loved the attention, but—thank god—she'd never accepted his offers.

Her blonde hair was swept in a diamond-studded hair clip. Her long curls cascaded to frame her heart-shaped face. She matched her boy toy with a long white sweater wrapped around her that was tied with a sash. Her tailored jeans peeked underneath and instead of beaded flip flops, she wore diamond-studded high heels. The diamonds matched the ones that circled her neck and hung from her ears.

I didn't feel the hand that Bryce placed in the small of my back as he guided me to the front porch.

Sheila skimmed over my pale features and glanced at Bryce behind me as my mother squealed, "Sheldon!"

She swept me against her chest and patted my hair delicately. "I've missed you so much, honey!"

"Really," I said dryly.

"Oh my gosh, honey. I had no idea. Are you okay? Our house was broken into, can you believe it? Officer Padley told me that this was the second time and you were here during the first. I can't believe it. My room was destroyed. All my valuables and jewels are all gone. I can't believe it."

I pulled away and saw the wry look in Sheila's eyes before I said firmly, "The men who broke in didn't do that to your stuff, mom. I did."

My mom had been standing in front of me for five minutes now, but at my words—I finally saw my mom.

A flicker of rage flashed in her eyes, but it was gone instantly.

"You did what?" Her comforting hand turned into a cold grasp.

"You heard me," I clipped out.

I felt Bryce shift closer, just one step, behind me.

Sheila coughed and asked, "Could I have a word in private with your daughter, Ms. Jeneve?"

"Its Carlton now," Sharon Jeneve said coldly as her eyes swept over Sheila, to Bryce, and settled on me.

I bit back a grimace.

"Of course, Ms. Carlton."

My mother's back straightened and she faced Sheila squarely. "I'd like a full list of everything my daughter damaged and everything the burglars damaged. I have a right to my own property."

"Well, with all due respect, Ms. Carlton," Sheila said softly. "You have a right to parent your daughter, but I've yet to see any of that happen."

My mother didn't gasp. She didn't curse. She just heard it, understood it, and stored the snub away until it would come back out to bite Sheila in the behind.

Sheila saw that too, but she finished, "We'll get the list to you in due time. Until then, my officers and colleagues have done all the police business that's to be done here." She signaled the deputies to leave and quickly both police cruisers had left.

"Sheldon," Sheila murmured with a gesture of her head. "Can I have a word?"

Sharon Jeneve-Carlton reached for her boy toy's hand and they both moved inside without another word.

When the door clicked shut, Sheila exhaled a deep breath, "That's some mother for you. I'll give you that."

I waited.

Bryce leaned on the porch's banister behind me.

"I don't have jurisdiction to inform your mother of everything that's gone on with my investigation. However, I strongly encourage you to be completely upfront with your mother."

"Why?" I bit out. "She'll just leave. She'll do that anyway."

"Maybe your mother would take you with her."

"I'm not going," I said firmly. I would not leave Bryce or Corrigan. Fat chance.

She shook her head and glanced to Bryce. She spoke clearly, "I didn't like you at first look and I don't like you now, but this girl cares about you so do right by her. Make her tell her mother what's going on."

Bryce didn't react or comment.

Sheila didn't expect it. She shook her head and left the porch to where her partner waited in their own car.

As they left, Corrigan's car screeched to a halt in the driveway.

He wasn't alone.

Bryce snorted in laughter as we saw Corrigan leap out of the car and jog over to us. Logan followed at a more sedate pace, opening and closing her own door without assistance.

"Hey, man. Wasn't that…what's her face?"

"Yeah," I said dully and skimmed over Logan's tight features. She looked like she'd been thoroughly screwed over.

"So…" Corrigan murmured as he leaned beside Bryce against the banister, "What's going on?"

I sighed and leaned on his other side. I surrendered my defeat, "My mother's home."

Corrigan choked in surprise, "What?"

Logan's eyes went wide.

Bryce remained unmoving.

"Mama Jeneve is home!?" Corrigan jumped back up. "Sweet!"

"And she's brought her boy toy with her."

Corrigan barked out a laugh. "That's awesome. I'm gonna go say hi."

Logan stayed behind and leaned, awkwardly, against the house.

I told her, a dull anger, "He doesn't love you. I don't get why you jump in his bed when he whistles. It's pathetic."

Logan gulped, but murmured, hesitatingly, "I thought you were going to be nice. Corrigan said you'd be nice."

Bryce watched.

"He lied," I laughed. "Corrigan is just another guy. They always lie to get what they want. Guess what? You were dropped before and he's going to drop you again. I don't understand why you guys keep signing up for the same humiliation." And then I delivered the most embarrassing, "He's inside hitting on my mother."

Logan glanced at me, but quickly looked away when she whispered, "I think that says more about you than me."

Bryce coughed to cover a laugh.

I seethed, "He picked you up at a fast food joint. We'd just bailed him out of jail and he got to order his food and sex for home. You let him do that. You guys always let him do that."

"Then why are you friends with him?" Logan asked quietly.

"Because he calls me in the morning," I said sweetly and left with my shoulders high. Strong.

I shook my head in disgust as I walked through the front door and heard my mother's flirtatious shriek of laughter. They were in the kitchen and Boy Toy was glowering from a seat at the kitchen table.

Sharon Carlton glowed as Corrigan stood right next to her, whispering sweet nothings in her ear.

"Corrigan," I said simply.

He looked up.

"Out."

He left.

And my mother sighed as she turned to regard me. She crossed her arms over her chest and noted, wearily, "You're furious with me. I've gotten the message, Sheldon. You didn't have to destroy everything I loved."

I flinched at her words. She hadn't come back for me. She'd come back for those *things* she loved so much.

I looked at the Boy Toy and pointed out, "You haven't introduced me to my newest brother. Are you thinking of adopting so late for his age? That's quite *charitable*, mother."

Her mouth tightened as she clipped out, "Now, now, daughter dear. No need to be snippy and rude."

"Is it not becoming of me?" I taunted and shifted to the back of my heels.

My mother was an intelligent, shallow, and selfish woman. Her intelligent eyes pierced through me as she drawled, "His name is Luther and we both know who he is."

"I guess we both don't," I said pointedly. "I didn't know his name was Luther, now did I?"

While mother and daughter played our game, Luther sat quietly.

"Tell me, Sheldon," my mother spoke again, seemingly bored. "Have you stopped yanking your friends around by their chains? Corrigan was positively enamored to see me. I wonder how Bryce felt considering it's his bed that you're in for the most part."

"Why would Bryce care if Corrigan was happy to see you?" I asked, but I knew I shouldn't have.

"Corrigan doesn't want my bed, darling. He wants yours. It's so obvious."

"Please," I laughed. "Do you know how many times that ploy's been thrown my way?"

"Really."

"Really," I delivered in contempt for my own mother. "Get some new material. You'd probably think of some if you weren't on your back more than I was."

Luther laughed, coughed, laughed again, and sputtered to compose his puppyish begging for scraps.

My mother froze and pierced me again with her eyes.

She asked softly, "Did you just call your mother a whore, darling? That's not very loving of you."

"That's funny. I don't ever remember you teaching me how to be loving."

Sharon took a breath and I felt her move farther away even though she never moved.

I waited, breath held in suspense.

A controlled smile graced her lipstick mask and she murmured, "We'll be going to a hotel from now on until I've found a new house for us. Now, if you'll excuse Luther and myself, we have important packing to do now. We need to sort what's worth saving and throw what's damaged."

Her words punctuated the right buttons and I felt a stab to the gut.

I stepped back and witnessed a flash of astonishment mixed with sympathy in Luther's brown eyes before he stood and followed my mother.

I stood by myself in the kitchen until I heard their bedroom door close upstairs.

I checked the window, but Corrigan's and Bryce's cars were both gone.

After another shower, I changed clothes and grabbed my phone as I moved into my backyard. It didn't pass my consciousness that I visited the backyard the first day my mother had returned home.

I stretched on one of the loungers and called Bryce.

"Yeah?" he asked and I heard the sounds of a video game in the background.

"You're at Corrigan's?"

"Yeah," he grunted and swore after I heard a crash.

"You just died, huh?"

"Yeah."

I rolled my eyes and snapped, "Bryce!"

"What? I'm here."

"Forget it," And I hung up. The phone rang a second later, but stopped with no message when I left it untouched.

It was the best time *ever* for my two best friends to abandon me.

It took me another second before I realized that Mena's house stared back at me. In fact, I had a perfect view of their driveway and living room. They only saw the back of my house with my garage at an angle. They could only tell if anyone was home if they actually walked over or saw headlights in the dark.

Not me. I saw perfectly that Mena was home as well as Denton's luxury Sedan.

I leaned forward from the lounger and squinted. I was able to make out four people in their living room. They all stood and suddenly the front door opened and slammed shut after Denton. He had a female companion with him that looked skanky with a barely-there red dress.

She was saying something as Denton walked her to his car—correction, her car—and just before she got into the driver's side, the kiss she tried to skim over his lips was met with air when Denton evaded her with a shake of the head.

Huh.

I saw her pull away and stiffen in anger before she peeled out of the driveway.

Denton stood a moment and watched her car before he raked a hand through his hair. He took a step towards their house, but stopped. He turned towards mine. I saw him jerk when it dawned on him that I had watched the entire thing. Another moment passed before he stepped towards me and I watched as he crossed the lawn separating our homes.

"You saw that, huh?" He dropped onto the lounger beside me.

I sat there, my eyebrows arched.

"Stop looking at me like that," he muttered as he buried his head in his hands, his elbows braced atop his knees. "God—this was an awful day."

"Tell me about it," I murmured, sarcastic.

"Mena has been…awful lately. I don't know what's going on with her. She just is angry and she takes it out on everyone. Dad's called me three times this weekend to come over because he can't handle her anymore. And Kari—it's our three month anniversary. She wasn't really understanding when I told her that I needed to stay with my family. We were supposed to fly to New York and have dinner at the Four Seasons." He laughed. "I'm going to be lucky if she even takes my call tonight."

I looked at him.

"What?" He looked back.

"You hit on me a week ago." Did it have to be said?

He shrugged. "So?"

"You were in a relationship and you hit on the 'girl that screws her movie star neighbor because she's pissed at how fake her parents are.'"

He flushed. "You're not ever going to let me live that down, huh?" He shrugged. "And besides, sex with you is like free champagne. You take it when it's in front of you and not ask questions or consider the consequences."

"I don't know if that's a compliment or if you just called me cheap." I seemed to be saying that to a lot of people.

"Neither. I'm just saying I'd jump on another bedspring with you any day."

Really? I remarked, dryly, "My mom's back."

He raised his perfectly plucked eyebrows that God had graced him with.

I sighed, "And she's back to get the rest of her stuff because her and my father are getting a divorce."

"Sorry about that," he said quietly. "I remember when my parents got their divorce. I really think both my parents went crazy during that time. Thank god they hadn't gotten a psych eval, because they would've been diagnosed with something."

It didn't really help.

"Speaking of psych—Mena said that she's supposed to keep her 'psycho brother' away from you," he mused and grinned my way.

"You are psycho," I said matter-of-factly. "You're psycho when it comes to your sister."

"Thanks for giving her the brush-off, by the way. You did it pretty harsh, huh?"

"I didn't give her the brush-off. Corrigan and Bryce didn't like her and Mena didn't exactly stand her ground."

His scowl was immediate.

He caught my hand in a tight grip and asked, "Can you blame her? That one guy is fierce. He's a dick."

I didn't yank my hand back.

Denton realized it and protective brother was gone in a flash, only to be replaced by someone eager for free champagne.

He slid his fingers into mine and caressed my thumb.

I held my breath.

"Got a garage nearby?" Denton asked as his eyes flickered and focused on my lips. He tugged me closer and slid a hand over my thigh to play between my legs.

"What'd you say before?" I asked, throatily as he tugged me even closer.

I felt his breath against my lips when he replied, "About not asking questions or thinking of the consequences?"

"Yeah." I licked my lips and that was all it took. Denton fused his own against mine.

Warmth and excitement enflamed me as he shifted to lift me. He walked to my garage, fumbled for the door handle, and we were inside quickly. Denton pushed me against the wall and his hands did quick work as he shoved my pants down.

His kisses were demanding and rough, but it's what I needed.

One hand worked at his own pants as the other pulled my hair back to hold my head captive as his mouth assaulted me.

His tongue demanded entry and I could only hold on.

I heard the crinkle of a condom wrapper and then he gripped my thighs and clamped me around him as he shoved inside.

I gasped at the first thrust, but he pounded into me.

It was feral, hot, and when it was done too quick to have started, I held onto him for support.

He grunted as his last spasm left him.

He groaned, deep in his throat.

"Yeah," I laughed weakly.

Denton chuckled, drained, as he held me in place for another moment. He smoothed the hair away from my face and pressed his cheek against my forehead. And then his hands slipped between our bodies and worked its way inside of me.

He whispered as he kissed the corner of my mouth, "You didn't finish." He held me up until I was done and then he held me again until I could stand on my own.

"I have to go. Mena's probably wondering what I'm doing over here." And with an impersonal kiss to the lips, he was gone.

The empty garage stared back at me as I'd yet to fasten my pants.

Chapter 19

I messed up. The one other time that I had slept with Denton, I hadn't been scared for Bryce's reaction. I hadn't kept it secret, but it just hadn't mattered as much at that time. This time...it was different.

When I got to school the next morning, I ignored everyone else and searched for Bryce. I wanted to get this over with. I found him listening to a story from Harris.

I interrupted and grabbed his arm.

"What? Sheldon," Bryce said, startled.

I dragged him outside to a private area and stood there.

He asked, amused, "What? What happened to you yesterday? Was it really that bad with your mom?"

"I did...I did something yesterday that...you're not going to like."

Bryce grew silent.

"I..." I gasped.

"What'd you do?"

"I...had sex with someone last night."

Nothing. Silence.

I didn't look at him. I couldn't, but I saw one of his hands jerk in reaction. It caught itself and stretched, as if struggling to stay at its side.

He asked hoarsely, "Who?"

"Denton Steele."

Bryce turned away.

I cried out, "Don't—please don't leave. Just...stay and yell at me."

I still hadn't looked at him.

He asked, softly, "For what? We're not together, Sheldon. You and I, we're not a couple."

I finally raised my eyes to his and saw pain mixed with an unnamed emotion.

I held my breath. "You're not mad?"

He shook his head, but he didn't reach for me.

"No. I have no right to be mad, remember?"

"But…"

Bryce shook his head again and said faintly, "I gotta go to class. Bell's already rung. I'll see you inside."

When he left, I stood there and felt the same coldness as before.

I knew, I already knew, that it'd be a long time before he held me again.

Dazed, I was in the same place when Corrigan stuck his head out and exclaimed, "There you are! Holy hell—where've you been?"

"Corrigan," I said weakly and crumbled to the floor.

"Hey," he soothed as he knelt beside me. "What's wrong? Hey, hey."

I shook my head, it was all I could do, and whispered, "I just lost him."

Corrigan sighed and sat beside me. He flung an arm around my shoulder and pulled me to his side.

I burrowed into his side as he said against my forehead, "No. No, you didn't."

"I did. I had sex with someone else. I screwed up, Corrigan. I really did."

"No," he soothed again as his hand brushed my hair back. "Bryce loves you, Sheldon. Like true, gut-wrenching, love. One screw-up and he's not going to leave. He could've walked a long time ago, but he hasn't."

I asked, hoarse, "How do you know?"

"Because whenever you think that he's gone off with some girl, he's usually on the phone with me talking about how he should actually do it. He should screw half the girls that you think he does, but he never does. He's just angry and tired of waiting. And he doesn't do it because Bryce loves you and he's waiting for your self-destruction to stop."

"Self-destruction?"

"Yeah," Corrigan laughed. "That's what Logan told me this morning. Last night, I told her a little about what else is going on. Logan was amazed that you could still come to school. She said she would've broken down and end up in the asylum or something." He laughed. "She said you're made of strong stuff and, no wonder, because of all that's happened to you."

"What? The notes and Leisha?"

"No," he murmured, tenderly. "Losing your parents. She said that Miss Connors told her once that the worst thing that could happen to a kid is to never be loved. That's the absolute worst thing. She said Miss Connors told her that every kid has a right to be loved and when they're not—it's never their fault."

It wasn't my fault.

Corrigan shifted away and remarked, "Um…about that…Miss Connors said that we were supposed to make an appointment in three days or something, but she's booked so…"

"What?"

"I signed up for her first available slot and it's…"

"Right now," I finished for him, numb.

He laughed nervously and watched me. He even scooted away from me.

"I have to go and see a counselor like this," I said flatly.

"Well…" Corrigan shrugged.

"Fine. Let's do this." And just as abruptly, I was up and through the door. I didn't care what my face looked like, if they could see the tears or not—I wanted this hour done and over with.

Bryce was already in the office, leaning in the same spot, but unlike the last time, he didn't straighten when we walked inside.

He ignored us.

Mena sat beside him, her face closed to everyone else.

When we traipsed in, Miss Connors looked us over and announced, "Well…is there special significance that Corrigan is in the middle this time and Sheldon isn't?"

Corrigan didn't say anything. Neither did I.

Bryce shrugged and commented as he looked out the window, "No significance."

Her eyes looked us over again and studied each one before she harrumphed and leaned back in her chair.

"You know," she spoke flatly. "If I'd judge from our last session, I'd think that this was another dog and pony show for me. So…is it? I come down on you guys about protecting Sheldon, so you put Corrigan in the middle this time? Is it going to be you, Bryce, next time?"

Bryce failed to react and Miss Connors' eyes sparked at that.

She asked, sharply, "Sheldon…I was told that you skipped every class yesterday. Did you?"

"No," I murmured and looked at the door.

"Really? Because I have the attendance sheets."

"I didn't. I went to first period."

"Right." She sighed and asked, "So how about you, Bryce? You were missing all day yesterday. Where were you?"

He laughed, chokingly, and shook his head. Our eyes met briefly and we both looked away.

He'd been inside of me. And then someone else had taken his place.

"Fine," Miss Connors took another deep breath. "Someone wanna clue me in on the very large, very white, invisible elephant that's in this room?"

Crickets chirped.

"Alright. No one wants to tell me. I'm not going to ream you out like yesterday." She sighed and reached for a book. "How about today we'll just read a story. You guys can sit and listen. It's probably appropriate and if you don't pass my quiz at the end, I'm going to require daily sessions."

"What?" Corrigan asked.

"Ah!" Miss Connors smiled. "And the middle-man speaks. Now, story time so sit and listen, little children."

She opened the book and sighed as she sat straight, "So there was once a little girl fish, named Spooky, who loved to swim, but she'd never been taught to swim. And there was this frog named Harry Green. He liked to chirp to the friendly pond that he called home." Miss Connors paused dramatically...

"Are you serious?" Bryce asked, annoyed.

She looked at him with chilled eyes. "No. Talk time was earlier. This is story time. So zip it."

He opened his mouth again—

"Zip it," she cut him off. "And if you're going to complain again—whip it!"

Corrigan laughed.

"Mr. Raimler," Miss Connors chastised.

"Why am I Sheldon? Corrigan is Mr. Raimler? And Bryce is Bryce Scout?"

"Can you three please make up your minds? I'm not a puppet for you to string along. If you want to talk, let's hear what the white elephant is and if you don't—you're going to listen to my stories."

"Your stories?" Corrigan asked, eyebrows arched.

"Elephant or story. Your choice." She raised her own eyebrows to match his.

"Story," Bryce said automatically.

"Elephant," Corrigan voted.

"I had sex with Denton Steele," I named the elephant and startled myself.

Without missing a beat, Miss Connors remarked, "Well, that makes sense." She was serious.

Everyone looked at her, puzzled.

She sighed and said, "You found someone you knew and considered a friend dead. You're normally cut-off, Sheldon, but quite a bit's been going on. You realized how truly crappy your parents are. You found someone murdered. You're getting threatening letters. And…I got a phone call from your father. He said your mother came home yesterday. I'd say for someone who usually flies under the radar, emotionally-speaking anyway…you needed a different avenue to avoid everything that's been going on. Sex with someone you don't love—that makes sense."

Sex with someone you don't love. Those words echoed in me.

She continued, "And I've seen his latest movie." She whistled, "Hot stuff."

Bryce asked as he stretched his legs out, "What do you mean? Sex with someone she doesn't love?"

"Ah!" Miss Connors grinned coolly and replied, nonplussed, "That's what you heard out of that whole speech." She nodded my way and said, "I bet she's thinking the same thing."

Corrigan laughed.

Miss Connors ignored him and looked at me, "Because you do love him, Sheldon. And guess what? That's a decent thing for you to do. To be with someone that you love." She looked at Bryce, "She might not know it, but she loves you."

"My father called you?" I asked, quietly.

Corrigan stopped laughing.

Miss Connors nodded and murmured, "I called him yesterday to let him know that I saw his daughter for a successful session. I couldn't tell him anything, but he called me back and told me what was going on." She leaned forward. "For the record, Sheldon—he sounded sorry about everything that's gone down."

"What'd you tell him?"

"Just what I said right now. Sheldon came in for a session with her two best friends and I felt it went very well. That was it."

"Nothing else?" I prompted.

"Did I divulge all your secrets? No."

Corrigan suddenly asked, "Can we get back to Sheldon's question? Why am I Mr. Raimler, she's Sheldon, and Bryce is Bryce Scout?"

Miss Connors grinned and said, "Because you're so informal that you're formal. A formal title only makes sense. Bryce is a legend. He deserves two names. And Sheldon because, half the time, she forgets her own name."

Huh?

"What?" Corrigan echoed my sentiments.

Miss Connors shrugged, "You'll get it. Someday, maybe."

"I get it," Bryce said softly and leaned forward. "Mr. Raimler because you flirt so much to actually be real. It comes off as kinda impersonal or...formal." He shrugged. "And Bryce Scout because she said it herself, she hears about me from all those girls. I'm not really real, but... I don't know, like a celebrity or something." He took a deep breath, "And Sheldon because...Sheldon forgets that she's human sometimes. She tries to be a robot all the time."

"A robot who has mad passionate sex," Corrigan joked.

"Not appropriate, Mr. Raimler," Miss Connors rebuked quickly.

Corrigan muttered, just as quick, "Sorry."

"I think," Miss Connors spoke firmly. "That the biggest question in the room today is if Sheldon is a decent person or not. She talked about it yesterday. She told me that she wasn't a decent person. Leisha was a decent person, but Sheldon wasn't. Her words, not mine. So..." She looked between Bryce and Corrigan. "What do you think? Do you think Sheldon is a decent person?"

Corrigan spoke first, "Hell, yeah."

Bryce didn't say anything for a moment, but then he sighed, "She's a decent person when she remembers that she is a person."

I looked over, surprised.

He shrugged and met my eyes, "You just...I just don't think you feel half the time. You're so harsh sometimes to other people and I think it's just because you're worse to yourself."

"I think the bigger question is what Sheldon is going to do when she leaves today. She felt something yesterday and look where we all got. So what about today?" She finally looked my way and asked me, "I know you're feeling something today—so what are you going to do when you leave this office and you enter that world where you can't feel to get by? What 'indecent' thing are you going to do?"

I shrugged and looked away.

To my surprise, it was Bryce who burst out, "Come on! Just…say something, Sheldon!"

"This isn't therapy with just me," I cried out. "I thought this was a group thing. Why are you so focused on me today?"

"Because you're the one who banged Steele," Bryce bit out.

Miss Connors said quietly, "Because you're hurting the worst of everyone in this room."

Shocked, I looked at her, but the words died in my throat. I shook my head.

Bryce fell back against his chair in disgust.

Corrigan raised a hand and said, "Can I ask a question? And I'm not doing this to distract from Sheldon, I'm really not."

"What?" Miss Connors asked.

"Why are the three of us in here? I mean—I know that we were originally in here because it was Bryce and Sheldon who found Leisha's body, but…no one else is doing 'group' therapy."

"You're in here because the three of you have formed a tight family unit," Miss Connors explained patiently. "I've heard and listened to other students. You three are so tight, that there's no room for anyone else and you bat down anyone who threatens your alliances with each other. In the therapy culture, we'd call you an enmeshed family."

"Oh."

"So…this actually leads into some homework that I have for you guys." She reached behind her and grabbed two pairs of handcuffs. "Hold out your arms."

"What?"

"Are you serious?"

"Hell."

As we did, Miss Connors clamped one pair of handcuffs from my arm to Bryce's. She extended the other from Corrigan's arm to my other and leaned back in her chair.

"Now," she skimmed our faces. "This assignment has been approved by all your teachers, parents, and even the police. The three of you are going to prove to me that it's healthy for you to be as close to each other as you are. You're going to keep those handcuffs on until you've proved to me that you're healthy."

"That doesn't make any sense," Bryce remarked.

Miss Connors shrugged and offered, "It's this or you listen to stories of fish, frogs, and ponds."

"Handcuffs." Corrigan nodded.

"Good. I'll see you in two days for a check up. I want to know how it's going."

And we stood up.

Handcuffs, chains, and arms swung between each of us in our tight enmeshed triad.

Chapter 20

Life in handcuffs was not new to Corrigan and semi-new to Bryce. Surprisingly, they were alien to me in and out of the bedroom.

How to get out of handcuffs?

It was Corrigan's forte and he only needed one stop along the way.

Hoodum's.

The gang leader laughed uproariously when Corrigan called him out to our car in the parking lot. He actually stood there, laughed, and needed to pat his leg for composure.

It was maybe the first time that all three of us were quiet for our humiliation.

After we were delivered a third-sheet of public ridicule, Hoodum hunted around his warehouse and produced a key. Of course, afterwards Bryce remarked that Corrigan should've just 'picked' the lock. After getting arrested a few too many times, Corrigan knew his way around a pair of handcuffs.

At Bryce's comment, Corrigan had blinked, startled, and then cursed his own stupidity.

From there, we went back to school with the handcuffs still on, but they were taped so Miss Connors wouldn't figure out that we were cheating. All three of us tried to figure out which classes to go to and we had finally decided on Corrigan's fifth period with Mr. Hankins. I had just settled back for a nap when Mena strolled in wearing a black halter-top and black leather mini-skirt.

Every guy sucked in their breath. And most of the girls' mouths fell open or they hissed.

Corrigan and Bryce both appreciated the imagery, but it was Mr. Hankins who spoke up, "Miss Cruiw, you can report to the office. I'm fairly certain your dress is inappropriate. They might have a large tee shirt for you."

Mena ignored him and sat at a table in the corner.

"Miss Cruiw," Mr. Hankins tried again.

Bryce leaned forward and remarked, casually, "You're not wanted, Mena."

She snapped to attention and whirled around, "Was my brother a good lay, Sheldon? He was over at your house a little longer than he needed to be."

The class gasped and I sighed. Bryce had started this, but Mena knew where to make him hurt...

"What does it take to get it through your head?" Bryce asked. "You're not wanted."

"What'd I ever do to you?" Mena demanded.

He leaned back, coolly in control, "You're not right in the head. That's what you did."

"What? And Sheldon is? She's more screwed up than me."

"Mena," Mandy spoke up.

She was ignored when Mena cried out, "I can't believe you. You guys go at it like rabbits and you're still defending her after she screwed my brother in her garage."

That was enough. I asked, a sly grin on my face, "Did you wish it was you?"

The class held their breath.

Mena paled.

"Do you wish it had been you instead of your brother? Or do you wish it had been you that he touched?"

Mena couldn't speak. We all saw her fight for words around the choking ball of fury in her throat.

I finished, "Watch what you say, Mena. Jealousy can be a bitch and make you do things you'd rather forget."

Mr. Hankins spoke up then, calmly, "I think, Miss Cruiw, that you're wanted in the principal's office now."

"But—"

"Just go," Bryce bit out.

She stormed out, but she threw a last seething glare to our table before the door shut behind her.

I watched Bryce.

Bryce resumed his sleeping stance.

And Corrigan laughed, "Talk about making an entrance and exit."

Mr. Hankins just shook his head as he turned back again to the chalkboard. I watched Bryce, uneasily, through the entire class period until he finally sighed and murmured, out of the corner of his mouth, "I'm fine. I'm not going to go off and do something, okay?"

I stopped watching him and noticed the doodles that adorned Corrigan's notebook. I nudged him with my shoulder and asked, "What's that about?"

"Bored."

"Oh."

And I was reminded why I usually skipped any and all classes. They're just...boring.

When class was done, Chantal brushed up against Bryce as she walked along his empty side. I trailed behind, which caused Bryce's arm to fall behind with Corrigan on my other side. I caught him glancing up and down the hallway and asked, "Looking for Logan?"

Corrigan cast a sharp, cautious, glance my way, but sighed as he saw genuine curiosity in my own eyes, "Yeah."

We had stopped at Bryce's locker and I leaned against his neighbor's locker when I remarked to Corrigan, "You should have her come over today. I'm sure my mother will be gone house hunting with her boy."

Bryce looked up at that and commented, "I'd rather hangout at Corrigan's."

I looked sharply at him and breathed in relief. I was still in his plans after school.

"Sweet. I'll tell Logan," Corrigan said quickly before anyone could change their mind.

I said flatly, "No Chantal."

Bryce shrugged and remarked, "No movie star."

"Fine."

"Fine."

"Fine," Corrigan piped in and wrenched me aside as Logan approached the group. With the handcuffs, I got a good grope under her shirt as Corrigan greeted her like a long-lost lover that had been separated and held hostage by warring neighbors.

"Okay." I tugged my hand back and commented, "No more of that until we're not actually handcuffed together."

Corrigan and Logan parted at my words.

Logan was flushed, speechless.

Corrigan just grinned and replied, "Deal." He let go of Logan.

Bryce raised our hands as Miss Connors walked through the hallway. He remarked, "See, Miss Connors. Handcuffs."

"That's very nice, Bryce Scout," Miss Connors commented, politely, as she continued down the hallway.

Corrigan punched Bryce in the shoulder when she disappeared, "What was that, idiot?"

"What?"

"Nothing like telling her that we figured out how to get out of the handcuffs," I remarked.

Bryce cast a shrewd eye over me and shrugged, "Whatever."

Logan surprised everyone and asked me, "How are things with your mom?"

Bryce and Corrigan didn't say a word.

Neither did I.

No one asked about The Mother.

"That's a loaded question," Corrigan commented and eyed his girlfriend in pity.

But—new leaf and all—I said, calmly and even a little bit nicely, "She's…hopefully gone pretty soon."

Corrigan suddenly laughed and suggested, "We should have a sleepover at your place tonight, Bryce."

I grinned and commented, "AnnaBelle Scout would pray the whole night with a Bible on her lap."

Bryce rolled his eyes, but I caught the slight quirk at his lips.

"Why?" Logan treaded onto uncharted waters once again. She asked, "What's your mom like?"

The pause wasn't so obvious this time and Corrigan answered easily, "AnnaBelle hates Sheldon."

"And she loves Corrigan. Corrigan's a saint in AnnaBelle's world," I added.

Logan kept quiet, which was wise.

Bryce muttered as the four of us moved towards my locker, "She'd go after Miss Connors and the school would lose a good counselor."

"She said she got everyone's permission for this thing."

"She called my dad, not my mom. The school knows to call my dad for anything real about me. They call mom if they want her to volunteer for a food drive or something." Bryce rarely talked about his dad and he couldn't hide the bitterness from his tone as he did now.

Logan glanced at me. Corrigan quieted, skimmed an eye over Bryce and turned to me.

I watched Bryce and he looked up to find my eyes on him.

"Don't even," he bit out.

I grinned, "What? You think you're the only one who can have a screwed up family?"

The second bell rang then and Corrigan asked, "What class are we going to?"

Mandy Justice approached us at that time. She gave us each a handout and said what the title read, "We're doing a candlelight vigil for Leisha tonight. It's nine in the tabernacle at Holy Mount."

Holy Mount was the local Christian college.

"Who's we?" I asked.

"Me. A few others. Becky, Jill, just...the regular girls."

"You guys didn't even know Leisha."

"No, but Carlos did and Becky wanted to do this for him." Mandy shrugged. "Your fight's not with me, but it's a good cause."

"You should get some of her friends to do it." And why would Becky want to do this for Carlos?

Mandy flinched. "Look, no one else is doing it so...just show up, okay?"

Mandy left before I could say anything.

Bryce nodded and stated, "We're going." It went without saying, but Bryce had already said it.

The final bell rang and I stuffed the handouts in my books.

Chapter 21

Compared to the normal hustle and bustle, all three of us spent a boring afternoon at Corrigan's. Bryce and Corrigan played video games, laughed, and punched each other. I curled on the couch for awhile and then moved to the bedroom.

Katrice came down a few times. The first time she brought a tray of crackers and cheese. Her second trip consisted of cookies that she'd baked that afternoon. The entire house was filled with the aroma of chocolate chip cookie dough. And her third trip was with hot chocolate and tiny marshmallows.

Corrigan and Bryce ate it up—literally.

I accepted the hot chocolate and curled up on the couch afterwards.

Logan hit the doorbell around seven and Bryce gave me his phone to call my house. I didn't ask for it. He didn't offer it. He simply dropped it in my lap with my number already on the screen.

I called, but there was no answer and I didn't leave a message.

Logan sat on the opposite couch and we watched the boys play their games. I sat up once for a round of Guitar Hero, but my blanket called my name after I was done.

For a group that was generally known for their action and immorality, we were saintly and boring that afternoon.

Katrice brought another round of sandwiches and then announced dinner.

Corrigan asked if we could eat downstairs and so dinner came to us. We were served lasagna and garlic bread.

Logan smiled politely and Katrice adored her instantly.

For a moment, I watched with a faint grin. I wondered if Katrice was relieved that I wasn't Corrigan's girlfriend.

Maybe Katrice would've turned into another AnnaBelle if Corrigan had become a Bryce.

Bryce's phone rang and jumped in my hand. I had held onto it after my empty phone call and now saw that it was AnnaBelle.

Bryce looked over, saw my expression, and said flatly, "Ignore it."

I glanced up and Bryce saw the devil-may-care glint in my eyes because he straightened and said further, "Leave it, Sheldon. I mean it."

I stood up and answered it in a sweet purring voice, "Hello, Bitch." I grinned in satisfaction as I walked from the room.

Annabelle caught her breath, but I heard a moment later, "I knew it. I just knew it. Bryce hasn't been returning my calls and he hasn't stayed at home since I found you in his bed."

I cocked my head to the side and returned, "Well, he hasn't been in my bed." He had, but only for an afternoon so it wasn't technically a full lie.

Annabelle laughed. It was full of contempt and my back straightened in indignation.

"I give up," she chuckled to herself. "I give up. You can have him, but I promise you, Sheldon, you won't hold him. No one's going to hold my boy because he's going to the professionals next year."

I frowned and stopped moving down the hallway.

His mother continued, self-assured, "He's going pro and he's going to leave you behind. You might want to start looking for a replacement pretty soon, another big guy that'll protect you and stay up at night worrying about you. My boy won't be that guy anymore. He's going pro and the world is going to notice him."

The phone rattled, just slightly, as my grip clenched tighter around it. "What are you talking about?" I turned and looked down the hallway.

I was far enough so they couldn't hear, but Bryce stood in the hallway. He watched and I saw that he knew. I couldn't see anyone else. The hallway cut off my vision of Corrigan, his perfect girlfriend, and the perfect doting mother.

A look of exhausted resignation came across Bryce's face.

"He 'has to work,'" I quoted Bryce's words to his mother.

"Yes, he does and he's going to be noticed and you'll be in his dust. Mark my words. You'll be gone."

Bryce took a step and said, "Hang up."

"He didn't quit soccer because a college scholarship wanted him to, did he?"

AnnaBelle laughed. "He quit because the pros don't want him to get injured before their trainers can work with him."

Bryce stopped just before me and he said again, softly, "Hang up."

My fingers gripped tighter and I breathed, "Where?"

"Far far away."

It was wrong for a mother to enjoy a daughter's torment. It didn't matter whose daughter stood at the end of that torment. That person, that soul, was someone's daughter.

"Sheldon," Bryce breathed.

Broken, I whispered, as her words whipped inside of me, "If I had a daughter and her eyes were his…would you want them to be crying?"

AnnaBelle stopped abruptly.

Bryce cursed.

He took the phone from my numb fingers and turned away as he quickly murmured into it. I saw the tension in his shoulders. I saw how stiff his back was.

When he hung up, I breathed out, "You're leaving."

"Sheldon."

"Why are you leaving?" I cried out. "This was before I messed up."

Bryce closed his eyes and I saw the turmoil inside of him at that moment. It raged inside of him and I slowly, in awe, pressed my palm against his chest. Bryce sucked in a breath at my touch, but didn't move. Neither of us moved.

"You can't move," I whispered.

His eyes opened, slowly, almost lazily, and he whispered, "I don't want to."

I closed my eyes at his words.

"Hey," Corrigan called out from around the corner, ignorant, and unaware. "We should get going. Mom wants to do something before we head to the shindig tonight."

My eyelids snapped open and I looked up.

Bryce watched me and I saw an answering ache.

Bryce turned to the side. My hand fell away. And we walked back to find Corrigan and Logan snuggled close together on one of the couches.

Bryce and I sat on a second couch. We didn't sit at the ends, but there was an easy breathing space between us. I sat back and Bryce leaned his elbows on his knees.

Katrice came back down the stairs a final time with two bottles of wine and five glasses in her hand. She uncorked one and poured the first glass.

To my surprise, she turned and handed it to me. Warmly, she murmured, "It's a toast to Leisha Summers."

I took the wine glass and felt the smooth fragile contour between my fingers. The wine was a deep red and it screamed of texture.

"Thank you," I murmured, surprised and quieted.

Katrice smiled warmly and I knew in that moment that she wouldn't have been another AnnaBelle. She would've been someone I'd never known if Corrigan had been Bryce.

Katrice nodded and turned to me, heartfelt and unaware of how startling a person she was, "She was your friend. Corrigan told me. He said that you liked her and there aren't many that you like."

She smiled again, sparkling, "This is a toast to your friend, Sheldon, because I know that she'll be missed by many if she passed the tests to your heart."

She poured four more until all of us held a glass of that textured wine.

Corrigan raised his and said, "I didn't know, but…I remember her crazy outfits. And she had some wild hair. I remember that."

Logan giggled before she drank to his toast.

Bryce glanced at me and I knew a temporary truce had been called. His eyes were clear as he said clearly, "I liked her. She put up with our crap that one day and…I don't know…I liked her. She seemed like a good person."

Numb, I watched as he drank to his toast.

They all waited for me now.

"She…wanted to be cool," I spoke the truth.

Corrigan, Bryce, Logan grew somber as they heard what I said.

It was the truth and it made the moment even more heartbreaking.

"She…did what I told her to do because she wanted to be popular. She wanted to be liked and I knew that. She skipped class one day and she never would've done that except that I asked her to. She only did it because…I was popular and she wanted to be popular. She put up with our stupid games."

I cut off, for a moment.

"I—what kind of person does that? Willingly lets someone…I never would do that. I would never go along for the ride, knowing that I might be humiliated by the people I'm with."

"It wasn't about that," Bryce spoke up. He shifted closer. "We invited her to go with us and she did. She sat at a table with you all year. She started to get to know you."

"Yeah. She…" Corrigan spoke up. "She was your friend, Sheldon. You looked out for her at the end. That's what we get because we're your friends. You look out for us. You're loyal even if it makes you a bitch."

"And besides," Bryce grinned softly. "This isn't about how horrible you are, whatever you're thinking right now—this is about Leisha. And she seemed like a right chill girl."

"Yeah, but…"

"No buts," Corrigan said firmly. He scooted to the edge of the couch and leaned towards me. "No buts, Sheldon. Leisha saw in you what we all see in you and that makes her okay in my books."

I grinned, "She wrote swear words in her notebook when she was mad." I laughed, "I thought that was hilarious when I saw it because…" My smile died. "I wouldn't have done that. I would've just told the teacher what I thought. I wouldn't have been…she was nice."

"She was," Logan spoke up, timid at first. "I had Spanish with her and I thought she was always really cool—kinda like you, actually."

"What?"

"She…she didn't care about fitting in. She just did what she wanted. That's what all her friends are like." Logan added, "You don't care about fitting in. You do what you want and that's what she did. She was nice, but…she did her own tune. She didn't… conform like so many others do."

"Like you," I noted.

"Sheldon," Corrigan reprimanded.

"No," Logan said quickly. "It's true. I conformed. I still am conforming. I get it, that's why…that's why you didn't like me for so long, right?"

I smiled tightly.

"That's why you still don't like me," Logan commented, wryly. "I think…at first I thought that I needed to be a bitch for you to like me, but that's not true…is it? I just…I have to be me, don't I? That's what all three of you guys do. You guys are just…you blow off anyone who stands in your way of that."

Katrice frowned.

I spoke up, "I wasn't trying to be mean just now."

"I know," Logan nodded. "It hurt because it was true, but... not many can get through high school without conforming. You're either...I'm not popular enough and I don't have the words or the snappy comeback and...I don't have...I care what people think of me."

"So did Leisha," I said. "She cared, but...I think she was just starting to not care. She was a 'good girl.'"

"She wouldn't have been for long if she'd been our friend," Corrigan laughed.

"No," Bryce spoke up. "I think she would've. I think she would've done what she wanted and liked who she wanted and blushed about lying to teachers."

Katrice frowned a bit more.

"She never apologized for it," I murmured as I looked at no one. "She skipped, but she was thrilled by it. I don't remember the last time that I skipped and I was excited by it. She was just refreshing because she was..."

"Not us," Bryce followed my train of thought.

"Yeah."

"I didn't know her, but I wish that I would've." Logan raised her toast and I saw a tear had fallen down her cheek. Another followed and she said gravely, "I wish that I would've known what you knew and that I could've looked at her through your eyes."

Corrigan smiled softly and chinked his glass against hers. They shared another smile and took a drink.

Katrice sniffled. We looked over and she reared back to try to hide her face with a hand. "Oh, don't look at me."

Corrigan laughed and stood next to his mother. He wrapped an embracing arm around her shoulders and lifted his glass, "To Leisha, who wasn't anything like us, but, hell, we got two people to cry because of her."

It was an awful toast, but I couldn't help chuckling anyways.

"A toast," Corrigan said further and all of us lifted our glasses. We toasted my friend and the different memory she'd leave us with.

After a second and third glass, Katrice was beet red and she was giggling nonstop. She excused herself after many reassurances to drive safe when we left for the vigil.

Bryce only had one glass of wine so he promised to drive safe and sober.

It brought a blush to Mrs. Raimler and she held a hand to his cheek. She gushed about how adorable he was until Mr. Raimler walked through the door. With a quick gasp and a quick squeeze to her son's hand, Mrs. Raimler was off and embracing her husband after a long hard day at work. Mr. Raimler was silent until he expelled a resigned mutter about wine and all of us broke into a grin below.

Corrigan rolled his eyes and shot a glare towards Bryce, "If you ever say a word about what just happened—you and I are not going to wake up in the hospital at the same time."

Bryce grinned and stood up. He dangled his keys and remarked, "Let's go. The thing is going to start soon."

Bryce drove. I rode shotgun and the two lovebirds sat in the back.

Corrigan mused, "What is a vigil? Technically?"

"It's a state of observance and prayer," Logan answered him softly.

"So why can't they just say that we're going to get together and pray for her?" Corrigan asked. "That's stupid. It's like making up a name for another name of what we're actually doing."

Bryce and I were quiet, but Logan had the answer. She said calmly, quietly, "There's a lot of opinions about what we're supposed to specifically believe in. I think it's just a way to make everyone happy by stamping a vague description on it."

"But that's..." Corrigan started. "That's stupid. If people are praying then that means they're all praying to their god, right? And yet, it's called a candlelight vigil?"

"There's a lot of specifics about a general concept," Bryce noted. "People want to have a say about those specifics because—"

I finished for him, "Because in the end, we have no say whatsoever."

"We die, we die," Corrigan put it simply. "We go where we're supposed to go."

Bryce tipped the rearview mirror so he could meet Corrigan's eyes. He murmured, "You want to think of Stephen going somewhere that you're not? What about your mom?"

Corrigan shrugged again. "I won't care. I'll be dead or they'll be dead. They'll be happier than me because I guarantee, if anyone's going to heaven, it'll be them before me."

Immorality and immortality. I wondered about the relationship between the two or if there was one.

"She's happy," I murmured, to myself, but the car heard. "That's all I care about right now. If there's a heaven or whatever—I'm sure she's there and I'm sure that she's happy."

"Yeah."

Corrigan had heard too. He added, "She's dead. She might've died an awful—"

He choked off abruptly.

Logan frowned and glanced over.

"She died because of me." I said softly.

"No," Corrigan said first.

Logan frowned.

Bryce shook his head and said roughly, "Shut up, Sheldon."

The car turned another corner and it wasn't until we'd covered a mile before I asked, chilled, "Do you think he's going to be there?"

"Shut up, Sheldon!" Bryce cried out. "I don't want to talk about it. I don't...this night is about your friend and that's it."

"This isn't about you," I cried back.

Logan and Corrigan didn't move.

"Yes, it is!" Bryce snapped. "Yes, it is and I'm done with it. I'm done with this loser who's just a coward. I'm done with it. We're going to this damned vigil and we're not talking about that psycho."

An uneasy chill settled over the car.

Corrigan broke it as he commented, "I don't think you're supposed to say 'damned vigil' together. That's like...what's the word? A dichotomy or something?"

A relieved giggle broke from Logan that was quickly covered up.

Bryce shook his head and sighed, "Shut up, man, just...shut up."

I said softly, "For the record, I wanted to talk about it and you didn't."

Bryce sighed another ragged breath and uncurled his clenched fingers from the steering wheel. "Can we...not right now?"

"Fine." I fell back against my seat.

"Fine."

Corrigan sighed dramatically in the backseat and groaned, "I think today has been the longest day in the history of my life. It won't end!"

Bryce fell silent and resumed his driving duties.

I sighed and folded my arms across my chest.

I heard Logan lean and whisper in Corrigan's ears. He laughed softly and said, "No, it's not like that."

The rest of the drive wasn't long and it took five more minutes before we arrived. The parking lot was overflowing at Holy Mount Church and Tabernacle. Even at night, the college's campus was a serene portrait. The sidewalks were bricked with burnt red and dusty rose colored tablets that matched the building's bricked fortresses.

It seemed the entire school's population had shown up for the candlelight vigil.

Inside the tabernacle, candles were placed along the aisles and at the end of each row of chairs. The stage was masked in thick blood-red robes, roses of every color, and candles.

Bryce grabbed my hand and led us to the narthex where we could sit above the rest. Corrigan and Logan followed close behind and Bryce snuck us into a back corner where little attention was spared in our direction.

As we sat, Bryce released my hand and I looked at him. He refused to meet my eyes so I slowly slid my hand down his arm and entwined our fingers.

Bryce held limp, glanced at me, saw the quiet yearning, and tightened his hold over mine.

"Whoa—how many candles do you think are on there?" Corrigan leaned over our chairs.

Bryce shrugged.

"It seems like a thousand," I remarked, not really giving it thought.

Corrigan nudged my shoulder and nodded behind me.

I turned and saw Officer Sheila in the doorway with her partner. She nodded in greeting, but didn't move our way. Instead, Sheila gestured downstairs and I turned to see my mother framed in a white chiffon coat with Luther cloaked in a textured black suit. They looked like they stepped from a magazine cover and I even saw some glitter in my mother's hair. They stood off to the side of the stage and I saw, horrified, that my mother was smiling graciously at Becky with a comforting hand to her shoulder.

"What the hell is my mother doing here?" I gasped through gritted teeth.

Corrigan and Bryce wisely kept quiet.

I stood up and started away, but Bryce hauled me back down with a firm tug.

"Stay," he said simply.

"My mother—"

"Is probably doing what my mother is doing." He nodded in an opposite corner and there stood AnnaBelle Scout with her hair primped and tied with a bow. Savannah glowed in a golden princess dress as she stood in the circle of her mother's arms. Luca was nowhere to be found.

Just then, as the thought occurred, Luca tapped his brother on the shoulder from behind. No one spoke, but everyone stood up and shifted down a seat so Luca could sit where Bryce had vacated.

Luca shook his head, grim, and muttered, "Mom's showing off again. I swear, every soccer mom or soccer-mom-wanna-be had to show up here tonight. It's turned into the 'thing' to be at."

Corrigan chuckled. "Man, my mom's so out of the loop."

I whipped around and said bluntly, "You have a good mom."

Corrigan raised an eyebrow and said, "I know."

Bryce lightly punched his brother's shoulder and Luca grinned, ducked his head, and murmured, "Mom's on the warpath for you so you better take off as soon as this thing is over."

I remembered Bryce's words from before and thought that Luca was a 'chill' fourteen year old.

"That's why my mom's here. She's entering the social circle again." I sighed as my fate resumed its old stance. I'd gotten a vacation with my parents gone, but now with the house hunting and the new boyfriend—mom was home to stay. I wondered if there'd be barbeques with the neighbors.

The vigil started as the lights dimmed and a hush settled over the crowd. I'd been right. The entire student population had shown up, complete with their parents and siblings and all their little friends.

And all for little Leisha, who a mere handful actually knew. And those who remembered her were even less than that.

A few touching words were shared by Becky and Mandy, the organizers of the event. They introduced Leisha's parents and her little brother who were seated in the front row, as if part of the show. They sniffled, hugged each other for support, and nodded their thanks to the two 'popular' girls who hadn't known Leisha existed until she was dead.

"Let's go," I said abruptly. "I don't want to be here. These people didn't even know her."

Luca shrugged and said, "Doesn't mean they can't pray for her or her family. It's just support."

Bryce stayed in his seat. So did Corrigan. And I shoved up and started down the aisle.

"Hey," Bryce whispered sharply.

"I'm just—," I turned back and gestured, helplessly, outside the doors. "I'm going to go out there. I won't be far."

I didn't wait for a nod of permission. I shoved my way through the crowd and stopped short at the surreal emptiness of the lounge that lay just beyond four opened doors. In the corner, tucked away behind the coat-racks, couches, chairs, and coffee tables was a girl with spiked hair. She looked like a peacock.

I remembered and approached her. Her head was downcast, studying her lap, and she seemed to shrink in size as I sat in a chair next to her.

She looked up after a moment and I saw the same injustice that raged inside of me. She had startling blue eyes, but she looked away again.

"You can just leave," she bit out.

"You were friends with Leisha. I remember seeing you at her table once."

She whipped up and snarled, "It was my table and Leisha *is* my friend…she's just gone right now."

"Don't tell me your name is Cassandra Bens." I remembered that Carlos had had a thing for her.

"God, no!" She blinked, startled, and in disgust. "I'm Bailey, Leisha's best friend."

"I'm—"

"I know who you are," she said quickly. "Leisha worshiped you."

"I know," I said faintly.

I caught movement at the doorway and looked up to see Bryce standing in the doorway. He met my gaze and turned to lean against the doorframe as he watched the vigil inside.

Bailey looked over too and shook her head, "He's really gorgeous, isn't he?"

"He's an ass." I smiled faintly.

"Yeah." Bailey laughed dryly. "Only you can say that because he's yours."

I frowned, but didn't correct her. "I liked Leisha," I said instead.

"I know. Me too," Bailey whispered hoarsely.

"I'm really sorry."

"Why? Leisha was the one who went to the party. She was the one who walked down the block."

I frowned and asked, sharply, "What?"

Bailey looked up. Blank.

"What do you mean—she walked down the block?"

"She was at my house that night. Carlos called her and she wanted to go. He said that you invited her. I live two blocks from Evans' house. He's a dipshit."

"I thought—I thought she was walking in the park because that was the straightest way from her house."

"Hell, no. Leisha's not stupid. She would never have walked in that park alone. Someone who's high might go there at night or if they want to get murdered and raped."

I was stunned. And speechless.

"I told her not to go. I thought it was stupid. She liked Carlos so much. I thought she was stupid for liking you too and I really thought she was stupid when she skipped with you and Mr. Gorgeous." Bailey shook her head as a haunted grin flitted over her features, "Leisha was so stupid sometimes, but…she said that you weren't what everyone said you were. I guess she was right after all."

"I liked her," I said again, faintly.

"I can't stand this mockery. I bet a third of those people in there are actually feeling sad. The rest, they're just there so everyone will see them there. I hate it. Leisha wouldn't have cared and that's so sad. She wouldn't care that they're just using her. She'd say something moronic like 'at least they're praying for a good cause.'" Bailey broke off and laughed bitterly. A few tears streaked down her face and she wiped them away.

"I gotta go," she said abruptly and sped down the stairs.
I didn't move. Bryce came and sat in her vacated seat.
He leaned back and neither of us said a word.
We sat and stared at nothing.

Chapter 22

Bryce and I left as the last prayer started. We wanted to beat the crowd and after Bryce dipped inside to tell Corrigan the plan, neither of us said a word when he came back with Luca in tow.

The three of us trailed to Bryce's car and Luca sat in the back. Silently, Bryce drove to his house. He didn't look my way, but disappeared inside with Luca for a moment. Bryce came back out with a bag slung over his shoulder and he reversed the car out of his driveway.

My house was doused in black while Mena's was white with movement, music, and dancing lights. They were having a party. It was surreal considering what we'd just left.

I walked around the garage for a better view. Bryce rounded the garage and stood beside me. He watched for a moment and murmured, "Those people seem pretty glitzy."

"Yeah. I don't think Mena's parents are there."

"Big bro is having a party." Bryce nodded with no reaction and moved around to the back door.

He knelt, found the hidden key, and unlocked the house.

It was a little startling how ingrained Bryce had become with my life.

.Once inside, I said, "You can't leave."

He stiffened and slowly put his bag on the ground before he turned to me. "We're not going to hash that out right now."

"Why not? This is as good a time as any. No one's here. And you're already pissed at me."

"Pissed," Bryce bit out. "That's what I am? That's why I held your hand and sat next to you at that prayer thing? That's why I'm here right now?"

"No." I was blind as I spewed out, "You lo—"

I stopped as the words choked in my throat. My eyes went round and I blanched as I took in the furious keenness that had overtaken my best friend as he heard me and heard the words stop. He stepped closer.

He asked softly, lethal, "What were you going to say?"

I readied myself. A fight was brewing.

Bryce finished it as a gentle fury swirled in him, "I love you. That's what you were going to say."

I looked away and started to walk, but Bryce gripped my arm and whipped me back. "You don't walk from this. You started it. We're going to finish it."

"I—" I started, but my doorbell rang and the words shriveled and died.

Bryce cursed and I shoved past him to walk the entire household's length to the front door.

I glanced through the living room windows and gulped as I saw who stood there.

Bryce still waited in the back doorway, so I moved around and opened the front door.

Denton stood and I saw the movie star that caused everyone to pant. He wore a crisp white buttoned-down shirt over a pair of just-as-crisp black leather pants.

Denton grimaced and laughed as he saw my perusal.

"Sorry. It's my get-up for the..." He waved in the direction of his home. "It's the crowd that I'm entertaining over there. The Hollywood crowd doesn't do jeans and tee shirts."

I leaned against the door and remarked, "I recall Mena wearing a shocking leather outfit today."

"Yeah," Denton rolled his eyes and rubbed a hand over his jaw.

"She…she's been a bit out of hand lately. I think she got it from Kari."

"So what are you celebrating tonight?" Let's swap evening stories. I've just been to a vigil for my murdered friend.

Denton seemed to choose his words carefully, but he said, "I'm trying to make it up to Kari for our argument last night."

"Yeah." I raised my eyebrows and taunted, "How's that going?"

Denton smiled softly, seductively, and stepped closer. "Mena told me about your friend. I'm sorry. I saw your car pull in and wanted to offer my condolences." He reached out and trailed a finger down my arm to my hand and threaded our fingers together.

I didn't move, but I just watched.

I felt Bryce move around the corner. No sound. No reaction. Nothing, but I just felt him. I looked over my shoulder and stared into his cold eyes.

Denton didn't notice him right away and murmured, "I was wondering if I could offer my condolences right now? Maybe in a bed this time?"

Bryce jerked awake and strode to us.

Denton looked up, startled, and was quickly pushed out the door. Bryce slammed the door shut and locked it.

He stood and breathed. His chest jerked up and down with each raging breath and then he hauled me against him and slammed his mouth down on mine. He ground into me and I whimpered once as pain and lust slammed full force into me.

I literally crawled up him and wrapped my legs around him.

Bryce clamped his hands around my legs and pawed where I knew bruises would appear within the hour. He turned and slammed me into the wall as he reached up and ripped my shirt into pieces. Different pieces hung off me. One wrapped around my wrist. Another hung from my naked waist. And one strand was still wrapped around my neck as it hung down my back.

Bryce took my weight as he walked up the stairs and to my

room. He threw me on the bed and pinned me down with his body as he unzipped my pants and flung them off.

I screamed in my throat from the force and anger that rolled off him, but I also screamed because I felt it and needed it. I needed him in that moment.

Bryce scooped me up and flipped me on my stomach. I heard a condom rip open and a second later, after he spread my legs wide, Bryce shoved inside of me. I felt him gasp just above my ear as his chest rubbed against my back.

I whimpered as I pressed my face into the blankets. I'd never felt anything like this before.

He shoved deeper and I felt myself stretch to take the full length. One hand held my arms pinned above my head. The other snuck underneath my body and grasped my breast. He rolled the hardened nipple in his fingers as I panted. I bucked underneath him, needing more. Bryce let my arms free as he moved to wrap my legs around his waist and he pistoned into me.

I twisted my neck, in search for him, and Bryce found me with his lips. He demanded entry and I gave it, gladly. After a short battle of the tongues, Bryce let go, clamped one hand to the bed's headboard and another at my hip. He held me still as he levered himself up and down over me.

I could only lay there, gasping, as the onslaught of pleasure crashed over me.

The thrusts increased in tempo and both of us were gasping for release as Bryce exploded over me.

I was just behind and my body quivered as he fell onto me with his full weight.

Neither of us moved. We laid there and focused on getting our breath back.

Finally, I asked, hoarse, "Was that supposed to be punishment?"

Bryce sighed wearily and rolled off of me. He moved on his back and threw a blanket over both of us.

I propped myself up, on an elbow, and asked as I stared at him, "What was that?"

"You came."

"Bryce," I snapped and overpowered him this time. I straddled him and glared. "What was that?"

He laughed bitterly, "The epitome of a dysfunctional and unhealthy relationship?"

"Are you smug about this?" I asked, incredulous.

"What do you want, Sheldon?" Bryce shoved me off. "I love you. You're about to say it and that movie star slut shows up."

"What do you want from me?" I snapped and shouted. I scrambled to my feet and flung a sheet over my naked body, but I stood and I demanded an answer. "What do you want from me?"

Bryce watched me intently from the bed. "What do you think?" he shouted back.

"I don't know," I grated out. "I don't know…okay? I want you, but…"

"But what?" Bryce scrambled to his feet now. He towered over me and I felt his body heat radiate off his skin.

"I…how can I want to—all the girls, Bryce! All the girls that you just screw."

"I don't screw 'em!" he cried back, frustrated. "I just…I don't push 'em away and why should I? It's not as if I have a relationship to push them away for. I'm not going to hand over my balls just to feel the breeze in a different way."

I choked in outrage.

Bryce said further, "I have told you. Others have told you. You know how I feel, Sheldon, and you don't do a goddamn thing. Are you that deluded?"

"You're leaving!" I shouted. "You're leaving me for professional soccer."

"No." Bryce shook his head, fierce. "You didn't find that out until today. That doesn't count. Stop playing games!"

"I'm not!" I got in his face.

"That's all you do!" He got in mine.

"My god—" I laughed, darkly, and shook my head as I stepped back. "I can't believe this. We just…you just screwed me, literally, and we're trying to tear each other apart. This isn't…this isn't right."

Bryce sucked in his breath and retreated. He raked his hands through his Mohawk and sat on the edge of the bed as the sheets covered his slim hips. Even there, even with the hatefully-charged words and recriminations, even with all of that—I wanted him. I wanted him deep and I wanted him forever.

"What do you want from me?" I asked, softly, and my voice echoed in the screaming wake.

Bryce drew a ragged breath in and said quietly, "Maybe the question is what you want from me?" He pinned me with his eyes and added, "I love you. I'm here. We'll have sex until the house falls down…what do you want, Sheldon? You don't want me gone. Is it—can you just not be vulnerable? Is it the trust thing? I've seen you naked in a shower. I've seen you pretty goddamn vulnerable."

"That's not vulnerable," I said faintly, surprised at my words.

"Yes, it is." Bryce stood up again and advanced on me. "I know you inside and out, Sheldon. I just…I want you to say it, once. I want you to finally break down your pride and admit that you need me. I know you do. Not Corrigan. Not even your parents. You need me and I need you. And I need you to just tell me, once."

"I want you."

"That's not what I want and you know it. Stop the games!" he retorted swiftly.

Backed into a corner, I snarled back, "Stop it!"

Bryce caught my hands and pinned them above me. He leaned close and whispered against my skin, "Just say it, Sheldon." He kissed underneath my ear and I gasped.

I arched into him and whispered, brokenly, "That's not fair."

"Yes, it is. I'll take anything I can get at this point," Bryce whispered back and his fingers slid around one of my legs. He raised me up to wrap around him and I felt him push against me. I melted inside and grasped at his shoulders. I fought to draw him closer and I fought to keep him away.

"This isn't—," I gasped as his mouth moved to my breast. "This isn't fair."

"Is this the only thing that you'll let yourself feel?" Bryce whispered against my skin and he thrust inside.

"No," I whispered as I wrapped my other leg around him and rose up against the wall.

"What else will you feel? What else can I get?"

"If I say it now, it's not fair." I kissed his jaw, his neck, his lips.

"I don't care anymore," Bryce whispered as he thrust again.

"Bryce."

"I love you," he panted against my lips.

"I—" I broke off as he thrust again.

"Say it!" Bryce demanded as he thrust again.

I snapped. I swiftly arched my back and shoved him away at the same time. It wouldn't happen—not like that.

Bryce fell on the bed, startled by the swiftness and strength, but I quickly straddled him. As he fought for entrance, I clamped my hips around his and held myself above him. Bryce could've overpowered me. He could've closed the distance and it would've been met with an excited scream, but he didn't.

Bryce stayed in my arms and he gazed at me as I waited for him to see what was in my eyes.

He stopped as he saw it. His breath left him in that exact moment. And I took it in. I let the warmth fill my lungs as I bent and softly met his lips, tenderly. I kissed him, a loving kiss, and I whispered against the corner of his lips, "I love you."

He lay suspended in my hold and the fight had left him.

Bryce blinked in shock until my words sunk inside.

I realized that he'd never expected it. He had asked, fought, and demanded—but he'd never expected it.

"I—," he started, but I kissed him and stopped the words. I moved farther up his chest and looked down.

The wall fell down and I let him see me.

"I love you," I sighed.

Bryce shifted and slid my hips down to meet his. He went inside and I gasped. My eyes closed as did his and we felt each other for the first time in four years of being intimate.

Afterwards Bryce curled me against his chest as we laid still, sweating, and panting from what had happened. He ran a soothing hand up the side of my arm to my shoulder and back down again.

In the darkness, I asked, "So what now?"

Bryce tucked his head into the crook of my neck and shoulder. He breathed in my scent and tightened his hold around me. His voice was muffled as he replied, "I don't know."

I heard the exhaustion and felt its answering pull inside of me.

"Just…no more Denton Steele," Bryce remarked.

"No more girls fawning over you."

"Deal."

"Deal."

Bryce chuckled and swiftly tucked me underneath him. He tucked a strand of hair behind my ear and cradled my cheek. His thumb rubbed sensuously, comforting, against my skin. I nearly purred as I moved closer and sought his touch.

"So what?" he asked and flashed a blinding smile.

"What?"

"Are you my…girlfriend?"

My eyes widened as panic robbed my breath. This was what I'd been afraid of—this unyielding fear. I twisted away from him and hurriedly dressed.

"What—." Bryce cursed and leapt for the door just as I turned towards it.

He got there first and twisted between me and my exit.

"Stop it," Bryce snapped and pushed me back. He held firm in front of the door. "We were just—you told me that you love me and now you're going to run?"

"That's all I can do!" I cried out, feeling the panic build up with each second, each breath, and each word.

Bryce quieted. He listened.

"It's all...I can't do anymore. I can't—I can't do conversations about us, not yet."

"Okay."

And I was left dazed at the abrupt softening of his voice.

Bryce jerkily nodded and said again, "Okay. I can do that."

The panic subsided and I warily dropped onto the bed.

Bryce still stood, naked, in the darkness and he came to stand in front of me. I met his glittering eyes in the moonlight and closed my eyes as his fingers found the side of my face and tilted me upwards. Gently, he pushed me back down and lay beside me, on his side. He laid an arm over me and kissed me.

Slowly, exquisitely, we explored each other as we kissed.

I broke away and said quickly, "You tell Corrigan, but he can't label us. Okay?"

"Okay." And Bryce quieted me again.

Chapter 23

"My dad's leaving my mom," Bryce broke the quiet.

I twisted and looked at him from underneath the sheets.

Bryce quickly wrapped an arm around me and pulled me against him. "I didn't want to deal with it so that's why I never said anything about it. It's why I'm going pro next year. My mom wants me to take care of the family. She says that we can't trust my dad for money. It's my turn to man up and take care of stuff."

We still heard sounds from Denton's party.

"I really hate that guy," Bryce said quietly against my shoulder. "And I really don't like his sister."

"I'm sorry about your family," I murmured softly and pressed a kiss underneath his jaw. He was so strong, in more than the obvious ways. I felt humbled, but I wasn't about to admit that. "And you don't have to worry about Mena anymore. Neither of those two are going to be visiting me anytime soon."

Bryce sat up beside me and draped a loose arm over my waist. He told me, "She's…she's not right. She doesn't have a base, I guess. I don't know. I just know…she reminds me of my mom sometimes."

That screamed of silence.

"It took my mom a long time before she could walk out of the house alone after my dad first left. Mena reminds me of my mom."

"You never talk about your mom like that," I murmured.

"I never talk about my mom," Bryce said grimly. "Period."

I grinned softly and reached for him. He came willingly and our lips met.

I gasped and shoved him away. "We didn't use protection that last time."

"I thought you were doing the shot."

"Oh." I'd forgotten and slumped back down, relieved. "Thank god."

Bryce ducked his head and grinned against my neck. His hand explored downwards and my breath caught as he poked and whispered, "I liked feeling you naked."

I laughed, "And that statement is the epitome of our dysfunctional and unhealthy relationship."

Bryce grinned, but whispered fiercely as his fingers found my core, "Shut up."

I did better. I shut him up instead.

And in the morning, my legs ached in ways that had me wondering how worse I would've felt if I'd run a marathon. It was still dark out, but the clock read 6:30 and I could *still* hear sounds from Denton's party.

Bryce flipped onto his stomach and wrapped an arm around my waist. He scooped me closer in his sleep and nuzzled my neck.

It tickled and brought a smile to my face. I sighed softly and turned to watch him. I saw the vulnerable little boy in his face as he slept. He was softer, without the knowledge that consciousness brought to him and hardened the wall that he resurrected.

I had a wall and my wall was thicker. But I'd told him twice more during the night that I loved him. Once as we made love and the second as he fell asleep. He hadn't heard the second time, but it's why I'd whispered it again. The words were foreign to my tongue and they slid off easier each time I said them.

I slipped from the bed and Bryce found me in the shower.

We didn't leave the room until another hour, but it was a refreshing morning that I knew would be remembered no matter what the future brought.

I needed that morning.

We skipped breakfast and Bryce paid for coffee on the way to school.

As we parked and sipped, Bryce grimaced and brought his hand up from the driver's door.

He smiled tightly and dangled two pairs of handcuffs from his fingers.

Steam rose from the cup in his other hand.

"Oh goody," I said dryly as I sipped my coffee. Neither of us made a move for the doors. We were content to sit with comfortable silence and steaming coffee.

Someone pounded on the back of Bryce's car and Bryce and I both turned to look. Anyone else would've jumped, cursed, spilled coffee, but not us. Years of training for iron restraint kept us cool, calm, and with the bored expressions on our features.

Corrigan hurled into the backseat and threw an arm around each seat as he leaned forward.

"So," he exclaimed, enthusiastic and beaming. "How are we?"

Bryce took a sip of coffee. So did I. And nothing was said.

Corrigan danced his eyes between us, watched, studied, and a slow smile spread over his face, "Oh man. Thank god!"

The barest hint of a smile ghosted over Bryce, but it was gone as I drawled, "Thank god for what? That we didn't kill each other?"

"Nah, man." Corrigan smirked, "Thank god that we remembered the handcuffs. I thought I might've lost our pair under my bed last night."

"Logan doesn't strike me as the handcuff type," I remarked.

"Oh," Corrigan was smug. "You haven't met the real Logan, yet."

"I'm okay with not knowing that Logan."

Corrigan was about to retort as I saw a police cruiser turn into the parking lot. I bolted upright and asked, "What are the police doing here?"

"I thought they were still following you," Corrigan replied.

"Yeah, but...those guys park across the street. These guys—look." I pointed. "They're right here."

Two police cars stopped just outside the parking lot doors of the school. Another two vehicles parked behind them and I watched as Officer Sheila climbed out of the driver's seat of one of them. She looked wary, but refreshed with her hair up in a high ponytail and a crisp trench coat tied around her waist.

"What...?" I murmured to myself as I climbed outside.

I was across the parking lot before I knew it and asked Officer Sheila, "What's going on?"

A frown flashed over her features and she held a hand up, "Sheldon, you should go back to your vehicle. Stay there."

"No. What's going on?"

Bryce and Corrigan had gotten out of the car and now approached us.

"Sheldon, go back to your vehicle. Make sure your friends are with you—they were with you last night, right?"

I frowned. "Bryce was. We left Corrigan at the vigil and went to my house."

She relaxed, slightly, which said something. A person can't normally read a cop.

I felt Bryce at my elbow and Corrigan rounded to stand beside me and Officer Patterson. Both guys were quiet when I asked again, "What's going on?"

Sheila frowned and nodded to two of the detectives that were waiting at the door for her. She made a gesture for them to go inside when her partner, Office Milon, appeared beside her elbow.

Firmness settled over her when she asked, "Did you know Bailey Umbridge?"

Bailey... "Crazy hair?" I asked.

Sheila nodded.

"Yeah. I talked to her last night at the vigil. She was friends with Leisha."

"What did you two talk about?"

"She just…I don't know. We talked about how fake people were and she…she told me that Leisha wouldn't have walked through the park at night. Leisha had been at her house when Carlos called her. Bailey lived two blocks from Harris'."

"Did you notice anyone? Did anyone watch you guys talking? Anyone that you remembered?"

"Just Bryce. He came and—he was in the doorway. That's all."

"No one else? Anything strike you as odd last night? Like a sense that you were being watched?"

I saw the intense scrutiny in her eyes and I knew she was watching me for a reason. When it clicked and I knew what she was asking, I felt the old numbness creep back inside. Its tentacles reached deep, deeper than before, and it grabbed hold of my organs and tightened its grasp.

Paralyzed, I murmured, "What are you talking about?"

Something flickered in her eyes and Sheila said quietly, "I think you know exactly what I'm talking about."

"He was there, wasn't he?" I whispered, hoarse. "He was there and he saw me talking to Bailey, didn't he?"

She didn't need to say a thing. Her eyes did the talking for her.

"What—" I gasped. "Is she…is she inside?" Dead.

Understanding dawned in Bryce and he shifted closer to me. His chest lightly grazed my side, but he didn't take a hold of my arm or hand. He just stood there.

"Do you remember anyone from last night, Sheldon?"

"I thought I had police protection," I said faintly.

"You do and they were outside, like they were ordered. They aren't one-on-one detail protection. They're on basic watch so they wouldn't have been inside. If you want one-on-one detail, I can arrange that. My men would be your personal bodyguards."

"She's got us," Corrigan spoke up.

"Sheldon…do you remember anyone?"

"No." I shook my head. "I just...I liked her. Bailey. I remember liking her, she was...she was cool."

"Well, she's dead now." Officer Milon clipped out, harshly. He raked his eyes over me, piercing me. His balding spot seemed to have grown, but it might've been the wind that flapped his hair around.

Bryce and Corrigan both tensed and shifted closer on either side of me.

"Back off," Sheila rasped sharply. "We're not accusing her of anything."

They stayed put.

I asked, my eyes flat, "Where was she found?"

Sheila hesitated and Officer Milon barked the answer, "She was found in the girls' locker room. That's what the report said, but we haven't gone inside yet."

"Who found her?"

"Another student. He came early to clean this morning."

"Who?" Corrigan frowned.

"You'd like that, wouldn't you?" Officer Milon's claws had been sharpened. He'd come to fight and he was thrilled to watch as Corrigan riled at his bait. "I know who you are, kid. You've been arrested for car theft, assault, vandalism. You're a nice tight little delinquent that's going to end up in prison one of these times."

Corrigan nearly growled, but he restrained himself, just barely.

"Hank," Sheila said sharply. "Let's go."

"I'm telling you, Sheila. It's this guy." Officer Milon stared at Corrigan, salivating. "What I would do to take you down right here and now."

Corrigan controlled himself and asked tightly, "Who's the kid that found her?"

"No," Sheila bit out. "That's official police matter. You won't be getting the name to shake him down. He's in police protection now."

The morning crowd had started to draw closer and multiply. More and more students, unable to enter school from the other entrances, all wandered and were attracted to the growing throng of gawkers. Just then, Principal Gregory pushed through the crowd and found our little group that had been moved off to the side.

"Officers," Principal Gregory nodded, grave. "Let's have our meeting."

Sheila clipped out a brisk nod, found my eyes once, and left with a final glare from her partner to Corrigan. They disappeared inside the doors that were now been marked off with yellow tape.

Corrigan snarled, "What I wouldn't do to…I want to know who found her. We should find out if there was another note for Sheldon."

Chet, Holster, and Harris all gestured for us as they stood in their group near the back of the lawn. We moved farther around the corner and I saw Braven, Carlos, Becky Lew, Mandy Justice, and anyone else who might've been deemed 'popular' crowded together in a tight pact.

In that moment, I saw that two social classes had separated. Our crowd stood around the corner. And the other crowd, the Grace Bartons, the Teddys, and the Menas now stood in the other large crowd. They congregated in the parking lot, just beyond the barricaded doors.

The gap had widened between the two groups and as we crossed it, I felt a chill down my back. It took hold and wrapped its slimy, wet, and frozen hand around my spine.

Chet gestured to the farthest corner of the school's campus. A side door that led into the school's theater opened. Two uniformed police officers walked outside and Marcus Donadeli walked behind with another two uniforms bringing up the rear. They approached a police cruiser as one opened the backdoor and held a hand to Marcus' head. He ducked inside and a uniform slid in beside him. The door was closed and two uniforms sat in the front while the last cop went to get into another police cruiser. Both cars pulled away from the curb and drove around the corner.

Evan remarked, somber, "It's all over school. Some chick got her number last night."

Corrigan was still watching Donadeli when he mused, "Wanna bet that's the kid that found her?"

Bryce frowned.

I stayed quiet.

"What are you talking about?" Holster asked just as Tatum approached the group.

"They said that a kid found her this morning. Some kid who cleaned here."

"Yeah, that'd make sense. That's the Donadeli kid, right? Doesn't he have, like, eight jobs or something?"

Corrigan lit up and exclaimed, "Sheldon, you can get the info from him. The kid's in love with you."

I shook my head, numb, and took an instinctual step backwards. "I don't want to have anything to do with it."

I moved back again and walked into Bryce. He slid an arm around my waist and anchored me to him.

Corrigan nodded as he searched my face. And he dropped it, just like that.

Becky broke the slight silence and murmured, "I think school's out for the week."

Carlos nodded and remarked, "They'll probably do a community curfew."

"Two students murdered and the last one was found in the school," Mandy noted. "I think they have good reason."

Chantal sidled next to Bryce and slid a finger down his arm.

Bryce's arm tightened around me and he shifted, just slightly, so that Chantal needed to step back unless she wanted to be in my face instead. It was subtle, but it spoke volumes. Chantal registered the movement and masked her irritation quickly, but everyone else seemed to be oblivious.

Another lull settled over our group when I looked up and realized that their eyes were on us, on Bryce, myself, and Corrigan.

In that moment, I remembered with a chill what the second note had read.

Queen of Geneva disregarded her lowly subjects. To the grave they went and more to come.

In that moment, I realized—more than at any other time—I held the crown and reigned with Bryce and Corrigan at my elbow.

Mandy spoke up, and it took a moment before I realized that she addressed me, "So what now?"

"What?" I bristled, irritated at the sudden proclamation of my power. I felt the full force in that moment and I knew that I didn't want it. I didn't want any of it. I wanted Bryce. I wanted Corrigan. And I wanted to be left alone.

That's all I wanted.

And I wanted Leisha's murderer to fry.

Bryce spoke up for me, "If no one's told us what to do, we should all just leave. Go to the Diner or something."

"Or go and get drunk," Corrigan commented, no joke.

"That too." Bryce faintly grinned at him.

Evans spoke up, "Ya'll can come over to my place. My parents aren't getting back from their trip until tomorrow. We could have one more todo dia festival."

Becky grinned ruefully, "Two girls are dead and we're going to party?"

"Do you really care? You didn't even know them," Harris threw back at her.

Becky shrugged, uncomfortable, as she glanced over her shoulder to Carlos, their hands had been entwined, but they broke free at that moment.

What the hell?

"Yeah, well, we care," Corrigan said sharply. "So show some respect."

Harris straightened abruptly and fell silent. He looked away.

Becky sobered instantly.

"But…" Corrigan heaved a sigh. "Bryce is right. There's nothing that we can do and it's not like we're going to have school. I'm not going to some mandatory peace talk and listen to the sheriff talk about buddy systems."

Chet asked, "So what?"

"I don't know. Go to the Diner." Corrigan shrugged and pulled me from Bryce. He started walking back towards the parking lot and Bryce followed.

It was an odd moment and an odd feeling.

As we crossed the separation again, I noticed that too many watched as we left. Pensive, desperation, hysteria, somber, and bitterness filled so many of their eyes as they watched us walk across and get into Bryce's car.

I'd never noticed the apparent social isolation before, not during a crowded hallway as students buzzed from locker to locker, but in that moment…I saw it all too clear and I realized what had been invisible became visible. And another chill upon so many slammed over me. The social hierarchy may have reared its ugly head to create a deadly monster.

Chapter 24

Everyone else was told to go to the Diner, but our crew went to my home. We hadn't been there long when the doorbell rang. I waited, my breath suspended, but I wasn't sure why. I hadn't had much luck with people coming over to my home lately.

Sighing, I opened the door, grateful as the rest stayed in the kitchen when I found myself face to face with Officer Sheila. She was alone, no hatred-spewing partner.

"Hi," I said tightly as Sheila nodded, gravely.

"Can we talk?" she asked.

I nodded and shut the door behind as I moved outside.

Sheila lounged on the porch railing as I sat in one of the wicker chairs. "Quite a morning, huh?"

I just waited. She was here for a reason and I knew it.

Sheila took a deep breath and told me, flat, "He left another note for you. This time, we got it first without your friends' prints all over it."

I readied myself.

Sheila added, promptly, "And it's got your boy's prints on it."

"My boy? I have a lot of boys."

"Not the boyfriend. The sidekick."

I laughed and shook my head, "Corrigan would never call himself a sidekick. You're lucky he didn't hear you or you'd probably come home to a trashed garage or something."

"He gets like that, huh? He's got a temper?"

I bared my teeth, "You know he does because of his history. Yes,

Corrigan can do some stupid crap, but there's no way you're going to tell me that he's the psycho stalker."

"Funny," Sheila remarked, emotionless. "I never said that at all. You did."

"It was implied and I'm not hearing any more of it."

"What if he is?" she pressed, heartless. "What if your boy in there is the monster who's killed two girls? Miss Summers was raped. Miss Umbridge was not. Maybe your boy had already been appeased. He's got his fair share of girls, doesn't he? Makes you wonder—why Leisha Summers? Why rape her and not her friend?"

"Corrigan couldn't have done anything that night. He was with Bryce."

"Are you sure? They left the party, didn't they? Are you sure Corrigan was with his buddy the entire time? He could've disappeared for a few moments. It doesn't take long to bash a girl in, move her body, and rape her." She paused. "And he wasn't with you last night."

"He was with Logan, his girlfriend."

"Was he? He didn't arrive with her this morning, did he?"

The arrow found its target. And I had had enough as I lashed back, "You've got two girls that are dead now, three notes, and you've got nothing if you're going after my friend. Some loser did this who wants to think they're high and mighty. Even I can get that and I'm not especially smart about this cold blooded—"

"I think you're incredibly smart and I think you know exactly what kind of person would do something like this. I've been questioning students. You've got the rep for being cold blooded and it makes me wonder—the three of you are real tight. You're sleeping with Scout. Maybe Raimler wants in on that action. Maybe you want him in on that action. Maybe this whole thing was a set-up and all three of you are in on it? Are you?"

"For your information," I said quietly, lethal. "If I wanted to sleep with Corrigan, I would've by now. I'm sure you also got that information from your 'questioning.' I do what I want and when I want. I don't exactly bend to rules. And I will tell you for the last time, Corrigan had nothing to do with this and none of us are in on this sick perverse game."

"But you are quite sick and perverse, aren't you?" Sheila raided my space. "You taunt other students. You taunt teachers. You skip whenever you want. You screw your boyfriend while you're screwing your neighbor. Tell me this, ever done a threesome? How about with your top dogs in there? They're both good looking. The best 'specimens' in school, as one girl told me. A girl with your morals, I'd be surprised if you hadn't."

The wall slammed back in place and I moved away, with ice in my veins and coldness shining from my eyes, "You can think all you want."

"I'm the police, honey. I can make your life hell."

"You have no right and no reason."

"I've got a note with your buddy's prints and I've got the subject that the note's addressed to protecting said suspect. I've got enough for a good solid theory."

Bait. Throw the line. Wait. And let the fish get caught before reeling them in. It's how I played the game and I'd just played hers. Enough was enough and I asked, "The notes addressed to me? I'd like to see it. It's mine, isn't it?"

"It's evidence and therefore ours, but I made a copy for you."

"Can I have it?"

Her hands were empty.

"I don't have it here. If you want it, you gotta come to the station to get it." Sheila smiled brightly and falsely. "Have a good day, Sheldon."

"You switched roles? Thought maybe you'd try your hand at being the 'bad' cop instead of the 'good' cop?" I taunted.

Sheila sighed abruptly and threw back, impatient, "No, Sheldon! This isn't a goddamn game. This is real and more girls are going to die. You were friends with both of them and all four notes are addressed to you. This bastard is obsessed with you and those two guys in there are in love with you. Maybe one of them is platonic, but what if he's not? I find it pretty suspect that a girl like you, who looks like you, and screws like you would make it easy for a guy to purely feel 'friendly-only' with you. I'm a cop, Sheldon. I see the lowest of the low and people can be like that."

I held firm and taunted, coldly, "What a compliment. A girl that 'looks like you, screws like you.' If that isn't painting it pretty, then I don't know what is."

Sheila snorted shrewdly, "Please. You might've deserved to have some parenting, but you've gone past where you should be. You should be a nice little girl who goes to school, worries about getting good grades, and holds hand with her nice popular boyfriend. That's not you and some pretty rotten things must've happened to put you were you are."

"I'm already in therapy. Thanks, though, Officer Patterson," I dismissed and stood up. "I'll tell Corrigan the next time we're having a threesome that maybe he should let up on his psychotic ways."

"If you want the note, come to the station."

"And subject myself to another round of harassment? Sure. Put me down for this afternoon...that's if I'm not flat on my back."

Sheila grinned and shook her head. "I can see why you're called cold blooded, but if this is you running from a stalker, I almost feel for the bastard when he goes against you."

I quirked an eyebrow.

Sheila concluded, a metaphoric hat in hand, "You think well when you're pushed. That's good, Sheldon. Very very good and that's what's going to keep you alive, because he's not going to expect it. Look, between you and me, I don't think it's your boy in there. If it was, he wouldn't be going how he is to scare you. He'd do it worse and I don't want to think that sick. But this stalker, he's trying to scare you. And I'm thinking the more you scare, the madder you are, and the more ruthless you'll get. That's what you need to survive this nightmare, Sheldon."

"Is that why you said those things today?" I asked, tensely, cautious.

"I needed to know. I needed to push you first and see what you weren't going to say. I read it and I'll back off—for now."

She left after that and I took a moment to cool down. I found the guys playing video games in the media room. Logan was curled with a blanket on the couch. They all watched me as I moved downstairs, but when I didn't say anything, neither did they. They went back to playing video games until Corrigan's phone started ringing. The first call was Chet. The second was Holster. The third was Harris. By the fourth and fifth, Bryce exclaimed, "Good god—what do they want?"

Corrigan glanced at me before he said, "They want to know what to do."

"Maybe we should have a party," I offered, thinking it wasn't the worst idea. At their blank looks, I added, "Seriously. What would it hurt anymore? The freak wants us scared. I say screw it and we should just have fun. Hell, let's do it here."

"Lew? Hunstville? Those guys invited?" Corrigan asked instead. "You know that Carlos is screwing Lew, right? That's the dude that your friend was into."

Maybe I was self-destructive because I replied, "I think we should invite everyone in our class. Teddy. The Bartons. Even Mena. Let's hash out who this loser is tonight, here, while everyone's here. And, trust me, I'll deal with Carlos later."

Bryce straightened.

Corrigan flashed a smile, "Seriously? We could make a game out of it. Like Mafia or Clue or something. Who's the Killer?" He turned to Logan, who'd been quiet the entire time, "How about it, honey? Are you up for a game of Who's the Killer?"

"I think...maybe I shouldn't say what I think," Logan said wisely and looked at me. "Sheldon's the one who's offering her home up. I, for one, will feel safer at my home."

"That's the problem. Girls who are alone are his prey. I say we shouldn't be alone," I argued.

Logan drew herself upright, thought about it, and nodded reluctantly, "Okay. I'm staying with you at all times, Corrigan."

Corrigan bounced to her couch and draped an arm around her shoulders, "Honey, we're not going to be mingling. We're going to be in a guest bedroom—all night long."

"Fine. As long as it's locked," she said tensely and burrowed into his shelter.

"Sweet." Corrigan withdrew abruptly and said, "I'm going to start passing the word." He was up and out the door, leaving a bereft girlfriend.

Bryce ignored Logan's presence and sighed, "This is stupid."

"I know," I said simply. "I'm tired and I'm not waiting anymore. If he's as obsessed as we think, he'll be here tonight. I'm going to hunt him tonight."

"He's crazy and illogical. You can't outwit a person like that. He's going to know the real reason for this party."

"No. No, he won't." I hadn't gotten the fourth note. He wouldn't know that I knew of it. "He won't know at all because he doesn't know me."

Logan sighed and curled back into a ball, blanket pulled over her head.

I stood up and climbed the stairs to my bedroom. I wasn't surprised when Bryce followed and shut the door behind him. He leaned against it and crossed his arms over his chest, "So is this what you're going to do?"

"Bryce." I hung my head. Exhausted.

"No. What'd that cop say to you? This came from left field."

"Why do you care?" I nearly whispered as I lay down and curled underneath the blankets.

"I care because this guy is psycho and he's obsessed with you. I love you. I'm not going to stand back and let you hand yourself over to him," Bryce said fiercely.

I smiled, softly, "You think that's what I'm doing? And it feels nice—to hear you say it."

He stopped abruptly and softened, "I heard you last night, you know. You thought I was falling asleep."

I grimaced, slightly, but rolled onto my stomach and burrowed my head under the pillow.

"Hiding's not going to erase what you said," Bryce said quietly and I heard the lock click into place. A moment later the bed dipped underneath his weight and Bryce moved on top of me, but he held most of his weight from me. He tucked his chin into the crook of my shoulder and kissed my cheek, "This is my favorite position."

"Shut up," I laughed.

He leaned over me and got in my face. "What'd that cop say?"

He had me trapped, pinned between his two arms, so I surrendered and confessed, "He left another note for me."

"Oh." A moment later, "What'd it say?"

"I have to go to the police station to get it." I pushed him off and sat up again. "And she said a lot of crap about how it's Corrigan because his prints were on the note. That's all."

"That's all!?" Bryce followed me into the bathroom, incredulous. "That's a lot."

"She just wanted to mess with my head. It's not Corrigan—" I stopped at the look on his face. "Right? It's not Corrigan."

Bryce blinked.

"Bryce!"

"Sorry." He snapped back to attention. "No, of course, it's not Corrigan. But...the thought has some merit. I mean...Corrigan must've touched that note somehow. So...someone would have to follow him around, pick up a blank piece of paper that he had touched and that's all it would take."

"That could be anyone."

"Corrigan doesn't go to classes, so that narrows the search. And he didn't take notes when we were handcuffed. So…what else has he touched lately?"

"He doodled in Mr. Hankins class today, but that was it," I murmured.

"So who's in Mr. Hankins' class?"

"I don't know." I sighed, washed my hands, and moved back to the bedroom. "This is useless. The cops can figure that out, but I want to know who comes to the party and who doesn't."

Something in my voice caught at Bryce's attention. He stopped and commented, "What?—you don't think he's coming, do you?"

"No." I rolled my eyes. "I think he'll come, but I think he'll skulk around outside. It's what he must've done at Harris' party. Leisha had to walk two blocks so I think he caught her outside. He was probably just watching the party."

"I think…you got a new alarm system, right? Did they install video at all?"

"What? Yeah, I ordered a new system the next day, but I didn't ask anything about video." That was creepy.

"Maybe we should install video output in a few hidden spots?" Bryce suggested. "And not tell anyone and I mean *anyone*, not even Corrigan."

"We have to tell Corrigan."

"No, we don't. Besides, he won't get mad. He'd understand."

"Why? Because some secrets are worth keeping?" I heard my own words, caught the flash of emotion on his face, and asked abruptly, "What? What secrets do you guys have from me?"

"Secrets that are for your own good." Bryce clipped out and shut his mouth.

A fist pounded at our door and Corrigan shouted, "Put on some clothes and get out here. We have a party to plan."

I threw open the door.

Corrigan looked disappointed to see us fully clothed, but he said, "Everyone knows. I passed the message to be here at nine tonight and ready to party. Everyone's bringing their own booze, but we gotta supply the food, music, and everything else."

Bryce said quickly, "Sheldon, go with Corrigan and Logan. Get the food and everything else. I'll work on that other thing."

Corrigan frowned, but shrugged.

"Fine," I murmured and led the way as Corrigan followed behind, excited. He threw an arm over my shoulder and murmured in my ear, "For the record, thanks for going to bat for me today. You know, against that cop."

I stopped, frozen, in the hallway and asked, "What are you talking about?"

"About those things she was saying, about me being the stalker guy."

"How do you know about that?"

A knot formed…

Logan waited for us at the door…

Corrigan shrugged, "I came up for something to drink after all of us went downstairs. You were out there and we thought we'd give you some privacy, you know—" He sent a furtive glance in his girlfriend's direction. "—you don't like everyone to know your business, but…it's hard not to overhear when you were almost shouting and I was just on the other side."

"I don't understand. The door was closed." And the walls were nearly soundproof.

"Yeah, but…the window was open, Sheldon." Corrigan told me and my world spun about in that moment.

"I reset the alarm this morning. It would've gone off if a window was open."

Corrigan froze and I realized that my own window hadn't sounded the alarm. Numb, I announced, "My alarm system doesn't work."

Jaded

Bryce came to the stairwell at that moment and our eyes met as I looked up.

Chapter 25

Bryce firmly volunteered to order a third alarm system and watch while the guy installed it. Corrigan and I were sent out for chips and dip while Logan went home to change and pack a bag. She figured she'd be spending the night and Corrigan told her that she was correct, but not to expect much sleep.

We had already gone to the grocery store and were in route to Donadeli's when Corrigan brought it up, "So…you and Bryce are together, huh?"

I looked at him and he shrugged, "He told me. He said that I couldn't label you anything, but…you guys are together now?"

"Guess so."

He nodded. "That's good. That's really good."

I grinned, "So you're not hoping for a threesome?"

Corrigan cracked a smile and shook his head, "Nah, but I give that lady cop her props. She had to say it and she had to say it to you. Me, it would've just rolled off me, but you—she needed to know what you thought about a buddy that might a hold a torch."

"So do you?" I held my breath, but my eyes didn't move an inch.

"Do I love you or do I hold a torch?"

"Are they different?"

"They are," Corrigan relinquished. "You're the only girl in my life that'll always be in my life. Yes, I love you. If I held a torch— you've always been Bryce's. I knew that from seventh grade."

"You haven't answered my question."

Corrigan started to speak, held his breath, and then said, "Let me put it this way, if there was no Bryce? What then?"

I got his point. "Okay." I nodded.

Corrigan changed the subject when he asked, "So tonight is a snipe hunt?"

I laughed, "Snipe don't exist. This psycho does."

"He needs to die. No one messes with the Queen and gets away with it."

"Don't call me that," I said quickly, startled.

"It's what he's thinking," Corrigan remarked. "If you're going to find him, you need to think like he does. He thinks you're some Queen and everyone else is a lowly subject."

"You guys aren't. He's gone after Leisha and Bailey. If he's going after people who I love, he'd have gone after you guys. He doesn't consider you guys lowly subjects."

"I'm anything other than lowly," Corrigan cracked a joke. Smug.

"Corrigan."

"Shutting up."

As we walked into Donadeli's, Marcus flushed brightly behind the hosting table. Corrigan nudged me and whispered, "He found the body. See if you can find out more about it."

"No," I hissed. "I told you."

"Come on. There was a note, right? Maybe he saw it. Maybe he read it." He flashed a smile, "Hi, Marcus!"

The kid tensed immediately, but he replied back, terse, "Raimler."

"I'm going to go sit...and wait for my drink."

"I'll put your orders in," Marcus mumbled automatically.

"No, no," Corrigan stopped him, charmingly. "Stand. Talk to Sheldon. We can wait. We're in no hurry."

I snorted in disbelief, but I murmured, quietly, "Hi, Marcus,"

He flushed again and fidgeted, "How are you, Sheldon?"

"I'm okay." I shrugged. "As good as can be with some loser killing people, you know."

"Yeah..."

"How are you? Everyone's saying that you're the one who found Bailey Umbridge this morning."

He gulped and looked away, but his fidgeting worsened.

I took pity, "I'm sorry. I didn't mean to upset you or anything."

This was such a rarity for me. For some reason, I took pity on the social defect. I have no idea why…

He looked back up, surprised and cautious, but I gestured towards Corrigan, "I'm throwing a party at my place tonight. We were wondering—I was wondering if we could order three Party Packs and get them delivered to my place?"

"Uh…sure." He blushed again and busied himself with the cashier. "Do you, um, do you want anything else?"

"I think Corrigan wants to actually eat here. I'll pay for the Party Packs now and Corrigan's order with two pops."

He rang the total and stammered, with another blush, "I can get you a free order of breadsticks, if you'd like…?"

"Sure. Thanks, Marcus." I smiled kindly and moved to our table.

Corrigan lifted an eyebrow and I shook my head. "He didn't want to talk about it. I can sympathize."

Marcus brought over the drinks quickly, along with the breadsticks, and Corrigan flashed a smile. "Thanks, man."

Marcus stood, uncertain what to do, but Corrigan had already hunched over his food and drink.

"Thanks, again," I murmured and Corrigan swiveled in his chair as the social defect left.

"What?" I asked.

"What? Are we nice now?"

"I kinda feel bad for him. He works eight jobs. He puts up with our abuse and he found someone dead…I feel for him."

Corrigan snorted and dramatically checked his forehead, "Am I sick? Or are you sick? Or…is this what the new Sheldon's going to be like?"

"New Sheldon?" But I didn't want to know.

"Yeah. The one in touch with her feelings, saying things like 'I love you.'"

Abruptly, I announced, "Bryce is leaving."

"What? No, he's not."

"Yes, he is. His parents are divorcing so he's skipping college and going straight to the pros. He has to support his mom and family, I guess."

"What?" Corrigan froze in his chair.

"Yeah."

"I mean...where? When?"

"He's not playing soccer anymore. They don't want him to play and get hurt before their trainers can work with him. I don't know where he's going, but he's leaving."

"That...that sucks!" Corrigan bit out and shoved back his chair. "Come on!"

Bryce and Corrigan rarely fought, in fact—I've never seen them fight, but as I saw the fury in Corrigan's clenched jaw, felt my own fury—I knew a fight was brewing.

Marcus was left in our trail as the door shut behind our heels. He stood with Corrigan's food in his hands when we hurried through the parking lot. Corrigan reversed the car and ate up the road until he turned into my driveway. Two vans were parked with a security company logo painted across and I figured Bryce had ordered a new alarm system. None of that mattered to Corrigan as he stormed inside, located Bryce, and threw the first punch. Bryce immediately recovered and rolled before he hit the ground and jarred his shoulder. He cast a glance to me, saw a mirroring anger, and immediately said, "Okay. You know."

Corrigan grunted and threw another punch.

Bryce dodged this one, swiveled underneath his arm, and grabbed him in a headlock.

"Get off me!" Corrigan ducked his shoulder and threw Bryce across the room.

The guys all scattered out of the way. The security men stood cautious and I was even further annoyed when I saw that Becky

Lew had already arrived. Mandy stood just behind her, but everyone was captivated by their two kings going at it.

"You're such a coward," Corrigan spat out.

"I'm a coward?" Bryce called back in disbelief. "Because I'm taking care of my family? Because I'm leaving you guys and sacrificing…"

Corrigan punched again, but Bryce evaded and rolled on his heels. He waited.

Corrigan taunted, "You're scared and you're heeling to your mother. Yeah—that's a coward to me."

Anger flared in Bryce and Corrigan knew he'd overstepped the boundaries—at least in public. It was a different matter in private, but Corrigan knew to never call Bryce and myself 'scared' or a 'coward' in public.

Corrigan choked off, glanced at me, but Bryce caught him with his first punch.

After that—no words were shared, just punches.

"Are you going to stop this?" Becky asked me. Mandy nodded, "They're trashing your house."

I shrugged, "Not the first time that's happened." Why would I want to keep that pleasure from someone else?

Becky rolled her eyes and griped, "That's just like you. Your two best friends are going at it, and the only person who could stop it, just stands back and watches. Do you have any feelings at all?"

Mandy sucked in her breath, but remained silent.

I swiveled on my heel to face her squarely and asked, eyebrows arched, "Excuse me?"

"You heard me," she clipped out, but some of her bravery had dissipated.

"Say it again," I taunted. Ready.

"I…I don't know why everyone worships you so much. I get it with Corrigan and Bryce. They're hot and funny and…loyal, apparently, but god—you're so cold to everyone."

"They're family. We're all family," I retorted as Bryce slammed Corrigan against the wall.

"That's just…of course, you'd say that," Becky bit out, hands on hips.

I shifted to my hip and asked, "Where's your lover boy? You know, the one that's only screwing you because he's got some serious guilt over Leisha's death. That's pretty pathetic, you know. *You're* pretty pathetic. The guy's messed up with guilt."

"He only called her because of you. Carlos didn't like Leisha, but he thought that you liked her so he was going to try. Can you believe that? A guy will date a girl if he thinks that's what you want. I just can't get over it. Do you have some magical spell that you just weave over these morons?"

And the two biggest morons had just splintered my coffee table.

A sudden thought came to mind and I checked to see where the booze was. I calmed a little when I saw it was safe so I turned back to Becky, "Is this what this really is? Jealousy? How lame can you get?"

Mandy sighed and murmured, "They're going to break your flat screen."

I glanced back so I didn't see Becky's hand slap across me.

Stunned, I looked back and saw she had balled her hands into fists and was one breath away from pouncing on me.

For the most part, girl fights were lame. The hair was pulled, a few slaps with open palms, and hateful insults were always cursed.

Mandy caught the delight in my face and stepped back, "Oh god."

The guys sucked in their breaths, a collective gasp, and my hand curled into a fist as I let loose with a roundhouse.

Becky fell back, stunned, and I shifted to the back of my heels.

I could like this, I could like this a lot.

From the floor, Becky looked up, stunned, and with a hand to her jaw before she rushed me.

I easily dodged, caught her hair, and slammed her to the floor.

The guys were delighted, but I was ready for her to swipe at my feet, which she did.

I jumped out of the way and warned her, "You don't win against me, ever. You're not going to win this one either."

"I am so sick and tired of you—" I saw the open palm coming and nearly rolled my eyes at the tortoise speed, but I caught it and twisted her arm behind her back.

"What are you so tired of? That I don't care while all you do is care? Maybe you should stop caring so much and just be yourself, Lew. You might find life a lot easier." I think it was her cry of pain as I twisted her arm again that caught Bryce and Corrigan's attention. Bryce had a hand to Corrigan's shirt, but both stopped, looked over, and immediately surged my way.

Bryce lifted me free while Corrigan swooped to keep Becky in place.

I didn't even fight Bryce's arm as it circled my waist and lifted me off my feet. I just laughed at Becky and said, "That was fun."

"Shut up," she snarled around from Corrigan.

"I'd like you a lot more if you were just honest."

"I am being honest. I hate you," she spewed back.

"See," I grinned. "I kinda like you now." Bryce had started to carry me upstairs, "I think this fight was good for us."

I caught a few amused grins from the guys, but Mandy just looked resigned to what was coming next.

Bryce locked my bedroom door behind us and set me on my feet. And I knew that meant the real fight was about to start. I backed up, hands in the air, and started, "Look, Corrigan is your best friend and he deserved to know. What do you expect? I'm not going to talk to my best friend when the guy I love is leaving me—"

Bryce slammed his mouth against mine, picked me up, and then slammed me on the bed with him on top.

I eagerly wound my legs around him and hung on.

Chapter 26

The party was in full swing by the time we emerged.

Holster greeted us, grinning like a mad man and a beer in each hand. "That was awesome!"

I chuckled and took a drink.

"We should have parties here all the time."

Evans came over and threw an arm around my shoulder, "Man, I can't ever beat that pre-party warm-up. Not only one fight, but a girl fight too! You already made this party. It could be lame for the rest of the night and it's still going down in history."

Chet materialized from the crowd and informed us, "Corrigan finished the alarm system stuff. It's all turned off for the night, since, you know—closed doors don't go with parties."

Tatum pushed his way through the crowd and said, "Corrigan's downstairs with his girl. Lew took off, but she'll probably show up with her boy and Locke."

"They dare to crash my party?" I laughed.

"Apparently anything goes with your parties," Tatum laughed.

Evans added, still grinning, "This party rules."

"And some losers showed up. We kept them outside," Holster spoke up.

"I want them to come," I murmured, suddenly somber. "I want them all."

"As long as they're not that psycho killer, right?" Tatum laughed and scanned the crowd. At our grave silence, he looked back, saw my face and sighed, "Oh no."

"Don't get drunk then," Chet murmured and handed his full bottle to someone passing behind him.

"Don't get drunk at all," Bryce said instead and the rest of the guys grimaced, but handed their beer away.

"Seriously? That's what this party is for?"

The doorbell rang and someone exclaimed, "Food's here!" The Party Packs were taken out of Marcus' hands and brought inside where they were immediately attacked. I'd already paid, but I grabbed a five dollar bill and pushed my way to Marcus' side. "Here you go."

He took his tip and smiled faintly, "You really *are* having a party, huh?"

I nodded and glanced around. "You already missed the excitement. There were two fights."

"I can imagine." He smiled faintly and blushed. "Thanks."

"You can stay, if you'd like," I offered.

His eyes narrowed as he searched my face. Slowly, he shook his head and said, "No, I'm okay. I'll be safer if I head home."

"Okay, but really…you can come back if you want."

"Okay." He nodded. "Thank you."

"Yeah."

I turned around before I saw the door close behind him. I didn't have to push my way through the crowd as I walked downstairs and found Corrigan nuzzling Logan's neck in a back corner. His hand was underneath her skirt as he straightened, lazily, and smiled with lust in his eyes.

He was already drunk.

"What, are you stupid?" I cried out and snatched his beer from his other hand.

Logan melted against him and wrapped her arms around him. She nibbled on his neck and I saw that she was drunk too.

"What?" He frowned slightly, but both his hands started to work their way up and Logan's skirt lifted, completely showing her thong to anyone who might've been watching—which was plenty.

"You're drunk and you know what this party is for tonight," I hissed.

"So? I'm sure you and Bryce got it covered." He turned his head and started nuzzling Logan's neck again.

"Oh my god," I snapped and hauled him off his chair.

Logan sat, dazed, and blinked at the open air.

I hauled Corrigan into a back room and shut the door. "Are you demented? Is that what this is?"

"What are you talking about?" He suddenly looked sober.

I sucked in my breath and asked, "Was that acting? Is that your plan? I don't need you drunk and getting it on with Logan at every chance. We're not hunting snipe tonight."

"What's the plan even? Just walk around and inspect every loser? See if they pull out a knife or something? We don't know who or what we're looking for—and I'm betting you money that the police are across the street, watching everything. You are under protection, right?"

"This is why this guy is going to come tonight. He can get close to me without the police seeing him coming. He's coming tonight and I'm going to be ready for him. I'm tired of finding more people dead or getting notes. I'm tired of it all."

"Sheldon," Corrigan sighed and sat down on the bed. "This isn't right. I mean—you threw me for a loop with Bryce leaving, I'm not exactly all clear-headed right now."

"Because you're drinking."

He cried out, "I'm not drinking! I'm just looking like I am. The guy's not stupid, whoever he is. He's going to know something's up when he comes and everyone's surprisingly sober!"

"Logan is drunk."

"So? Logan can drink. She's not a part of this."

"You want your girlfriend to be inebriated when some killer shows up, looking for an easy target?" I spat out. "That's who I'd go for if I was him. She's close to our circle and she'll be vulnerable.

And probably passed out by the time he gets here—where she'll be alone because you'll be hanging out with me, waiting for him to show up."

Corrigan hissed and shook his head, "You're a little too good at this game, Sheldon."

"It's not a game. It's my life and it's others' lives. I'm tired of this guy pushing me around. I'm pushing back now."

"…he's trying to scare you and I'm thinking the more you scare, the madder you are, and the more ruthless you'll get. That's what you need to survive this nightmare, Sheldon."

I remembered Officer Sheila's words and felt nothing.

"I'm ready for him," I only said and left the room.

Tatum stopped me just as I walked out of the room and informed me as he glanced at Corrigan, "Yerling just showed up with his buddies. They're outside. Chet and Holster won't let them inside."

"Where's Bryce?" Corrigan asked.

Tatum shrugged, "I don't know. I thought he was down here with you guys."

I found him upstairs in a back room, in my dad's office.

"What are you doing in here?"

Bryce didn't turn around, but opened some cupboards and exposed four video screens.

"What are those?"

"Video output. I wanted it installed because your last alarm system was useless."

"Why? I mean…" Okay. I got why. I just didn't…the why didn't help keep the shivers away. Huskily, I murmured, "Bryce, I don't like video cameras."

"Don't worry. There's nothing that'll break privacy or anything. I just had the guys install them on your doors, like—here's the front doorway, there's the back doorway, here's the other door, and…" He studied the screen closer and asked, "Is that Yerling?"

I moved closer and peered at the screen to add, "And look— Mena's come to join them."

"If her brother shows up…" Bryce let the threat hang open.

"It wouldn't be at my invitation. Trust me. Unless he's the stalker, then he can come."

Bryce grinned and asked, ruefully, "Did you just hear yourself?" I shrugged.

Bryce chuckled and switched the screens for the last doorway. It was rarely used and it led into the garage from the street. In fact, I normally leaned tables against it from inside the garage, but I gasped as it came onto the screen. The door had been left open and I saw that no tables blocked it anymore.

"What?" Bryce looked at me.

"It's never open. I…tables were there, the lawnmower's in there—that door isn't used because we *can't* use it."

"Would you have mowed the lawn today?"

It only took one incredulous look for Bryce to realize the moronic value of his question.

"Just saying…" he finished haplessly, but he refocused. "I don't get it. Anyone can walk in here through the front door, why use that door?"

"Like someone who doesn't want to be seen here?" I suggested, rolling my eyes.

"So…oh hell," Bryce swore. "The guy's already inside…what now?"

"What if…the guy is coming for me, right? I mean…why don't we stay put and have him come to us? We can monitor these screens then and sees who comes in and who goes outside."

"Yeah, but…" Of course. There was always a *but*. "If Yerling starts something, I'm going to have to go down there. I don't want to leave you alone."

"Maybe he won't." And we didn't live on Mars so I don't even know why I uttered those words. I flushed and remarked, "Sorry, wishful thinking."

"That's okay," Bryce soothed and ran a hand down my arm and around my waist. He scooped me on his lap and sat on a chair.

Corrigan said disgustedly, "You guys are just rabbits."

We'd left the door unlocked and I turned to see Logan, who stood rooted in the doorway, as Corrigan moved around us and studied the video screens intently. Logan shut the door behind her as I rested against Bryce and turned my head towards Corrigan.

"Not that I mind, normally," Corrigan relented with a rakish grin. "But tonight is for other things."

I asked, "What are you doing up here?"

"Crowd control," Corrigan remarked and glanced our way. "Your place is overflowing now. What do you want to do?"

"The cops are going to get called pretty soon," Logan piped up with a flush.

I guessed where that flush came from and rested my chin on Bryce's shoulder as I mused, "You have sex with Corrigan and yet—you're too prim and proper to realize other people do it?"

"It's not that…"

"Then what is it?"

"I've just…never…watched…" She blushed with each word.

"It makes you hot, doesn't it?" I flashed a knowing grin.

"Leave her alone, Sheldon," Corrigan suddenly said. "We have more important things to deal with."

"Right," I sighed and stood off of Bryce's lap. "Like how you're not my psycho stalker."

"Right," Corrigan grunted and watched the screens again.

Bryce stood behind me and asked, "What do we do about the cops?"

"They're already here," I pointed out. "They're parked across the street. If they were going to break it up, wouldn't they have done it by now?"

"Maybe. Maybe not. They might just be waiting."

"For what?"

"For someone to scream so they can rush in and actually get a shot at this guy?" Corrigan mused. "We're doing their work for them. They're not going to break this up, not while we might actually draw this loser in."

"Corrigan," Logan suddenly spoke up. "I want to go home."

"No!" Corrigan rounded on her. "That's what this guy wants. He wants people to be alone."

"I want to go home. Now. I don't want to be here. My parents are home. So is my little sister. I want to go home."

"Where you're safe and tucked in bed?" I asked.

"Yes," Logan said honestly. "For whatever reason, you guys think this guy is obsessed with you. Call me crazy, but I don't exactly want to be standing next to you when he shows up."

Corrigan stiffened.

I wasn't surprised.

And Bryce was…quiet. He knew, just as I did, what her words actually meant to Corrigan.

"I'm not leaving my best friend," Corrigan said softly. "You can go if you want, but you have to get your own ride home."

"Corrigan…"

"I'm not leaving Sheldon's side," he said swiftly and pointedly turned his back.

Logan gaped and realized, for the first time, what target her words hit. She gaped again, but slowly, stiffly, found her way out the door. It wasn't long before we saw her on the screen leave through the front door with a friend behind her.

Bryce moved away and I heard the door lock. He slumped onto the couch and kicked his feet on the table as he remarked, "Someone's going to end up in the hospital tonight."

"Or dead." Corrigan turned to him.

"Maybe the party wasn't such a good idea," I mused and sat on the far end of Bryce's couch.

He rolled his head towards me and smiled faintly. It didn't reach his eyes.

"I'm sorry about Logan," I murmured to Corrigan.

He sighed, but remarked, "It's too soon, you know. We hadn't really been together long enough…"

"Still…sorry."

Corrigan smirked and remarked, "There aren't many girls who'll let you put handcuffs on them."

The old Corrigan still sparked.

I saw Bryce open his mouth and swiftly raised a finger, "No!"

He closed it and slumped back on the couch.

Corrigan snickered, "You had to try, though, right?"

Bryce grinned and I knew the two were fine. They just needed to throw a few punches before all was fine and dandy.

Corrigan glanced at the screens and remarked, "Too bad you didn't put any videos in the rooms. We'd get some great porn right now."

My insides cringed, but I teased, "Already resorting to porn, Corrigan? She just left."

Bryce suddenly shot up from the couch and strode towards the computer keyboard that manually controlled the video output.

"What are you doing?" I asked and moved behind him.

"The guys were…just before I got punched the tech guy was telling me that it was weird because there was already a feed going on in the house. I didn't think about until…"

"They didn't say anything," Corrigan spoke up. "I told them just to fix the video where you told them and not worry about it."

"Yeah, but," Bryce frowned. His fingers went to work on the keyboard.

I asked, "What are you doing?"

"Are you a geek?" Corrigan asked.

Bryce rolled his eyes. "Luca has a thing for this stuff. Playing one on one with him—he tends to ramble about this stuff. I've picked up some of it after shooting hoops with my brother for years."

I arched an eyebrow. "That's a nice skill to suddenly come in handy right now."

"Shut up," Bryce snapped.

I grinned.

"Seriously." Corrigan shifted closer. "What are you doing?"

"The other feed is bothering me. It could've been the other alarm system. They didn't remove it. I told them just to use the old wires, because they were already there, but...what if..."

He hit a last button and my eyes filled in horror.

Bryce finished, numbly, "What if...an alarm system wasn't installed the last time..."

My insides hurled as I saw images of myself on the computer screens. In the shower. On the couch. In bed, sleeping...and...my eyes fixed on the bottom screen where Bryce pistoned into me. We were both grasping the bed in desperation and instead of the remembered passion from that night, disgust rolled over me in waves.

"That's the night..."I swallowed, but forced myself to finish. "That's the night..."

Bryce finished my thought, "...of the candlelight vigil."

Chapter 27

I shot to the bathroom and emptied my stomach that had been filled with nothing. I stayed there, even after a tentative knock sounded at the door. Someone shuffled in, saw my ashen features through their drunken glaze and shuffled back out.

I held onto the toilet and rested my forehead against my arm.

I don't know how long I stayed there, but it was long enough for Bryce to have regained control over himself. Or—that's what I assumed when he entered the bathroom, silently locked the door, and curled around me. He rested his arms on both sides of me and dipped his forehead against my back.

Neither of us said a word, but the images flashed through me. I saw every single time where I had thought my home was private, where I was alone. And everytime my stomach rolled from the violation.

"Did…" my voice cracked. "Did you guys stop the feeds?"

Bryce heaved a deep breath and said, "No."

It took me another moment before I was able to formulate a rational response, but I asked, "Why not?"

"Because…" I wasn't the only one fighting for composure. Bryce trembled, just barely, but he managed out, "Corrigan called Hoodum. He's got a technical guy that might be able to follow this feed to wherever it's going."

My throat dried.

"Are you saying…this stuff could get leaked to Hoodum?" I asked.

"No. Hoodum won't do anything with it. Corrigan will make sure and Hoodum's already agreed. The guy's supposed to just follow it back to where it's transferring somewhere and that's it. He's supposed to find the address and hand it over."

"How can we be sure? Not a lot of trust going on with me."

"Because…we don't know, but we both know that Corrigan will kill Hoodum if this is leaked."

I rested my forehead on my arm and Bryce scooted closer behind me. His arms tightened and he rested his head in the crook of my shoulder. I felt him breath my neck when he murmured, "He's gonna fry. You know that."

I sighed, but it didn't help.

"He's already seen…" So much. Too much. "Can…" A worse thought came to mind. "…was there sound?"

"No," Bryce whispered in my ear.

So he didn't hear everything, not everything…

"God," I choked out again.

Bryce took a deep breath, "If…"

"Don't!" I said sharply and shoved him off. I stood up, suddenly fed up with feeling the victim. "I want to know who this guy is and I'm going to kill him before the police get here."

Bryce stood, slowly, and watched me tentatively. Cautious. He reminded me, "They *are* parked outside."

"I know." We'd just have to get around it.

I led the way back into the small room and saw Corrigan bent over the computer keyboard with another guy speedily punching the buttons. Both of them glanced up, caught our gaze, froze for a moment, and then returned to their work. I stood in front of the screens and watched. I wanted each image branded into me. I wanted to see what he'd done to me when I was going to do what I needed to do, to him.

Bryce kept his eyes on me, but he circled beside Corrigan.

Both glanced every now and then to me, but they always shifted back to the tech's heart-pounding race to trail the feed before any more damage was done.

I glanced around and spotted the remote. Lifting it up, I changed the channels. More and more images replaced the ones already there of me. They were all of me, at different times. I was just dressing in one. Another—I was putting make-up on. A third, I was just sitting on the couch, staring at nothing. And then…Bryce and I were in the shower. I was straddling Bryce. Bryce was on top of me, behind me. Sometimes we were wrapped around each other, talking, laughing, or arguing. One screen was of us fighting. No words were heard, but it was evident. It started, we fought, and then it replayed immediately so just our fight was being watched.

And still…I changed the channels again.

This time, one screen was Bryce and myself again, but Bryce reached inside my nightstand and froze. I looked puzzled and the shot repeated to the beginning where we were kissing, starting to undress, and Bryce would always reach for the condom, but freeze as his hand found the gun instead. The screen image never let the gun be shown.

And then…I must've made a sound because Bryce and Corrigan both looked over, saw my eyes riveted, and trailed to a camera that had been placed in the garage. I was pressed against the wall by Denton. The camera saw everything. Denton's jeans sagged, the thrusting, how I gasped against the quick onslaught, and then how Denton helped me finish. Just as the door closed behind him when he left, the image repeated again for us to watch the entire thing over and over again.

Bryce clenched his jaw, but turned back and snapped at the tech. to finish working.

I met Corrigan's gaze and saw sympathy in that moment. Any other time, any other person, I would've lashed at them. I didn't need anyone's sympathy, but it was Corrigan. The sympathy was replaced with a hardening and I knew Corrigan wanted to beat this guy just as much as myself and Bryce.

I left suddenly, ignored the sudden calls from Bryce and Corrigan and swept into my room.

I hurried to my nightstand, reached inside, and heaved a breath of relief as my fingers found the cold metal of the Colt.45.

Instead of leaving it, I tucked it into my pants and left again.

This time, I moved through the house and headed towards the garage.

A few of the guys tried to stop me, but I ignored them like I'd ignored Bryce and Corrigan. As I cleared the garage, Yerling, Mena, and a few other straightened abruptly at my sudden appearance.

Mena remained quiet, but Yerling smiled, smug, and threw the first taunt. "Come to beg, Sheldon?"

"Come to die, Yerling?" I threw back.

The frown was there, slightly, but it was replaced with malicious amusement and then...just wariness.

I tilted my head and mocked, cruelly, "This isn't the Yerling that promised me it'd be you and me one of these nights." I moved closer and pressed, taunting, "What happened to that brave little boy? Did he get beat up one too many times? Does he no longer have some balls? Or maybe you do, maybe you're the one who's doing all of this?" I wanted that. I wanted him right in front of me. I wanted a target, finally.

"You might want to watch it," Yerling flashed a growl, but shook his head and moved a step back.

Mena stood just at my right, so I attacked her instead, "What happened to you? It seemed like you turned crazy overnight."

Mena smiled sadly and remarked, "You know, I actually just wanted to be your friend." Mena added, not unkind, "That's all I really wanted, but...I learned my lesson. We all learned our lesson not to mess with you, Corrigan, and Bryce. You guys don't need anyone else, just each other. It's...sad, really."

Everything she said wasn't untrue.

"Bryce didn't like me from the start because I could've been the best friend. I would've taken you away from him—or I'm sure that's

what he thought. And you know what pissed me off the most—
you liked me, Sheldon. You actually did, but you listened to them
even though they were so wrong about me." She finished with a
triumphant, bittersweet, arch to her eyebrow, "And you know it."

"No," I shook my head. "You gave up. That's what you did and
then you started hanging out with this crowd. You make it sound
like we're the crowned throne that reigns over the entire student
body. It's not like that at all."

"Really?"

One of Yerling's buddies grew disgusted and snarled, "We didn't
come to hash out girlfriend issues. We came to mess up your house,
Jeneve."

He wanted fear, but he got a laugh instead.

"Seems to be the theme," I said easily. "I already trashed it. Bryce
and Corrigan had a go today. You're welcome to it."

He flashed confusion and Chad chuckled, an ugly sound. He
moved forward and remarked, "This is what she does. She plays
with your mind, laughs in your face, and then she taunts you with
her body."

I arched an eyebrow, "Really? Did I tease you? Is that why you
turned psycho too?"

"Seems to be the theme," Mena mocked me, twisting my words.

"For all your show—you're nothing, but a tease, Sheldon.
Everyone hates a tease," Chad spoke again.

He stepped forward again and I cooed, "Oh—you're getting
more confident. Now the real Chad is coming back, makes me
wonder where you went?"

"You want to know? You really want to know?" He baited me,
ruthlessly, but I didn't care.

I followed the crumbs and took the hook, "Yeah, Chad, I want to
know. It's why I asked."

"Your boys made it pretty clear that if I ever talked to you again,
I'd end up in a body cast instead of a grave."

That sounded like them.

I shrugged, "We'll find out, won't we?"

He barked out a laugh and shook his head in amazement, "I can't believe you. You're outnumbered fifteen to one and you're still flinging insults in our faces. When do you get real?"

"Are you serious? Do you think you're my big problem?" I threw back, actually enjoying this. "You're nothing. You're just a guy trying to be bigger than who you are. If you were really who you say you are—you wouldn't be crashing a high school party." I stepped back and delivered, cruelly, "How sad is that?"

Mena finally reared her head and spat out, "I think you're the sad one, Sheldon!"

"Finally!" I exclaimed with a wide smile. "I'd like to meet the real Mena, not the façade that you've shown me this whole time." I added, "I am not friends with weak people. If you want to be my friend, you have to prove you've got some spine behind you. That's who I am, Mena. I respect nothing less."

"I am not weak!" Mena cried out with tears that rolled down her face. She hiccupped, "I just...Bryce was so mean. He—,"

"—because he thinks something's wrong with you!" I shut her up. "Is something wrong with you? *Are* you fixated on me?"

The guys held their breaths and it was just me and Mena.

Mena finally broke when she bit out, "I never knew you could be so vindictive."

I rolled my eyes and stepped back, suddenly disgusted and tired of weakness.

Another group of students turned the corner at that moment and I recognized the Barton siblings, alongside Teddy and two other guys. One was Darrell—the kid that Bryce and I had threatened to keep him from ratting on Corrigan. Teddy sent me a tentative grin, but he glanced towards Tim and Grace, who were captivated with Mena in that moment.

I stepped further back. This was no longer about myself, but Mena.

"Hi, Mena," Grace said softly with a kind expression.

Mena saw it, twisted it, and sent it back snarling, "Hi, Gracey."

Grace caught the inflection of tone and knew it wasn't in warmth. She still held her head high and said calmly, not afflicted, "I was wondering how you were. You haven't returned my phone calls."

"Are you serious?" Mena laughed, caught my gaze, and stopped short.

To tell the truth—I was mystified. I watched as Grace smiled, still, and commented, "My mom really liked meeting you. She was wondering if you'd come for dinner Sunday evening?"

"Are you...demented?" Mena asked harshly.

Grace still stood before her and replied, "No. We're having spaghetti. I know, I know. It's kinda a lame meal, but I like to stir the noodles. If you come, we could watch a movie afterwards."

"And brush each other's hair?" Mena taunted.

"No," Grace said simply. "I know you think I'm a nerd."

"Mena!" A shout sounded across the yards and Mena groaned.

Denton darted across the separating lawns, frowning fiercely and he stopped just short of the crowd. Denton's gaze traveled to me, stopped short, and his jaw clenched one more time before he spat out, "We're going, Mena. Now!"

"No."

"Yes." And Denton grasped her arm, but she wrenched it away and scurried towards Yerling.

"No! Go order Kari around. I'm tired of hearing your orders," Mena said hotly.

"Mena. Now," Denton clipped out.

"No!"

"I'm tired of this. If you don't stop it, you'll—"

"What?" The younger sister cut off her older overpowering brother, defiantly. "What? You'll do what? I'll do what?"

"You'll go back," he said quietly as the fight left him. "I've done what I could, but you're spiraling out of control again. You're off your—"

"My psychotic meds?" Mena provided for him, angrily.

"Where will you go back?" I asked and pushed from the wall. A path cleared for me and Mena bit her lip as she glanced towards me. "Where were you—really?"

Denton sighed and murmured, "Mena."

"No!" She said sharply.

"Mena. Please."

She abruptly shrieked, "You didn't want me to be friends with her because she was yours! You just didn't want to share her."

An ugly taste formed in my mouth as I heard her cries as she continued, "I just wanted to be her friend, but you couldn't handle that. And, surprise surprise, when I'm not—you're over here the first chance you got. And you were back here last night. I saw you. You showed up because you're in love with her!"

Denton didn't say anything, but he looked devastated as he heard his little sister's illogical ramblings. It was almost as if his worst fear had come to life before his eyes, he'd fought so hard, and it had still happened.

"It wasn't even like that, Mena," I spoke up. "He just didn't want you...to become like me."

"I..." Denton spoke up. "You'd been fascinated with her for so long, Mena, and I knew that you wanted to be like Sheldon, but... you can't handle her life. She's tough, she's..."

I stepped closer and added, "Not who your brother wants you to become."

Denton flashed a grateful look in my direction as he said further, "I just...wanted you to be you, Mena. You have a hard time doing that. With all the therapy and meds, I was just worried that you'd cling to someone's world that wouldn't be the healthiest for you."

"I'm not sick, Denton."

"Yes, you are!" He swallowed tightly, but said again, "You *are* sick and you have to go back to the group home."

"Denton!" Mena cried out, horrified.

He'd spilled the secret. I saw the instant horror and regret that flashed in Denton, but it was already said. They were words he couldn't take back.

Bryce rounded the corner that moment and quickly found me.

Denton shifted back a step.

And Chad instantly readied for a fight.

Mena didn't see any of it. I could see that her brother's voice still sounded in her head.

And then Bryce grasped my arm and said quietly, "Let's go."

Chapter 28

Bryce yanked me behind him and we slipped through the garage, through the opened door that shouldn't have been opened. Corrigan found us that instant and called out from the other doorway I usually took into the house, "Hey, we got something."

Corrigan led the way, Bryce followed behind, and I was about to step through until I found myself blinking at Denton's face.

He hauled me back, slammed the door, and locked it tight.

Bryce and Corrigan both shouted instantly and pounded at the door.

"Denton," I said quietly.

He ignored me and called through, "I just want to talk. That's it. You can have her back in ten minutes, okay?"

The door that connected the garage to the door rattled and then the fists abruptly stopped.

"They're going to my car to get my garage-door opener," I murmured.

Denton swore and raked a hand through his movie star hairstyle.

"What is up with them? They're so protective of you."

"Mmm," I cocked an eyebrow. "Kinda like an...older brother?" Except Bryce wasn't. And Corrigan wasn't...not really.

I was going to stop thinking about that.

"Whatever. They're obsessed," Denton dismissed, irritated.

"They're being my friends," I pointed out.

"I get that Mohawk guy. Mena said that he's your boyfriend or something like that."

"He was not happy to see you last night."

"I figured that out when I was shoved out the door." Denton sighed and leaned beside me against my mom's Chrysler.

"Well…to be fair…you did interrupt something pretty intense that night," I mused with a small thrill as I remembered the rest of that night.

"Look…" And the reason for his sudden arrival was about to be announced.

I held on with no excitement, I had no room for that anymore. "What do you want?" I asked flatly.

Denton grinned and ran another hand through his hair.

"If you have a pretty gala for tonight, you're going to have to call your hairstylist again. Your hair's gone dead."

Denton grinned again, but shook his head. "I didn't come—you make it so easy to flirt and I just instinctually want to hit on you."

"Free champagne, right?" I teased and I knew a sparkle shone in my eyes. I liked being called champagne. I made a note to remind Bryce of that fact, just not who made the reference.

"No, I came because of Mena."

"Where is she?"

"She's at home. I think most of their friends took off."

Wow. They really *had* come to vandalize the house, not to kill anyone. Shocker, but not a relief.

Denton started, warily, exhausted, "I'm…the truth was that she left a group home because she turned eighteen. They thought she was good enough to come home, but I wasn't too sure about that. I made the mistake of telling her about our neighbor, about the 'free champagne' that I got that night and…Mena just grabbed that, I don't know. I don't know why. She just…I mean, you and me— that happened awhile ago, you know, but Mena idolized you for so long. She thought you were cool, sophisticated, and suave. You name anything worth aspiring for and you were it for her. She got a picture of you and that sealed the deal. She was coming home and she was going to be friends with Sheldon Jeneve."

"What's wrong with her?"

"There's nothing really wrong with her, but...she witnessed some trauma when she was younger and I think it altered who she grew up to be. Mix in some fancy neurotransmitter language and poof—the psychiatrists gave us a handy mental diagnosis for her."

"What is it?"

"Does it matter?" Denton asked, more to himself than towards me. He shook his head, saddened, "It's just a label that she got slapped with. That's all the therapists look at for them to figure her out, but...she's more than some psychological assessment that was dictated by some graduate intern."

"I think if I got my assessment done, they'd say I'm a psychopath," I remarked, dryly.

Denton laughed and shook his head, "No. You're fine. You just have trust issues."

"Is that my problem? My only problem? I thought I was just a bitch. Is that a mental disorder? They can write progress reports on me."

His laugh was genuine as he tipped his head back.

It brought a smile to my face.

"See," Denton pointed out. "This is why I want to hit on you and why I want to take you into the backseat of this car and peel down your—"

I interrupted him, before I was tempted, "I have said the sacred word. The 'l' word and I can't take that back."

Denton quieted and asked, "Is it...Brian?"

At my pointed look, he shrugged and said, "Mena's told me all about you guys. It's petty of me to pretend that I don't know his name." He sighed and straightened from the car. "Another time, without a Bryce in it, I'd have you on my arm for every gala and Hollywood party."

"That would've been fun."

"It might be. You tend to have a charisma that can't be squashed. People hate you, but they also love you."

The Queen of Geneva...

I sobered and noted, "So I'm told."

"When you and Bryce break up—call me?" Denton requested.

"It might be sooner than you think," I remarked. "Bryce is going pro-sports. He won't be around for much longer."

"Well...even though I have a hard time believing that you'd let him go without a fight, if that does happen—you have my number."

I nodded and asked, "Is she going to be okay?"

Denton sobered instantly, the flirting vanished, and he remarked, heavily, "This just means that her progress isn't as far as we'd hoped. She might have to go back to a group home and she'll need weekly counseling sessions."

"Is she...can you cure that stuff?"

"Therapy can work wonders. I think so—if the person is willing to do the work. I've witnessed some miracles with Mena so far, but...she's had a relapse that she needs to go through again. We've got some work ahead. She crumbled when she wasn't approved by your two guard-dogs, but she's convinced that you liked her."

"I did." I didn't know why. I remembered Grace and murmured, "She should let Grace Barton visit her."

Denton looked up, confused.

I shrugged and gestured outside, "That girl outside, the blonde. She's kinda loser-ish, but...she really cared about Mena. She even risked her neck and came to me a few times about Mena because she was concerned."

Denton nodded. "I'll tell Mena that you think so."

"And maybe I'll come too," I offered, though I needed to make it through the night first.

"That'd be good. Mena would like that." Denton smiled kindly.

I wrapped my hand in a circling motion and asked, "So is our talk done? Because we're going to get interrupted anytime soon."

Denton smiled dashingly as the garage opened.

Corrigan stood, smirking on the pavement, as a crowd formed behind him.

Denton Steele's name was whispered with revenue and awe and I laughed, "Oh god. I forget half the time that you're a celebrity."

The first rush of fans swarmed him, but Denton threw over his shoulder, "That's another reason why I want to..." He looked to the car's backseat, but Bryce strode to my side and plucked me off the ground. As he carried me inside, Corrigan smiled and shook his head behind us. He followed Bryce back up the stairs. We walked back into my dad's office

I saw that the television screens had now switched back to the doorways. I asked, "What happened to the other stuff?"

"We saved it all on a hard drive, but erased it on the network system," Corrigan answered me.

"What does that mean?

He shrugged and gestured towards the tech, who stood up and walked towards us, "So...what that means is that the feed, everything, originated here and was sent to an off-base account, this guy's computer. I can't cut the feed that's automatically transmitted without losing the signal all together, but I was able to erase all the data and video recorded here at ground zero. That means that he can have downloaded the same input and still have it at his place. So he can still..."

"Watch us having sex," I murmured.

"Yeah, but he won't get anything new. The signal's still transmitting, but the data is dead."

Bryce cleared his throat and told me, "When you ordered the new alarm system, they didn't install an alarm system. They installed these videos."

The tech asked as he readjusted his coveralls, "Who'd you call for this?"

I didn't want to know why a tech would wear coveralls so I shrugged, "I just opened the phone book and found someone to do it. I wasn't really thinking rational at that moment."

"Do you think it's possible that this guy ordered the break-in so that Sheldon would get freaked and get a new alarm system?"

"It is, but how do you know which system she'd pick?" Bryce mused.

"Sitting right here," I snapped, irritated. "And he'd know. He's obsessed with me enough—I'm sure that he'd know."

"You don't remember what their names were?"

I shrugged, but something pricked at my memory. Something...I murmured, "Williams Alarms? Is there a place like that?"

"When did they install it?"

"It was after the break-in, the next day. I ordered it. They came and installed it. They gave me the instructions and then I went to bed. I wasn't paying attention to them. I went downstairs until they were done. I haven't thought about it since."

"Didn't they bill you?"

"I...I gave them my credit card number. I suppose it'd be on my statement?"

The tech snapped his fingers and said swiftly, "I can do that. Give me the account number."

I did and I noticed that his name badge said Kevin. As he brought up my last statement, I murmured, "Thanks, Kevin."

He smiled a genuine smile and swung around in his chair, "Thank you, Sheldon."

Bryce frowned, glanced between us two, and moved the computer screen towards him.

"Williams, Martels, and Alarms."

"That sounds...not at all familiar," I said. "Sorry."

"How much did they charge her for?" Corrigan asked.

"$35.50"

"Are you serious?" Corrigan pushed his way to the screen. "That's the cheapest alarm company ever. The cost alone would've steered me to another company."

"Thanks, Corrigan."

"It's not your fault. You were all traumatized and stuff."

Bryce pondered, "So maybe this guy didn't work for the company, but showed up and installed all the stuff himself."

"And maybe that's even scarier. He would've needed to take her phone call and forward it to his own phone…"

Kevin pointed out, "He's got the skill to do it. He did all of this."

"Is a window open? I'm cold." I glanced around, but none of the guys looked for an open window.

Bryce caught my gaze and nodded solemnly. The goose bumps hadn't come from the outside temperature. My chills weren't circumstantial. I turned away, and then moved to the farthest couch where I curled my legs underneath me. Bryce and Corrigan sat on either side of me while Kevin took the desk.

"Can I just ask," Kevin started. "Why are you guys doing this? Isn't this police business?"

"Police that aren't doing a whole lot," Corrigan growled.

Bryce murmured, "Someone else died and the guy's obsessed with Sheldon. We're not…"

"I'm not waiting any longer," I said firmly and looked up.

I saw the tech for the first time. He was leanly built with intelligent green eyes and brown curls that gave him a boyish innocent look. That look alone would earn him the nickname of 'Pretty Boy' for the rest of his life. He was young, but when I looked into his eyes—he wasn't young.

"Thanks for helping us," I said again.

Kevin nodded, glanced at Corrigan and Bryce, and murmured, "Mark said to come and help, to do everything possible so that's what I'm doing."

"Mark?" Corrigan asked.

"Sorry." Kevin rolled his eyes. "Hoodum. That's what you guys call him."

"What do you call him?" I asked, throatily.

"Brother." Kevin smiled. "He's my big brother."

"So…you're not…"

"I'm not a part of Mark's stupid gang. I go to MIT, actually. I'm post-secondary by, like, four years." Kevin chuckled and shook his head. "I'm their secret. I help them out. They get me a nice car every now and then, some 'nicer' things like diamonds or...I don't know—I get favors like protection if I ever need it."

"That's gotta be sweet."

"It is, but the cops know about me. One of them, in particular, is on my rear all the time."

"Which one?" Corrigan asked casually with an easy grin. "They're not fans of mine either."

"Officer Milon. He's such a jerk. I swear, I think half the time he's the one who breaks the laws and just tries to set us up. I'm surprised he's not here to bust me. He's that obsessive sometimes. I feel like I have a homing device implanted in my skin or something sometimes."

I straightened and looked at Corrigan. "The same officer who was pretty adamant that you're behind all of this," I poked him.

Corrigan lifted an eyebrow, crossed his arms, and grunted his agreement.

"No way," Bryce shook his head. "No way."

The same thought crossed all our minds.

Bryce continued, "He's a cop. There is no way he would've set all of this up, just to..."

"He's a vigilante cop," Corrigan corrected him. "They can do pretty 'grey-area' stuff, Bryce. I've been arrested enough. I've met a few of 'em."

"I wouldn't put it past him," Kevin added his two cents. "I mean, he might not have set it up, but...he probably didn't share all his evidence either."

"Are you for real?" Bryce snapped and glared at no one in particular. "This is...this is a nightmare."

"He could've been behind Sheila's attack today," Corrigan suggested.

It did make sense. Partners listened to partners. And partners could be coerced by partners.

"He was really nice to me when I met him," I murmured.

"Yeah. He is. He's great to the victims, pretend or real."

"I don't know, guys…" Bryce shook his head again and started to pace.

"It doesn't hurt to go and ask, does it?" Corrigan ventured and held my gaze.

Kevin and Bryce looked at me too.

"They're parked right across the road," Corrigan added.

"I might have an address by then for this feed," Kevin added.

"I think this is stupid. You can't just go up to a dirty cop and ask them if they're dirty," Bryce cried out.

"That's exactly what you do," Corrigan disagreed. "You don't listen to what they say. You listen to how they act, what they don't say. That's how you know."

"This is stupid!"

"No. This is the best lead we've got."

"Guys." I stood between them.

"You're not going out there with Sheldon," Bryce said firmly.

"What?" Corrigan asked, tensely. "You don't trust her with me?"

Bryce froze in place.

I stood between the two, stiff as a board.

"Guys…" I murmured. This would not end well.

Chapter 29

"Are you insane? You can't just accuse a cop of being dirty!"

"Why not?" Corrigan smirked. "They accuse me all the time."

Bryce shouted, "You're not a cop!"

"I protect my own law." He glanced my way and smiled, "And I serve to protect those I love."

I closed my eyes.

"This isn't funny!" Bryce cried out, aggravated.

"Yeah...kinda...okay, not really, but...it's not like..."

Bryce pushed, firmly, "You're all eager to jump on this bandwagon because you have serious issues with authority. You always have, Corrigan."

"It *is* the anti-social quality in you," I murmured softly.

Bryce dropped beside me and cried out, "I give up."

"Fine. Let's go." Corrigan grinned and extended a hand.

Bryce slapped it away. "You can go, but she's not."

"Oh my god!" Corrigan cried, "I thought you surrendered."

"On trying to get through your head, not on Sheldon going out there."

"No! No. No. Are we twelve, fighting over a girl?" Corrigan laughed in disbelief.

"No," Bryce said calmly. "She's my girlfriend and she's not going out there."

I slapped both hands on my ears and cried out, "Don't say that word!"

Bryce ignored me and said again, "The line's drawn, Corrigan. Step over."

Corrigan smirked in his best friend's face and drawled, "So we're playing who has more credibility? Are you serious? You're pulling the boyfriend card?"

"Not that word either!" I shrieked.

"I guess I am," Bryce said clearly.

"Fine. I'm her best friend."

"So am I—and I'm the guy she's in love with."

"She loves me too," Corrigan debated.

"Not in your bed."

I slumped over and dropped my forehead on my knee.

Corrigan sighed, "You can't be her best friend and her lover. You can't be both."

"Are you kidding? Of course I can." Bryce stood up and added, "I love her and you're not taking her."

"Oh my god!" I burst out. "The crazy people are outside, not in here!"

They both ignored me and Corrigan retorted with, "Sheldon is going to get the best reaction out of this guy. He'll look at her and something will happen. A twitch, a whisker, I don't know. Something. I have to take Sheldon with me."

"No, you don't," Bryce got in his face. "Look, all you need to do is tell him that we've got a trail on this guy's feed. Tell him that we're going to have the address in the next thirty seconds or something. Then you'll see a reaction or you won't."

"Stop it," I said forcefully. "Stop it right now!"

Corrigan shifted back and Bryce faced me. He said calmly, "There is someone out there who's obsessed—"

"And he's likely to kill you just as much as me," I pointed out.

Bryce quieted.

"I did not...I didn't bitch slap Lew to end up hiding in my own house. That's not me and you both know it! I am done hiding, that's the entire reason for this party."

At Corrigan's brief flash of triumph, I squashed it immediately and said, "But I'm not going to go accuse some cop of being dirty or setting this up or even…I don't know…trying to actually find this person by letting me be the bait."

"Sheldon…" Corrigan sighed.

"I am embarrassed that I'm here," I cried out. "I'm embarrassed that…we're insane. I got fed up and instead of thinking rationally and going to the police, I threw a party. And you let me!"

Bryce and Corrigan almost jumped from the accusation, but both merely looked scared—in their tough and manly way.

I cried out, hoarse, "We're a bunch of high school kids! I'm not some 'Ruling Queen.' I'm just…I'm just a girl that goes to school, that wants to keep her two best friends close, and…God forbid!—I even want to, *maybe*, hold hands in a slightly couply boy/girlfri—I still can't say that word."

"So what are you saying?" Corrigan asked, cautious.

"I'm saying that we're insane!" And then I crumbled and fell back on the couch, stricken.

I knew that there was a brief exchange of looks between Corrigan and Bryce. Bryce won out. He shooed the best friend and computer tech from the room as the boyfriend—still a knee jerk reaction—sat beside me.

"Hey…" Bryce murmured, huskily.

"Don't!" I said sharply.

Bryce grew silent. His hand fell away from my knee. "Sheldon," he sighed.

And that one word, from that one voice that belonged to that one person—this is where my walls crumbled and I curled over my knees with a hoarse cry.

I didn't want to die.

"I'm so stupid. We're stupid." I cursed. "This isn't some high school prank. We're not—we have no idea what we're doing. We're talking about dirty cops. Are you serious?! When did we lose our minds?"

"Probably about the time when you said, 'let's have a party,'"

Bryce remarked, ruefully. His hand slid down my back. "I don't think Corrigan ever had his mind, if that's worth anything."

"It's not and you're not helping," I pointed out.

He was joking. I was crumbling and he was joking.

"Stop the show," I murmured, hoarse. "I'm scared, Bryce. This is real…"

"I know!" Bryce snapped. "What do you want me to do? We're already…the party's here, Sheldon! The people are here. They're out there. We can't send them home. We can't…the trap's already been laid."

It hadn't been baited.

"I have to go out there."

"What? No!" Bryce denied.

"Yes."

The trap needed to be baited. We'd brought it this far…

"No," Bryce said again. "This guy, he's strong, Sheldon. He's sick and twisted and you can't go out there. I mean, my god, he killed Leisha and Bailey. He killed them both and then moved their bodies. What kind of sick person does that?" Bryce shook his head again, but stopped when the door was abruptly kicked open. Chet stumbled inside, along with Mandy. They fell to the floor, rolled over, and stared at us, dumbfounded.

"Oh, hey." Chet grinned stupidly and then pushed himself upright. He soothed a hand down his wrinkled shirt and announced, "Corrigan's been arrested. The cops want you to go down and post bail. Some Officer Sherry told me to tell Sheldon that."

Bryce and I didn't even blink. We should've, but I almost expected something like that to happen. So we just stood and traipsed out the door. As we headed downstairs, I was grateful to see that a lot of people had cleared out, but was even more grateful when Mandy said she'd make sure everyone was gone by the time we got back.

Chet stayed behind, but Harris rode in the back. Bryce drove and I rode shotgun with a thick air of tension among us.

As we drew near the station, Harris asked, "Man, which door do we use?"

Bryce parked in the visitor parking lot and both of us got out without a word shared between us. We both fell in line beside each other as Harris trotted behind.

"Guess you guys have been here a few times, huh," Harris said dryly.

"Corrigan getting arrested. Not new."

"Hey," I glanced over my shoulder. "Thanks for doing the bail."

Harris shrugged, "No problem. Now I have a story to tell, you know. I bailed a buddy out of prison."

"Technically," Bryce murmured as he held open the door for us, "This is jail, not prison."

"We can have Corrigan call you from now on. Think of all the stories you can tell then," I suggested.

It bounced off of Harris' shoulders as he remarked, "Screw that party. We should head to a strip joint after this. Drinks on me."

I frowned and seriously wondered about his sanity.

As we swept into the main waiting area, we moved to the front desk where I asked for Officer Sheila Patterson. The officer on desk duty skimmed a cold, unfeeling, gaze over us both before he turned and disappeared down a side hallway. A moment later, Sheila followed behind and nodded in our direction. She gestured for us to proceed behind and we did while Harris stayed in the waiting room. More than a few police officers glanced up, watched, and bent their overworked shoulders over an endless pile of paperwork. The rustling of paper never paused, stopped, or slowed.

Sheila waited with her arms crossed at the end of the hallway. Her buttoned shirt had been pulled haphazardly from her jeans. Her gun and walkie were covered by the tails of her shirt with only a corner of her radio peaking out. Her hair was pulled back in a braid that looked like it had just seen a thirty four hour shift and knew it'd see another thirty four hours before it received any tender loving care.

Her eyes were tired. And flat. Sheila hadn't ever stopped being a cop, but I saw that the deadness stood prominent. It had me wondering what she'd unearthed in the last eighteen hours since I saw her.

"You look like you could use a bed," Bryce murmured in greeting.

Sheila smiled tightly and replied, "Morning."

I nodded, now tense.

Sheila raked another raking perusal over me before she nodded towards a closed door. "You know what's going on in there?"

Bryce didn't answer so I did. "You're interrogating Corrigan."

"You're right." She nodded briskly and moved into a back room. A one-way mirror separated us from Corrigan's room. He sat, bent over a table, his arms crossed underneath him and he looked like he was asleep.

"Care to venture why we're interrogating your friend?"

"Because he's a cocky teenager with authority issues," I said lightly.

Corrigan was unfazed as an officer slammed a file on the table. The table jumped, Corrigan did not. And the cop flipped open the file.

"You know what he's showing him in there?"

I knew. I didn't need to say it.

Sheila answered anyway, "Those are the pictures of Leisha Summers and Bailey Umbridge. Two girls that were raped, strangled, and cut to death. And your buddy in there thinks this is a joke. This isn't a joke."

Corrigan didn't even look. I watched, transfixed, as my best friend didn't even look at the pictures.

"He's not looking," I said faintly.

"He doesn't have to. He's already seen them," Sheila rasped out. "He saw them in person and we can place him at the scenes of the crimes."

"What?!" Bryce spoke now.

"Corrigan wasn't anywhere near—"

"Leisha Summers did not die in the park. She died a block away from your party that night. And Bailey Umbridge, she died in the same block. She wasn't killed in the school. She was found in the school, just like Leisha was found at the park. They were both moved."

"Corrigan was with me the whole night—" Bryce started to say.

Sheila cut him off, "You told me that he was with you 'most' of the night. He disappeared, didn't he? For a little while, didn't he? You told me that this afternoon. You can't take that back now."

I froze and whirled around.

Bryce stood, pale, and stiff. His eyes watched me in horror and he whispered, a choking sound, "I..."

His hand had held my elbow, but I moved forward, a slight shuffling step. His hand fell away and I was now cold.

"It didn't take long for him to slip away and murder Leisha. She was only a block away. He drove her over later, after you guys finished with your 'buddy.' Didn't he? He left again—"

"He went to the bathroom!" Bryce cried out, "I told you this."

"Yeah. You gave your 'friend' some holes in his alibi. That's what you did."

I glanced between the two and pressed, "He was with Logan the night that Bailey was murdered."

Everything was unraveling. Hideously.

Sheila turned almost sympathetic eyes towards me and said softly, "She went home. He wasn't with her the whole night."

"I can't...this is preposterous!"

I felt the string quickly racing from my hands. The end was nearing and I watched, horrified and in slow motion, as it came and passed through. My hands were too slow, too clumsy, and I stood without an anchor.

"You need to wake up about your friend, Jaded. I understand the blinders considering all the things that have happened to you.

I understand why you're denying what's in front of your eyes, but open your eyes. His prints were on the fourth letter. He's virtually got no alibi for either of the murders and he's got the criminal history to back up our claims. He's got a one way ticket to being a career criminal with anti-social qualities. And I'm not talking someone who's just unfriendly. I'm talking anti-social personality disorder. Go to any prison and you'll find more than you can count. That's where they go, to prison."

"I…"

Everything was collapsing.

"We've got a psychologist coming in for an assessment. He's going to tell us that Corrigan is capable of murdering two teenage girls. Judges listen to those guys."

"Corrigan didn't murder anyone. My god—he was arrested because he thinks one of you guys know who did and they're not doing anything about it," Bryce said harshly.

Sheila quieted and seemed to withdraw, though her feet didn't move.

Bryce saw it too and he murmured, not missing a beat, "Is that what this is about? He fingered one of you guys so you're taking him down? Does it work that way?"

"You better watch what you're claiming…" Sheila said faintly, but she backed off.

"Can we talk to him?" I asked, a sudden white flag rose in the air.

Sheila glanced over my shoulders, sighed, and said faintly, "No."

"Fine." I nodded tightly and Bryce moved ahead of me for the door. He saw the disengaged expression on my face and abruptly bundled me outside, away from prying eyes and ears. The cold air was cool and crisp. It was exactly what I needed.

Bryce waited behind me…

And then I turned swiftly and punched him.

Bryce didn't move. He didn't react. He didn't even flinch. He knew it was coming.

"You came here and talked to her?!" I exclaimed, harshly.

Bryce knew it was coming. He murmured, "I wanted to help. I want them to know as much as possible to find this psycho."

"And instead, they twisted your words and they're *still* after Corrigan!"

Bryce didn't say anything, not for awhile. And I held my breath, knowing that was the worst reaction I could've hoped for...and then I heard, faintly ...

"Maybe they're after the right guy."

I sucked in my breath and lashed out blindly, "You did not just say that!"

Bryce backed up. "I'm just saying—"

I turned my back, but my words were lethal, "You did *not* just say that!"

"I did, Sheldon." He sighed heavily behind me.

"Go away," I said tightly.

"No," he said just as tightly.

"You cannot...it's not Corrigan..."

Bryce sighed, ragged, and said softly, faintly, "I think we both need to face the facts that we don't know who it is..."

Chapter 30

They wouldn't let Corrigan out on bail. He was too important and sacred. I agreed, but for different reasons. As we left, we bypassed his parents. They'd been called by another student, a Good Samaritan that would be rewarded when Corrigan hunted him down in thanks.

Harris dropped us off at home and we found Mandy to be true to her word. Everyone was gone except Chet and Tatum. The house was nearly spotless and all three were lounging on the couches, watching television.

Bryce took a beer for me and one for him before he dropped down on the closest empty seat next to Mandy.

I was exhausted, but I still noticed how Mandy tensed.

Mandy may be more mature than the average girl, but she still had the same schoolgirl tendencies for the average crush. Bryce was oblivious and I was oblivious to his outstretched hand as he waited for me to notice the beer.

"You guys get Corrigan out?" Chet asked.

I curled on Bryce's lap as he answered, a deep timber that reverberated through his chest to mine.

"No. They wouldn't let us post bail until he saw a judge, but his parents got called. They showed when we were leaving."

Chet barked out a laugh, along with Tatum.

Mandy frowned and asked, "What? I don't get it."

No one bothered to explain it, but Chet remarked, "Corrigan's going to love that."

"Who called?" Tatum asked. "The cops can't do that."

"A student."

"Corrigan's going to love that kid." Chet cracked another grin in amusement.

"Thanks for cleaning," I told Chet.

He shrugged and gestured to Mandy and Tatum, "They helped. Mandy got all the sobbing hystericals out and Tatum helped with the guys. And some Kevin guy took off. He said that nothing came up, but the stuff was still running. He said you'd know what he meant."

Tatum grinned proudly, "All the guys helped out, but most wanted to go to Harris'. He's having an after-party party at his place, but I don't think he actually knows that since he was with you guys."

"Don't suppose you two are going?" Chet murmured.

Bryce slid a hand down my back and answered, "No, we're not going." His hand stopped caressing my leg, but he tightened his hold and clasped me strongly against him.

"Let's go to Harris'," Tatum exclaimed as he stood from the couch.

Mandy sighed and stood, slower.

Chet grinned as they left. He stopped just short of the stairs and said as an afterthought, "That Donadeli kid showed up tonight. He said that he was invited, but he took off again. He's going to come back later in the morning to pick up the Party Packs. Have a good night, guys!"

His chuckle could be heard as he jogged upstairs and shut the door behind him.

As the door closed with a deafening click, the laughter was cut off abruptly.

The absence echoed around the mansion and all I heard was Bryce's breathing.

I moved and straddled him instead.

Bryce's hand fell to my legs and he relaxed against the back of the couch.

Our eyes met and we both waited for the other to break the laughter's absent echo.

I broke it and murmured, "Mandy has a crush on you."

"Left field." Bryce grinned. "So?"

"So. Nothing."

He asked and watched me intently, "Or were you hoping for a reaction?"

"No," I lied.

"What are you doing? I don't care about Mandy. You know that."

I said evasively, "Mandy's not stupid. She's kinda cool. I like her."

"She's stupid for being friends with Becky Lew."

"You're stupid for letting her sit on your lap all those times," I pointed out.

It didn't escape my notice that his hands swiftly pulled me farther down. I felt him jerk upwards at the contact and grinned, smug.

"You know what that was about." Bryce bent forward and kissed my shoulder. He trailed towards my neck and settled there.

"I know," I sighed and curled a hand around his neck to hold him in place.

No more words were shared until we were both panting and I had been transferred to lie on the couch. Bryce lifted himself up and said, out of breath, "I don't want to do this here. Not with those feeds still going…"

I shuddered at the reminder, but nodded and crawled up as he moved off the couch.

We walked in unspoken agreement to my bedroom. Bryce led and I followed. The light was left off as I silently packed a bag and Bryce waited on the edge of the bed. When I was done, I turned and Bryce lifted the bag out of my fingers. He carried it and his free hand found mine.

We walked down the stairs, flipped the lights off, and

programmed the alarm system. The door was locked and we were in Bryce's car, heading towards his place within moments.

"What about your mom?" I hadn't asked before, but I asked now.

"She took Savannah and Luca to our Aunt Kelly's. Mom called and left a message. She doesn't feel safe with everything going on in the community."

"Her words?" I grinned and relaxed in the seat.

"Her words exactly." Bryce shrugged. "I'm okay knowing that my little sister and brother aren't around right now."

"Yeah."

Bryce reached over and took my hand. I never knew that my fingers grasped his, desperately.

The rest of the way was in silence. When we got outside, it was peaceful. It was shattered when we both shut our doors. Bryce led me inside, in the dark, and we moved into his bedroom.

He waited on the bed as I moved into his bathroom and cleaned for the night. We bypassed each other and then I curled underneath his blankets. As I waited, a tear slid down, but it was brushed briskly away and I sat up to open Bryce's window an inch.

He always liked that. He liked the cool breeze of fresh air.

When he came back in, he sat on the edge of the bed and looked at me. Our eyes met as the moonlight filtered inside and cast shadows across our features, but our eyes were glitteringly alive and we saw the other.

"I can't..." He sighed, raggedly.

I shook my head. There was too much in the air with Corrigan in jail, the stalker still out there, and Bryce was leaving me. He couldn't say anything to make any of it right so I just shook my head.

Bryce sighed again and moved towards me.

Tenderly, he kissed me.

The kiss inflamed and I found myself clutching to him. Bryce shifted so I could lay down and he rose above me. I closed my eyes against the onslaught of pleasure. He stretched out on the side with one leg thrown over mine, proclaiming his hold, as his mouth kissed mine again and slid down. With each kiss that trailed south, I heard his breath exhale. I felt his breath on my skin and raked my hands through his hair.

Bryce lifted his head, met my eyes, and slid back up to kiss my lips.

We made love for the rest of the morning. The last twenty four hours had rolled slowly by and we hadn't enjoyed the night. It was morning when we got to bed and it was still morning when we breathed after the last climax that pulsed our bodies. Bryce collapsed on me with an arm thrown around my waist and his head rested on my shoulder.

He fell asleep and I stayed awake. I trailed a hand down his back, feeling the sweat, and muscles that aligned and gave him the structure of who he was.

I fell in love with him. I had said it again.

I wasn't his girlfriend and laying there, with him breathing for us, I realized that I wasn't going to be his girlfriend. We weren't simple like that. We were best friends and lovers, but girlfriend/boyfriend limited us beneath what we were. We were more and I was loath to take a label that didn't justify who I was or how I felt.

I heard movement in the house and slid out from underneath Bryce's warmth. I pulled on my loose scrubs that hung low on my hips and grabbed one of Bryce's sweatshirts to cover my top. Silently, I opened the door and moved out as Bryce rolled over in the bed, fast asleep.

When I moved into the kitchen, I stopped short in surprise.

Jefferson Scout stood at the coffeepot, frowning fiercely like it was alien technology.

"Water and coffee grounds," I said by a greeting. I leaned against the counter, stuffed my hands inside Bryce's sweatshirt, and smirked. "And then you push 'on', but you'll want to make sure it's plugged into the outlet first."

Jefferson nodded, "Ah. I got it now." He smiled and I saw he had Bryce's smile.

"Bryce told me that everyone was gone," I murmured, feeling slightly foolish.

"Yes, well…" He glanced at me, cautiously.

I replied, "I know about the divorce. Bryce told me."

"Yes, well…" he continued. "It was too tempting to pass up. My wife left town once she heard that I was back and well—my own home without my wife sounded wonderful."

I hadn't quite expected that answer. He sounded tired, resigned, and sad. He didn't sound like a father who was about to leave his family behind, with no means to pay their bills.

"Bryce is sleeping…" I stopped, realized how that sounded, but I finished anyway, "I know that he'll be happy that you're here."

Jefferson smiled, more to himself than to me, and he noted, "I'm not my wife, Sheldon. I know what you mean to my son even if he doesn't realize that I know, but I do. I'm not going to burn you at the stake like I'm sure that my wife would like to."

I laughed, genuinely, and replied, "What are you talking about? Your wife is one of my biggest fans. She prays for me, did you know?"

"Yes. She prays for everything, but I doubt she lives a very Christian lifestyle."

"No, I doubt she does."

He sighed as he finished filling the coffeepot. He pushed the 'on' button and remarked, "You know—I don't think I've ever had a conversation with you before. How long have you been with my son?"

"Seven years." I acknowledged the truth in my response and knew I had kept him away for most of those years. Hindsight is crystal and bitterly true.

"Well, it's very nice to meet you…finally." Jefferson Scout smiled an adorable smile and I realized why AnnaBelle Scout had fallen in love in the first place. He may have been quiet, but he was gorgeous underneath his seemingly nerdy exterior. A businessman and inventor (from what Bryce had told me once), but I saw a lot of Bryce in his father.

Color me biased, but I liked the guy.

"If there's something I've learned from even starting this whole ordeal, it's not to believe what you're told." Jefferson nodded quickly, poured himself a cup of coffee that had slowly filtered through, and added, "Some things don't add up and living with my wife—I pushed a lot of those nagging little things to the back of my mind, but I've paid the price now. She'll take me for everything I have. I'm sure of it, but at least now I have a clear mind. And I can judge for myself what makes sense and what doesn't. Silly, yes, I know, but…I've learned that I can only say what I know. If I didn't, I wouldn't think of saying it at all."

It was an oddly placed speech and I knew that he spoke from his personal demons, but it jarred my own.

Everything unraveled as I heard two of his sentiments.

Bryce had lied. He wasn't working to support the family. His father had enough money and his wife would take most of that from him.

And Bryce had talked about something that he shouldn't have known. He had said, before the police even told me—"*He moved both bodies.*"

Bryce knew that Bailey hadn't died in the school. He knew before the police told us.

He knew and he shouldn't have known.

Jefferson left as I stood in the kitchen. As I stood there and my world had just cracked open, I was left alone and no one saw how I fell to the floor, blinded from my revelations that now screamed inside of me. I watched, suspended and paralyzed, as my hand must've caught and pulled the coffeepot to the ground. I saw it fall, crash into a million pieces, and I watched as the black content seeped across the floor.

The broken glass was camouflaged underneath the dark liquid.

My hand reached out to help myself stand up. I saw the shattered glass and I placed my hand there anyway. I felt none of the pain, but I stood and I gazed in horrified suspension as the blood quickly covered my hand.

That didn't make sense. I didn't understand where the blood came from.

And another hand was there, covering mine as they pushed against the blood, to stop the blood flow.

I looked up, numb, and saw Bryce's ashen features.

Chapter 3 1

The streetlights whizzed past into a steady constant blur.

I had wished, for a moment, to forget what I realized and to pretend. I wanted to curl up with Bryce, pull his blankets over us both, and sleep, protected in his pretense.

I had almost chosen to forget and deny rather than fight and survive.

I wasn't the innocent, sweet, and helpless princess.

Bryce would be after me. I knew it. And I think he knew it as he stepped aside and let my excuse command our actions. I had pled a headache and time to be alone and he had heeded. He chose to play the game and I bit back the tears as I stepped from his front door. I had wanted him to not play the game and strip away everything.

A big part of me wanted to turn the car, crawl back in his bed, and pretend I didn't know what I knew. But there was another part of me that wanted to survive, that wanted to live and birth fat babies. That was the part of me that kept me driving ahead, but if it had to come to percentages—it would've closed at 51% to live and 49% to die in bliss.

How sick and twisted is that?

I pulled into my garage and hurried inside. Immediately, I slid the locks in place, changed the alarm system's codes, and headed for the shower. And there I sat, naked, chilled from the cold stream, and teeth chattering in the corner. I hugged my knees to my chest.

I stared at nothing and my hair plastered against my skull, but my eyes were flat. Dead.

I never felt the frozen water slam against my vulnerable skin.

I lost track of time and I don't know how long I sat there, but my limbs were trembling uncontrollably when I moved out of the shower and wrapped a robe around myself.

I sat at the mirror and left my soaked hair alone.

The distant chime of my doorbell finally penetrated the haze. I wondered, briefly and faintly, how long the doorbell had sounded, but I ceased wondering when I saw Marcus Donadeli on the other side. He looked nervous and awkward.

I said nothing as I decoded the alarm system and stepped back with the door open.

"Hi, Sheldon." He blushed as he smiled.

I've never blushed before. I wondered what it felt like to blush, to have the capability to blush.

"What are you doing here?"

His eyes lingered on my robe, on the naked skin that showed near my neck. I didn't care. I didn't pull the robe tighter, but I did ask again, "What are you doing here?"

"Oh. Um…the Party Packs." He gestured, haltingly, inside. "I came by last night, but the party was done, huh?"

Yeah. The party was done.

"Corrigan got busted by the cops," I remarked and walked inside with him following.

"He did? Why?"

I shrugged. "I think he accused one of the cops of being dirty. I don't think that goes over too well."

"Yeah…cops can be pretty quick to defend themselves," Marcus muttered.

The Party Packs sandwiches still covered the entire table, half eaten.

I sighed and leaned against the counter as Marcus started cleaning off the food. "You like me, don't you?" I asked suddenly.

His hands paused, clenched, and he looked up, pale, "Yeah."

"Why?"

He said swiftly without pause, "Because you're amazing." He added, "Why do you think everyone wants you?"

"Everyone doesn't want me."

"Chad Yerling. Bryce Scout. Corrigan Raimler. That movie star guy."

"Yerling never wanted me. He just wanted to piss off Bryce and Corrigan."

"What about the rest?"

I gave no comment to the rest, but I did mutter, "Corrigan's my best friend."

"And..." His jaw clenched as he asked, "Bryce?"

I didn't comment. I didn't trust my voice.

"What?" Marcus asked softly. "You guys have a fight or something?"

"What?"

"You look sad."

I glanced to the floor and tightened my robe.

"But you always look sad..." he added.

I did?

"You didn't eat yesterday when you were at the Eatery. You didn't eat...I noticed that..." He swallowed, jumpy. "Are you hungry? I have some food in my car. I could go and get it...if you'd like."

"No, I'm okay. Thanks. I just...I don't eat that often."

"You should, you know." He jerked his head up and down, a self-conscious nod. "You hardly ever eat. Is that...are you, like, anorexic, or something? I...I know someone with that eating disorder and she said she can't eat because she feels all panicky if she does, like she's going to fall apart or something."

"No. I eat when I'm hungry. I'm just not hungry that often."

"Oh." He fell silent and returned to cleaning the Party Packs.

"Thanks for noticing, though," I remarked, kindly.

He glanced back, blushed, and smiled, "Yeah."

TIJAN

I had taken two steps towards the door when I heard him whisper, underneath his breath, "I notice everything."

I turned back and asked, clearly, "Why?"

He jumped and whirled to me. "What?" He looked alarmed.

"Why do you notice everything?"

"Because no one notices me."

"Everyone notices me," I said flatly.

"I know." Another flush and his hands jerked.

"I wish no one noticed me."

His hands stilled and the flush disappeared. "You do?"

"I do. I could breathe a lot easier."

"I...I feel like that sometimes," Marcus confessed.

"Why can't you breathe?"

Call me crazy. Call me out-of-sync or illogical, but for some reason—I was clinging to every word he said. I didn't have the lash inside to remind Marcus that he was a social defect, but then again—I was always nice to him. I just never understood why or thought about it.

I thought about it now.

"I don't know." He glanced towards his hands, which seemed steady and strong now. "Just...there's a lot of bullies, you know, and girls who are mean. They laugh in your face sometimes and they're not very nice."

"I'm sorry."

He looked up, "Why? You've always been nice."

"I'm not nice to everyone."

"Those people deserve it, though. You're nice to who deserves it."

"No." I shook my head, numb. "I'm not."

"You're not nice to fake people, but...you're nice to people who are real. You like that. I've watched you, I've seen you be nice to people who are real, who don't care about being...popular or laughed at."

That was true, but I was more surprised that he knew that.

"So, you've been watching me, huh?" I joked, but I knew I was waiting for Bryce to ring the doorbell.

I was stalling, biding time. That 49% had reared its ugly head.

It took a little bit, but I realized that Marcus never answered my joke. He froze in place, his eyes glued to mine, and he looked like he was about to jerk into action.

"I was joking," I drawled. "Relax."

And that was when the doorbell rang.

I think a part of me had sensed his approach, maybe I felt his footsteps on the front porch, or maybe I just knew how long he would've let me leave before he pursued. Even in madness, I still knew Bryce intimately.

Marcus jumped at the sound.

"You should go," I murmured as I was turning around.

"Uh…"

"There's a back door, through the garage. You can get out that way. You shouldn't go this way."

I walked into the front hallway and I felt Marcus leave behind me. He ceased being a blip on my radar as I saw Bryce's shadow looming behind the glass door.

My heart started to pound. I heard it and felt it and it sounded ominous.

"Sheldon!" Bryce pounded on the door.

This time, I was the one who jerked. I knew it was coming, the force just rattled me.

"Come on. I see you, you're right there! Let me in!"

Still nothing. My feet were glued to the floor. I didn't run, I didn't flee, but I didn't approach either.

"Look—I know you're mad. We can figure it out later. This is about me going pro, right? I'm not leaving tomorrow, okay? Corrigan got let out. I figured—I should be here because he's going to show up pretty soon. His mom called me. He's furious."

It was lies. All lies. And even the slight hitch of emotion in his voice was perfectly placed.

The door was securely locked. I reached up, numb, and coded in the alarm. I called out, huskily, "You killed those girls."

Bryce froze on the other side. He didn't say anything for a moment. And then, a choked, "No. What are you talking about?" He was desperate now. "Let me in, Sheldon! We can talk about this."

"You killed Leisha and you killed Bailey. And..."

He was going to kill me. I knew it in that moment, but I still stood there—frozen and paralyzed.

"I didn't," Bryce cried out, hoarse. "I don't...where is this coming from? I didn't kill anyone."

"You knew that Bailey hadn't died in the school. You knew that before Sheila told us. And you knew that Leisha hadn't been killed in the park. I knew that, but I never told you that. You were the only one who knew Bailey had talked to me. No one else was watching. It was only you!"

He went utterly, perfectly, absolutely still.

And then, a sigh of surrender left him and instead of hearing his maddening confession, I heard a different take, "I went to the cops yesterday. I knew that stuff because I talked to Officer Patterson. I talked to Sheila. She told me that stuff. And I saw your fourth note. It said on there that they were moved and he was going to move you too."

"You went down there to frame Corrigan."

That pissed me off.

"I went...I went to Sheila and I told her about the party last night. I just...I wanted you to be safe and I'm smart enough to know that this should've been handled by the cops from the start. That's why I went down there. I told them about the videos, about the second alarm system, about...I told them everything because this is their job. This isn't what we do. I just..." He sighed again and leaned his head against the door. I heard his muffled honesty ring forth, "I just wanted to make sure you were okay."

It was the right words, the right time, and the right person.

I wanted to believe it, but… "How can I believe you?" I cried out, hoarse. "I can't believe anything anymore. Corrigan, you, who else? I don't know where to turn anymore."

"You can believe me. I'm telling you the truth. God—would I…? I already have you, why would I need to—that's sick and wrong. I love you, Sheldon."

"Yeah." An ugly laugh left me. "I'm sure he thinks so too."

"Sheldon," Bryce breathed out. "Listen to me—go upstairs, to the office, and get the gun. I put it underneath the couch, remember? Go and get it and bring it down. You can point it at me, but please— let me in. Let me talk to you, not through this door."

I turned, but stopped before my feet could move.

I stood there and waited. For what—I couldn't say. It was a weird sensation. How do you turn your back on someone to whom you've professed your love?

"Look—," Bryce cried out. "If you're not going to grab it, just listen to me. Please."

I waited.

"He…he wants you alone, Sheldon. He wants you to be vulnerable. This whole time—it's been me or Corrigan. We've been there, at your side, the entire time. Through everything, through all the crap—my mother, your mother, Denton Steele. Even—even the cops thinking that Corrigan is this dick. This whole time—I'm your best friend, Sheldon. I wouldn't—I couldn't do this!"

"I don't know anything anymore," I cried out, shrill. I wanted to crumble. I felt it inside.

"I know! That's what he wants!" His fist pounded the door, helpless. "Seven years, Sheldon. We've been together for seven years. You've been my best friend for that long, before all the drama and everything that happened in school."

The popularity curse.

Bryce added, "Sheldon…I know you inside and out. Of anyone in this world, I know you the best. I messed up. I'm sorry. I didn't…I was just afraid. I was scared that if I told you that I'd gone to see Officer Patterson that you'd be mad and...well—it wouldn't have been as bad as this. I'm sure, but still this sucks pretty badly."

"Bryce..." I said weakly.

"Sheldon...please..."

I couldn't. I still couldn't.

"Please—of all—god—talk about emotional, huh?" His laugh was weak, but genuine. "Remember when we had angry sex and you told me that you loved me? I remember that. Sheldon, you just run all the time. You've got such a heart, but you cover it with poison sometimes. People have to be immune to poison to be your friend, but—thank god—only Corrigan and I are stupid enough to come back for seconds."

Of endearing speeches, his ranked the lowest.

"You're not helping," I said flatly, but I stood a little straighter, a little firmer.

"I know. I know. I'm sorry, but it's just...you're such a bitch, like, 90% of the time."

"That's supposed to be better?" I cried out.

"Well...I'm telling you the truth. I mean, that's my job, isn't it? To tell you the truth even when you think I'm a psycho madman? Right? It's the truth."

"It's not any better!"

He cried out, aggravated, "What do you want me to say? I'm pouring out my heart here because you think I'm some killer, but I'm just trying to tell the truth. This is new territory, Sheldon. We're not exactly emotional people."

On the contrary...

"Okay," Bryce corrected himself. "We're emotional, but we don't talk about that crap. Up until three days ago, I think the most emotional conversation that we had was when you told me that white bread makes you angry."

My lips quirked at that. Wheat bread was the real deal, white bread was the fake bread.

"I just…" Bryce hung his head. "Go get the gun, Sheldon. Please. Go get the gun so that you feel safe and I can look at you and you can see that I'm telling the truth."

I still didn't move. I wanted to believe him. I wanted so badly…

"Please," his plea was weaker.

"I can't."

"Then…call the police. Take your phone and call them. Just— open this goddamn door."

"You call them."

"I don't have my phone. I left it at home because I was in such a rush to get here after Corrigan's mom called me. I'm sorry."

I pulled out my phone and felt it's smooth contours. I didn't press the buttons, but I didn't turn my eyes from the door. I called out, "If you're lying to me and you're the psycho, I'm going to kill you."

"Deal," Bryce sighed in relief and I opened the door.

His smile was decorated with a few tears, but he swept me up and I didn't see the tears. I just felt everything that he had told me. Bryce pulled away swiftly, grabbed my hand, and dragged me upstairs.

"Where are we going?" I asked.

"We're going to get that gun," Bryce said firmly. "I'm not taking anymore chances. We don't know what's going on and I'm not… we're getting that gun." He pushed open the office door. Bryce quickly strode towards the couch. He bent and lifted the cushions as I wandered around to the computer screen.

"Are we…?" I let the question hang.

Bryce paused and glanced up. Our eyes met and he said slowly, "We'll talk about it, but not now. There's more important things to do."

I frowned, confused, and I saw the computer screen. It had stopped blinking and an address stood prominently against the screen. I saw the address and realized I knew the address. That was when I looked up and said softly, "It says a lot when I did think you were the killer and…I wanted to stay with you."

Bryce froze, the gun now in hand, and he stood. His eyes lifted and met mine.

I felt the punch and added, "I even understood a little, and I wasn't actually…I must be pretty sick to still love you even when I thought what I thought."

"You're not sick, Sheldon," he whispered.

"I'm not?"

"No. You're just…human," he finished, saddened.

I bit back the tears and watched the computer screen. I professed, "I don't feel like a girl. I don't feel anything half the time."

"Well…" Bryce laughed, incredulous. "Are we supposed to? I mean, I don't care what you feel as long as you're feeling it with me."

"You're such a guy." And my words were out-of-sync as I watched the address blare at me. Finally, I said faintly, "There's an address…"

"What?!" Bryce rushed towards me.

But I stopped him as I murmured, "Its Corrigan's."

We both stood. Bryce froze and it was weird, like I was watching a blurry movie in slow motion as the office door opened to reveal a furious Corrigan.

Bryce lifted his hand, cocked the gun, and our best friend froze.

I sat down in the desk chair.

Chapter 32

"What. The. Hell."

Those were Corrigan's first words as he gaped at us.

Bryce sighed, but held his arm steady.

"Seriously. Get the gun out of my face," Corrigan snapped.

"I can't," Bryce merely said, firm.

"Bryce. Sheldon. Gun needs to be gone, now!"

The alarm hadn't gone off, but the door had been opened from the inside. I opened the door and it hadn't shut. The only door that could be opened from the inside, without the alarm going off was the front door.

I opened it and it hadn't been shut. That was how Corrigan got in, but...the alarm should've gone off before I had coded it off...I had told him to go out the back. I had waited for the alarm to go off...

And yet...

"It's not you, dude," Bryce clipped out and I looked up to realize there was a fourth presence in the room. A fourth person that had been there the whole time.

He was supposed to have left, but he hadn't...he'd been there the whole time.

Marcus stood behind Corrigan and as I shifted to the side—he brandished a lethal knife in his hand and an insane glint in his eyes.

It wasn't Corrigan. It wasn't Bryce.

It had been Marcus the entire time.

And the knowledge that he had put doubts between me and my

friends—that pushed me past the brink. I shoved off the chair, up and fighting, and I snarled, "You little bastard!"

"Sheldon," Bryce urged, quickly, and tightened his hold on the gun again.

"What?!" Corrigan exclaimed, hands still in the air. He jumped from the force of my voice, but he saw that I was intent on something behind, *someone* behind, and he whirled around.

Marcus grabbed him and warned, "Put the gun away, Scout, or your buddy's insides are going to get spilled."

"Corrigan will live. Shoot him," I ordered.

Bryce's eyes widened, but he didn't say or do anything.

"No! Don't shoot, man! Please—don't shoot!" Corrigan said frantically.

"Shoot him!" I barked with clenched fists.

"Don't shoot!" Corrigan cried out.

Marcus' laugh halted everything and it was a heinous evil sound. It sounded unnatural, but then again—he was insane. I saw it, plain as day, and I wondered how I hadn't noticed it before.

"You didn't come for the Party Packs this morning, did you?" I asked.

Marcus turned his attention towards me and pretended to slice and dice the air. He still held Corrigan as a shield.

Bryce distracted him, "You have no chance, man. It's three to one and I've got a gun to your knife."

"And I've got a back to my knife." Marcus nudged Corrigan ahead, a jerking step. "I think you might have some penance to pay, you know, since you thought he was the killer."

"I didn't—"

"What?!" Corrigan asked sharply.

"Well—I didn't know," Bryce said just as sharp.

"I'm your best friend!" Corrigan cried out.

"I know!"

"And you thought..." Corrigan glanced at me and cursed. "That's low, dude. That's really...messed up."

"There were reasons." Bryce gestured towards the computer screen.

I stepped closer and murmured, cautious and dangerous, "You were here last night."

Marcus held my gaze.

"And you saw what we were doing."

"It was pretty ingenious," Marcus admitted, but smiled victoriously. "I have to admit that. Finding the feeds in the first place was your lucky break."

"And you routed the feed to Corrigan's home, didn't you?"

"Why are you asking when you already know?" Marcus whispered smoothly.

"I notice everything."

I lashed out, "You notice everything, pervert, because you install videos to watch! You don't notice anything—you *violate* everything!"

Marcus chuckled and relinquished, "The hours I've watched you, Sheldon Jeneve, Ruling Queen and Princess Entwined."

This wasn't a fairytale and I wasn't some dark princess. "Shut up!" I snarled.

"You're so cool and cold to the world, but in the bedroom—that's where you're hot. Passionate. That's where the real Sheldon Jeneve lives and I knew...I had to see the real Sheldon Jeneve. I had to see who she was." He smiled, tenderly, "And you knew, didn't you? I felt it. You knew I was watching and you performed for me."

Corrigan grimaced, disgusted.

Bryce's jaw was locked in place.

I waited and watched the end of the gun barrel. I was looking for the smoke to uncurl itself and to feel Marcus' dead body slump to the floor.

It never came.

Marcus wasn't done.

"You need a lover's touch," he whispered, silkily. "You're left unsatisfied. That's why you sought solace by Denton Steele, but he didn't last. He didn't satisfy you and you returned to *him*, but he's not the touch that you want and yearn for. It's not his touch."

"I'm going to puke," Corrigan muttered.

Marcus touched the tip of his knife to Corrigan's back and he smiled at me, "You weren't like the others."

Disgust competed with rage inside of me. I didn't know which would win.

"You were the only one who came to me. All the others never came, like I was beneath them, only there for them to walk on, but not you. You always came and you smiled. You were nice."

"Yeah," Corrigan cracked a joke. "Look where all the niceness got you now, Sheldon."

"Shut up," I whispered. I asked Marcus, "What are you talking about?"

Bryce answered instead, intense, "You're the only girl that goes to the Eatery. None of the other girls go there. It's *why* we go there, Donadeli."

His contempt was whiplash. Marcus wasn't happy to be addressed by his competition and he stabbed his best friend. At Corrigan's sudden cry in pain, Marcus snarled, "You do not address me. You are beneath me."

"Beneath you?" Bryce asked, a taunt.

And Corrigan cried out louder, "Shut up, man. Just—shut up."

Blood had started to drip on the floor. It ran the course of Corrigan's jeans and a small droplet pooled on the wood flooring.

I asked hoarsely, "Why'd you kill Leisha and Bailey? Why them?"

"I was wondering when you'd ask me that and I'd hoped for a more intimate moment between us. Here, with these two, it's not the right time for those answers. I'm sorry, Sheldon Jeneve, but it's not the right context."

Screw context.

I yelled now, "Why'd you kill them, you sick bastard?!"

That was the moment Marcus Donadeli woke up, where he blinked and saw the reality that screamed in his face.

I was the reality and I was screaming in his face.

That didn't bode well for a psychotic murderer and Corrigan took the brunt of his rage.

He slid the knife in further and Corrigan's choked cry reigned against my ears. I'd hear that quiet weep of agony every night of my life, but I asked anyway, "Why'd you kill them?!"

"Sheldo…" Corrigan begged in pain. His eyes pleaded.

"You slice him one more time, I don't care about the risk. I'm putting a bullet between your eyes," Bryce clipped out and stepped closer. His hand was perfectly steady.

Marcus saw that, even in his madness, and he stopped.

Corrigan fell to his knees. The blood's pool had grown and multiplied at his feet. His jeans were velvety red from blood and black from the grime of his evening in jail.

"Why'd you kill them?" I asked again.

And this time, I got an answer. Marcus whirled his gaze back to me and replied, calmly, "I was watching you that night. You wanted her to come to you, but I couldn't let that happen. You had been with him again." He sent a scathing look to Bryce. "You needed to be punished. She was your friend."

"God," I whimpered.

"She walked right past me. I was in the bushes and your punishment had been delivered to me. I knew it was the right thing to do." He smiled. "I haven't regretted it. I haven't regretted anything. It all opened for me."

"That night her house was broken into—did you do that?" Bryce asked.

"No." Marcus smiled evilly, "But I was there. I was just outside and you looked at me. You knew right where I was. You felt me that night. I knew it then. I knew you wanted this to happen."

"…That's the Donadeli kid, right? Doesn't he have, like, eight jobs or something?"

I remembered. "You work at the alarm company that I called."

"A twist of fate. He was telling me that we belonged together. I knew it then, when I heard your voice on the other line."

"You...didn't find Bailey that morning, did you?"

Finally. A flash of uncontained control. There was a chink in his perfectly orchestrated plan of luck. He smiled, still, and shrugged, "Who's going to believe Marcus Donadeli, the kid who just works all the time? Such a 'good kid, that one is.' The kid who gets trampled by bullies that you screw. No one doubted my story for a moment."

"Someone caught you, didn't they? You didn't 'find' her. You were caught leaving her."

"Yes." He sighed and rolled his eyes. "The other janitor came in early. I told him that I'd mixed up the days. I thought I was supposed to clean that morning, but 'look here what I found.'"

"You're sick, man." Corrigan coughed from his knees. He had curled an arm to hold his bleeding side, but it hung loose and weak.

"Why'd you kill Bailey?" I needed to know. I needed to know...

"Because she talked to you. I watch you, Sheldon. I told you that. I notice everything. I couldn't risk her anymore. She knew more than she knew that she knew. I couldn't risk it...she had to go."

"What'd she know?" I stepped closer.

"Sheldon," Bryce murmured, softly. A heed.

"What'd she know?" I ignored his heed. I had to know.

"Bailey saw me that night. I live between her house and Evan Harris' house. She had seen me go for a walk that night. It was only a matter of time before she realized it and told. She already told you enough as it was. I didn't kill Leisha in the park. That's just where I enjoyed her."

"You're lying!" My words were acid, sharp to the touch. "There's no way you'd dump her in the park, risk that time by getting caught. No. You dumped her and left. You don't do that—you don't make this like it was supposed to happen. You controlled it. You controlled everything!"

"Why'd you come back?" Bryce asked. I knew he wanted to distract the inevitable rage that would snap inside the boiling madman.

It worked.

Marcus smiled, calm again, and eerily, "Because she lied." He turned those inhumane and serpent-like eyes my way. "You lied to me this morning."

"What?"

He caressed his cheek with the knife and whispered, "I can forgive your lustful nature. I understand it. You need that touch to make you feel alive, but I can't forgive your hypocrisy. You can't lie to me and you lied this morning."

"I wish no one noticed me."

His hands stilled and the flush disappeared. "You do?"

I remembered when the blushing schoolboy disappeared in an instant.

"You love the attention, Sheldon Jeneve. You're the Queen. You command attention. To say that you wished no one noticed you was an insult to me, to us. You insulted us and you became the hypocrite. You lied to me. You were fake to me. You're never fake to me…that can't happen."

"Are you insane?" I gutted out, automatically, reflexively. He was insane and someday I would wonder when he had ceased living among us, but now was not that time.

"I think you should shut up," Bryce warned, lethal.

Marcus whipped back to him, narrowed his eyes, and I saw the intent before I could scream.

Marcus plunged deep within Corrigan and I blinked.

It was done.

Corrigan's eyes rolled inwards and he slumped to the ground.

Bryce lifted the gun, but Marcus ran.

The gun went off, but it only splintered the empty doorway.

Wood chipped off and flew around us. I felt a few slivers break open the skin on my cheek, but I watched Corrigan on the ground.

Bryce cursed, dropped the gun, and sprinted out the door. And Corrigan laid on the ground.

Chapter 33

I knelt, watched, and felt the gun by my hands. I stared at it, surprised. I heard Marcus' words in my mind.

"...*that was supposed to happen*"

I was the girl that no one messed with. I remembered Officer Sheila's words.

"...*I'm thinking the more you scare, the madder you are, and the more ruthless you'll get...he's not going to expect that.*"

Well, she was right. I was livid, a gun lay at my hand, and my best friend's blood coated my floor.

My hand grabbed the gun and I stood. I would not and will not stand by when I can enact my own revenge, should it be justified or not.

Corrigan moaned at my backside and I whirled to the corner. My stomach emptied its contents and Corrigan was again unconscious.

My fingers twitched from my rage and my jaw firmed.

The hallways stretched long and wide. The paintings seemed to shrink as my shadow crossed over them. And in the meantime, I listened. I heard one set of footsteps, but I doubted the heavy sprint belonged to a student who'd made the pros because of his footwork.

Bryce was graceful and exquisite to watch, but this hunt belonged to me.

I followed the footsteps and found myself turning down the stairs.

All the lights were suddenly cut and the house plunged into darkness.

That wasn't Marcus' handiwork.

I now knew where Bryce had disappeared to and I instantly realized the significance.

This was my territory. This wasn't Marcus' backyard and he was a blind rabbit running for its hole.

As I cleared the last step, the heavy sprint suddenly choked itself off.

And I grinned, a mask of malicious humor against the dark backdrop of the night. I wasn't scared. I had been—I hated to admit it, but I wasn't scared anymore.

My best friend was nearing his death's doorstep.

I had almost turned away from the man who loved me.

And I had felt, briefly, but blaringly, the cold winds of isolation and loneliness.

I circled around the back hallway and bypassed my hidden spot. The bench now seemed cold and useless, but it had been my life's shelter at that time when my home had been violated for the first time.

I heard the garage door turn and I heard the garage door stay shut.

It was still locked.

I almost felt the house's grin of eager approval.

I plunged through the dark and walked through the back sitting area where I had laid my head to rest, where I had woken to the sounds of a burglary.

I had one more door and one more hallway, but I heard a silent curse.

And then I heard—"Corrigan?" Logan's voice was quivering, fearful, and hesitant. It was also far off and I knew she was in the foyer, just through the opened front door.

A black shape stood just before the locked garage door, but he had turned at Logan's voice. Marcus froze in place and I almost felt the wheels spinning in his sadistic head. I could see him as I slunk down the hallway.

And he now started towards Logan's voice.

I froze in place, right against the wall, and he moved past, a mere shirt sleeve away.

My lungs ceased breathing.

He passed without any realization and I now stood to follow him.

"Corrigan?!" Logan called out again, anxious. She started up the stairs, "Where are you?"

She'd find him and her scream would be heard in a moment.

A heartbeat and then another—and the scream rang throughout the house.

Marcus stopped and waited.

I could hear his heart pounding and if he had looked behind him—he would've stared into my white eyes.

He didn't and he strained his ears, waiting for murmuring hushes to proceed.

He heard none of it and I knew he was confused.

I wasn't up there and I was supposed to be. I was supposed to have rushed out to silence her or to warn her. I was supposed to have remained behind, but I hadn't. He realized that now and he stopped—confused for his next plan. I saw his hands tighten around the knife. The edge still dripped blood and my hands tightened around my gun's handle.

I raised my arm swiftly, ready to enact my vengeance, but something crashed through a window in that moment. Marcus instantly turned in that direction and my arm swiftly returned to my side. I stepped past and he moved beside me, back into the darkness cover where he could wait and plan his next move.

I flattened against the wall once more and he moved past... again.

I knew my luck was about to run out, but I couldn't stop.

He went back to the garage door and rattled the locked handle once more. Still nothing.

He didn't dare move towards the front door. That was too obvious. So he tried for a window instead.

They were all locked. The alarm system ensured it and it only allowed the front door to be opened. It was pretty marvelous and I thanked Bryce for installing it properly.

Marcus cursed, not for the second time, and I heard Logan's weeping in the background. We both heard her call 911 and I waited for Marcus to decide his next move. He either chanced it and ran through the rabbit-hole or he stayed for the cops.

And then I heard the front door slam shut, lock, and a second beep sounded throughout the house.

Bryce shut the door and we were all locked, ready and waiting for the next move to be had.

And then I heard his voice, high above, and omnipresent, "Hey, Marcus…"

Marcus froze, but said nothing.

Bryce laughed shortly and commented, "Do you want to know what it's like to be hunted?"

Still nothing from Marcus.

Logan wept in the background. I could imagine that she cradled Corrigan in her arms as her knees became covered in his blood.

My eyes went a little more lethal in that moment, as I thought that sight.

It was symbolic, in a way. Corrigan bled because of me. Bryce hunted because of me.

In the end, I was the one who stood beside the murderer.

Bryce called out, "I can see you, Marcus."

And I knew that he could see me too. The videos were still being used and I looked up to where I remembered one was poised.

I smiled, almost soullessly.

Marcus shivered in front of me and gripped his knife tighter.

It wouldn't do any help.

I had the gun and I had the smarts to ensure I pulled the trigger and not him.

I wasn't stupid. I knew that he could knock it out of my hands. He could probably overpower me and wrestle it free, but he didn't have the clear head. His heart pounded wildly and he was barely holding onto any calmness.

His breathing was ragged while mine was anything but.

And I knew that Bryce saw it all.

"You're being hunted right now, Marcus," Bryce continued, cruelly. Cold. "I'm watching you and I know where you are."

"Stop this!" Logan suddenly screamed. There was a thump and then her footsteps were heard on the stairs.

The sudden movement unhinged us both and as Marcus whirled to the stairs, so did I—but he saw me instead of the empty hallway.

I froze.

He froze.

And then he smiled while I leapt into action.

Marcus lunged for me, but I spun out of his grip. I dropped to the floor, remembered a wrestling move from Bryce, and I kicked desperately up—trying for any weakness he might have.

My foot connected to his groin, but his hand connected to my jaw.

We both spun from the hit and saw stars from the pain.

I still held the gun while the knife was securely gripped in his own hold.

"You bitch!"

I blinked back the pain and rolled to my feet. I backed up and raised the gun.

Marcus saw it now and he stopped abruptly.

From the look in his eye, I don't think he even cared.

He saw his point of obsession in front of him and he smiled, triumphantly. He wasn't thinking clearly and that was a point on my side.

I lowered the gun, slightly, to my side and I remarked, seemingly casual, "So what is this? Between you and me? Is this because you got bullied all your life?"

We heard the sirens in the distance. They were coming…

"Wouldn't you like it to be so cut and dried." Marcus actually laughed.

"Is this because I'm popular and you're not?"

"As if," he mocked with a twisted grin.

"You better start talking, Marcus," I said faintly and stepped back. "I've got the gun while you've got the knife."

"And I'm a man," he countered.

I smiled, a taunt, and moved another step back. I held the gun tight, but still kept it at my side. "Were you expecting me to quiver in my shoes? Maybe pee my pants? Is that what you wanted?" I heard Logan scream again and smiled, cruelly. "Maybe you wanted me to scream like her. Is that it?"

"God, yes," he breathed out and I knew his libido sparked at that image.

I murmured, "I only scream for Bryce. You should know that—you've watched enough."

His smile was wiped clean.

Give me a reason, I prayed.

"I'll tell you something," I murmured. "You're right. I'm not like other girls."

He preened. He was insane.

"I don't give a shit about proper etiquette, about being nice, or about people liking me."

"That's why you're the one," he murmured.

His insanity knew no boundaries.

."Is it?"

"You reign supreme over everyone. You hold power over everyone."

Are you kidding me? "Do I?" I asked, dryly.

"You do." And he smiled brilliantly at me.

"You're wrong," I replied. "I'm at the top because I settle for nothing less—and you—you settled for where you ended at. You're a loser. A social deficit. You're the one who chose that place. You chose your life—not your godforsaken bullies. They're just doing their jobs. They're being bullies because it's what they were taught. But you—you chose this. You. Chose. It!"

"She whimpered," he whispered and smiled.

"So will you," I returned swiftly.

The smile was wiped clean. "She was so tight when I went inside of her."

I smiled. "I can shoot you up the ass if you'd like."

He stopped—he just…stopped.

"You've got nothing that'll unhinge me," I tsk, tsked. "That's a lesson learned the hard way, isn't it? I don't scare and when I do— you get this instead."

Logan screamed in that moment.

Marcus raised his knife and prepared to lunge…

There's my reason…

And my finger pulled the trigger.

His body slammed to the ground.

Logan's scream cut off.

And I stood there, silent, with the gun in hand.

He'd given me the reason that I prayed for.

Logan stood behind me, near the base of the stairs, and I turned to see her hand clasped to her silent mouth. Her eyes were wide and panicked. She looked like she was about to faint.

I wiped the gun and let it drop beside Marcus' body.

"You just…" she chortled. She didn't make sense in her shocked state.

"That's what I do," I murmured and glanced back to his soulless eyes. "It's why he picked me."

"But…"

I sighed and grasped her arm lightly, "Come on. The paramedics are coming."

They did, but they were accompanied by the police.

I left Logan standing in the hallway and went upstairs.

Bryce had lifted Corrigan to the couch where he was applying pressure to the stab wound. The blood covered his body now and I stopped in the doorway, grateful of what I'd done.

"Hey…" Bryce greeted, hoarse and exhausted.

"You watched…" I gestured towards the monitors.

"Yeah. I erased it all until the last second where he lunged. It's self-defense. They'll take that and leave it," he said grimly.

I moved to his side and sat down, wearily.

Bryce grinned, sadly, and brushed a thumb across my cheek to tuck back a loose tendril. I felt the trace of blood that was left instead of his loving touch, but I didn't care. I turned and gazed at Corrigan.

"He's so pale," I murmured.

"He'll pull through. He woke up a little while ago."

"He did?"

"He's fighting." Bryce bent and kissed my forehead. "That's what we do."

Epilogue

Miss Connors exclaimed brightly, "So!"

I cringed against the harsh sound and sunlight that filtered through her office windows. I curled into a ball on her chair and rolled my eyes in annoyed resignation.

"Sheldon!"

"What?" I cried out, annoyed. "I graduated yesterday. I'm hung over. Sue me."

"You're annoying, you know that?"

"You're supposed to be my counselor. What happened to all the sympathy and condolences?"

"The 'sympathy and condolences' went out the window when you used a certain expletive with me that pertains to intercourse." Miss Connors smiled tightly. She twirled her finger in the air and exclaimed, "So you can 'screw off' when you ask for that."

I grinned. "That wasn't what I said."

Miss Connors sighed, folded her arms, and asked, "So how's it going with your parents?"

"What parents?"

"You know—the dad that's still out of the country? The mom that's suddenly trying to be a mother with all this media attention? Those parents."

Oh. I shrugged. "They're fine."

"They're a disappointment," Stephanie said for me because I couldn't. Two months of therapy and my counselor finally realized that I couldn't ever say those words, but I liked hearing them. Hell, I needed to hear them.

I shrugged again.

And she sighed. She shifted and sat on her hands, prim and proper, and fast studiously, "You know, Sheldon, you have a right to feel anger at your parents."

"What for?" I asked.

She nodded, solemn, and encouraged with a nod, "What do you mean?"

"Mom's a fraud. My dad's gone. What am I supposed to feel angry about? I can't do anything about it and I'm just wasting energy."

"You still call them Mom and Dad and, yet, you talk about them like they're not your parents."

"Stop it."

"Stop what? Being your counselor?"

"You're annoying." I glanced out the window.

"I care," Miss Connors said softly and watched me intently. "And that's why you put up with me—because I care and I'm here and I'm listening. And I want to listen to more."

"Gag me."

"Maybe later."

I grinned. I couldn't help it and Miss Connors didn't hold it against me.

"So!" Miss Connors said abruptly with a bright smile as she slapped her hands on her lap. "Are you going to ask me the question why you came in for a session that wasn't mandatory today? We've been seeing each other for six months, ever since it all went down, and there's one question that I know you haven't asked and I know you want to ask…so just ask it, Sheldon."

I took a breath and asked the million-dollar question, "Why the handcuffs?"

Stephanie rolled her eyes and chuckled lightly. She leaned back, crossed a leg over her other and sighed, "Because I wanted to annoy you as much as you annoy everyone else."

"Seriously?" I muttered.

"Seriously." She laughed. "No, there's a real reason for them, but you guys cheated when you got them off so I'm not telling."

I remarked, "You should get laid."

"I did. Last night. Twice," she clipped out and leaned forward. "It's scary isn't it? Letting people in, not controlling everything. It's downright terrifying and you don't want me to press the point, but I can't resist."

"God! You piss me off!" I snapped out.

And Miss Connors smiled, triumphantly.

What counselor would enjoy making their client squirm in fury? Mine.

"I know," Stephanie proclaimed. "And that's how I have to communicate with you."

I glared, but she was right.

"Okay, I know the hour's up. Give my best to Bryce and Corrigan. And...send a postcard from Europe, Sheldon. I never would've thought that I'd actually miss all of you guys, but Europe won't know what's hit them. Tell Bryce good luck with Barcelona."

I nodded, jerkily, and clamped a hand to hers. I squeezed it abruptly and then left quickly. I didn't want to look back. As I walked down the hallway, Corrigan was teasing Logan with whispered promises of—I'm sure—sexual positions. Logan blushed like she always did. I was slightly nice to her because she had held Corrigan's hand in the hospital when Bryce and I weren't there.

That earned some spine of steel points in my book.

And Grace—that was the shocker heard throughout the school's social hierarchy. Grace Barton, former loser and social defect, was now friends with me. Bryce and Corrigan didn't understand it, but I saw it with my own eyes. She was sickeningly sweet at times, but she had strength that amazed me. I didn't understand her and somehow—we came to be best friends.

And Bryce and Corrigan—they hadn't changed. They were just wanted more by every female in the school. Bryce was officially and publicly hailed as an up-and-coming star in the professional leagues. Girls were starting to arrive in our town, but I had more than enough venom to send them packing.

Corrigan lifted his head as I approached.

Bryce grinned and raked a hand through his Mohawk as he leaned beside my locker.

"How's Miss Connors?" Bryce asked.

"Still pisses me off."

Corrigan barked a laugh. "You're just saying that because you like her."

I glared.

Logan kissed him and I rolled my eyes.

Grace dodged a group of laughing seniors and drew abreast our group. Her smile tightened at the sight of Corrigan and Logan's locked lips, but she said brightly, "Everything's set. Next year will pale in comparison, but as the senior class President—I can conquer uncharted seas and bring unity to our school once again."

My lips thinned and Bryce waited for my response.

Corrigan grinned, waiting, as he lifted his head from Logan's lips.

And I remarked, "I'm about to vomit."

Grace was undisturbed and she raised a hand in the air, "Vomit all you want, One with Negative Sarcasm, but you're gone and I'm still here next year. This school will rebound after Sheldon Jeneve." And then she ended it with, "Do you want to go to church right now?"

"Do you want to suck Bryce's dick right now?"

Logan blushed, but Grace merely smiled—this was why we were friends—and said sweetly, "That's your job, not mine."

"And yours would be…?"

"Keeping your conscience intact."

It was a weird friendship.

Later, curled in bed with Bryce, I rolled out from underneath him and asked, "Do you remember when we were going to Leisha's candlelight vigil?"

Bryce shifted to his side, smoothed a hand down my flushed cheek, and asked huskily, "Why?" He bent and pressed a tender kiss to my cheek and worked his way to my neck. I fell on my back and Bryce settled half on top of me. He continued his caresses as I stroked a hand in his hair and asked the ceiling, "When I told your mom that if I had a daughter and she had your eyes…"

Bryce finished for me as he lifted his head again, "If my mom would want her to cry?"

"Yeah."

"Yeah," he said faintly. "I remember."

"What if…?" I raked my hand through his hair and grinned wolfishly.

"What if what? If we have kids?"

I shuddered at the thought. "God no, that's like…years away and we'll probably have broken up by then or killed each other, but…maybe someday."

He ignored that, "I think that if we had a child, she'd have my good-looks and your tongue."

I thought so too, but I murmured, "I'm pretty hot too."

Bryce kissed me and the warmth sparked again.

He shifted and rolled me underneath him.

I murmured as my speech was quickly evaporating underneath Bryce's exploring caresses, "I want to go to Leisha and Bailey's candlelight vigil next year."

Bryce paused again and stared down at me, lustfully and intently.

I whispered, hoarsely, "I want to go with you and Corrigan, just you and Corrigan."

Bryce nodded and when I saw the love in his eyes, I reversed our positions and straddled him instead. He grinned, just as wolfishly as I had earlier, and said, "I have Miss Connors' handcuffs, you know…"

THE END

For more information, go to Tijan's Books on
Facebook or purchase *STILL JADED*, the second in the Jaded series.

Lightning Source UK Ltd.
Milton Keynes UK
UKHW011844090721
386928UK00011B/689/J